"Johnson's ... en two
characters ... s. The
romantic s... sizzle."

"This story is so m...ful it takes you inside this
small town a...really makes you think you are
there...your heart will be in your throat as you
await [the characters'] fates."
—*Harlequin Junkie* on *Everywhere She Goes*

"*All That Remains* is a riveting and emotionally
compelling story."
—*USATODAY.com's Happy Ever After* blog

"The prose is strong and there is a lot of movement
in the scenes and by movement, I don't mean
action but rather an ebb and tide of emotion that
was carried through even the love scenes."
—*Dear Author* on *Bone Deep*

"I know that when I see a title
from Janice Kay Johnson, I will be in for a read
that I will be unable to put down
until the last page is turned."
—*Fresh Fiction*

"*Match Made in Court* did not disappoint,
capturing my interest from the first page....
The plot drew me in within a few paragraphs
and held my attention throughout."
—*All About Romance*

"Janice Kay Johnson wins our hearts with
appealing characters."
—*RT Book Reviews*

JANICE KAY JOHNSON

The author of more than eighty books for children and adults, Janice Kay Johnson is especially well-known for her Harlequin Superromance novels about love and family— about the way generations connect and the power our earliest experiences have on us throughout life. Her 2007 novel *Snowbound* won a RITA® Award from Romance Writers of America for Best Contemporary Series Romance. A former librarian, Janice raised two daughters in a small rural town north of Seattle, Washington. She loves to read and is an active volunteer and board member for Purrfect Pals, a no-kill cat shelter. Visit her online at www.janicekayjohnson.com.

USA TODAY Bestselling Author

JANICE KAY JOHNSON

Cop by Her Side

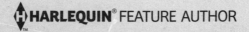

HARLEQUIN® FEATURE AUTHOR

Recycling programs
for this product may
not exist in your area.

ISBN-13: 978-0-373-60642-9

COP BY HER SIDE
Copyright © 2014 by Harlequin Books S.A.

The publisher acknowledges the copyright holders
of the individual works as follows:

COP BY HER SIDE
Copyright © 2014 by Janice Kay Johnson

MAKING IT TO 25
Copyright © 2005 by Harlequin Books S.A.

Printed in U.S.A.

HARLEQUIN®
www.Harlequin.com

CONTENTS

COP BY HER SIDE

For Pat (aka Alexis Morgan),
the best of friends and a fantastic plotting partner

CHAPTER ONE

LIEUTENANT JANE VAHALIK'S skin prickled from her awareness that she was being watched. She didn't have to look around to know who had his eyes on her.

It seemed an excellent time to fade away into the early-evening darkness, circling behind her big black SUV to change clothes in preparation for tonight's assault. Others had been taking turns to do the same; earlier, two designated officers had returned to town to collect the additional weaponry the group would need, as well as body armor and black clothing. Much as Jane had hated the idea of a fellow law enforcement officer—male, of course—letting himself into her apartment and pawing through her drawers, there hadn't seemed to be a good alternative. Her GMC Yukon was one of the more conspicuous vehicles collected out here, and going and returning unnoticed was essential. Besides, any of the guys might have hated having her in his home as much as she did the other way around. And did she *want* to know that a detective under her command had an impressive porn collection or decorated his living room with a beer-can pyramid or had a kitchen or bathroom so filthy it would turn her stomach? Really, really, no. At least *her* place was clean.

The Yukon was currently backed into a dirt turn-around, shielded from the main road by a thicket of scrubby trees and blackberries. Rusting barbed wire, only a few feet away, marked the beginning of a pasture holding a couple of horses, one obviously elderly and swaybacked, and, of all things, a donkey. Now she heard a few far-off rustles, followed by a whuffle from the darkness. Animals. They would be supremely uninterested in seeing her seminaked.

Knowing how brief her privacy might be and listening for human footsteps, Jane hastily shed the clothes she had been wearing for two days now, since she'd learned that police chief Raynor's nephew was being held hostage. Her nose wrinkled in distaste as she bundled them up. She'd managed a shower this morning at Raynor's house, but had had to put the same clothes back on. Even if she'd been comfortable asking, she couldn't have borrowed from Julia Raynor, the police chief's sister-in-law and the boy's mother; Julia had a slender dancer's body, while Jane…did not.

She had stepped into the black trousers first and was tugging down the hem of a long-sleeved black T-shirt when she heard the crunch of a footstep.

"Jane."

She closed her eyes for a moment in resignation. "Sergeant."

There was a brief second of silence. She had no doubt Clay Renner's jaw was clenching in annoyance. An attempt to distance herself, her formality was bound to irritate him, and he surely wouldn't like any reminder that she outranked him, even if they were from different law enforcement agencies.

He stepped around the fender of the Yukon. The night wasn't quite ink dark yet, but getting there. The moon, only a sliver in the sky, was their friend. Given virtually no cover during the approach, getting half a dozen people in place around the barn where they believed the thirteen-year-old boy was being held hostage would have been a heck of a lot more challenging under the bright silver light of a full moon.

Jane could make Clay out, barely. He was really just a darker bulk against the indistinct background, but she didn't need to see him to picture him. She'd dated Clay Renner half a dozen times almost a year ago. He was big, athletic and surprisingly light and agile on his feet given his impressive muscles, with a roughcast, angular face that was very male without being handsome. Blue eyes that were too observant. His light brown, sun-streaked hair always looked as if it was in need of a haircut, but felt like the heaviest of silk slipping through her fingers. At thirty-six, he was two years older than she. Idiot that she was, she still remembered his birth date.

"Are you trying to prove something?" he asked, voice low and intense. "That you can do anything the rest of us can do?"

This was why she'd quit seeing Clay.

"I *can* do anything the rest of you can do," she said levelly. "And damn well, too."

He made an exasperated sound in his throat. "You know what I mean."

Unfortunately, she did. "No, I don't," she said perversely, reaching for the vest.

The weight settled on her shoulders. Of course, the blasted thing didn't fit the way it was supposed to. Tactical vests and body armor that actually fit women's bodies were being manufactured. Unfortunately, the Angel Butte Police Department had yet to purchase any. Of course, a vest that accommodated her inconveniently large breasts was otherwise way too large and too long. She consoled herself that her abdomen was covered.

"You're going to get stuck going through that goddamn window," Clay snapped. "That's what I mean."

"I'm smaller than the rest of you."

"Except for your, uh, chest."

The mealymouthed description surprised her. "Don't you mean tits?" she said, the heat of anger searing her cheeks. "Or— No, it's a rack, isn't it?"

She was pretty sure she *heard* his molars grinding this time.

"I told you it was nothing but stupid male posturing and I was sorry."

Like she could forget the way she'd overheard him talking about her to some of his buddies, all fellow cops.

The anger disappeared as fast as it had risen, leaving her feeling…hollow. She shook her head, even though he probably couldn't see her. "The fact that you're given to stupid male posturing is enough in itself, Clay. Let's drop it. I'm a cop. I have breasts. Get over it."

"You don't give anyone a second chance, do you, Jane?" His voice was rough.

"You know what I heard was just the icing on the cake. The fact is, you'd never be comfortable having a relationship with a woman cop. I don't suppose you raised a champagne glass to me when you heard I'd been promoted, did you?"

Silence.

"Didn't think so." She tossed her discarded clothing into the back of the SUV, holstered her .38 Ruger and closed the rear door as quietly as possible. "You'd better get changed, too. Your white shirt kind of stands out."

That wasn't a lie, even if mostly she was trying to get rid of him. Earlier she'd seen he had on well-worn jeans and a snug-fitting white T-shirt that revealed powerful biceps and pecs. The better to advertise, she'd thought cynically.

"Listen to sense, will you? You being there will distract the rest of us. We'll all be worried about keeping you safe."

Was she supposed to be touched? she wondered wearily. "No, Clay, you won't *all* be distracted. Astonishingly enough, Captain McAllister and Chief Raynor, at least, respect my abilities. And you know what? I'd really like it if you wouldn't worry about me."

He made an inarticulate sound of frustration, snapped, "On your head be it," and stomped away.

Jane didn't move to follow him immediately. Instead she gazed toward the dark pasture and struggled to center herself. Pictured the small window she had studied earlier through binoculars. Began to walk herself step-by-step through what she had to do. Shatter the glass. Toss in a flash bang. Sweep the shards off the frame. Hoist herself—

"Is Sergeant Renner going to be a problem?" asked Captain Colin McAllister from only a few feet away.

She gasped and swung to face him. "Damn. I didn't hear you coming."

"I can see why," he said drily.

It was Colin who last year had promoted her to lieutenant, heading the investigative division directly beneath him. Colin, a man who bore some physical resemblance to Clay Renner, enough to, on occasion, push her buttons.

Well, he'd never looked twice at her, not that way. The upside was he treated her with unwavering respect for her abilities. Downside? She was thirty-four years old and had yet to meet a man who treated her with respect *and* wanted her as a woman. She'd begun to suspect it wasn't happening.

And was that so bad? She loved her job, and the relationships she'd tried to have had left her pretty sour on men anyway.

"Did you hear all that?" she asked.

"Afraid so. I didn't want to interrupt. Sorry. When you recommended Sergeant Renner for this team, I didn't realize you had a history."

"Not much of one." She shrugged to suggest how little she cared. "Impulse on both our parts. As you may have gathered, he's a sexist pig."

Colin chuckled. "Or intensely protective of you."

She felt like a cap had been pulled out of a bottle of champagne—or a bottle rocket. "So protective," she said fiercely, "I walked into the squad room to hear him describing my, er, attributes and telling everyone in earshot what he intended to do to me."

She could make out his grimace. "Yeah, that would do it."

Feeling sick, Jane said, "Now, I'm sorry. I shouldn't have told you that."

"I assumed you took some guff, being a woman in a field that's still primarily male and testosterone driven. Let's say I'm not surprised. Disappointed in Sergeant Renner, though." He shook his head. "He's been strictly professional here."

"I wouldn't have suggested we call him if I hadn't been confident he would be."

Colin pushed a button on his watch and it briefly lit up. "Less than an hour. You okay with your role?"

"You mean, going in the window? Sure."

"Good enough." He nodded and melted away, leaving her with a whole lot of regrets involving both men. Why couldn't there be one man who both wanted and respected her?

CLAY WISHED HE'D been feeding Jane a load of crap, but the truth was, he didn't think he was going to be able to turn off his awareness that she was one of the first members of the assault team in. Maybe *the* first member.

Jane Vahalik, no more than five foot four. Jane, with a sweet face and an incredibly lush body. A centerfold body, not a tough-as-nails cop body.

And, goddamn it, he *knew* she was good. She'd spent time on the multijurisdictional drug enforcement team, so this sure as hell wasn't the first raid she'd participated in. From what he'd heard, she had played a solid part in the ugly stuff that had gone down last year in Angel Butte that had resulted in the police chief resigning in disgrace and a succession of reputedly crooked officers getting the ax. There was no way she'd earned the promotion to lieutenant by sleeping with her boss, as he'd heard suggested. If nothing else, Colin McAllister had the reputation as a straight arrow. Plus, he'd been living with another woman, one whom he had since married.

Knowing all of that didn't help. Clay had been raised to believe in traditional gender roles. His father was a domineering man, his mother gentle and clearly subservient. Clay supported equal rights and never had any trouble working with women. But he'd tended to date women who didn't challenge him in any meaningful way, and in his hazy view of the future, he saw a wife who'd stay at home with the kids, making her life about *him*.

He still didn't know why he found Jane, a woman who'd excelled in a macho profession, so compelling. But, damn it, she'd gotten to him from the first time he'd met her. He'd *liked* her. He'd been living for the chance to get her into his bed. The really shitty part was, he'd deserved to be dumped. He still winced at the memory of having let himself be goaded into talking about her as if she was nothing but another piece of ass while bragging about his own sexual prowess. That moment—when he'd turned and seen her face— was one of the worst of his life.

That was it. She turned and walked out. He'd left groveling messages on her voice mail. She hadn't returned them. Pride and his own awareness that the wrongdoing was his kept him from leaning on her doorbell. Also, as a cop, he was especially sensitive to any behavior that would smack of stalking.

He'd spotted her from a distance a few times, but

when she'd seen him, she'd turned in the other direction. The closest had been one day in the corridor at the courthouse. The way her expression had gone blank when their eyes met had hit him hard.

And yes, he knew he should have kept his mouth shut tonight. He *had* kept his mouth shut while he, Raynor, McAllister and Jane, as the ranking officers, had planned the assault. He wouldn't embarrass her like that.

But if he had to see her go down—

Clay swore softly under his breath as he ripped off his white T-shirt and pulled on a black one followed by the vest, which he topped with a black windbreaker that said POLICE across the back.

It might kill him if he saw her reeling back, blood blossoming. If he had to watch as the light went out of her hazel eyes.

He swore again, more savagely this time. He might *really* die if he couldn't keep his head in the game.

And he didn't know if he could do it.

Clay never liked waiting. This time was worse than usual. Jane was at the top of his list of reasons he hated everything about this operation, but she wasn't the only thing. He had worn, with pride, the Butte County Sheriff's Department uniform every day for years. He might not wear a uniform to work anymore, but he still clipped the badge to his belt nearly every morning. Finding out at least two of the kidnappers were Butte County deputies eroded everything he'd believed about the men with whom he worked. The one that really got him was Bart Witten, a detective in the major crimes unit, a man Clay had worked closely with in the past. Not a friend, but

Clay had trusted him. And now it was looking as though the son of a bitch had been willing to participate in the kidnapping of a *kid* to put pressure on a witness in the trial of a drug lord.

It sucked to know he might have to shoot either of the men who wore the same uniform he did, but he couldn't afford to hesitate. He knew that.

This operation was high risk for a lot of other reasons, too. They weren't sure how many men were inside the barn. They'd seen four, but there might be more. Getting close without being spotted would be tricky. Three different entry points for his team meant a real possibility they'd shoot each other by accident.

The fact that Jane was lead on one of those entry points made his head swell with fury and frustration and fear.

To make it all perfect, the creeps inside were holding a kid. A vulnerable boy who could get hit by cross fire even if someone didn't try to take him out on purpose.

And, oh, yeah, Chief Alec Raynor, in charge of this whole freaking operation, loved that kid, his nephew.

"Just the way I want to make a living," Clay muttered, to nobody, but another shape near him turned.

"What?"

"Nothing," he growled, identifying Abe Cherney, who was with ABPD rather than the sheriff's department. Cherney was a big guy who, with Carson Tucker, a sheriff's deputy, would be using the battering ram to break down the double doors into the barn. "You ready to go?" he asked, and Cherney gave him a thumbs-up.

EVERY SENSE HEIGHTENED, Clay stood in the darkness, intensely disliking his role. Hovering in back, command central, he would make the final decision. Although they had a warrant based on a tentative witness identification of Tim Hansen as the deputy who'd picked up thirteen-year-old Matt Raynor at his house, everyone here would be happier if they had confirmation the kid really was being held inside the barn before they went in with guns blazing. Some skinny ABPD officer who looked about sixteen—Ryan Dunlap—and Jane were the two who were taking a huge risk to try for that confirmation.

And goddamn—Clay wanted to be one of the first in the door, not the last. But there was no way he could get his shoulders through either of the windows, and Raynor and McAllister had claimed prime entry positions.

It was Dunlap's voice Clay heard first through the radio, next thing to soundless.

"Can't see much. Back of someone's head sitting at a table, a corner of an interior wall. Sorry."

Then Jane's whisper, chilling him. "Two—no, three guys at a table. Playing cards. There's a door— Wait."

Oh, shit. Oh, hell. All one of them had to do was turn his head and he'd see her face in the window. Clay's jaw hurt and the tendons strained in his neck.

She'd told him not to worry about her. She couldn't have made it any clearer that there was no do-over for him.

Didn't matter. The need to keep her safe raged in him.

Head in the game, he reminded himself, trying to

take slow, deep breaths. He wouldn't do her or Raynor's kid in there any good if he didn't get in the zone that would let him shutter the emotion and do what had to be done.

"It's opening," Jane continued. "Man coming out. That makes four—" She stopped abruptly. "Kid on a cot." Soft as her voice was, he heard the triumph. "Looks like tape over his mouth."

Clay closed his eyes. But he thumbed his radio and said it. "Go."

GLASS SHATTERED. Flash bangs. Oh, Jesus, gunshots. *Jane.* The motion-activated light above the barn doors came on as Cherney and Tucker charged forward and smashed the battering ram into the doors. McAllister and Raynor were poised to enter.

Wait, Jane. Goddamn it, wait until there's some confusion. Don't play heroine.

At the next rush, the doors cracked and fell open. Already running, Clay was only steps behind McAllister.

Inside the barn was chaos. Trapped in stalls, horses kicked and screamed. Men were shouting. A couple of voices yelled, "This is the police! Hands in the air." The light was unnaturally bright. Clay made himself slow down in his head, see that the broad aisle opened into a space probably designed for a veterinarian or farrier to work. He saw only one room separate from the stalls—a tack room? Smells were sharp in his nostrils: hay, manure, beer and burgers, gunpowder, fear. As reported, a group had been sitting around a card table, already kicked over. Clay saw Raynor vault it. Metal folding chairs were flying, tangling underfoot.

Nearly in front of him, Carson Tucker went down, clutching his belly and screaming something. No time to stop.

There was Jane—*alive, yes!*—but someone swung a chair at her. As she ducked away, it connected with her shoulder and knocked her to her knees. Even as Clay fired, he saw her gun bark, too, and the guy collapsed, sprawling hideously over the chair. She didn't even look at Clay, only swung in a circle with her weapon held ready.

A burst of gunfire from the small room brought Clay's head around and an expletive escaped him. That was where she'd seen the kid.

Don't be stupid. Make sure it's secured in here first.

They all had assignments. Raynor had gone after the boy.

Like Jane, Clay was turning carefully, looking for targets. All four were being cuffed or lay still on the floor. Clay checked to be sure the guy he'd shot no longer held a weapon, then crouched by him. His eyes were open and sightless. Dead. And no wonder—his body was riddled with bullet holes.

Clay was the closest to the open door that led into the tack room. He spun in, weapon extended, and found two more bad guys down, one dead, the other bleeding and cuffed. The kid was alive but bloody. Chief Raynor was trying to yank the boy's T-shirt off, hampered by the duct tape binding his hands and ankles. Clay had forgotten the poor kid wore a cast on one arm already.

"Where are you hurt?" Raynor was saying in a voice Clay hadn't heard from him before.

"I'm okay." The boy's voice was thin and high. "I'm

okay." And, damn, the skin where the duct tape had been ripped off his face was painfully red.

Clay saw the moment relief hit Raynor. "I need a knife," he said hoarsely.

"I've got one," Clay said. He'd worn a backup .38 on one ankle and a knife sheathed on the other. He pushed up his pant leg, took out the knife and sliced the duct tape, freeing the boy's ankles and then his hands.

Matt Raynor leaped into his uncle's arms, clutching on with his one good arm while the chief grabbed tight and bowed his head over the boy's.

Clay backed away, feeling an unfamiliar sting behind his eyelids.

It was all over but the mop-up.

WITH THE TAILGATE of her Yukon open again, Jane peeled off the vest. She felt...weird.

She was in the here and now, but every blink brought a miniflashback. The effect was like a strobe light.

Dark, slow shapes moving in the pasture—horses.

Diving in the window, shards of glass ripping at her vest and clothing. Fear.

Blue, white and red lights swirling atop aide cars.

Knowing she couldn't totally evade the chair swung at her. Dodging, feeling it connect.

She gingerly fingered her shoulder and upper arm and knew there'd be a bruise. A whopper.

The weapon jumping in her hand. Blood. Astonishment on the man's face as he stumbled and began to fall.

Men's voices on the other side of her SUV, a rumble that might be comprehensible if she could bring herself out of this fugue state.

The slackness of death. Death she *had caused.*

Jane heard herself make a sound. Either she had killed a man tonight—or Clay Renner had. Or both of them.

"You okay?"

Of course it was his voice. Of course she hadn't heard him coming.

"Why wouldn't I be?" she said sharply.

"You ever shot anybody before?"

The angle at which she thrust her jaw forward made her neck hurt. Pride was a powerful force. Even so, she hesitated. "No," she admitted, grudgingly.

He swung the back door of the Yukon wider open and half sat on the back, one booted foot braced on the ground. "I have," he said, tone flat, reminding her of his military service. "This is the first time as a cop I've killed a man."

"You sure you did? I thought *I* killed a man." The words were no sooner out than she cringed at the hostility in her voice. What? Was she turning this into a *competition?*

And what did that make her?

Clay didn't say anything for a minute, only watched her. Uneasily, she wondered how much he could see.

Finally he stirred. "The M.E. will let us know eventually. My guess is, we killed him a couple of times over."

She squeezed her eyes shut and saw it all over again.

Astonishment on the man's face as he stumbled and began to fall. She swallowed and opened her eyes.

"We all hope we'll never have to do that," Clay said, in a tone so gentle she didn't recognize it coming from him.

Jane was suddenly horrified at how terribly she was behaving. If he could be decent, she could, too.

"No," she said. "Or yes. I never wanted—" At the taste of bile, she had to swallow again. She turned her back on Clay.

The faint sound of the Yukon sighing made her realize he'd risen to his feet and stood behind her.

"Jane."

"Don't say anything," she whispered.

A pause. "Why?" His voice, too, was so soft he wouldn't have been heard by anyone more than a foot or two away.

"Because—I can't talk to you."

"You don't trust me." Now he sounded harsh.

"No." She steadied. "I can't."

"You can, but you'll never believe it, will you?"

She held herself together by pure force of will. "No."

It was as if they were in a bubble of silence. Everything around them seemed far away. Jane didn't move, wasn't sure she breathed.

Then the bubble popped and she heard him walking away. One of the aide cars was pulling out, accelerating. She realized she should have been out there while the wounded were loaded, not hiding here in the darkness.

Following Clay, she reached a second aide car and saw that Ryan Dunlap had been hoisted aboard on a gurney. He was swearing, an impressive litany that made her smile despite everything. Thank God he'd regained consciousness. Apparently the bullet had only grazed his skull.

She leaned into the back of the ambulance. "Headache?"

"Like I got slammed with a two-by-four." He swore a little more. "Sorry, Lieutenant." Then, "Is it true? The kid's okay?"

"It's true. He's safe. We did our job."

One of the EMTs hopped to the ground. "Lieutenant, we have to go."

"See you at the hospital," she told Ryan, and stepped back as the doors were slammed and, a moment later, the aide car pulled away.

She watched it drive away for a minute, then trudged toward the barn, wishing Sergeant Clay Renner wasn't sure to be there.

CHAPTER TWO

CLAY WAS SITTING behind the desk in the captain's office frowning over a weekly report he'd been too busy yesterday to study, the reason he'd come in on a Saturday he'd intended to take off, when he heard raised voices and a scuffle in the squad room. Nothing unusual in that, but he glanced out the open doorway of the office anyway in case someone needed a hand.

"What are you doing? Why are you grabbing me?" A man was trying to explode upward as one of the detectives pressed him into a chair.

He wasn't the usual lowlife being hauled in. The guy was in his thirties, good-looking, thin and maybe earnest when he wasn't distraught. More like a computer geek than anything. He wore wire-rimmed glasses and had dark, curly hair poking out every which way.

There wasn't a lot of help to be had out there right now in case this guy went off the deep end, so Clay headed toward the disturbance, cutting his way between desks. "What's going on?" he asked, when he got close.

"I just want to report my wife and kid missing, and nobody will listen!" the computer nerd said frantically.

"We need an Amber Alert or—I don't know. *Something.*"

"We'll listen," Clay said, "but you've got to calm down so we can understand what happened."

Wild eyes pinned Clay for a couple of heartbeats, and then the guy sagged. Bent forward with a moan until his elbows were braced on his knees and his head hung.

The detective, Steve Atwood, cautiously removed his hands and, when the guy didn't erupt into motion, stepped back. After a moment, he took his own seat behind the desk. He was nearing retirement, solid but not imaginative and not real big on empathy, in Clay's opinion.

"All right, sir," Atwood said. "Let's start with your name."

It looked like he could handle it now, and Clay turned to leave them to it.

"Andrew Wilson," he heard the guy say. "Drew Wilson. My wife is Melissa."

Garden-variety names, but Clay stopped where he was. He'd heard those names before.

"It's my daughter Brianna." The name rode a dry sob. "She's only seven. She's with Lissa."

Lissa. Drew. Bree…and Alexis.

Stunned, Clay turned around, taking in this man's face. He was Jane Vahalik's brother-in-law. Had to be. She'd talked about him and her sister and the nieces she loved.

Drew Wilson looked up and saw Clay's stare. He didn't even seem to question it. "Where can they be?"

"Your other daughter," Clay said. "Alexis. Where's she?"

"Alexis." He tore at his hair. "She's… A neighbor has her." Confusion altered his features, and Clay realized Atwood was looking at him in puzzlement, too. "You know her?" the guy said.

"I know Lieutenant Vahalik. She's talked about all of you."

The softening he saw rubbed Clay the wrong way. He had a sister-in-law who was a nice enough woman, but he knew his face didn't look like that when someone mentioned her.

"I would have gone to her, but we don't live in Angel Butte."

"Okay," Clay said, shoving down a reaction he knew to be irrational. He had a hell of a lot of feelings for Jane Vahalik that fell on the hopeless to downright crazy spectrum. Seeing her again two weeks ago for the joint operation had stirred up too much. "Tell us why you think your wife and daughter are missing."

The story poured out. They'd gone for a brief errand, to Rite Aid in town. Melissa really hadn't wanted to take Brianna because the store had a whole aisle of toys, not to mention the candy, and Bree would beg, but his wife had finally succumbed and let her go along. Alexis was still napping, so she'd stayed home with her dad.

"Lissa called me on the way back. I'd asked her to pick up some stuff for athlete's foot." He started to lift one foot as if he was going to take off his shoe and show them his problem, but his thoughts moved on and his foot thumped back down. "She'd forgotten it and she wanted to know if it was important enough to go back for. I said no, I could pick some up the next time I went out. She said okay and then she—" He struggled for words. "She yelled. And I heard Bree screaming something like, 'Mommy, what are you doing?' or 'What are *they* doing?' And then the phone went dead."

Breath shuddered in and out a few times before he resumed his story. He'd tried calling his wife back, but the phone rang and rang and then went to voice mail. He tried again; same thing. Although alarmed, he figured she'd pull in any minute. Melissa had probably dropped the phone and couldn't reach it.

Only, she hadn't shown up. He'd waited for a bit, although it wasn't clear whether that was ten minutes or thirty. Finally, he got his younger kid up, put her in the family's second car and took her to the neighbor's. "We're on an acreage," he explained. Clay knew, pretty close, where the address he gave was. It was an area of nice, modern homes that were each on two-and-a-half or five-acre lots. Clay couldn't have afforded any of them on his salary from the county. He tried to remember what Jane had said the brother-in-law did for a living, but failed and didn't want to interrupt him now.

Drew went on to explain he'd then gone home again to be sure Melissa hadn't showed up, after which he'd driven her logical route to the outskirts of Angel Butte where the Rite Aid was located. He didn't spot her Toyota Venza anywhere.

Clay made another mental note. If he wasn't mistaken, the Venza, a crossover, had been new in 2013. It wasn't the most expensive vehicle on the road, but it didn't come cheap, either. The Wilsons must have money. He wondered what Drew drove.

Drew had called his wife's mobile phone half a dozen more times. He'd driven alternate routes. He'd gone home again to find she still hadn't returned. Scared, he'd come to the sheriff's department, from which, ironically, the Rite Aid could be seen.

"Let's back up here," Atwood said. "Any chance your wife is prone to impulse shopping expeditions? Say she remembered Target is having a back-to-school sale, and since she had your daughter with you she decided to stop?"

"What about the last thing I heard on the phone?"

"Maybe another driver cut her off."

Drew shook his head and kept shaking it. He seemed to have forgotten Clay had propped himself against a nearby vacant desk and was listening without intruding himself. He didn't kid himself that Atwood had also forgotten he was there.

"Maybe she didn't call you back because she was annoyed at you," the detective suggested in a tone of "it happens to all of us." "She as good at sulking as my wife is?"

"No!" Drew scowled. "She's—" He seemed to fumble with how to describe his wife. "She's…"

"Fiery, huh?" Atwood's eyebrows rose. "Say, you didn't have an argument before she left, did you? Maybe she's pissed because you expected her to buy something like athlete's foot powder? Or because you pressed her to take the kid when she didn't want to?"

An expression crossed Wilson's face so fast, Clay couldn't quite pin it down. "She didn't want to take her," he admitted, sounding as if he wished he didn't have to. "I told you. But…it wasn't like that. Anyway, she wouldn't disappear if she was mad at me. Especially not with Brianna."

Clay was getting a bad feeling about this. He excused himself to check on recently reported vehicular accidents, abandoned cars and the like while Atwood nailed down more details, especially a more precise time frame. Exactly when *had* Melissa called? Three hours ago or forty-five minutes ago?

The bad feeling got a hell of a lot worse when he reached the desk officer, who immediately said, "Yeah, there's been one possible fatality accident."

Jane's sister, *dead?* Shaken, Clay learned that Melissa Wilson had suffered a head injury and had been transported to the hospital in critical condition. Deputies were investigating the cause of the accident.

Clay called a deputy who was actually at the accident site.

"A kid?" He sounded appalled. "There was no kid in the vehicle when it was spotted." He swore. "You're sure?"

"I'm sure," Clay said grimly. "Unless there's another explanation—or we're being fed a line of bull by the father."

He strode across the squad room to where Drew Wilson sat with his head buried in his hands.

"Mr. Wilson," Clay said formally, "do you have a home phone?"

Jane's brother-in-law straightened, having aged even in the past five minutes. "Sure, but Lissa wouldn't have called it."

"I'm afraid," Clay told him, "there was an accident involving a Toyota Venza registered to you and your wife. The woman driver has been taken to the hospital. Last we know, she was unconscious. A police deputy has been trying to reach you, but unfortunately would have used your home phone rather than a cell number."

"The hospital?" Drew repeated numbly. But then his face changed and he lunged to his feet. "Bree. Is she okay?"

Clay didn't like saying this, but there was no alternative. "Your daughter wasn't in the vehicle, Mr. Wilson." Seeing the horror in a father's eyes, he raised his hand. "It's likeliest that your wife dropped her off somewhere before the accident. At a friend's house, perhaps?" He hesitated. "Especially given that the Venza wasn't found between your home and Rite Aid."

"But…I heard Bree when she called." His wild glance swung between Clay and Detective Atwood. "I know I heard her!"

JANE WAS CHEWING the hide off two detectives who had allowed half the citizens of Angel Butte to tromp through a crime scene when her desk phone rang. She gave it an irritated glance. She'd asked not to be interrupted and decided to let it go.

"And what about the log?" She stabbed the document in question with her forefinger. "I know for a fact that patrol officer Gwen Schneider walked through the house. Perhaps you can explain what she contributed to the investigation."

Kyle Griffin's mouth opened and closed a couple of times.

She leaned forward. They'd get back to the reason why a pretty young patrol officer had been given a tour of a nasty home-invasion scene. Now, though, she turned the log around so they could see the list of names with times of arrival and departure. Both sets of eyes were drawn irresistibly to it. "Perhaps," she said with silky menace, "you can point out to me where her name is."

"How did you know—?" Phil Henry was stupid enough to blurt.

Her cell phone began to ring. She shot it an exasperated glance, having already ignored a call from her brother-in-law, then felt a weird clench in her chest when she saw the displayed name. Clay Renner. Somehow she'd never deleted his phone number from her address book. Why would *he* be calling in the middle of the afternoon?

She wanted to mute the damn phone and ignore him—but he was one of her counterparts at the sheriff's department.

Jane blistered the two detectives sitting across from her with a stare, said, "Excuse me, I need to take this," and picked up the phone. "Vahalik."

"Jane, Clay Renner here."

Conscious of her audience, she said stiffly, "Sergeant."

"This is about your sister." He hesitated. "Your brother-in-law came in to report her and their daughter Brianna missing. Melissa's vehicle was located in a ditch. I'm at the scene. She suffered a head injury, Jane. She's in ICU, still unconscious. I'm afraid I don't know more. I'm focusing on another problem. The girl is missing."

"Oh, dear God," she whispered. "Drew… Is he all right? What about Alexis?"

"Alexis is safe with a neighbor."

"Did anyone see the accident?"

"No. A young couple on a day hike popped out of the woods just down the road from the SUV. They say another car had stopped. When the man called, 'Hey, is anybody hurt?' they heard a car door slam and the vehicle sped off. Fortunately, they were carrying a cell phone. They didn't try to move your sister once they realized she was unresponsive."

"If the other car caused the accident and the driver freaked…?" Even in shock, she knew that was stupid.

"A logical assumption, except that we've so far been unable to locate Brianna. Your brother-in-law went home to get his wife's address book and lists of names and phone numbers for Brianna's summer day camp and her first-grade classroom. Mr. Wilson started with the kids he thought she might be friends with, but so far no one has heard from her or Melissa today. We still haven't given up hope that your sister dropped her off somewhere—a friend's mother might have called to see if they could take her on a picnic or something that means they're not answering their phone. But at this point—"

"You have no idea where she is." Oh, God. She sounded so harsh.

"Thanks for the vote of confidence, Lieutenant."

She closed her eyes. "I'm sorry. I didn't mean…"

"Working on the assumption that she *was* a passenger when the accident occurred, we're organizing a search. Volunteers are already arriving."

"I don't know whether to help or to go to the hospital."

"Your brother-in-law is now at the hospital."

She swallowed, trying to think. "Then I'll come help search. If Bree's hurt or hiding for some reason, she'd recognize my voice."

"All right," Clay said. He told her where the SUV had gone off the road, and when she asked what Melissa could have been doing there, he said only, "At this point, we don't know. You okay to drive?"

"Of course I am!"

"Then I'll look for you." He disconnected.

Jane pushed her chair back and rose, looking at the two men in front of her. "You disgraced your shields today. Straight out of the academy, you should have known how to secure a crime scene. You are both on suspension until we can discuss this further."

They argued. She told them to go home, then detoured by Captain McAllister's office, found him there—another workaholic—and told him what she'd done and why, and where she was going.

He listened and shook his head. "Family comes first," he said, and asked if she should be driving.

She stared at him. He was serious. Colin McAllister *was* more like Clay Renner than she'd wanted to admit. She couldn't imagine either man would have asked that question if she'd been male.

"I'm fine," she said shortly, and left.

EVEN AS SHE drove, Jane puzzled over what Lissa had been doing out on 253rd, a little-traveled back road that would, heading west as Lissa had apparently been, have ultimately bisected a somewhat busier road that meandered between Angel Butte and Sun River far to the north. If she'd wanted to go to Sun River, though, it would have made a lot more sense to backtrack east to Highway 97, the major north-south route. And there were way more logical ways to return home or even to go into Angel Butte.

Okay, people did live along 253rd, so she might have taken Bree to some friend's house out there. But then, if she'd already dropped Bree off, why wasn't she heading back toward home? And—there weren't that many houses out here. Probably fortunately, as Jane was ignoring posted speed limits.

Bear Creek ran on the right of the road, which was several miles outside the Angel Butte city limits; she vaguely recalled a picnic area that shut down in the winter. She passed the decrepit sign for a long-since-closed resort and recalled a shooting that had happened there last December involving Colin's wife, Nell. Maybe this stretch of woods had some kind of bad karma.

Slowing at the sight of a dozen vehicles ahead parked along the shoulder, she shook off thoughts of Lissa's motives. Lissa would open her eyes anytime and *tell* them what she was doing here. Jane loved her sister fiercely even though she didn't always like her. She refused to even consider the possibility the head injury was severe enough that Lissa wouldn't *be* opening her eyes.

She parked at the end of the long line of cars, pickups and SUVs, then locked her vehicle and hurried forward. The burble of the creek, running low in late summer, and voices calling from the woods drifted to her ears as she rushed along the pavement toward the closer sound of other voices ahead.

Several men stood just outside the yellow tape surrounding her sister's red Toyota. Aware one of those men was Clay and that he'd turned when he heard her hurried footsteps, Jane initially ignored them to gape at her sister's Venza, a sporty crossover. *Ditch* had been a misnomer. Really, it was more of a bank that dropped toward the creek. It appeared as if a cluster of small alders and shrubbery was all that had kept the Venza from plunging another ten feet down into Bear Creek.

Clay separated himself from the group and approached her, his blue eyes intent on her face. He wore chinos and a polo shirt. She wondered if he'd been working today anyway, or if he had been called in. But no, she realized right away—that made no sense. Like her, he worked major crimes, not traffic accidents. In fact…what *was* he doing here?

"Jane," he said with a nod.

As always, she reacted to his physical presence in a way that aggravated her. Even his stride was so blasted *male*.

"Have you learned anything?" she asked, although she knew better. He'd have called if her sister had regained consciousness or a search-and-rescue volunteer had found her niece.

"I'm afraid not." He sounded regretful. "We've been going over the ground around the vehicle without finding a damn thing." Lines furrowed his forehead. "We need to find the driver of the other car that stopped. I'd hoped for a tire impression that would give us something to go on to locate it."

"Can't the hikers you said called tell you a make and color?"

He grimaced. "They think it was a car rather than a pickup or SUV. But it was apparently parked in front of your sister's SUV, which blocked their view. They were standing—" he turned and pointed back the way she'd come "—probably fifty yards away. They were aiming to come out at the picnic ground where they'd left their car, but they heard the sound of what they thought was a small waterfall and cut through the woods."

"Is there a falls here?" Jane asked, puzzled.

"No. Not enough elevation change. We're thinking they heard an engine."

She nodded. "What can I do?"

He led her to a man who appeared to be the organizer of the volunteers here to hunt for Bree. They had initially concentrated their efforts on the creek side of the road, in part because a child getting out of the vehicle would have had to scramble up to the road, while sliding down to the creek would have been easier.

Jane met Clay's eyes and knew what he was thinking. *If Brianna had been scared and running away.* But why would she have been?

Please, please let her be safe with some friend and her family.

Not hiding for some reason in the woods. Or—worse.

Her mind slammed shut on even the possibility of *worse.* No, no. *Worse* would mean somebody had snatched her, and that was ridiculously unlikely.

"What about that old resort?" Jane asked. "It has a bunch of cabins."

"A couple of deputies went over there," Clay said. "Talked to the people who own it. They run some kind of group home and use the cabins that are in better repair for teenage boys. Some of the boys helped scour the place. The deputy I talked to said they even got down and checked beneath porches." He shook his head. "Nothing."

"I wish there was more I could do," she said helplessly.

"I'm sorry," he said. "I thought you'd rather be here."

"Yes." She made herself say, "Thank you for calling me. I'll, um…" She gestured toward the search-and-rescue guy.

"Wait."

Surprised, she looked up at him.

"Your sister and her husband. Were they having any kind of problems?"

Jane grappled with the question. "You're not thinking—"

"I'm not thinking anything yet. Just asking questions."

"They've been having to tighten the belt," she said after a moment. "If that's what you mean by problems. Drew lost his job, oh, probably four months ago and hasn't been able to find anything comparable. Being out of work is upsetting for him. I don't know any man who would like the idea of his wife supporting the family. He's started looking farther afield, and I know Lissa isn't happy about that, but I wouldn't say they were fighting about it or anything."

"Would she tell you if they were?"

"One of them probably would." She couldn't say Drew would have, because then she'd have to explain that he was more than just her sister's husband, that it was because of her he'd met Lissa, and that she and her sister had a tense relationship at the best of times—and that these recent months had not qualified as the best of times.

If she wasn't imagining it, Clay's eyes had narrowed slightly. He'd heard something in her voice, even if it was only restraint.

"How much do you see of them?"

She looked away from him, watching as more volunteers arrived and were dispatched across the road into the dry woods. From each direction, she heard voices calling her niece's name. "Oh, you know. Dinner probably once a week. Sometimes I take the girls somewhere." She watched a middle-aged man in hiking boots and camo pants accepting instruction, nodding, and starting across the road. "I should be with them."

"You can join them if you want, but you'll do more good helping me understand if there's anything going on here besides a woman running off the road by accident in broad daylight and a kid either being misplaced or taking off."

"Bree wouldn't." Despite herself, she couldn't help looking into Clay's face again, hoping for… She didn't know. Reassurance? As angry as she still was at him, she knew he was a smart cop and a strong man. It disturbed her now that she couldn't tell what he was thinking. His expression was kind, but also detached. "Why would she?" she asked him, even knowing she was pleading. She hated how small her voice sounded.

His gaze turned from hers to move restlessly over the woods. "If she's out there, it's because she's scared. My first thought was that she'd gone for help. She's old enough to think to do that. But surely she'd have headed for one of the houses."

"Bree is really mature for her age—" She didn't even want to say this, but had to. "Unless she stopped a car and...and got unlucky. The driver was some kind of creep."

A pedophile. Please, God, no. Brianna was a beautiful child. She'd taken after Melissa, who'd always stopped traffic. Melissa, who used her beauty as a way to handle people.

Clay's gaze had locked on her face again. "Let's not get ahead of ourselves."

"Then where is she?" she cried.

His jaw tightened. "I don't know. If we have to seriously start considering this an abduction, though, we need to look at family first. You know that."

It took a minute for the implications to sink in. "Me?"

"Of course not you!" he snapped.

"Then *who?* It's only Jane and me."

"What happened to your parents?"

She couldn't *not* answer, but she also couldn't look at him while she said any of this. Instead she fixed her gaze on the trees across the road. "My mother walked out on us," she said, ignoring his close scrutiny. "I was eleven, Lissa eight, so it's ancient history." She did her best to sound matter-of-fact. "I have no idea if she's even still alive. My father died when I was twenty."

Maybe she was wrong in fearing that Clay heard things she wasn't saying. After all, look what an insensitive jerk he'd turned out to be. But no matter what, she didn't like telling him stuff that was so personal. She never talked about her childhood. If she had one desperate need in life, it was to be invulnerable. Why else had she gone into a male-dominated profession where *she* could hold the authority?

If she'd made him curious, he didn't comment. "What about your brother-in-law's side?"

"His parents are in Florida. They were out here for Christmas. They seem like nice people." She shrugged. "Drew has a brother and a sister. They came, too, with their families. Um, I think the brother may work for Boeing. His dad did, too, before he retired. That's where Drew grew up, near Seattle. The sister... I don't remember where she lives, but not locally. She's married and has kids, somewhere around the same ages as Bree and Alexis."

"Your sister get along with his family?"

Lissa had bitched for weeks about having to host Drew's whole damn family. That was how she'd put it. "The house is going to be stuffed, and we'll be lucky if any of them even offer to pay for any groceries," she had groused. "*Or* help with cooking and housework. They'll probably be happy to have me providing maid service. And I can't stand Kelsey. You know that."

Jane did know. Lissa didn't like Kelsey because she thought Drew's parents did more for the baby of the family than they did for Drew and his brother. Kelsey's husband taught English at the middle school level and they'd agreed that Kelsey wouldn't work outside the home at least until their youngest reached first grade, so they did make a whole lot less money than Drew and Lissa. Or at least, than Drew and Lissa had at the time, when he'd still had a job. Drew's parents had wanted Kelsey to have a safe vehicle to drive their grandchildren around in, so they'd bought her a Dodge Caravan at about the same time Lissa had insisted on trading in her four-year-old Rav4 for something newer. She had been bitterly resentful that they hadn't even offered to help with the cost. "Our income doesn't have anything to do with it!" she'd snapped, when Jane was unwise enough to try to reason with her.

"They didn't see that much of them," Jane said now. "Things seemed fine at Christmas."

He looked at her thoughtfully, and she knew— *knew*—that he had noticed how uncomfortable she was.

"All right, Jane." His phone rang and he answered it immediately. "Renner here."

He'd half turned from her as if to shut her out, but he didn't walk away, so she couldn't help hearing his side of the conversation.

"No change?" Pause. "Uh-huh." He frowned, listening. "Yeah, we're out beating the bushes for the kid. We're going to feel like idiots if it turns out she's at the public swimming pool or, I don't know what little girls do, a toenail-painting party." A grunt. "Tell him to keep trying." Whoever had called talked some more. "What about that last clerk at Rite Aid?" Clay asked. Something changed on his face at the answer and he turned to look at Jane. "Okay. Let me know." He returned his phone to his belt.

She didn't like his expression. "What?"

"We've now talked to everyone working at Rite Aid today, including the pharmacists. Not one of them remember seeing your sister or the girl. It's looking a lot like they never went there at all."

"But—" Jane stuttered "—she told Drew…"

"I know what he claims she told him." The emphasis on *claims* was subtle, but unmistakable.

"Why would Drew lie? This was an accident!"

"Was it?" Clay's angular face was hard now, all cop. "I'm starting to wonder."

CHAPTER THREE

Rɪᴄʜ Bᴀʟᴅᴡɪɴ, a sergeant in the patrol division, crossed his arms atop the open driver's-side door of his unit and eyed Clay. "I've got to admit, I wondered why you were there early on."

He paused, eyebrows raised, but Clay didn't rise to the bait. Damned if he was going to admit to having a thing for a woman who despised him.

The eyebrows flickered, but Baldwin gave up and finished his thought. "I'm glad now you were. It's looking more like your baby all the time."

Clay grunted his agreement, although he could not freakin' *believe* he was dealing with the second kidnapping of a child within a matter of weeks. Except for the everyday domestic blow-up variety where Dad didn't bring the kids home when he should just to spite the ex wife, kidnapping almost never happened around here. He kept telling himself the girl was going to turn up anytime, that there was a reasonable explanation for her disappearance.

But as the hours passed, the odds that seven-year-old Brianna Wilson would turn out to have spent the afternoon with a friend were looking longer by the minute.

At 7:30 in the evening, your average family's dinnertime had come and gone and the sun was dropping low in the sky. Kids that age did overnights, but according to her dad, Bree hadn't taken pajamas, toothbrush or anything else with her.

A deputy had stayed at the Wilson house to answer the phone, mostly in hopes some mother would call and say, "Was I confused? Weren't you going to pick Brianna up by six?"

Clay almost wished he could anticipate a ransom call. That would have been better than the far uglier alternative. But though the Wilsons' house was nice, even before Drew lost his job, they didn't have the kind of money that would make a scenario of that kind probable.

Ankles crossed, Clay leaned against the fender of Baldwin's squad car, parked not far from the emergency room entrance. Clay was arriving, Rich departing from the hospital.

"I don't like that we couldn't find Mrs. Wilson's phone," Clay said.

"Or that it's dead to the world."

Destroyed, he meant. If she'd given it to the kid to take with her, they should have been able to triangulate its location even if Brianna had somehow turned it off.

Yeah, the completely missing phone was a puzzle piece slotting into an increasingly ugly picture in Clay's mind. He just wished there weren't so damn many missing pieces still.

A missing *kid* was what he really meant. Clay had seen Brianna Wilson's first-grade school picture now, as well as a formal family portrait of the whole family taken just before Christmas. Bree, as Jane called her, was a doll, Clay hadn't been able to help thinking, on her way to being a stunner. Her hair was the same chestnut-brown as Jane's, highlighted with red, and wavy like hers, too. And, damn, but Clay did love Jane's hair. Little Bree had just enough freckles scattered over the bridge of her nose to be cute. In both photos her untroubled grin showed missing front teeth. Unlike Jane's, the kid's eyes were a warm brown.

Clay was ashamed in retrospect at how closely he had studied that family photo, fascinated to see how the sisters resembled each other and yet…didn't. He guessed most people would have said Melissa had gotten the looks, but nothing about her face stirred him. Yeah, she had finely sculpted cheekbones, a pouty mouth that made him wonder about collagen and a perfect arch of eyebrows shaped by a master hand, but she looked hard to him. As if she'd summoned that smile when the photographer said, "Cheese!" but didn't really mean it.

Or maybe he was prejudiced because he liked everything about Jane's looks, including her round, gentle face and curving forehead that was almost too high, the tiny dimple that formed in one cheek when she was trying to hide amusement, the pretty mouth, the eyebrows that—well, she was a girl, so she probably did some plucking now and again, but not often.

Jane would never believe him if he told her he'd been drawn to her face even before he'd noticed her generous breasts or well-rounded hips. She seemed convinced now that he'd never lifted his eyes above chest level.

Not relevant, he told himself for about the dozenth time today. This wasn't about Jane. It especially wasn't about Jane and him.

"Baldwin, I'm keeping you from leaving," he said, slapping a hand on the hood of the car and pushed himself away from it.

Baldwin nodded and lowered himself behind the wheel, but didn't immediately pull the door closed. "Lieutenant Vahalik says search and rescue was called off?"

"An hour ago. I take it she isn't happy?"

"I think she's mostly scared. Doesn't matter that she's a cop. This is her family."

"Can't blame her," Clay agreed, lifted a hand and strode toward the hospital entrance.

He knew his way to the ICU. From well down the hall, he saw Jane alone in the small waiting area outside it. She was staring fixedly at the double doors that kept her out. It struck him that he'd never seen her so absolutely still before. Jane was too full of life to waste time sitting still.

Whether she heard his footsteps or not, she didn't react. He had almost reached her when her head finally turned. He was shocked at the sight of her. Her eyes were red-rimmed, her mane of curly hair slipping from its usual ponytail and, for one unguarded moment, he saw all her stress and fear before she managed to mostly blank her expression.

She rose to her feet in a single jerky motion. "Have you found—?" The answer must have been apparent on his face, because she dropped back down as if she were a puppet whose strings had been cut. "Oh, God."

"I'm sorry." He took the chair next to her and reached for her hand. It felt so small, too delicate to hold a heavy handgun, never mind to fire it. To kill.

Damn it. If he couldn't get past thinking things like that— Oh, who was he kidding? He'd had his chance and blown it. And…did he *want* to change his thinking so drastically?

Yeah. For Jane, he did.

"Any word on your sister?" he asked.

Her eyes, puffy and desperate, never left his. Her hand held tight to his, too. "There's no change. They're letting Drew sit with her. Every so often he comes out to give me a report, or…or he takes a break and I go in. They're calling it a coma now, Clay. They drilled a hole in her skull to relieve the pressure. The doctor isn't saying what he thinks the prognosis is. Or else he told Drew, who is lying to me."

"She's your only family."

"Her and the kids." Her shoulders moved a little. "And Drew."

"Damn, Jane." He cleared his throat. "I wish you weren't having to go through this."

Tears shimmered in her eyes, but she blinked furiously, not letting them fall. "Shit happens, right? Who knows that better than we do?"

He couldn't argue.

"Where's Bree?"

The way she looked at him, as if he was capable of miracles, made his sinuses burn. Produce the kid and redeem himself.

He'd give damn near anything to be up to this particular miracle.

"I don't like what I'm thinking," he said gruffly. He couldn't lie to her. Jane wasn't most women. She was tough. He knew that. "Did Sergeant Baldwin tell you Melissa's cell phone is missing?"

"He says it might have been destroyed."

Clay's thumb circled on the back of her hand. "Yeah. And we both know that's not good."

Her head bobbed. Either she hadn't noticed they were still holding hands or she needed the contact too much to let go no matter how much she detested him.

"The phone at your sister's place hasn't rang once. Home phone numbers are on those lists handed out by the day camp and the school, so we know the odds are any of her friends' parents would have it, not just Melissa's cell number.

"We've got an Amber Alert up," he told her. "That may or may not lead to FBI involvement. At this point, with no unexpected dents or scrapes on the vehicle, we don't have any evidence to suggest your sister was forced off the road. It's still entirely possible Brianna is with a friend, and has maybe spent the night before so the mom or dad figures Melissa had some crisis but will call tomorrow."

Despite the fear in her eyes, a tiny hint of hope sparked. "It is possible, isn't it?"

"Yeah." He wished he believed it, but didn't see how it would hurt if she did, at least for a little while.

"Okay." She ducked her head suddenly, probably to hide tears. "Thank you."

He bent over her and kissed the top of her head, letting himself inhale the scent that was uniquely Jane. For a moment she seemed to sway toward him, as if she was going to let herself lean, but then she squared her shoulders and straightened, tugging her hand free at the same time.

"You probably have things you need to be doing—"

"I wanted to talk to you some more, and then to your brother-in-law."

She visibly armored up. "To me?" she said, polite but surprised.

"Yeah. You. You know your sister. You know your niece."

A cautious nod.

"I expected Drew to have a better idea who his daughter's best friends are."

Tiny lines puckered that high forehead. "I think that's because Bree's two best friends are both gone. The summer hasn't been a very good one for her."

"Gone." Clay echoed. It had to be a reflection of his job that he equated *gone* with *dead*.

"Moved. Well, Poppy's family moved, and to Texas, no less, which means no visits. They'd been friends since preschool. And then Bree's other best friend, Schuyler, was in a foster home, but Lissa said the courts finally terminated the mother's parental rights and they're trying Schuyler in a potential adoptive home. Which unfortunately is in… I forget. Bend or some-place. Close enough for sleepovers, but not to be in the same school, which means they'll forget each other by October, probably."

"Sleepovers," he repeated.

Her hope brightened. "Schuyler would have been on that class list, but the phone number would have been for the foster parents who don't have her anymore. It could have been impulsive…."

He was already shaking his head, even though he hated to dim the light in her eyes. "I'll check. You can count on that. But if your sister was going to take Brianna to a friend's house, why wouldn't she have stopped at home first to let her pack a bag? Plus, it doesn't explain why the accident happened where it did."

Her shoulders sagged. "You're right." Then she cried, "Oh, why doesn't she wake up and *tell* us what happened?"

She sounded as if she was angry at her sister, which might be natural, or might not.

"Melissa," he said, pursuing the thought. "The two of you close?"

Jane's gaze slid from his in what he recognized as evasion. "Yes." She hesitated. "I mean, we have our moments. Don't most siblings?"

"Sure," Clay said easily. "My brother and I beat the crap out of each other every now and again just for the hell of it."

Jane rolled her eyes. "I can safely say that Lissa and I never get violent. We just, um, have stretches where we don't talk very often. You know."

No, he didn't, but he wanted to. "What about lately? Have you been talking? Would you know if anything was going on with her?"

"Anything?"

"Say, trouble with her husband."

Some anger fired up on her face. "The husband who is in ICU right now holding her hand and praying for all he's worth?"

"Two people can fight and still care about each other."

"But you're suggesting something a lot worse than fighting."

Yeah, now that she mentioned it, he was. He couldn't help thinking of a couple of moments where something had been really *off* with Drew Wilson. It was a gut feeling more than anything else, but Clay trusted his gut.

"I'm trying to get a complete picture, that's all. You'd be doing the same if you were in my shoes."

She slanted a suddenly suspicious look at him. "Why *were* you at the accident site so early on? Is there something you're not telling me?"

Clay shook his head. "Nothing like that."

"Then why?"

He moved his shoulders, trying without success to ease the new tension. "I'd come in for a few hours to catch up on reading reports."

She nodded. She'd been at work on a sunny Saturday, too.

"One of my detectives was taking a report from Drew. He'd given his name, and then I heard him talking about Melissa and Brianna. It clicked that he had to be your brother-in-law and that it was your sister who was missing." He grimaced. "I was curious."

Jane studied him, long enough for it to become uncomfortable. Her pupils dilated slightly, as if…he didn't know. Finally she gave a funny little nod. "Thank you."

Which meant she knew he'd stuck his nose in where it didn't belong because he was worried about *her*. "If it had been the other way around…"

"You're right." Now she didn't want to meet his eyes. "I'd have been curious, too."

There was a bump in his chest, as if his heart had

maybe skipped a beat. Was she implying…? Something else he didn't know.

Damn. *Focus. Do your goddamn job.*

"You didn't really answer my question. *Was* Melissa speaking to you lately? For some reason you want me to think everything was sweetness and light between her and Drew, but I need to know if it wasn't."

She averted her face. He sat through the silence while she struggled with herself. When she finally looked back at him, her expression was guarded.

"No, we haven't been getting along well lately. Like I said, we have…tensions. There's three years between us, and after Mom took off I sort of stepped in as a mother figure. Then Lissa was only seventeen when Dad died and she lived with me until she graduated from high school. Especially once she hit about thirteen, she resented me having any authority over her. Her favorite line was, 'You're not my mother and you can't tell me what to do.'" Jane shrugged. No biggie, she was trying to convince him. What had she said? *Ancient history.*

Too bad he didn't buy it.

"Rivalry for your dad's attention?"

Her expression shut down with the finality of a steel door. He didn't have to hear the lock to know it had slid into place.

"No," she said, and that was all.

Oh, man, he wanted to pursue the subject, but had an uneasy feeling he was straying into personal territory. Yes, he wanted to know Jane, but right now, the people he needed to know were her sister, her brother-in-law and the missing niece.

"Drew and I are friends." Jane didn't sound as if she wanted to tell him, but felt compelled to. "If they were really having problems, he would have told me. Like I said, there was the job thing and the question of whether they'd move if he found a good enough one, but he hadn't yet, so—" She lifted one shoulder.

"Is he good with the kids?" Clay made his tone casual.

"Drew?" Jane looked genuinely surprised. "Sure. Hey, right now, *he's* the one who's home with them. That's probably why Lissa took Bree with her. Especially with her two friends having moved away, Bree probably needed some exclusive mom time."

She didn't know that Drew had implied Melissa had felt extreme reluctance to take her daughter along. Because she'd been cranky and wanted some peace and quiet? Or because she'd never intended to run the errand that was her ostensible reason for leaving the house?

Or—and this was the big *or* in Clay's book—was the whole story fiction? Melissa Wilson's supposed trip to Rite Aid, the possibility she and her husband had squabbled about whether she was going to take Brianna, the later phone call... It all came from the same man.

Not the phone call; Clay had verified that there was a call lasting just under one minute from Melissa's phone to Drew's. But what was said, who'd actually dialed the call, that was all in question as far as Clay was concerned.

His least favorite scenario involved the pedophile who got lucky and happened on a really pretty little girl trying to flag down a passing motorist.

But he had some others that would keep him awake, too, and they involved Drew Wilson.

What if he and his wife had done more than squabble? What if they'd had a nasty fight? If she fled, he might have pursued and been responsible for running her off the road. He could have Brianna stashed somewhere so she couldn't tell what had really happened. He might figure he could brainwash her, then have her miraculously restored to him.

Or what if he was sexually molesting his eldest daughter, and he really couldn't afford it if either she *or* his wife talked?

Jesus. What if he'd killed his daughter and then chased down his wife to shut *her* mouth? So far, Clay hadn't found a witness to confirm anything beyond the fact that Drew had dropped his younger daughter off at the neighbor's without saying anything but that he thought maybe his wife's car had broken down and he needed to go check on her. His frantic appearance at the police station could be a con job.

And Clay didn't like being conned.

He was honest enough with himself to admit that he also didn't like the idea that Jane had a closer relationship with her brother-in-law than she did with her sister.

Once he finished talking to Jane, he was going to have a chat with the nurses in ICU and make sure they kept at least half an eye on Melissa Wilson and her so-devoted husband.

"You said you take the girls alone sometimes. I'll bet you tried to keep Brianna from feeling too sad this summer."

"I've tried to do something fun with her every week.

Sometimes both girls, but Alexis is happier at the day camp than Bree is this year. I know Drew lets her stay home some days even when he takes Alexis."

A father *should* want to spend individual time with his kids. Unfortunately, in his job, Clay had seen too many cases where a father liked being alone with one of his kids for a sick reason.

"I've mostly been working Tuesday through Saturday," Jane continued. "So I've devoted a lot of Mondays this summer to the girls. Sometimes they spend Sunday at my place. In July I took just Bree over to that really cool water park in McMinnville."

He decided he had to be direct. "Does she talk to you? Would she tell you if something was weighing on her?"

Jane's uncomprehending stare slowly altered to one of outraged understanding. "You're suggesting that… that Drew or Lissa was *abusing* her?"

"I'm asking if the possibility exists."

"No!"

He held her gaze with a steady one of his own. "Jane, you're not that naive. I know this is your family. Nobody ever wants to think a person she loves could do something like that. But it happens. In fact, it's a hell of a lot more common than most people have any idea."

She visibly choked on it, but she had been a cop too long to deny what he said was the truth. "No," she repeated, but more moderately. "I really don't think so. The girls are both cheerful and affectionate and—" Jane scowled. "If I could imagine it with either of their parents, it wouldn't be—" She stopped again, unhappy.

"Your sister," Clay said slowly.

Her mouth tightened. "Actually, I was going to say Drew. He's a really nice guy. I think Alexis and Bree are more comfortable with him than they are with Lissa. She's, I don't know, uptight and—" something else she didn't want to say "—self-centered, I guess."

An unpleasant suspicion had entered Clay's mind as she talked. Clay remembered the way Drew's face and tone had softened when the subject of Jane came up. Now listen to the warmth in her tone. Was there any chance something was going on there? Even the idea enraged him.

But, truth was, he couldn't think how a flirtation or even an affair between Jane and Drew could have played into today's events, unless it had been a catalyst for a monumental fight between husband and wife. And then how did that involve the kid?

No.

He didn't believe it anyway, he discovered. He thought Jane's sense of integrity was too unbending to allow her to sleep with her sister's husband.

But he also found he hated almost as much the possibility that she wanted to. That the two of them looked at each other sometimes with the knowledge between them that they might have been happy together.

And yeah, what grated maybe most of all was the way she'd described Drew. He was a really nice guy— while Clay Renner was scum of the earth.

Like acid in his belly, it ate at him knowing he'd given her damn good reason to believe exactly that.

And…maybe she'd be right to believe it. A self-confident man, Clay had taken a serious hit that day. Since she'd walked away, he'd looked hard at a lot of crap he'd grown up taking for granted. What shook him most was discovering how much contempt for women had been embedded in his father's "traditional" views of male/female roles.

Yeah, well, too little, too late.

He stood abruptly. "I'm going in to see how your sister is doing. Then I want you to switch places with your brother-in-law so I can talk to him."

By her narrowed eyes, he could tell she thought he really intended to bully poor, *nice* Drew, which upped his pissed quotient. But by God, he was too good at his job to let personal feelings influence an investigation.

He nodded at Jane, probably nothing too friendly showing on his face, and left her alone there.

Drew sat in the hard plastic chair beside Lissa's bed in ICU, listening to the hum and beep of monitors and the squeak of shoes as a nurse walked past. Farther away were voices. Somebody else getting bad news? he wondered with a jab of pain.

Sometimes he tilted his head back and stared at the pattern of Lissa's heart beating in jagged green lines across a monitor. Mostly he gazed at her face, so ominously still and unlike her. He sat on her good side, so he didn't have to see the horrible swelling and bruising. Not that he could forget doctors had actually drilled into her skull.

He squeezed the lax, cool hand that lay in his. "Liss," he murmured, "can you hear me? I really need you to open your eyes. You're scaring me. I can't believe you of all people—" He broke off with a harsh breath.

Melissa had been a revelation to him when he'd met

her, filled with a vitality that made her stand out from everyone else he'd ever met. Enthralled, he hadn't been able to resist her. He hadn't *wanted* to resist her, even though he'd known he was hurting Jane.

The terrible thing was that sometimes he thought he'd been an idiot, that Lissa was all surface and flash, and he should have been able to see beneath it. He'd begun to wonder if she really loved him at all. Lately—

But he didn't want to think about the suspicions that nibbled at him like mosquitoes raising welts. If only she'd open her eyes, they could talk. She would convince him that she had nothing to do with whatever had happened to Bree, and these doubts churning in his belly would go away. If only he could have Bree back, have Melissa back, he could forgive almost anything.

He leaned toward her, resting his elbows on his knees. "I need you to talk to me. Please, Liss. Please."

But her face stayed still and sunken, and on a surge of anguish he tried to imagine never seeing her laugh again, or whirl on him in a fury, or light with some new enthusiasm. What if he had to plod on without her?

But on a clench of dread and fear, he knew: if he could somehow, magically, save either his wife or his daughter, but not both, he would have to choose Bree.

"That's what you'd want, isn't it?" he whispered.

She didn't answer, of course.

CHAPTER FOUR

"AUNTIE JANE?" Huddled in a tiny ball beneath the covers, Alexis peered out. "Will you...will you stay till I fall asleep? And maybe even lie down with me?"

Jane's heart squeezed painfully. "Oh, pumpkin. Of course I will."

She untied her athletic shoes and dropped them on the floor, then turned off the bedside lamp before lying down atop the covers so that her head shared her five-year-old niece's pillow and she could kiss her on the nose. The little girl wriggled a few times to fit into the curve of Jane's body. Then she gave a small sniff.

"Auntie Jane, will you find Bree tomorrow?" The question floated, only a wistful thread.

Jane gave her a squeeze. "You know I'll try, with all my might. But Sergeant Renner is really the one in charge of finding her. The good thing is, I know he'll try with all his might, too."

"'Cuz I miss her."

"Oh, sweetheart." Jane squeezed her eyes shut in hopes of damming the tears and leaned her forehead against her niece's. "I know," she said huskily.

"Where's Daddy? I mean, is he with Mommy?"

"Yeah. He's with Mommy."

The silence was so long, Jane began to hope Alexis had fallen asleep. Somehow she doubted it, though; even through the covers, she could feel the tension in the slight body.

"Why won't Mommy wake up?"

"Mommy had a *really* bad bump on her head. You remember the time Bree fell off her bike and she had that great big lump that looked like an egg and we had to take her to the hospital?"

Alexis nodded slightly.

"Well, this is a bump way worse than that. Sergeant Renner thinks your mom's car was going really fast when it went off the road."

"Mommy always said if she was in a…a accident, this humongous balloon would puff up so nobody was hurt." She sounded indignant.

"The balloon is called an air bag. And they work really well, except they only puff up in certain kinds of accidents. Like if your mom's car had hit a tree. But the way the car tilted kept the air bag from puffing up."

The "oh" was sad. After a minute, "When will Daddy come home?"

"I think he might be here when you get up in the morning. He misses you, pumpkin."

"Okay."

Feeling Alexis slowly relax until, finally, her breathing became deep and regular, Jane thought about Drew's terrible dilemma. Did he stay at Melissa's side, willing her to open her eyes? Or did he go home to comfort his youngest daughter, so terrified because, in her perception, almost everyone in her family had disappeared?

Jane was only glad she could be here. She'd already decided that if they didn't find Bree tomorrow, she would pack a bag and come to stay. She'd take days off from work, too, as much as she had to. That way she could offer Alexis some stability and Drew the relief of knowing she was being taken care of. She could take care of him, too. Cook dinners, that kind of thing, even though she wasn't exactly Susie Homemaker.

Once she was sure Alexis was sleeping soundly, Jane slipped off the bed and out of the room, leaving the door half ajar so she'd be able to hear the little girl if she awakened. The twin bed was way too small for the two of them to share, and Jane's adrenaline ran too high for her to be sleepy yet anyway.

What she wanted was to be hunting for Bree, but she knew she was lucky that Clay had involved her as much as he had so far. He didn't have any obligation to. And as much as she hated it, he was right that family members were always the first suspects when an act of violence or an apparent abduction happened. And what had she done but told him, so brilliantly, that she and her sister weren't getting along very well. If she hadn't been at work when the accident occurred, he'd have had to consider her; she knew that. Considering that she didn't like him, she was disconcerted by the sting she felt at the idea that he'd readily suspect her of hurting her own sister, or her niece.

He'd said he didn't as if the idea was ludicrous, but... she didn't know whether to believe him.

He'd seemed angry at her when she'd last seen him at the hospital. Was that because she'd been too honest about Lissa, and he'd realized he had discounted her possible involvement too quickly?

I don't care what he thinks about me as long as he does his job, she thought fiercely. *As long as he finds Bree.*

But…she knew that wasn't true. She did care. She could have cared a whole lot, if only he had turned out to be the man she'd believed he was.

That thought felt like grief, heavy in her chest, not so different from her fear for Lissa and Bree and her sadness for Alexis.

Something she so didn't need.

IT WAS PROBABLY too late to call Jane. Clay didn't even know why he wanted to. He'd seen plenty of her today, God knows. But after he'd left the hospital, as the evening and then the night had crawled on, he kept thinking about her. Wondering whether she was still there, or had gone home, or…?

He reached his own place, a log cabin on the outskirts of Little Elk, a town too small even to have a post office. He loved the quiet and the peace here, and had looked forward to showing Jane his home.

Yeah, well, that wasn't happening.

He parked his Jeep Grand Cherokee in the carport attached to one side of the cabin and got out. The moon was heading toward full now, and the silver illumination cast shadows from the tall pines. He'd never installed a motion-activated light; there was enough wildlife around here that it would have been popping on all the time. As he walked toward the front door, he heard a soft hoot. A welcome home, or a complaint because he'd disturbed the night?

He let himself in, not bothering to turn on the porch light or a light in the main room. Instead he made his way by habit to the kitchen, where he poured himself a glass of milk and downed it in a few swallows, hoping it would soothe the acid in his stomach. Too many cups of coffee today. Had to be that, and not the gut-churning emotions he'd felt every time he looked at Jane or thought of her.

The clock on the stove told him it was 11:19 p.m. Maybe not too late to call? As scared as she was, would Jane really have dropped into a peaceful sleep by now?

Clay didn't know why he felt such a hunger to talk to her. He didn't have anything that qualified as real news to share, but…he wanted to hear her voice, to know she was okay.

He was dialing before he could have second thoughts.

Jane answered on the second ring. "Clay?" Her voice rang with anxiety.

"Nothing new," he told her hastily. "I just, uh, thought I'd check in. I hope I didn't wake you up."

"No. Of course not." She hesitated. "I'm at Lissa's with Alexis. So Drew could stay at the hospital."

"He's planning to stay all night?"

"I don't know. He shouldn't. He has to get some rest sometime. But I offered to pick up Alexis and tuck her in. She'd already had dinner with the neighbor."

"Did *you* have dinner?" he asked, leaning back against the knotty pine kitchen cabinets.

There was a moment of silence. "I'm not hungry."

"I know it's hard when you're scared, but you should have something."

"Maybe."

He sought for something else to say. "Alexis okay?"

"Not really. It was—" She broke off, or maybe her voice had broken. "Um, she wanted to talk about why her mommy hadn't opened her eyes, and she was hoping I'd promise to bring Bree home tomorrow."

"She's five, right?"

"Right. She's supposed to start kindergarten in… wow, not much over a week."

"Bad enough at that age having something scary happen to one member of your family. But two…" He shook his head, remembering something he hadn't thought of in years. His mother had had breast cancer when she was in her forties. Really scary shit, even if he was an adult. Sort of an adult, he amended, doing some mental arithmetic to decide he'd been…nineteen? Twenty? Anyway.

"What are you thinking about?" Jane asked. "You've gotten really quiet."

So he told her. "All they did was remove a lump. They were confident they'd caught it early. But we all watched her like a hawk for years. I don't even know when I quit getting this sinking feeling every time I saw her and thinking, what if it comes back?"

"Maybe after the magic five years?"

"Maybe." What did this have to do with anything? He wasn't sure. But he said, "My dad's a hard-ass. You know? That's the only time I can ever remember seeing him emotional. Scared. And gentle with Mom. That's not his style."

He'd never actually thought of his parents and the word *love* connected until that scare. Then he'd known. His father might not be good showing it, but he loved Clay's mom. It was plain he'd have been lost without her.

Clay had liked his father a little better after that.

His mouth twisted. *A little* summed it up. Increasingly, he felt distaste for a man he'd once admired. A man who'd loved his sons and always had time for them while he taught them everything he believed a man should be.

"I'm sorry," he said. "I don't know why I told you all that."

"Maybe because it came out all right?" Jane suggested. "Your mom is fine?"

Was that why? He'd wanted to remind her that, yes, scary shit did happen and most often everyone came out safe on the other side?

If so—that was dumb as hell. Jane and he were both in a good position to know how often when things went to shit they stayed that way. Faces flashed through his memory, too many to catch one and stop it—the faces of accident victims, battered wives, kids who did something stupid and paid the ultimate penalty. Murder victims.

"Thank you," she said softly.

What could he say but "You're welcome."

"Have *you* gone home?"

"Just got here." He kneaded the back of his neck. "With the Amber Alert out there, a bunch of phone calls came in from people who thought they might have seen

Bree. You know how it is. We had to follow up on all of them, but nothing panned out."

She made a sound that might have been an "oh."

"Didn't really expect they would," he continued, "but you never know."

"No. Maybe tomorrow. I mean, she can't have just vanished from the face of the earth."

Thinking of the miles of empty country around Angel Butte, Clay knew she was wrong. A little girl's body could go undiscovered for a long time. Even forever. But he wasn't about to say anything like that to Jane. Didn't have to, he realized; she knew. But she was trying for hope, too, and that was okay.

"You should get some sleep," he told her gently. "Don't wait up for your brother-in-law. You know he'll call if anything changes."

"You will, too, won't you?" she said with sudden urgency. "This is really hard, being on the sidelines. I don't care if you wake me up. If you hear anything. Anything at all."

"Yeah," he said. "I swear."

"Okay." There was a pause. "I'm glad you called. Thank you, Clay."

"You're welcome," he said again. "Go on. Hit the sack."

"You, too."

They said good-night and his phone went dead. Clay checked to be sure he'd put the milk back in the fridge, then flicked off the overhead light and made his way through the dark to the stairs. He thought he might be able to sleep now. Talking to Jane had…settled him. No real reason, but he felt better knowing she was hanging in there. He liked the softness in her voice when she said his name, too.

He hoped she went to bed before Drew came home wanting to weep on her shoulder.

JANE WOKE TO the sound of voices down the hall. She grabbed the second pillow and slapped it over her head. She wanted desperately to sink back into sleep. An uninterrupted hour or two. That was all she asked.

But of course it was hopeless. The light slipping through the blinds in this guest bedroom told her it was morning. Anyway, once she was really awake, she was awake.

She dragged herself to the bathroom and groaned at the sight of herself in the mirror. Given that she had no change of clothes, without borrowing something from Lissa—and she shuddered at the very thought—there wasn't a whole lot she could do about her appearance. She did use the girls' hairbrush—with a sparkly pink handle, no less—to try to restore order to her wild locks. Her mouth felt gummy, but a brief search of the drawers for a spare toothbrush came up empty. She really had to make it home today to pack that bag.

Drew sat slumped at the kitchen table. Alexis had scraped her chair as close to the corner of the table as she could get it. As close to her daddy as she could get.

"Can I have 'nother waffle, Daddy?" she begged in her piercing little voice. "I think I want jam on this one."

"What? Oh…sure," he agreed, voice dragging. He started to push his chair back, and she bounced out of hers to follow him. Drew saw Jane then. "Hey. I'm sorry if we made too much noise."

He was hardly recognizable. His brown eyes were puffy and bloodshot. Deep lines had somehow carved themselves between his nose and mouth and across his forehead. Jane would have sworn he'd aged ten years in the last twenty-four hours. Twenty years.

Of course, she didn't look so sharp this morning, either.

"I'll put her waffle in the toaster," she offered, having seen the box on the counter. Thank goodness Drew hadn't felt obligated to make some from scratch, not after the night he must have had. "Did you get any sleep at all?" she asked.

He sank heavily back into the chair. "Couple hours. How about you?"

Jane bent down to hug Alexis. "Your daughter had nightmares." Lots of nightmares. "But we survived, didn't we, pumpkin?"

"Uh-huh. I didn't want to be alone last night." Alexis and Bree had their own bedrooms now, but they'd shared a room until about a year ago. "So finally I went to bed with Auntie Jane."

Drew gave her a wry smile. "Lucky Auntie Jane."

"She said she couldn't sleep, either." Alexis followed Jane. "I can have jam, right?"

"You bet. Can I have some of those waffles, too?"

The little girl nodded. "But what if they're all gone?"

"Then we'll grocery shop today."

"Or you'll eat cereal for breakfast tomorrow," her father said, giving her an admonitory look.

She looked mulish. "I only like waffles."

While the waffles toasted, Jane asked what the plan was for today.

"I think I'll take Alexis to her day camp," he said.

His daughter let out a wail, threw herself from her chair and ran to him. Her arms clamped around his waist and she buried her face in his torso. "No! I don't want to go. Don't make me go, Daddy. *Please.* I want to be with you."

The look he cast Jane was so hopeless, she felt an anguished pang.

He smoothed his hand over his daughter's hair, the same brown as his. "I have to go back to the hospital. And Jane has a job."

"I can go to the hospital, too, can't I?" Alexis pleaded. "I'll be good. Really, really, *really* good."

The waffles popped up and Jane began buttering. "Lots of jam or a little?" she asked.

Alexis ignored her. "*Please,* Daddy."

Jane slapped huckleberry jam on both waffles, stuck two more in the toaster, then carried the plates to the table.

Alexis had lost interest in the second course of her breakfast. She kept weeping and pleading. Drew kept explaining that he couldn't take her, that she wouldn't be allowed back where Mommy was and she couldn't stay by herself in the waiting room.

Jane wanted to do something truly useful today. Scour the woods around the accident site again. Knock on doors. Go on TV with a plea. *Something.* "You can stay with me today, Alexis," she offered instead.

Her niece sobbed wildly. "I want to go with *Daddy!*"

He rose abruptly, pulled her arms from around him and almost ran from the room.

Alexis dropped to the floor and began to drum her

heels while she cried. Wow. Jane hadn't ever seen a kid actually do that. She knew how her father would have reacted if she or Lissa had ever tried it.

Jane looked after Drew, wanting to follow him, but what he needed most from her was for her to take care of Alexis.

Which did not necessarily mean rewarding a temper tantrum with sympathy, no matter how well Jane understood a little girl's terror and need to cling to her one remaining parent.

The two waffles in the toaster popped up, and Jane hadn't even taken a bite of her first one. She had an attack of guilt for being such a pig. Poor Drew probably hadn't had a bite, and here she was wanting to stuff her face to make up for missing dinner.

"I'm going to eat your waffle, too, if you don't want it," she said, pitching her voice above the wails.

Alexis cried harder.

Jane sat down, staring at her breakfast and discovering suddenly that her stomach was churning. Sighing, she pushed the plate away and stood, going to Alexis and picking her up.

DÉJÀ VU.

With no windows in the small room where Clay assumed family members were brought when the news wasn't good, day could just as well be night. He had used this same room to interview Drew yesterday evening. Now they were at it again.

Seeing his ravaged face, Clay felt some sympathy for the guy. But not so much that he wasn't going to push today, and push hard. Clay couldn't get the missing little girl out of his mind. If Drew Wilson had a secret, he was, by God, going to spill it.

"Let's talk again about what your wife said before she left. Had she told you in advance that she needed to do an errand? Say, the evening before, or that morning?"

The chair scraped as Drew lurched back. "I've told you and told you!"

"Tell me again."

"No! Why would she give me a lot of notice that, oh, gee, she needed some hair gel and tampons and she was going to run to the pharmacy?"

"Is that what she said she needed?" Clay asked thoughtfully. "Was it that time of month for her?"

The other man let out a hoarse sound. "How would I know? She didn't say, I didn't ask. We didn't— "

Clay watched for every twitch on that face. "Did you sleep together the night before?"

"Yes!" A flush spread on his cheeks. "We just didn't—"

Was the embarrassment because this guy was too repressed to talk about sex, or had he and his wife not had sex in so long, he'd lost track of anything like monthly cycles? If it was the second, that had a whole lot to say about the state of the marriage.

Clay made a point of relaxing in his chair, letting that subject go, if only temporarily. "Okay. So when did she tell you she needed to run an errand?"

"Five minutes before she went." A nerve twitched beside his eye. "Longer than that, I guess," he said reluctantly. "She and Bree went at it for a while."

Clay walked him through the scene. Melissa had already had her purse over her shoulder and her keys in her hand when she announced that she was going out for a few things. Drew had asked where. Rite Aid, she said. Had she asked if he needed anything? Drew claimed not to remember, which meant no. He'd been the one to say, "Will you buy me some athlete's foot powder?" Right after that discussion, their daughter had pounced. *She* wanted to go. Mom said no. Bree pleaded. Drew had finally asked his wife why she couldn't take Bree since it was just a short errand. Clay saw the way his face tightened. His answers became more and more terse. Something about that squabble had bothered Drew, or the whole thing had blown up into a major fight. But the more Clay drilled, the more evasive Drew got.

Clay circled back with more questions about the guy's job hunt, his wife's job, how she felt about the possibility of selling their home and moving. Had all this created some tension in the marriage?

Jane's brother-in-law conceded that there had been some tension. Lissa loved her job and didn't want to give it up. He didn't like knowing she was having to carry the financial burden right now. The kids might have overheard enough to guess their parents weren't happy.

When had he lost his job? April. Since he was home daytimes anyway, and their budget had to be a little tighter, had they considered not putting their daughters in the summer day camp? Of course they'd talked about it, but both of them were sure Drew would be getting a job any day, and then it might be too late to find quality day care. Besides, Lissa had been sure the girls needed the socialization with other kids their age. How much did it cost? Clay winced at the answer. It was a major chunk of change, in his opinion.

They went on and on, Drew's answers terse while his eyes got wilder, until he suddenly jumped to his feet. "None of this has anything to do with where my daughter is! Why are you here instead of doing your job?"

"Mr. Wilson, I understand it's distressing having to answer these kinds of questions, but I *am* doing my job in asking them." Clay kept his tone deliberately soothing. "Part of any investigation is making sure family members don't play a part. We are looking hard for your daughter, I promise you. Finding Bree is the first priority of the entire sheriff's department."

Drew stared sullenly at him. "Well, I'm done." He pushed the chair away and walked out. By the time Clay followed, all he saw was Drew's back as he disappeared through the double doors into ICU.

Clay leaned a shoulder against the door frame and mulled over the conversation. None of the answers had been surprising in any way, but he still felt a tingle that told him there was something there. Drew Wilson knew or suspected more about his wife's errand than he was letting on. And maybe he had deliberately pushed her to take their daughter because he thought having her along would mean Melissa indeed went to Rite Aid instead of wherever she'd intended.

An affair?

That could be interesting, Clay thought. But if so— why *hadn't* Melissa changed her plans and done the routine errand instead? Maybe called her lover and said, "Sorry, can't make it?"

Clay didn't know, but he was wondering. He was wondering about a lot of things.

For instance, her job. She was a bookkeeper. Nothing

fancy like an accountant. Nonetheless, bookkeepers up on QuickBooks and whatever other software they used nowadays were surely in demand enough that she could get another job easily. Drew, on the other hand, was a mechanical engineer. His skills had required considerably more training, and were more specialized. There wasn't a lot of the kind of manufacturing that required mechanical engineers in these parts. He'd be bound to earn a hell of a lot more than his wife when he was working, too. How could they *not* move so that he could find a job in his profession?

This time the tingle was tantalizing enough, it seemed to raise fine hairs on the back of Clay's neck.

Visiting Melissa Wilson's workplace had just risen to the top of his list of priorities.

CLAY DIDN'T MUCH like James Stillwell, Melissa's boss and the owner of Stillwell Trucking. Of course, there were a lot of people he didn't like, yet who were nevertheless law-abiding citizens.

Stillwell was a little older than he'd expected, at least if Melissa was sleeping with him. Fifty, maybe, although not bad looking for his age and if a woman liked the type. Five foot nine or so, he was lean and fit. Tanned as if he spent time out on a boat. Silver threaded his salon-cut hair and shone at his temples. His eyes were as blue as Clay's, but projected sincerity in a way Clay didn't trust.

"Heartbreaking," he declared, shaking his head. With a surprisingly resonant voice, he'd have made a hell of a disc jockey. "I've stopped by the hospital twice now, but they won't let me in to see her."

That would be on Clay's orders, even assuming Intensive Care staff would otherwise have been willing to allow people who weren't family to troop through.

"Sit, sit," Stillwell said, waving expansively at the conversation area on one side of his sizable office.

Could be it was the office he didn't like, Clay reflected. A trucking company should be utilitarian, shouldn't it? The exterior of the building was. A long row of loading bays dominated it. He shouldn't have been surprised at how extensive the facility was, because the trucks, displaying a logo of a stylistic elk head circled by the name of the company, were a common sight on the highways in Oregon. It hadn't really clicked, though, until he'd noticed the logo on the cab of a semi backed up to one of the bays.

Once he'd stepped through a steel door, he'd found the reception area to be fancier than he'd expected. Ditto the receptionist, a twenty-something beautiful blonde who looked as slick as her boss.

Other offices opened from the hall extending behind the receptionist's desk. Stillwell's was at the end, which put it on the corner of the building and allowed two large windows, in one of which Angel Butte, a small volcanic cinder cone, was framed. The deep blue carpet was so thick, his footsteps were silent on it. Clay wouldn't have liked that. When he was absorbed working on his computer, he wanted to hear anyone approaching.

Call it paranoia.

The desk was a huge slab of wood from some ancient tree. He kind of thought ponderosa pines didn't get that big. A sequoia? The chair behind the desk was

scaled to make the man sitting in it look more impos-
ing than he was.

Clay let himself be directed to the set of four leather
chairs surrounding a low table topped with a matching
slab of wood.

"Nice office," he commented.

Stillwell couldn't hide his gratification, although he
tried. "The appearance of success breeds success," he
murmured.

Could be. In Clay's world, success didn't look quite
like this. It was often the sweet click of handcuffs closing on a pair of wrists.

"I'm getting the feeling Stillwell Trucking is a much
bigger company than I'd imagined. Doesn't have anything to do with what I'm here about, but I admit I'm
curious. Are you entirely regional?"

When he began the company, James Stillwell said,
he'd had only a couple of trucks. Used ones, but with
shiny new coats of paint and the logo that had now
become well known. "Mostly we operated within the
state," he explained. "There were runs between Portland
and Bend, The Dalles and Klamath Falls. Ten years ago,
we expanded to encompass the Northwest. Washington,
Oregon, Idaho, Montana. Now we cover the entire west
coast." He chuckled. "San Diego to Vancouver, B.C.
We've kept the original business, of course. We have
long-haul trucks and short-haul ones. There's scarcely
a business of any significance in the tri-county area
that doesn't turn to Stillwell Trucking for their transportation needs."

That was the brochure version, but Clay couldn't really blame him.

"So, Ms. Wilson. I gather she's in your bookkeeping department?"

Department, it developed, was a misnomer. There were only three people in *Finance*—Stillwell laid it on heavy when he corrected Clay—including, yes, a CPA as well as Ms. Wilson and a Betty Jean Bitterman. Betty Jean had been with the company the longest, but Stillwell implied that, as much as he valued her for her loyalty, she hadn't caught on to new software well. He couldn't imagine functioning without Melissa. He shook his head in dismay and repeated, "I just can't imagine."

Clay asked a few polite questions. Did Mr. Stillwell have the sense anything had been troubling Ms. Wilson? Did he socialize with the Wilsons? Was he aware that a move out of the area was a possibility?

Troubling her? He raised his eyebrows in surprise. Not at all. But of course he didn't see that much of her on a day-to-day basis. Perhaps Sergeant Renner would care to speak to the people who did...? Delicate pause. Yes, Sergeant Renner would.

Stillwell claimed he'd never been to the Wilsons' home, but naturally had met Melissa's husband at Christmas parties, company picnics and the like. The children, too. He'd found them delightful. Delightful.

He did love to repeat himself.

"Yes," he agreed, frowning enough to make plain that he had been concerned, "she did tell me that her husband's job hunt hadn't borne fruit. We would hate to lose her, but certainly will understand if she and Drew have to make that choice."

What else could he say?

Clay was ushered to the finance department, where

utilitarian made a reappearance. Walls were white, floors vinyl, desks nothing fancy. Betty Jean, who at a guess was in her early sixties, expressed her deep emotions and assured Clay she had been praying for Melissa and that poor, poor child. As for troubled, on the contrary, she'd had the impression Melissa had been feeling especially pleased about something. Betty Jean, too, had known that a move was a possibility, but didn't recall Melissa saying anything about it in some time. Perhaps as much as a couple of months? she said hesitantly.

Clay had to wonder how friendly these two very disparate women really were.

The CPA was fortyish and gave the impression that the interruption wasn't welcome. Glenn Arnett had his own office, so although he surely interacted on a regular basis with the two women, he wouldn't be spending the day listening to their chatter. Clay got the feeling he'd hardly known Melissa Wilson *had* children or a life outside Stillwell Trucking. If in fact, he had a closer relationship with her, he was a damn good actor.

Clay thanked them all, thought about detouring back by James Stillwell's office but decided not to. He hadn't learned anything especially useful. It was possible Stillwell knew all his employees intimately, but his enthusiasm for Melissa, his insistence that he *relied* on her, had pinged on Clay's radar. She was a lowly bookkeeper. Why would she have any special significance to him?

Unless...

Damn it, he thought, shaking his head as he walked to his department-issue Explorer, how could Jane *not* know what her sister had been up to? Was there any chance she was shielding her?

He unlocked the vehicle and got in behind the wheel, mulling over his next step. After a moment he grimaced. Somehow, all he could think about was Jane.

CHAPTER FIVE

STEAMING FROM HAVING to run a gauntlet of reporters outside, Jane held on tight to Alexis's hand. Couldn't they see they were scaring a little girl? Thank God the hospital administration was refusing to let them inside even as far as the lobby.

She hated thinking that the two of them might appear on the evening news. Thank God she'd taken Alexis by her house so she could change clothes and pack. Viewers would have really loved the sight of her in yesterday's wrinkled clothes.

A day or two and the vultures will lose interest, she told herself. No, better yet, they'd lose interest as soon as Bree was found. It was the missing child that had them all thinking this was a gripping, front-page, top-of-the-hour story.

Walking down the broad hospital corridor, her steps shortened to accommodate her niece's, Jane was startled to see Drew sitting on one of the chairs clustered in the open alcove in front of ICU. Even from a distance, she saw despair in his posture. He was bent over, both of his hands fisted in his hair.

Fear shot through her like an electric shock. Oh, dear God—had Lissa *died?*

"There's Daddy!" Alexis cried. "Daddy!" she called.

For an instant, he didn't respond at all. At last he slowly, painfully straightened and Jane saw his face. He'd aged yet another ten years. Oh, no.

"Drew?" She didn't realize she was whispering until Alexis looked up at her.

"What's wrong, Auntie Jane?"

"I… Nothing."

Drew had risen to his feet. "Lexie."

She ran to her daddy, and he swung her up into his arms and held her as if she was a glimpse of heaven. Eyes closed, he laid his cheek against her head.

Jane walked as slowly as she dared, fighting the desperate desire to turn and run away. She didn't want to know. Her chest ached. *My sister.*

But Drew was looking at her now and holding out an arm. Jane walked into the circle of it and, for a moment, laid her head on his chest, feeling the comfort of an embrace that also contained Alexis's small bony body.

But finally, she had to know. She straightened and stepped back, and his arm dropped away. "What's happened?" Jane was horribly conscious of the way Alexis's head came up and her alarmed stare, but how could she *not* ask?

He only shook his head. "Nothing's changed. It's just…getting to me. Here, sweetheart." He bent to set his daughter down. "Look, they have some toys over in the corner."

She hesitated, obviously reluctant to leave her father, but temptation sent her trotting to the play corner, where there was a child-size plastic table and pair of chairs, coloring books and crayons, and toys that looked designed to keep little hands busy. She took the seat that allowed her to keep an eye on her father and aunt, however.

"Something's wrong," Jane said with certainty, keeping her voice low.

"That cop." The kindest, most easy-going of men, he snarled the two words. "He thinks I did something to hurt Lissa, and God knows what he thinks I did to Bree. He asked if we have life insurance on each other or the kids."

Despite herself, Jane was shocked. "Sergeant Renner?"

"Who the hell else?" Drew never swore, either.

"Do you?" she blurted.

He stared at her without comprehension for a moment. "Life insurance? Oh, I had some through my job, but it's probably expired now. I guess Liss might have it as part of her benefits at work. I don't know. But on the kids? Why would we buy something like that?"

Jane decided she had to divert him. "What else did Sergeant Renner say?"

Nearly black with despair, Drew's eyes met hers. "He didn't say anything. He asked questions. He kept finding more to ask. Did Lissa and I sleep together? Have sex? Have we been fighting? Why do I think she didn't want to take Bree with her? Why did I want her to take Bree? He thinks—" Looking shattered, he stopped and pinched the bridge of his nose. His knuckles turned white. Jane watched as his Adam's apple bobbed. At last he was able to look at her again, and this time tears glazed his eyes. "He thinks I wanted to hurt her. And Bree!" His voice held even more horror. "You know how much I love her!"

Jane knew. She also, with a cop's eye and ear, saw and heard that he wasn't sure he did love his wife. That maybe something *was* wrong between them. And, heaven help her, as much as she wanted to hate Clay Renner for upsetting Drew like this, she also couldn't blame him.

I would have done the same, she admitted silently.

But she stepped forward and wrapped her arms around him anyway, and let him squeeze her back so hard it hurt.

THE SIGHT OF the two of them in a clinch brought Clay to a halt halfway down the hall. You couldn't have squeezed a toothpick between them. The son of a bitch had his head bent and his face buried in Jane's wild, curly hair.

The tide of possessiveness sweeping through Clay felt so primal, he didn't know himself. He'd never been jealous about a woman in his life, if that was what this was. God help him, he had to get a grip before Jane saw him.

He stood there breathing hard, his hands opening and closing into fists. Not until he thought he could hide his emotions did he resume walking.

He was only a few feet away when he thought suddenly, *Oh, hell.* What if Jane's sister had died? They could be consoling each other.

Drew didn't show any sign of being aware of Clay's approach, but Jane did. She made slow, separating-herself motions before turning her head and locking her gaze with his. A trace of shock entered her eyes, making him wonder if he'd hidden what he felt as well as he'd thought he had.

"Clay?" she said.

The brother-in-law seemed to sway on his feet. He looked like hell, Clay realized, his stab of alarm sharpening.

"Any change?" he asked when he was close enough.

Jane shook her head, although her mouth was tight. "I haven't been in there, but…Drew says not. It's just all hitting him." She gently took the guy's arm and led him to a chair. Her nudge signaled him to sit. He definitely wasn't firing on all cylinders. Clay guessed he couldn't blame him.

If that had been Jane in a coma, lying in ICU…

His throat tightened. She wasn't his. He had to accept it. What was he going to be, the kind of asshole who was consumed by what *he* wanted?

No.

But the anguish didn't let up, either. If it was Jane in there…Clay knew. He'd look as bad as Drew did.

Shake it off, he told himself, but saw that it was too late. She'd seen something on his face; her forehead puckered and her lips parted.

"Clay?" she said again, as though she were asking him… He didn't know.

He managed to swallow most of the lump and simply shook his head. "It's nothing."

"It's not."

He couldn't talk about it. Not in front of her brother-in-law and—he'd finally noticed—her niece. No, not at all, given how she felt about him.

"I'll check on your sister," he said.

The nurse fussing with a monitor only shook her head. Clay stood for a minute beside Melissa's bed, gazing down at her. Nobody would call her beautiful now. The swelling and discoloration on the left side of her face made it grotesque. Her skin tone was pallid, even though he could tell she'd probably had a light tan. It was the slackness that allowed flesh to appear to be melting from bone. If not for her chest rising and falling slowly, the breaths seeming shallow, he might have thought she was dead.

"It's really only been a little over twenty-four hours," the nurse said.

He glanced at her, surprised. Did she think he needed to be comforted? Disconcerted, he realized maybe he did. This was Jane's sister. Except for the kids, she'd said Melissa was her only family. Clay didn't want her to lose her sister.

He nodded, said, "Thanks," and left, pushing through the doors a minute later to find Drew still slumped in the same chair and Jane perched on one of the kid-size chairs helping the little girl put together a simple puzzle. His chest cramped, seeing her tender expression and the gentle way she directed Alexis's hand to set a piece into place. She looked so much like a young mother, the kind of woman he'd expected to fall in love with.

Once again Jane seemed to become aware the moment he stepped through the doors. He shook his head slightly, much as the nurse had done, and saw her shoulders sag.

She murmured something to Alexis, then stood and came to Clay.

"Why are you here?" she asked, chin tilting up to suggest a hint of antagonism.

"I was hoping to talk to you."

"Not Drew?"

"You," he repeated.

Seemingly disconcerted, she said, "Oh, okay." Her head turned. "Um…do we need to sit down somewhere? Or…?"

"How about the cafeteria?" he suggested. "I haven't managed any lunch yet."

She acquiesced, taking a moment to tell her brother-in-law where she was going and then joining Clay again.

He didn't say anything during the short walk to the hospital cafeteria. There they separated and each filled a tray. He noticed she'd gathered some food he assumed wasn't for her—a couple of sandwiches, cookies and the like.

He led her to a round table in the far corner, well away from the few scattered diners, mostly medical personnel.

She poked without a lot of enthusiasm at her salad. "Is this going to be an update, or an inquisition?"

Mood momentarily lightened, Clay grinned. "Six of one, half dozen of the other."

She chuckled, then looked surprised that she had.

"My mother always said that," he explained.

Her smile dimmed. No happy memories of *her* mother, he diagnosed.

He took a few bites of his burger while he tried to

decide how to frame his questions. He needed her on his side, not firing up in defense of Mr. Nice Guy Drew.

After a moment, Clay set down the burger and looked at Jane. "I may be entirely off base here, but I keep thinking something was going on between your sister and brother-in-law that might help explain what happened." Too blunt? Trying to read her expression, he forged on. "Talk to me. Help me figure out whether this is a dead end or important. If it's a dead end, I can quit wasting my time and focus on other things."

Her head stayed bent although she didn't take a bite. "I was thinking about this earlier."

Uh-oh.

"You really upset Drew. His whole world has been shattered, you know."

"I understand." Better than he could admit. If she'd been the one in there, unconscious… It was disconcerting how fast that fear resurfaced. No, he couldn't afford to go there. He cleared his throat. "But there's something he's not saying, Jane."

At last she lifted her head and met his eyes, looking shattered herself. "I think so, too," she said, so softly he barely heard her.

He reached for a French fry to give her time.

"I don't know what was wrong, though," she said at last, sounding miserable. "And…why didn't I have a clue?"

"Did you really not?" Clay asked. "Or is it possible you noticed and just didn't want to believe their marriage was in trouble?"

She stabbed at the salad some more. "When I think

back, I really didn't see much of them together this past month or so."

"It's summer. Time for family picnics. Fourth of July fireworks. You sound like you've been over there a lot."

"The kids are such a distraction," she tried to explain. "Every time we get together, they're hanging from me and chattering away. Anyway, my days off don't coincide with my sister's. I see more of Drew."

Clay didn't dare say anything.

"And…well, I told you already," Jane continued. "Lissa and I haven't been talking much."

"Why? Did you have a fight?"

Jane stole a look at him. Color had risen in her cheeks, making him suspect he wasn't going to like what she had to say. "This was back in, I don't know, June, maybe? She was being snotty, talking about how important her job was and how lucky that *one* of them was working and how Drew seemed happy enough to take all the time off he wanted. And he was there! I could see him shutting down. Sort of shrinking before my very eyes. So when I got Lissa alone, I chewed her out. It didn't go well."

Given what Jane had said about their relationship, Clay wasn't surprised.

"Anything between her and Drew was none of my business," she said. "So I could just back off. Except she put it more profanely."

Yeah, he could imagine.

"I have, but I guess I came down on Drew's side. He is job hunting! He tells me about it. He's actually been offered a couple of positions, but of course they weren't around here, and they weren't so irresistible he was willing to put his foot down and say, 'we're going.'"

Pansy. Clay was a little disconcerted to realize he heard the description in his father's voice, despite the conscious effort he'd been making lately to shut out his voice. He didn't like it, even though he shared the basic sentiment. Pretty clearly Melissa was the dominant partner in that relationship. Dad was old school enough to say she wore the pants.

What irritated him was the sympathy fairly oozing from Jane. Poor, sensitive Drew, whose wife was being unfair and unkind. Clay didn't suppose she'd hinted that he might consider standing up for himself.

"I suppose you wouldn't have had any trouble putting your foot down," she said tartly, and he realized she'd read his expression with unerring accuracy.

"No, I wouldn't have." He raised a hand when she showed signs of wanting to launch an assault. "Jane, this isn't about me. It's not about us. I need to know about Drew and Melissa. Is this new behavior for them? Has she always taken the lead? Have you ever before sensed she feels some contempt for him, or is it new?"

She bit her lip. The pink in her cheeks became brighter. "You're right. I'm sorry. And no, I really thought they loved each other. Maybe Lissa is the stronger minded of the two, but I thought that was okay. She needed someone easygoing enough to let her moods slide off his back. You know?"

Was that what *she* needed, too? Clay wondered, appalled. Or, at least, thought she needed? Man, he hoped not.

Repeat to self, this isn't about me. It's not about us.

"So things have been going sour since he lost his job," Clay said thoughtfully.

"I... Maybe."

"You noticed more than you thought you did, then."

Jane nodded unhappily.

Clay went back to eating, and she did the same. After a minute, between bites, he told her about his visit to Stillwell Trucking. "You ever met any of her coworkers?" he asked.

"Sure. Speaking of the Fourth of July, the owner always throws a big shindig. He has a really nice place out of town. He always has everyone who works for him over for the holiday. Barbecue grills, potluck, great view of the fireworks, families welcome. I've gone a couple of times with Liss and Drew and the kids."

"This year?"

She nodded.

"Who does she like? Not like?"

Jane stared at him, her eyes wide, the color... bewitching. A word that had never so much as crossed his mind before.

"Why does it matter?" she asked. "What are you thinking?"

He hesitated. This investigation was his. She was family. Could he trust her not to repeat things he said to her brother-in-law?

Yeah, he was surprised to realize. He thought he could. And face it, his speculation was just that so far.

"I'm not thinking anything yet. I'm...casting a fly on the water, looking to see what rises," he admitted. "If your sister really just had an accident and Brianna was grabbed by a stranger who happened to stop, then

I have absolutely nothing to go on. Finding her is going to be purest luck. One of the tips people are calling in panning out. You know how those work. The guy stops for gas, has to take the little girl to the restroom and somebody sees and recognizes her picture on the five o'clock news."

Jane nodded again.

"I'm not saying that isn't what happened. I hope not."

She shuddered, not needing him to explain. Stranger abductions were the worst.

"We're checking into registered and suspected child molesters in the area, for what that's worth."

Another nod told him she understood how unlikely it would be for them to find Bree that way.

"But there are these little mysteries digging at me," Clay continued. "Why was Melissa so insistent about not taking her daughter with her? With her working full-time, it's surely natural for the kid to want to spend some time with her. Why didn't they go where your sister said they were going? And why did the accident take place so far out in the country, not on the way to anywhere logical?"

Her lips tightened. He guessed she had asked herself all those same questions.

"Do you remember all the stuff that happened last winter," she said, "when Colin produced the long-missing Maddie Dubeau?"

Surprised by the abrupt right turn in topic, Clay said, "Sure."

"Did you know one of the attempts on her life took place at that falling-down resort so close to where Melissa ran off the road? The one you said is some kind of group home now?"

"No," he said slowly. "I didn't."

So she told him about the incident. How Maddie, who had suffered from amnesia, had driven straight to the resort by instinct, thinking it was important. How, after she had talked to the couple who now owned the place, she'd started down the driveway, only to have bullets shatter her car window. "She wasn't hurt then. I mean, later the guy grabbed her and tried to kill her, you know that."

"You're thinking the two things are connected."

"I really doubt it. How could they be?" Jane pushed the tray away, although as far as he could tell she'd hardly eaten a bite. "Coincidences bother me, that's all."

They bothered him, too. And that wasn't all.

"There's something you're not saying."

She lifted her eyes to his with obvious reluctance. "I kind of found out something I wasn't supposed to. And I don't want to tell you, because you might think you have to do something about it. And I really *don't* think it has anything to do with what happened to Melissa or Bree."

Maybe not, but she was wondering anyway. And Jane Vahalik had good instincts. They were what had made her a top-notch detective.

"What if I promise not to do anything about what you tell me?"

"Can you really do that?" She sounded skeptical.

He gave that a moment's thought. No, he didn't like giving blind promises. But now his curiosity was aroused, and…this was Jane.

"Yeah. As long as it doesn't impinge on this investigation," he said finally.

So she told him. The old Bear Creek Resort was indeed a kind of group home, but not a licensed one. In fact, it flew so far below the radar, it was as invisible as the stealth bomber.

He gave his head a disbelieving shake. "So the boys there are all hiding from authorities. This couple running the place is defying court orders, the kids' parents and just about everyone else. And you knew about it."

Her look was more sidelong than direct now. "Well... yes."

"It didn't occur to you that one of these runaway seventeen-year-olds might have a thing for little girls?" His gorge was rising. "That this nice couple providing a bolt-hole probably don't actually know much about the boys they have living there?"

"No. Not until... Well, I just got to thinking about it. When you talked about the weird location where the accident took place. And, um, the resort might have been a logical place for Bree to go for help."

"You just got to thinking." He was *just* getting mad. "Goddamn it, Jane!"

"I'm sure they vet the kids carefully. I really don't believe—"

He swore and pushed his chair back, getting up.

"Wait!" Jane shot to her feet, too. "What are you going to do?"

"What do you think I'm going to do?" he said from between tight jaws.

"You promised."

"You know I have to go check it out."

Her misery was so apparent, his anger softened. "Jane, I have no choice. I didn't say I'm going to turn these people in. But I have to pursue an all-too-realistic possibility. Would you want me to do any differently?"

She searched his face anxiously. "No," she finally said. "If one of them hurt Bree…"

Hurt was a euphemism on a par with *passed away,* but Clay understood why she couldn't make herself say words like *raped* and *murdered* in the context of her own niece.

A strange impulse seized him then. "You can come with me if you want," he suggested, before common sense could jump to his rescue.

"Really?"

He liked the way she was looking at him, as if she thought *he* was a nice guy, too.

But after a moment she gusted a sigh. "I can't. I promised to keep Alexis today. There's no way Drew can have her with him if he's going to stay here at the hospital."

That was true. Staff would never let a kid that age go back into ICU, even supposing it would be a good idea for her to see her mother looking the way she did.

"But you'll call me, won't you?" she asked.

"I can do that," he agreed, picking up his tray.

They bussed their dishes, Jane collecting the lunches she'd picked up for her niece and brother-in-law. Clay walked her partway, before their routes diverged. When they reached the place where the corridors crossed, he stopped.

"We got distracted. You never did say what you thought about the people Melissa works with."

Tiny crinkles formed on Jane's forehead. "I...actually don't know. She seemed to get along with everyone."

"What about the big guy? Did you see them together?"

There was a noticeable hesitation this time. "I guess she was a little flirtatious with him," she said. "Nothing that obvious, though. He was sort of, I don't know, gallant. Like he was flattered. I didn't see any secret glances and they didn't sneak off to meet somewhere."

"You sure?"

"Positive," she said firmly.

Clay found he didn't want to give up that particular scenario, but he would set it aside for now. "All right," he said. "Jane..."

His voice had come out rough. She suddenly looked shy.

"Take care of yourself, too, okay? Not just everybody else."

"I do—"

"You barely ate."

"Oh." She appeared startled he'd noticed. "I'll get something later, at home."

"Okay." Damn, he wanted to touch her. Kiss her cheek. Comfort her in some way. Or was he really wanting to lay a claim? Unsure of his own motivations, he only nodded and walked away, aware she hadn't moved and was watching him go.

"THE BOYS WERE with us all morning," Mrs. Hale told Clay.

With her graying hair in a braid and wearing Birkenstock sandals and a tie-dyed T-shirt, Paula Hale looked like, and maybe was, an aging hippie. Gray streaked her husband's hair and beard, too.

Clay had seen their wariness from the minute he parked out front of the old log building and walked to the front porch. They were itching to find out how much he knew about their operation, but didn't dare ask any questions that would make him curious if he wasn't already.

If not for what Jane had told him, he might not have thought much about it. People always looked alarmed when police cars turned into their driveway.

"You were gathered together when the officers arrived to ask about Brianna Wilson," he said.

"That's right." Roger Hale stood protectively behind his wife, who was perched stiffly on a bench that served as seating for a long table. One of half a dozen long tables. Clay straddled the same bench at the other end.

The shabby interior of the former resort was set up to serve as home for a lot more residents than the Hales were admitting to. Clay had made note of the commercial appliances in the kitchen, the one indication significant money had been spent to update the old lodge.

He'd seen a couple of teenage boys when he'd arrived, although both had faded away immediately. Maybe he should suggest to the Hales they coach the boys to fake it better. That slow slide out of sight would catch the attention of any self-respecting cop.

"How long had this meeting you were holding with the boys been going on?" he asked.

"We started at ten," Paula told him. "We do one every Saturday, regular as clockwork. Attendance is required, no exceptions allowed. Routine works well for these boys. We'd actually finished and were getting lunch on the table when the deputies arrived."

"Did any of the boys leave at any time during those two hours?"

The couple exchanged a glance. Not a conspiratorial one, Clay didn't think.

"A couple of them used the john," Roger said. "For that matter, I did. Nobody was gone for more than a couple of minutes. I'd have noticed if the back door had opened or closed, or the toilet wasn't flushed." Reading Clay's expression, he said, "Yeah, we get a bad apple once in a while. And some of the kids need time to settle when they come to us." Code for *they're really screwed up.* "We have a pretty stable group right now."

"Looks like you could accommodate a lot more than you have," he suggested.

"We could. Our numbers rise and fall. Just depends on referrals."

Clay nodded. "All right. You understand I had to ask when I learned you have a number of teenage boys here who might have significant issues."

"Of course we do." Paula sounded as if she meant it. "You haven't found the little girl? Does her mother not remember what happened?"

"Ms. Wilson hasn't regained consciousness, although we still hope she will," he said. "And no. Frankly, at this point we don't have a clue. That leaves me pursuing all possibilities."

Expressing sympathy, they saw him to the door together. There he paused, turning finally. "Sounds like you're doing a good thing here. You ever need us, you let me know."

Their faces relaxed. They wouldn't like knowing how obvious their relief was.

"Thank you, Sergeant. We'll keep that in mind."

Getting into his Jeep, he caught sight of a couple boys, lurking almost but not quite out of sight. He nodded at one and smiled at the flare of alarm. Judging from their reaction, his smile was not reassuring.

He didn't quite know how he felt about the Hales' operation, but he'd keep his promise to Jane. And he'd seen too many kids returned by an overwhelmed court to an abusive home. He couldn't help sympathizing, even though he also believed absolutely in the rule of the law.

Clay was struck during his drive back to town by how much he'd come to diverge from his father's more rigid beliefs. A cop, too, his father would have turned in the Hales without a second thought. But then…he'd been only a small step away from abusive himself.

Instead of making Clay uneasy, the reflection eased something in him. He did not want to be a reincarnation of his father. He didn't like thinking he had been heading that way.

Maybe he and Jane could find common ground.

The trouble was, discounting the contempt for most of humanity his father had taught was one thing. Changing a gut-deep belief that a man took care of a woman, especially the one he loved, and didn't stand back while she took care of herself—that was something else.

A gulf he didn't know if he could cross.

CHAPTER SIX

"DREW," JANE SAID the next morning at breakfast, "you need to stay home today."

He stared at her in shock. "I have to be at the hospital."

"No, you don't. You should spend some time with Alexis. Take a nap when she does. If you want to go back tonight, fine, but you look really bad." She shook her head when he started to speak. "I'll sit with Lissa this morning for a bit. Then I need to go by the station, check on my apartment and grab a few things I forgot yesterday, maybe pick up some groceries. I promise I'll go back by the hospital after that. They have your phone number. They have mine. If anything changes, I'll call. I promise."

Comprehension was slow to enter those bloodshot eyes, but it got there. He nodded slowly, as if even so minor a movement required energy he didn't have. "I'm running on fumes," he admitted.

"Alexis needs you. She's scared."

The five-year-old had fought sleep the night before even after Jane had welcomed her into bed with her. It seemed like once an hour, she woke up sobbing and clutching Jane, who was wearing down herself. Right this minute, she and Drew, bleary-eyed, probably looked like the parents of a newborn.

The home phone rang and he sprang to his feet. A moment after picking up the receiver, he slammed it back down without saying a word.

"Aluminum siding." He sank back into his chair, looking dazed from what had probably been an adrenaline-inducing cocktail of fear and hope.

"Which phone number does Bree know?" she asked. "Home or cell?"

"Ah…both, I think. I know she's called me on both."

Jane wondered if a seven-year-old actually could memorize three separate phone numbers, but maybe. It was also possible that some of those phone calls had been prompted by a friend's parent, who had told her the number or even dialed for her.

When Jane went to the guest room, Alexis was sitting bolt upright in bed looking scared, and with a gasp threw herself at Jane. "I thought you were gone!"

Jane explained that she was leaving temporarily, but that Daddy would be home with her, and watched as the little girl tore off in search of Drew. It gave her a pang. The girls loved her, she knew they did, but truthfully she was like a stuffed animal Alexis was fond of yet only cuddled as a substitute when her pitifully worn blankie couldn't be located. Jane shook her head, bundled her dirty clothes into the duffel she'd brought, then carried it along when she stuck her head in the kitchen to say goodbye.

Alexis seemed content enough eating the Eggo waf-

fle her father had toasted for her, but Drew trailed Jane
to the front door, hovering a little closer than she liked.

"When do you think you'll be back?" he asked plain-
tively, looking as if he was about to cry.

She wanted quite desperately to go back to work and
be Lieutenant Vahalik again, not Drew's fill-in…what?
Not blankie. Wife? The thought brought a wrench of
anxiety.

No, that was ridiculous. Maybe he and Melissa *had*
been having problems, but he loved her. Look how devotedly he'd stayed at her bedside! *He's grateful to me,
that's all,* Jane told herself.

"Probably dinnertime, but I'll call, okay?" she said,
and couldn't help feeling a wash of relief at her escape.

Chagrined, she wondered if she'd lived alone too
long and was past being able to adapt to the demands
of real family life, when you couldn't have fun for the
day with the kids and then return them to their parents
and go home free as a bird.

She wondered if Clay would be disgusted to know
she had any doubts at all about whether she wanted
children. In his world, single women were probably
supposed to be hankering to immerse themselves in
motherhood.

For just a moment, she found herself wondering what
their children would look like, if she and Clay had any.

She snorted and got into her car. Yep. Those would
be the children *she* was supposed to stay home and
care for while *he* headed out the door every morning
to earn their daily bread. To solve cases, play hero and
rise in the ranks.

And that would be while *her* career stagnated and died.

But, damn it, not two seconds later she was wondering if she'd see him today.

DREW WAS SITTING on the floor trying to fit a teeny tiny sweater on a Bratz doll whose hair reminded him of Jane's. Alexis was much more deftly dressing her doll, the one with hair more like hers. Born bossy, she had picked out the outfit he was to dress his doll in. It looked kind of slutty to him—the skirt was miniature, and then there were tights that looked like those leggings ballet dancers wore, followed by hot pink boots. His fingers felt big and clumsy.

At the sound of the doorbell, his whole body jerked. *God.* This was even worse than when the phone rang. Who could it be? Maybe Jane had come back for something and couldn't put her hands on her key...?

He blindly thrust the doll at his daughter. "Daddy has to answer that," he said.

Through the stained-glass sidelight he could make out the tall, bulky shape of a man, and he knew. It was the cop again.

Sure enough, when he opened the door, there was Sergeant Renner, impassive and somehow merciless. There was no lightness on his rough face to suggest he had good news, but no pity to foretell bad, either.

"Sergeant," he said past the tightness in his throat. "What is it?"

"May I come in?"

"No" wasn't a viable answer. Nodding stiffly, Drew stepped back.

"You don't have news?" he asked.

"I'm afraid not. Is there someplace we can talk?"

"I'm alone with my youngest."

"Jane's not here?"

He explained she'd persuaded him to stay home today and that she was on the way to the hospital.

Not seeing a lot of choices, Drew finally led the cop to the dining room table, where they had a degree of privacy but he could see Alexis—and she could see him.

Drew didn't offer coffee. "What can you possibly have to ask that you haven't already?" he asked wearily.

"I want you to tell me about your wife's work," the sergeant said.

Drew hid his dismay. How had the guy learned that Lissa's job was a sore point between them? Or had he? Maybe he was poking until he noticed a wince.

"She's been with Stillwell for six years. Before she had Bree, Lissa worked for a dental supply place. She said it was boring and decided not to go back. Pay's better at Stillwell, too."

"Uh-huh. I've been wondering about that. Do you mind telling me what your wife earns?"

Drew stared at him incredulously. He and his family were the victims, but they were being treated like criminals. "What does it matter?" he asked.

"I'm just wondering a little why Melissa's job seems to be so important to her," Sergeant Renner said blandly. "But let's get back to that. Tell me what you think of her coworkers."

Afraid he'd stiffened, Drew talked about Betty Jean Bitterman, always described by Melissa as the old biddy. Lissa wasn't always kind, but Drew had to admit that Betty Jean was halfway to being fossilized.

Glenn Arnett had been new to the company sometime after Lissa had started there.

"Maybe four years ago?" he said. "Yeah, I think it was after Lissa went back from maternity leave. You know, after Alexis was born."

The sergeant nodded.

"She didn't say much about him." Drew told him about the one good friend Lissa had at Stillwell Trucking, the front office receptionist. Courtney Hendricks. Mostly the two women did girl things together, which was good—Drew had next to nothing in common with Courtney's husband, who owned an auto-body shop.

He should have known, though, that Renner was only working his way around to his true object of interest: James Stillwell.

Clay paged back through his notebook as if he needed to find a reference before pinning Drew with those sharp blue eyes. "Mr. Stillwell assures me that he *relies* on your wife. Seemed a little strange to me, her being only a bookkeeper. Not even the only one. And he's got Mr. Arnett."

This was what Drew didn't like thinking about. What Lissa and Stillwell were to each other. When Drew asked, she told him he was being ridiculous. They'd had some pretty hot sex one time when she was reassuring him that she wanted him and not her boss. The reassurance had worked, too…for a few weeks.

"My impression," he said carefully, "is that Stillwell keeps Betty Jean on only out of gratitude for her years with him. I suspect he leans a little more heavily than usual on Lissa because she's so much more computer savvy. She does a whole lot more than her half of the work. When Stillwell wants a figure, she can pull it up."

"Rather than him asking Mr. Arnett for that figure."

"Why are you asking me about this anyway?" he said sharply. "Why not talk to them?"

"I might do that." He paused. "I've been told that your wife and Mr. Stillwell seem flirtatious. I believe that was the word used."

He stiffened and hoped it wasn't obvious. "Lissa's style is flirtatious. It doesn't mean anything."

"Uh-huh. Well, then, let's get back to her salary."

Unable to see any way out of it, Drew grimly told him what she brought home.

Sergeant Renner glanced around, his eyebrows raised, as if assessing the house. "I assume you have a mortgage?"

A big-ass mortgage. Drew had thought they'd over-reached themselves when they bought this place, but Lissa had loved the house and at the time both their jobs had seemed safe.

"Yes," he said tersely.

"You must have been having to dip deep into savings since you've been out of work."

Drew glared at him. "My wife handles our finances."

"I suppose that makes sense, since she's a book-keeper. But you'll be able to handle the bills until she's able to take them over again?"

"Yes."

"You do online banking? Maybe you have invest-ments beyond a savings account?"

"We both have retirement accounts through our jobs. Once I hire on somewhere, I'll roll mine over."

"You do know it may take your wife a while to bounce back after a head injury of this magnitude."

Whether Melissa might be brain damaged was one of Drew's many fears. This time, the cop sounded compassionate.

"I can't let myself worry about that until she wakes up."

"One thing at a time. I understand that." He took another one of those assessing looks at the living room with a vaulted ceiling and soaring windows, the kitchen with gleaming granite countertops, garbage compactor, double ovens and copper rack over the large island with a second sink. "If I were you, though, I'd be taking a look at my finances, just to see where I am."

With a nod, he rose, thanked Drew for his time and left. Locking the door behind him, Drew had the unpleasant thought that Sergeant Renner had a point.

The truth was, he admitted, if only to himself, he hadn't asked as many questions as he should have about how the bills were getting paid. And—*God*—if Lissa didn't wake up pretty soon, he wouldn't have any choice but to find out how they were holding on to this house on a bookkeeper's salary. Especially since right now she wasn't earning a salary at all.

The kernel of dread that had been with him for months twinged painfully.

Tomorrow, he told himself.

Maybe tomorrow.

CLAY STEPPED INTO the Kingfisher Café on the main drag in Angel Butte and looked around. He hoped this wasn't one of those places where the servings were skimpy and the combination of ingredients weird. Where food was concerned, he was conservative.

Like Dad?

Irritable, he shook off the thought. Not like Dad. His father had grumbled whenever Mom had served anything unfamiliar for dinner. Clay was more adaptable. He wasn't much for leafy greens, that was all, especially the ones that looked and tasted like weeds gathered from the roadside verge. And, hey, sue him—he liked meat. He was a big man, and he needed his meals to be substantial.

He didn't see Jane on his first scan of the interior, but his gaze did find a blackboard listing specials. The chili and a burger with blue cheese both sounded good to him, and he relaxed.

Yeah, and he'd have eaten bitter greens for lunch without a word of complaint just so he could have a meal with Jane. She was the one to suggest this café.

"Hi," she said from beside him. "Have you been waiting?"

He turned, surprised as always at how far down he had to look. Jane had a personality way bigger than her shorter-than-average height suggested.

"No, just got here. Had to park a couple of blocks away."

"Me, too." She wrinkled her nose. "Tourists."

Clay grinned. "And where would we be without 'em?"

That dimple flickered in her cheek. "You and I would have a whole lot more leisure time."

"Assuming we still had jobs," he pointed out. "Think of the layoffs in our respective departments if all those tourists, bless their hearts, didn't bring crime in their wake."

Jane actually laughed. "You're right. I just wish they wouldn't take the parking spot I want."

The hostess appeared then to seat them, putting them at a small table against the wall. Clay's knees bumped Jane's under the table. He didn't mind and couldn't tell if she did.

"I've never eaten here," he said.

She looked up from her menu, her surprise obvious. "Really? It's the best place in town for lunch. Everyone from the police department and city hall eats here. Besides—" she leaned forward and lowered her voice conspiratorially "—the owner and chef is best friends with Colin's wife, Nell."

"Ah. As long as she can cook."

They put in their orders, then looked at each other.

"You're not getting much sleep," he said.

Jane grimaced. "I was a little shocked when I saw myself in the mirror this morning. Alexis keeps waking up with nightmares. And who can blame her?"

Clay shook his head. Poor kid. "I stopped by the house earlier. Drew said you'd talked him into staying home."

"I hope he'll take a nap when Alexis does. *And* that she actually sleeps. She must be getting tired, too." She searched his face. "Why did you stop by?"

"More questions for your brother-in-law."

"You are wasting your time going after him, you know."

"Are you so sure?"

"I'm sure." And damned if she didn't sound it. "Drew

and Lissa may have been fighting. I don't know. But he'd never have hurt her or Bree. He might be able to tell you something useful, I won't argue about that, but..." She started to shrug.

"He's so *nice* he'd never hurt another soul?" Clay's interruption came out barbed.

Her eyes widened. "What, you've decided you don't like him?"

I don't like the way you defend him.

"I think nobody is that nice," he said curtly.

"You're wrong."

"You meet a lot of nice people every day on your job?" Clay asked with exaggerated interest.

"Yes!" She pressed her lips together. "They're usually the victims," she said finally, grudgingly.

Clay let out a huff of air. "You're right. I won't argue. There are decent people out there. He may be one. But, damn it, he's hiding something."

He didn't like to see the lines of worry on her forehead.

"You're a stranger," she said. "And a hostile one at that. His whole world has imploded. Do you really blame him for not wanting to express every doubt about his marriage and his wife to you?"

Put that way—no. But the fact he understood didn't make Clay like Drew Wilson any better.

"Why are you so hot to defend him?" he asked. "Are you that good of friends?"

"Yes!" She glowered at him, not relenting even as her salad and his cup of chili were delivered by a cheerful slip of a girl who looked like a middle schooler to him.

Maybe he should remind the proprietor of child labor laws. Or— Hell, maybe he was just getting old.

Even when they were left alone, Clay didn't reach for his spoon. "There's not some awkwardness, you being such good buddies with your sister's husband? I've got to tell you, I don't think my brother would like it much if I was suddenly best friends with his wife."

"That's…that's ridiculous!" Anger didn't look natural on a face as gentle as Jane's. On the other hand, Clay thought with the first amusement he'd felt since they sat down, he would swear her wild curls writhed like Medusa's snakes when she got mad. He'd never seen hair so alive.

Thinking about what it would feel like falling over his chest was enough to keep him awake during nights when he couldn't get her out of his head.

"Is it?" he asked. "I don't see you two having that much to say to each other."

"Why not?" she challenged him. "You must have had plenty of female friends who were *nice*. Did you run out of things to say to them?"

He felt as if a punch had robbed him of air. It was a minute before he could say quietly, "I guess I must have. None of them stuck, did they?"

This was *not* a good time for a revelation.

Jane and he stared at each other, neither of them seemingly able to look away. He was afraid his shock must be showing, and damned if there wasn't a hint of shock in her eyes, too.

"Drew and I aren't best friends," she said suddenly, her voice stifled. She looked away, as if someone had caught her eye across the café, but Clay knew better.

He felt as if an essential connection between them had been severed. Stupid.

"I'm being a jackass," he admitted.

"Why?" she asked, tilting her head when she looked at him again.

"I didn't like seeing the two of you wrapped around each other yesterday." The words came out as a rumble.

"But…" The word formed on her lips, almost soundless. She gave her head a slight shake. "It's not as if you and I are even seeing each other."

He was blowing it here, Clay knew, and couldn't seem to stop himself. "That's not my choice."

"Oh." Her eyes shied from his. She looked down at her salad as if it was some foreign substance. "You aren't…seeing someone else?"

"Right now? No." Pride wouldn't let him admit that he hadn't had a date since last October, when she'd ditched him. For months, he'd deluded himself she'd forgive him and they could start again. Even once he knew that wasn't happening, Clay hadn't worked up enough interest in any of the women who might have been receptive to ask one out. He'd begun to worry about himself. He hadn't been celibate for an entire year since he was about fifteen. Maybe middle age had hit, he'd thought with some horror.

Then, two and a half weeks ago, he'd seen Jane again and knew what his problem was. Continuing celibacy had now become painful.

"You?" he heard himself ask gruffly.

Her teeth sank into her lower lip and she shook her head.

Yeah, but just because she wasn't dating anyone right

now didn't mean she *hadn't* been sometime in the past ten months. Or decided what she really wanted was a man like her brother-in-law.

"We'd better eat," he said in that same gruff voice. "The rest of our lunches will be out any minute." And he knew damn well at this point in an investigation, he should have grabbed a bite on the run, not sat down for a leisurely meal with the woman he craved.

"Oh," Jane said, seeming startled by the reminder of her surroundings, and picked up her fork.

No, this lunch wasn't social, he reminded himself. It was a disguised attempt to penetrate her defenses and get her to help him.

The chili had cooled off some, but was still good. The chunk of corn bread that came with it was even better, Clay discovered. It was unexpectedly spicy.

Jane saw him looking at it. "Not what you expected?"

He guessed she was trying to get the conversation back to a more conventional place, and made an effort himself. "No. You want a bite?"

She shook her head. "I've had it before. It's really good."

He nodded at her food. "Eat. This is the second salad I've seen you push around on a plate."

She wrinkled her nose at him, looking absurdly young for a moment, but did start eating.

They were able to talk after that, him asking a few questions about the owner of the café because it was an easy topic.

Sure, get her comfortable, then *go in for the kill.*

"You and Nell McAllister friends?" he asked.

"Yes, and I'm getting to be with Noah Chandler's wife, Kait, too. They're both interesting women."

Clay knew enough about Angel Butte's mayor Chandler to guess it would have to be an unusual woman who'd be able to stand up to him.

The thought fed back into his earlier epiphany, which he had no intention of pursuing right now. Instead he asked, "Have you talked to your sister's doctor?"

"Yes, this morning. He's still claiming to be optimistic, but…" Her throat worked. "I could be wrong, but I had the feeling he's getting worried."

Clay reached across the table and covered Jane's hand with his. He felt her tremble. "Hey. It's barely been two days."

She smiled gratefully at him. "I keep telling myself that. It's been a really long two days, though."

"She's your sister—"

As if she didn't hear him, she said, "It's mostly Bree I'm thinking about. Whether…whether she's even alive. And if she is, is she hurt? She has to be petrified. Oh, damn." She freed her hand from his grasp to swipe at the tears that suddenly overflowed. "I'm sorry."

"Don't be sorry." Clay discovered how much he hated seeing her cry. Sometimes he'd resented her strength. Now all he wanted was to see her strong again. Not afraid. "I keep thinking about her, too, and I've never even met her."

"I love her." Those beautiful eyes, still swimming with tears, met his. "I love both the girls, but Bree… She's more vulnerable, I guess. Unsure of herself. She hates change. That's why the summer has been so hard for her, losing her best friends. Even if we find her…"

"We'll find her, damn it." The words felt raw. "I won't let up until we do."

She seemed to be looking deep into him, her eyes searching, intense. "I know you won't," she said at last, softly. "Whatever happened between us, I always knew you were really good at your job. Smart and tenacious. That's why I called you. I mean—" she made a small gesture "—two weeks ago. And…I told Alexis yesterday that I trusted you to find Bree if anyone could."

Man. It was like having a boa constrictor squeezing his chest until his ribs creaked. She trusted him.

And the cop in him thought, *You need her if you're going to find the little girl. Use her mood. That's what you're here for.*

It took him a minute to overcome his paralysis. "If you trust me, Jane, you've got to help me. Find the answers I need. Don't let your sympathy for your brother-in-law blind you."

Her expression changed, and he felt like a ruthless bastard. He didn't take back what he'd said, though. His first priority *had* to be that little girl. In the absence of Drew Wilson's cooperation, Clay needed Jane's. It was that simple. This wasn't some kind of competition, him needing to prove she was on his side.

He didn't like that he had to wonder if he was lying to himself.

He softened his tone. "Help me, Jane."

She took what seemed to be an angry swipe at her eyes, and after a moment nodded. "For Bree," she said tightly. "What is it you want to know?"

Was it that easy? Was she surrendering because she really did trust him—or because her loyalty to her niece was more powerful than her also steadfast loyalty to her brother-in-law?

"I want to know about Melissa and Drew's finances."

"What?" Despite the chair, she lurched back enough to have given herself whiplash.

"Did they have a big down payment on their house?" he said, voice hard. "Or do they have one hell of a mortgage? You know his car is two years old and hers only one? Do you know what that summer day camp costs?" He told her. "And has your sister told you what she earns?"

He saw from Jane's expression that either her sister or Drew had.

"Tell me how they afforded all this, Jane."

"With them both working..."

"With them both working, they might just squeak by. What do you think, did they make so much they were able to stash a bunch in savings for a rainy day?"

She looked stricken.

"Drew was laid off four and a half months ago, Jane." His jaw tightened. "You tell me. How are they paying all those bills?" He paused. "Or are they?"

"Ask Drew!" she cried.

"Oh, I've asked, and he doesn't want to tell me. That's why I need you."

She stared at him for a long moment, and he could tell she didn't like what she was seeing. "I thought," she began, barely above a whisper, then stopped, gave a brief, unhappy laugh and shook her head. "Who'd have thought I was so stupid?"

"What are you talking about?"

"It doesn't matter." She bent down, making him wonder what she was doing until she reappeared above the tabletop with a couple of twenty-dollar bills in her hand. To his shock, she dropped them by her plate. "Since this was my idea, I should pay." Then she pushed her chair back and stood. "The answer is no. My sister is in a coma, my niece is missing, my brother-in-law is distraught and grieving and you want to believe they did this to themselves. I will not spy on my family."

Shocked and suddenly pissed, he shot to his feet and grabbed her arm as she started past him. He tugged her close so their bodies were almost touching. He *wanted* the plush mound of her breasts pressed against him.

"Tell me, Jane," he said roughly, aware enough of surrounding diners to keep his voice low. "Why are you so determined to fight me?"

Color came and went in her cheeks. She had to know he was talking about more than what he'd just asked her to do. Looking into her eyes, a green so dark there was no hint of gold, he was perilously close to kissing her whether they were in the middle of a damn restaurant or not.

But she wrenched herself back, actually stumbling in her desperation to escape his touch. "Did you really think I was the docile little woman who'd do anything you wanted her to?"

Her utter disgust made him feel as if she'd just belted him.

Stunned, he watched her wind her way between tables and leave.

CHAPTER SEVEN

JANE COULD NOT believe she'd almost fallen for that load of bull from a man who was apparently a master manipulator. She was mad as hell, but underneath flowed an unseen current of something that felt an awful lot like grief.

She heard him saying, *That's not my choice.* And, *I didn't like seeing the two of you wrapped around each other yesterday.* Asking if she was seeing anyone else. Giving her a funny, floaty feeling of hope. She'd remembered the night of the raid to rescue Matt Raynor, when Clay had told her so quietly that she could trust him, if only she'd believe it.

No, she thought, that wasn't exactly right. He'd said, *You'll never believe it, will you?* And she had said no. But the Clay she'd been getting to know this past couple of days wasn't quite the man she'd thought he was. When he had mentioned wanting to talk to her and agreed readily when she suggested lunch at a favorite restaurant, she had, oh, so foolishly *begun* to believe.

Until she'd found out all he was doing was playing her, trying to get her to wait until Drew was out of the house so she could hunt for passwords that would allow her to break into their computer and see exactly how much he and Lissa earned and owed. Incredibly private things they didn't tell her, even though she was family. The kind of things she didn't tell them, either.

Tell me how they afforded all this, Jane.

What difference did it make? Maybe they *couldn't* afford it. So what? Plenty of people lived beyond their means. They didn't kill their child because they were freaked about their finances, if that was what Clay was trying to suggest. It made no sense. Drew and Lissa could have put the house on the market, or Drew could have accepted one of the jobs he'd been offered. If he was determined to hold out for a great opportunity, he could take something temporary that would bring in more than his unemployment did.

What *sense* did Clay's insinuations make? His fixation on Drew felt like a vendetta.

I didn't like seeing the two of you wrapped around each other yesterday.

Could he possibly really believe she and Drew had something going? And that he minded so much, he'd go after Drew like this just to…she didn't even know. Prove something to her?

She didn't know whether believing that was worse, or knowing he'd deliberately set out from the minute they'd sat down at the café to get her thinking he actually felt something real for her, only so he could use her feelings.

But that was what he'd done, wasn't it?

Jane stomped down the sidewalk, only as aware of passersby as she had to be to avoid crashing into someone.

She'd let herself cry in front of him!

Well, never again. To hell with Clay Renner and his "you can trust me" crap. *Was* he really looking for Bree, or was that a lie, too?

She didn't realize she was mumbling under her breath until she intercepted a pair of startled looks from two people who then steered wide around her, the crazy woman of Angel Butte. Imagining the dark smudges of exhaustion under her eyes and her wild hair flying loose, she would have laughed if she hadn't known it would come out sounding hysterical. Thank God, there was her Yukon ahead.

Of course, some idiot had all but blocked her in. It took her five minutes to squeeze out of the too-small parking space by dint of backing up a few inches, cranking the wheel, going forward and doing it all over again—and again. Her mood did not improve. She wanted to make herself feel better by slapping a traffic ticket under the idiot's wiper blade. Unfortunately, the driver hadn't actually done anything overtly illegal.

Now, if she'd found a certain dark green Jeep Cherokee blocking her in, she could have rammed it with pleasure. It would totally be worth the boost in insurance rates.

By the time she reached the hospital, the anger had seeped away, leaving only the sadness and fear, which she assured herself didn't have anything to do with Clay. She wanted to walk in and, when she took Lissa's hand in hers, feel a faint squeeze in response. See a flutter of breath not driven by the machine. A flicker of eyelashes. *Something.* Hope.

Of course, there wasn't anything like that. She'd have been called if there had been any change in Lissa's condition at all. Feeling obligated, Jane sat with her sister for an hour, holding the chilly hand that could have been molded from wax like in Madame Tussaud's, and remembered for some absurd reason a time when Lissa, fifteen or sixteen, had called her, whispering that the boy she'd gone out with was drunk and she was scared and please, please, please could Jane come and get her.

I did rescue her sometimes. If only she hadn't been mad later that she'd *needed* rescuing.

Oh, didn't that sum them up perfectly: Lissa, fiercely, angrily independent, desperately unable to depend on anyone but herself, and Jane, hungry to be needed, always the responsible one. Lissa lithe and beautiful, Jane in comparison squat and ordinary.

No, she thought, *I like myself. I do. It's just that sometimes I wish...* She hardly knew what. Not that anyone would rescue her, because she didn't need it. Maybe she hoped that in one particular person's eyes, she would be beautiful and awe-inspiring, not either the stereotype of the too-buxom woman with a plain face or the worse stereotype of female cop who was subject to sexual innuendo if anyone thought of her as a woman at all.

Ugh. She hated feeling sorry for herself. Hated looking at her sister now, waxen and not at all beautiful and utterly dependent on tubes and lines snaking in and out of her body to sustain life.

Feeling like a coward, Jane slipped away, amazed at Drew's courage in staying at Lissa's side hour after hour.

"ALL RIGHT." CLAY pinched the bridge of his nose until the cartilage complained. "You were on the Cabot Lake Trail..."

"No!" the woman caller exclaimed. "I mean, you can turn off to Cabot Lake, but we'd been up to Carl Lake. We were coming down the switchbacks when we met this man with a little girl."

"This time of year, there must have been a lot of hikers up there." If he was remembering right, Cabot Lake was up in the northwest corner of the Metolius Basin, a good distance from Angel Butte. The country was spectacular, and this was August, the height of tourist season. "These folks caught your eye because...?"

"The age of the girl, for starters. I mean, this isn't the toughest hike in the world, but it's five miles into Carl Lake. There was no way a child that young could be expected to make it, but the man was getting mad at her and I thought she looked scared of him."

His interest abruptly sharpening, he asked, "Did you stop to talk?"

"We tried. I said something like, wow, you know there's another three miles to go, and the man just snapped, 'We're fine.' Completely uninterested. He had this grip on her shoulder and sort of pushed her ahead of him so we couldn't see her very well, except I'd already noticed how curly her hair must be because it was escaping from these really crooked braids. I looked back when I got to the next switchback and saw that he was staring after us. I don't know what it was about him, but he gave me the creeps."

It wasn't the first time Clay had heard someone say that: *He gave me the creeps.* People didn't always listen to their instincts, but sometimes they couldn't help themselves. The guy must have given off really strong vibes of wrongness to worry this woman so much.

"Were they carrying overnight gear?"

"Yes, he had on a fully loaded backpack, which meant he wasn't going to be able to carry the girl pig-gyback. We'd spent a couple nights up there and Irv had some trout hanging from a line. Most people we passed wanted to talk about how the fishing was, but not this guy."

Even as he continued to question her, Clay asked himself why in hell some creep would abduct a seven-year-old girl, then take her backpacking. On a grunt, Clay reflected that maybe a better question was why not? Once you got up in that country, there were trails sprouting off every which way. If memory served him, the Pacific Coast Trail was nearby. Head into the back country, enjoy the cute little girl you'd picked up for as long as you could afford to disappear from your every-day life, then dispose of her. Not hard out there.

Wouldn't she have begged for help? But he was already shaking his head. A kid Bree's age could be terrorized into silence in any number of ways.

"So it wasn't until you got down that you saw a newspaper with Brianna Wilson's picture."

"We stopped at a store to pick up some cold drinks. And I felt this awful sinking sensation and said, 'Irv, isn't this that little girl we saw?' and he thought she might be, too. So we decided we had to call."

Clay noted their contact information, hung up and groaned. Most of the tips they'd received were easy to check out. They could send a unit out to that Arco station where someone was absolutely *positive* he'd seen Brianna using the restroom and returning the key to the clerk who didn't pay any attention, only it turned out the clerk had paid enough attention to know the little girl's mother had also come in and bought candy bars for the girl *and* her brother, and by the way the girl didn't look much like the one on the front page of the paper. In fact, the mother had commented on the picture and how scary it was having a child that age disappear. A good hour, hour and a half of an officer's time wasted.

This latest caller, though, had hit some hot buttons. Unfriendly man who had his hands on the kid to quell her; the suspicious stare back. *He gave me the creeps*. The kid's curly hair, her air of distress, the absurdity of a lone father—if that was what he was—taking a girl that young on a ten-mile round-trip hike.

Clay dragged out a map and determined that Carl Lake was in Jefferson County. He could start with the Forest Service…but he didn't want to send anyone in who wasn't armed, just in case. If the trailhead had been closer, he'd have gone himself. The elevation gain wasn't great; he could jog five miles, no problem, and hope with the kid pooped out the man wouldn't have tried to take her farther. But the afternoon was advancing, and the drive alone would take him…an hour, hour and a half.

He put in a call to Jefferson County, gave them specifics and received a promise to send a couple of deputies who were also experienced hikers in to find the man and girl. He knew they were taking him seriously. Everyone was already watching for Brianna; there wouldn't be a cop in Oregon who hadn't memorized her face. He knew—he'd been working the phones whenever he had a minute, calling every jurisdiction he could think of, asking them to visit gas stations, mom-and-pop grocery stores, cheap motels and out-of-the-way resorts. Get Bree's picture out there. He'd met with nothing but cooperation; a missing child, likely abducted, was every cop's worst nightmare.

Hanging up, he should have been satisfied by the sergeant's promise to call the minute they learned anything, but instead he felt edgy.

Clay didn't usually mind delegating; these days, that was half his job. It made no sense anyway for him to focus without any good reason on this one tip, not when so many were pouring in.

But he didn't have to like it.

"Hey," Nguyen called from a few desks away. "You might want to talk to this one."

Clay waved his thanks and picked up the phone again.

A minute later, he was saying, "Yes, sir, we do appreciate you calling. Now tell me again…."

THE CALLS KEPT coming, not only to the Butte County Sheriff's Department, but also to the FBI, Deschutes County, every city jurisdiction. Probably the DEA and the ATF and the CIA, for all he knew. The frustrating thing was that the vast majority of callers were so off base, if not downright delusional. They'd seen a kid trip on the sidewalk and sit there sobbing over her bloody knee, but no mother or father had come running, so it had to be the missing child even though, it was true, this girl had black hair and might have been a little bit older. Was he *sure* Brianna was only seven?

There were always the lonely folks who wanted an excuse to feel important for a minute, to be listened to.

There were the nut jobs who ranted about extraterrestrials and how Brianna's parents would be lucky if those gray creatures with the pointy heads weren't cutting her heart out right this minute to study it.

And then there were the semireasonable callers, the ones consuming the time of half the law enforcement officers in central Oregon.

Jefferson County got back to Clay in the early evening. Yes, indeed, they'd caught up to the scared little girl and her daddy, who really was her daddy, except that he had only very limited visitation allowed by the court and hadn't brought her back after supposedly taking her to breakfast. The mother had been hysterical. The cops in Jefferson County didn't consider their trek to Carl Lake a waste of time. They'd already phoned the nice lady who had worried about that girl and told her she did a good thing. Daddy, who had anger management issues, was behind bars with charges still undecided. And yes, the child did have curly hair, although it didn't have any hint of red in it, and she was actually six years old.

Clay thanked them for jumping on it and ended the call wishing like hell that Brianna Wilson had been rescued instead. The other little girl hadn't been in as much danger as Bree was.

He kept going until after eight, even though tiredness was clouding his thinking. He needed a decent night's sleep. There was nothing he was doing here that others who hadn't been going for twelve plus hours straight couldn't do better. Walking across the parking lot to his Cherokee, he called the hospital and got put through to ICU, where he was told that Melissa's coma seemed to be getting lighter. Muscles were spasming, eyelids twitching. Once she'd pursed her lips.

None of which, Clay was well aware, meant she'd soon open her eyes and be herself again. Even if she did open her eyes, chances were good she'd prove to have suffered some degree of brain damage. Massive, or more subtle, but still impacting her ability to hold a job or function normally as a wife and mother.

Still, it was good news. *He* wanted her to wake up and tell him what had happened to her daughter.

He got into the Jeep, stuck the key in the ignition, then just sat there. This had been one of the crummiest days he could remember. All he'd done was spin his wheels.

And alienate Jane.

Yeah, don't forget that.

He hadn't, although he'd done his damnedest to block out her expression as she'd tossed those bills on the table and told him she wouldn't betray her family.

She'd made him feel about two inches tall and slimy besides.

He had been left asking himself whether he was fixated on Jane's sister and brother-in-law for all the wrong reasons. His gut instincts were wrong sometimes; he couldn't deny that. But not often. When they spoke, he listened. That and sheer tenacity made him good at his job.

This time, though—had he allowed jealousy to make him irrational?

Sitting there, arms laid on the steering wheel, staring out at the advent of night over Angel Butte, Clay couldn't answer his own question. He really didn't know.

Yes, he was jealous. Yes, he believed Drew Wilson wasn't saying everything he knew or suspected. But any problems between him and his wife might have nothing to do with her SUV plunging off the road and her child disappearing. In all honesty, it was a stretch to imagine how they *could*.

And yet—

Clay groaned and reached for the key. He needed to hit the sack. Tomorrow was another day and all that crap.

Another day when Jane Vahalik would not forgive him for being a Class-A jackass, and how could he blame her?

She'd been in his head from the minute he got up that morning, and was still there. In all honesty, she'd been there from the first time he saw her, at a lecture on advances in DNA technology and what it meant for detectives working cases. He'd been late, slipping in just before the door was shut and taking a folding chair at the back. It was her hair that had caught his eye— primly pulled into a ponytail, from whence it erupted in a wild cascade, the color fascinating him. He'd thought of melted caramel, wavy striations in red sandstone in the Four Corners country, curlicues of ribbon atop wrapped gifts. There was just a hint of red in her hair, enough to warm it and fascinate him.

He wasn't looking at the back of her head. The angle allowed him to see one ear and a little of her jaw and cheek. He kept waiting for her to shift in her chair, maybe glance back, so that he could see more. He'd been inexplicably riveted.

Who was she? He knew she wasn't with the sheriff's department; everyone there was familiar to him by sight, at least.

He kept trying to yank his attention back to the lecture, then discovering five minutes later he was back to staring. She had trouble sitting still. She kept squirming, rolling a shoulder, nodding or shaking her head in response to some point the speaker made. Once she reached up a hand to check the elastic was still firmly in place. She lifted her hair, momentarily baring a pale nape that had his hungry attention.

Sure as shooting, she'd finally turn her head and he'd discover she was homely as sin. Or too young, too old. Have a face plastered with makeup. His interest would go dead in the water.

But then it happened—the door behind him opened and the woman looked over her shoulder to see who'd come in or gone out. Only, he'd been gawking at her, and the idle sweep of her gaze didn't get any farther than him. Her eyes had widened and dilated, and for a moment that stretched all they'd done was stare.

When the talk ended, he'd waited until she came even with his chair and stood, edging into the exiting crowd right behind her. About one minute later, she'd agreed to have dinner with him.

Meeting Jane had something in common with getting struck by lightning. He had never before or since reacted to a woman like that, far less one whose face he hadn't even seen.

Once he saw the whole package—her lush, petite body packed into mannish trousers and white shirt—he'd been sold. And once he'd gotten to know her, smart, too serious as if she couldn't let herself relax, clear-eyed and self-aware, shy about her own sexuality, cynical and innocent at the same time, he'd gone down for the count.

Now he was bothered by one of his first thoughts—*she doesn't look like a cop.* Whatever that said about him, her appeal hadn't waned as he discovered that she did *think* like a cop.

Maybe it was love at first sight, if such a thing existed. He didn't know, only that he wasn't making any progress in getting over her. He thought he might have had another chance if he hadn't tried to push her this morning into doing something that so repulsed her.

But, goddamn it, he thought with intense frustration, what could he do but put Bree first? He was carrying a photo of Jane's niece with him so he had it to show, but also to remind him where his focus needed to be.

Every time he pulled it out he was jolted by how much she looked like Jane, even as he was reminded that she was also her mother's daughter. Bree would have spectacular cheekbones when she reached womanhood instead of Jane's apple cheeks. Still. The indefinable something that hinted at Jane was there, and not only the riot of curls. It might be as much personality as anything.

Bree... She's more vulnerable, I guess. Unsure of herself. She hates change The painful pause. *Even if we find her...*

He didn't like to think how damaged the little girl might be, if they did find her alive.

I had to ask, he thought. Jane is a cop! Was it really so terrible to say, "Yes, they're your family, but something's wrong there"?

Clay swore under his breath, bumped his head

against the backrest a couple of times, then finally put the Jeep in gear.

Quit thinking about her.

Can't.

Call her.

Oh, yeah, she's going to leap eagerly to answer.

You know she's not asleep yet.

Doesn't mean she'd want to talk to him.

But she might.

And what was he supposed to say? "Help me find Bree"? Or "give me another chance, Jane"? Please.

It was pitch-dark by the time he got home. He went in and grabbed a beer, then without turning on the porch light came back outside to sit on the steps. He liked the quiet, the cool air after the day's heat, the occasional rustle or squeak off in the dark branches or the understory of the surrounding woods. He wondered if Jane was addicted to town living and would hate the isolation of his cabin.

One hand curled around the damp, cold beer bottle. In the other, he held his phone, bouncing it lightly.

Call.

Wait until she has an attack of reason and comes to you to say, "You were right and I was wrong."

He snorted, startling himself. Like *that* was happening.

Yeah, but it might. Right now, her smarts were at war with her bone-deep sense of loyalty. Clay surprised himself by having faith her smarts would win, in part because she would realize her loyalty was owed, first and foremost, to the girls. More so than to her sister, even.

Bending his head, he scrolled to his last call to her, hesitated…and touched Send.

JANE HAD TALKED Alexis into going to bed in her own room by promising to stay until she was asleep. She'd read stories, then given a gentle back rub until Alexis's eyes drifted shut. She was deeply, peacefully asleep now, thank God. She might not stay that way, but for now, Jane could relax.

She slipped out, realizing she was actually hungry for the first time during this entire, devastating day. She'd made tacos for Drew and Alexis and only pretended to eat hers.

Drew had left long since, galvanized when she told him Lissa seemed to be struggling toward the surface. No, Jane had thought, it was more like a butterfly encased in a chrysalis. Tiny movements that grew larger until the first tears appeared.

And what would emerge? That was the scary part. Nobody, including the doctors, really had any idea.

Jane reheated the taco meat in the microwave while she grated some cheese and found the corn tortillas, lettuce, salsa and sour cream. When the meat came out, two tortillas went in the microwave to warm, after which she quickly assembled her meal and carried it to the table. It smelled so amazing, she couldn't imagine why she hadn't been able to eat earlier. Now she sat and devoured both tacos. She gave serious thought to licking the last of the sour cream and salsa from the plate.

Her phone rang, and her heart took an extra, hard beat. It would be the hospital or Drew, telling her something had happened with Lissa. And then she saw Clay's name. He'd found Bree....

She snatched it up. "Clay?"

"No news." He'd heard her eagerness, her hope. "I'm sorry." He sounded genuinely regretful. "I should have thought."

It took her a second to deal with the adrenaline in her bloodstream, but then she was able to say, "No, that's okay. Why are you calling if nothing has happened?"

The momentary pause made her wonder if she'd been rude, or even hurt his feelings. Who cares? she tried to tell herself, but knew she did.

"Thought I'd update you," he said in a voice devoid of emotion. "That's all."

"Oh." Jane slid her thumb back and forth over the smooth side of her phone. "Did you know about Lissa? That she might be emerging from the coma?"

"I checked with the hospital half an hour ago. The nurse I talked to is pretty upbeat."

"I want to be," Jane said, and suddenly there was a lump in her throat.

"Yeah." Now he sounded gentle, the Clay she had begun to think she could trust. "Let yourself hope, Jane."

"I don't know," she heard herself say. "Then it's worse if you crash and burn."

"Is that what you always think? That you will?"

Yes. The instant answer startled her. She immediately amended it. "Maybe. You're the one who has pointed out that we don't see a lot to make us optimistic."

"This is different. It's your sister."

She didn't want to think about her sister, who had

lied about where she was going and who had driven off a road that led nowhere she should have been. The sister who often seemed to hate Jane as much as she loved her.

"What did you do this afternoon?" she asked, just for something to say.

He told her, talking for long enough that she realized this was why he'd called. He was frustrated, tired and he needed to tell someone.

"It was lucky for the other girl that those people paid attention," Jane said tentatively.

Clay's "Yeah" came out hoarse. "But I hoped—"

She nodded even though he couldn't see.

"Your mom," he said, surprising her. "Do you remember her very well?"

What a strange thing to ask. Jane didn't like to talk about her mother. She didn't like to *think* about her. But, weirdly, she thought maybe she could tell him. It helped he couldn't see her, so she wouldn't give away more than she meant to.

"Yes. Kind of. I mean, I was eleven— I told you that, didn't I?— so of course I remember her. But I also think I blocked a lot out after she was gone. I was devastated, even though—" Whoa.

"Even though?" he prompted after a moment, his voice a deep, quiet rumble that made her think of a big cat's purr. Did lions and tigers purr? She had no idea.

"I was an afterthought for her." Saying it out loud hurt more than she'd expected.

"Just you?" Clay asked. "Or both you and your sister?"

Her fingers tightened on the phone. "Both of us, but especially me. Lissa looks like Mom. Me, I take more after Dad, which does not fill me with joy, I have to tell you."

"Looks are the smallest part of what we take from our parents, don't you think?"

"I don't know," she admitted. "In the case of my parents, well, I'm not thrilled to know *any* part of me came from either of them."

"That bad, huh?" He sounded tender.

"Dad hit Mom. Us, too, when his mood was right. Or wrong. Mostly we learned to stay out of his way. I didn't mourn a whole lot when he died."

"I'm sorry. My father—" Clay cleared his throat. "I told you some about him. Did I say that he's a cop, too? Over in Linn County."

Despite the topic, her mouth began to curve. "Is it chance you live on the other side of the mountains from your parents?"

His laugh was short and not all amused. "No. I'm glad to be able to see my family once in a while, but I didn't want to be close enough for the every-Sunday dinner, and I sure as hell didn't want to work for the same department my father does."

"He's still on the job, then?"

"Yeah." A wryness in his tone warned of some irony to come. "He's a sergeant, too."

"Was he glad when you got promoted?" She suddenly winced, remembering the last time she'd posed a similar question to him, but she didn't try to take it back, either.

"He said he was, but something changed between us after that. He's more competitive with me. Happier when he has a chance to jump on something I say."

Jane thought back and realized he'd cut himself off earlier, not sure he wanted to finish some thought about his father. Because it would offend her? Or bare more than he wanted her to know about him?

"Knowing you has changed how I look at my dad," Clay said, startling her. *This* was what he'd hesitated to say. Or hesitated to acknowledge even to himself? "I used to channel him sometimes." His voice got even gruffer. "Maybe I still do, but…I'm trying."

Jane's heart felt like a sponge being wrung out with a ruthless hand.

"That day," he continued, "what you heard me say about you—I realized later that's the way my father always talks about women. Even a compliment is wrapped around contempt. I told you I think he really loves my mother, but he doesn't show it very often. I don't understand why she puts up with his attitude."

With an effort, Jane said, "They must have been married a lot of years," as if that had anything to do with anything.

"Yeah…" He seemed to be thinking. "Heading toward their fortieth anniversary, I think."

"Maybe when they're alone, he's different. She might know which parts are surface, which parts real."

The minute the words were out, Jane felt a shock of realization. She had always known that what she heard Clay say that day was, as he put it, posturing. She'd *known* he wasn't like that underneath. Her shock and hurt had been real nonetheless. His gut-deep belief that a woman should be a woman and not try to work in a man's profession, that part she feared *was* real, and not an obstacle the two of them could overcome.

Except…she'd never expected him to admit as much as he had tonight, in this strange, intimate conversation.

I'm trying.

Was that enough? she asked herself, and didn't know. Maybe…maybe she had other issues where he was concerned, ones she hadn't let herself identify. Maybe she was afraid to let herself count on him.

Because I've never been able to count on anyone.

Oh, God, she thought in horror, *it's true. And I didn't even know.*

"Here I wanted to know about you," he said suddenly, sounding more like the man he usually presented himself as, "and all I've done is talk about me. Listen, I've got to hit the sack. I'll call tomorrow if I find anything out, all right?"

"All right." She hesitated. "I'm glad you called, Clay. Talking to you helped."

"I'm glad," he said, his voice dropping a notch again. "It helped me, too."

He said good-night, and she did the same. A minute later, she was alone, the phone still clutched in her hand as if it was a talisman.

One thing she knew, Jane thought in a state of semishock—not everything he'd said at lunch today had been intended to manipulate.

That's not my choice.

Despite all the intervening months, Clay still wanted a relationship with her. She guessed she'd known it, too, from the way he looked at her. Which meant…she could unmake her choice, if she really wanted to.

CHAPTER EIGHT

COME MORNING, JANE heard Drew's voice even before her eyes were open. It sounded as if he was right outside her bedroom door, and she realized he was trying to shush Alexis.

Too late.

Jane dragged herself up, feeling like the last rose of summer. Startled by the thought, she remembered that her mother had always put it that way. Great. All she needed was Mom appearing in her head. Jane hadn't lied to Clay—she didn't want to believe she had it in her to be anything like her mother.

Just because I say things once in a while that she did doesn't mean I'm like her.

No, but it did mean that, on some level, she was channeling her mother. That was how Clay had put it. She could tell he was as appalled at the idea of being unconsciously influenced by his father as she was by summoning bits and pieces of her mother.

"Ugh," she said aloud, and got herself ready to face the day.

When she reached the kitchen, Alexis hopped out of her chair to give Jane a quick, hard hug around her waist, and Drew greeted her with obvious pleasure despite the deep furrows of exhaustion in his face.

"Long night?" she asked.

He grunted.

"Is she still improving?"

"Looks like it."

Okay, so…why wasn't he more enthusiastic? But with Alexis here, this wasn't the time to ask. She glanced to see that they were both eating—what else?—Eggo waffles again. Jane poked around until she found a brand of cereal that wouldn't send her into sugar shock, added milk and carried her bowl to the table.

"You have plans today?" Drew asked.

She paused with the spoon halfway to her mouth. "That depends on you and Alexis."

"Lexie—" he dredged up a smile for his daughter "—has agreed to go to her camp today. Her friend Ava called and wanted to know if she was coming. They're going to Grouse Lake for a treasure hunt and a swim."

Jane, too, smiled at her niece. "That sounds like fun."

"Bree's gonna be mad she missed it."

Jane's smile faded. It was a moment before she could say, "She will be, won't she?"

Alexis looked up, her eyes damp. "I wish Bree was here *now.*"

Drew's face spasmed in agony. Jane doubted he could have said anything. So it was up to her.

"Yeah." It was hard talking past the lump in her throat. "Me, too."

She gazed at her cereal and wondered how she was going to force even a few bites down. But she had to set an example, didn't she? She made herself lift the spoon to her mouth, chew, swallow and try not to choke when even the small amount seemed to get stuck halfway down. Another bite. Repeat.

Drew finally sent Alexis off to her bedroom to get dressed and said he'd make her a lunch. He didn't move right away, though. Jane couldn't help noticing he didn't seem to have eaten much, either.

"I'm glad she's willing to go," Jane offered.

"I was really hoping. Jane…" He hesitated.

Inexplicably alarmed, she braced herself.

"I don't want us to have to keep trading off. I feel better when I'm with you. I was, uh, hoping to see more of you today."

Jane made herself meet his gaze and immediately thought, *Oh, boy.* Was that *yearning* she saw in his eyes? Please, God, let him be asking for support and friendship, not…whatever else she was imagining.

"I do have some things I need to do today, but I can sit with you at the hospital for a little, if you'd like."

"I'd like," he said, too fervently.

"Drew—"

"Lissa isn't the woman I thought she was when I married her," he said. "Why didn't you tell me?"

Jane bristled. "Tell you what? You went head over heels the minute you saw her! Like you'd have listened to *me*." Horrified by how caustic she sounded, she pushed away from the table. She hadn't been *that* hurt. Really. "No one in love wants to listen to reason. Anyway, Lissa is…exciting. Beautiful, fun. You've been happy with her, haven't you?"

"I thought so," he said despondently to her back as

she carried her bowl to the sink and dumped most of its contents down the disposal. "But this past year—"

Jane turned to face him from a safe distance. "What do you mean?"

"She was a bitch about my family coming for Christmas."

Yes. She had been.

"I think that's when it started. Then, when I got laid off…" He stopped, as if unable, or maybe reluctant, to continue, but then did. "It was like I was suddenly *less* in her eyes. You know?" he appealed.

God help her, Jane knew that, too. Lissa had been scathing sometimes when she talked about her husband, as if he was a loser. Later, though, she'd begun to sound almost pleased. As if she liked holding the upper hand.

My sister, the bitch.

Who was it I didn't want to betray? Jane wondered. *Lissa? Or was it really Drew?*

Both. The lump in her throat had swelled again, like a clog in the pipes that grew to increase the blockage as it caught every stray emotion trying to slip past. They were her only family. Of course her loyalty was to them. Nobody said you always liked the people you loved most.

"It's been a stressful year," she murmured. "Lissa gets…pugnacious when she's scared. You know that. It doesn't mean she feels any different about you."

Was that hope, or some darker knowledge, she saw on his face?

"Listen," she said, "I can drop off Alexis when she's ready. Why don't you go back to bed? Then we can meet at the hospital later."

He agreed and, once they set a time, stumbled off toward his bedroom. She heard his voice when he stopped to talk to Alexis, and then a minute later the sound of his bedroom door closing.

Jane remembered that Alexis needed to take a lunch with her, and delved into the refrigerator for peanut butter and jam. Lissa would insist on sending either some carrot and celery sticks or an apple, too, although Jane had her suspicions those didn't always get eaten. Cookies... The crock was empty, but she found packaged chocolate-chip cookies in the cupboard. Juice in a box. Grabbing a marker from a drawer, she wrote ALEXIS in big letters on the brown paper bag.

With all her heart, she wished she was reaching for a second lunch bag and writing BREE.

"I SHOULDN'T HAVE left things hanging," Jane said apologetically.

She'd dropped by Colin McAllister's office, hoping to get lucky and find him there. With him running for sheriff and the election just over two months away, he wasn't there as much as he used to be. She needed to find out whether he'd dealt with the two detectives she had put on suspension just before she'd taken off in a panic to help search for Bree. Saturday.

Oh, dear God—three days ago. An eternity.

Colin's expression was kind. "All I've done so far is confirm the suspension when that idiot Griffin called."

"We must be shorthanded."

"We are, but if we can't trust them, they don't belong on the job," he said flatly.

"No."

He raised his eyebrows. "Your call. Do we fire them both? Knock 'em back to patrol? Call the suspension good?"

She shook her head at the last. "Suspension isn't enough. An honest mistake is one thing, but this was pure egoism. They were showing off."

"All right," he said. "What about Officer Schneider?"

"She should go on suspension. She knew better, too."

He didn't say anything, only waited while she thought through how she wanted to handle Detectives Phil Henry and Kyle Griffin.

"Griffin was promoted only a couple of months ago. Not to excuse him, but so far in that pairing, Phil's calling the shots. Kyle at least had the grace to look embarrassed when I talked to them. Phil let slip something that told me he would have lied and kept lying if I didn't have him cold." The decision wasn't hard after all. "I need to fire him. I thought Kyle had a glimmer of promise. I'd like to send him back to patrol if Brian's okay with it, then give him another shot down the line."

"Good." Colin's gray eyes warmed. "Do you have time to go talk to Brian and then Human Resources? Or do you want me to take care of it?"

"No, I know how crazy busy you must be these days." She smirked at him. "It takes time to think up all those wise quotes I'm reading in my newspaper." At his snort, she laughed. "Really. I have a few hours before I need to go to the hospital. I'll handle it."

She'd already told him about the signs of improvement Melissa was showing, and he had assured her she could take as much time as she needed.

Now he said, "Is there anything I can do to help,

Jane? That any of us can do to help? Alec keeps asking about you, too. He of all people knows how you feel."

"I guess he does. I keep thinking about how we did find Matt and that he's fine." Her smile wobbled. "There really isn't anything you can do unless Sergeant Renner needs help. For that matter, there's nothing *I* can do but support my brother-in-law and help take care of my niece. I hate feeling so useless."

"I can imagine." His eyes stayed keen on her face. "Renner keeping you informed?"

"Yes, he's been really decent." Except when he was trying to use her. "Especially considering we didn't have that good a relationship. Um…they've been getting a ton of tips."

"We've had our share," Colin agreed. "Mostly from our usual crazies. Only one or two even worth following up on."

He walked her out of the office, his presence big and solid and reassuring. She guessed maybe she'd had a little bit of a thing for him—something like a middle school crush, really—but at the moment she had the fleeting wish she was with Clay.

Stupid.

The only good thing about her next hour and a half was that actually doing her job steadied her, made her feel more like herself. No surprise—the job was her life. She didn't have much outside it. The way she'd felt lately was like…like the doctor that suddenly found herself the patient, needing reassurance as much as anyone even though the knowledge was there in her head.

I could do something to help. Clay asked for my help. No! There was no way she could do that to Drew.

Her phone rang as she was walking out of the public safety building. Clay.

"Hey," he said. "You at the hospital?"

"On my way there. I was just firing one of my detectives."

There was a pause. "That's rough."

"Not my favorite part of the job." She hesitated. "Drew hasn't called. But he might not have gotten to the hospital yet. Have you heard something?"

"No, I was going by as much to see you as anything." He hesitated. "How about if I grab a couple of coffees at the Java Club and we sit and drink them at the park? We can watch the river run and you can tell me why you're having to fire someone."

Jane felt a cramp of pure longing. She didn't even try to resist it. "As it happens, I'm looking at the playground. I'll go stake out a bench."

"Deal," he agreed.

He showed up fifteen minutes later, carefully carrying two tall cups, one of which he handed to her before he sat down with a sigh and stretched out his legs. The cup was cold—he'd brought iced coffee.

She'd found a bench in the shade right beside the paved path that ran alongside the Deschutes used by bikers, runners and in-line skaters. In the heat of the day like this, though, she and Clay were mostly alone. A few mothers had young children over at the playground, and some older kids splashed in the water close to the bank of the river, running low now in late summer.

Clay gazed toward them. "School's about to start."

"A week from today."

"Alexis will be starting kindergarten, won't she?"

Jane concentrated on the uninteresting cap atop her drink. "Yes."

"And Bree, she'll be a second-grader?"

Hearing the rough sympathy in his voice, she nodded without looking at him.

They took simultaneous sips. Jane was disconcerted to discover that hers was an orange spiced coffee with just a hint of cream. He'd remembered her ordering something similar last year.

"Thank you," she said, lifting the cup to him.

He smiled, still looking out over the river.

He was so damn *male,* she thought. He was too big and powerful for her ever to forget he was a man. In this light, she could see how sun-glazed his hair was, but the bristle on his jaw was darker, as was the hair on his muscled forearms. He wore a short-sleeved sheriff's department uniform today, which made her wonder what he'd been doing. The olive green was a good color on him.

After another sip, she started talking, telling him without naming names about the fiasco at the crime scene.

"Part carelessness, part showboating for a pretty patrol officer."

"That's what you get for having women and men working together."

Jane's spine stiffened. "So it's the woman's fault for distracting the men?" she asked in outrage, before she saw the smile playing at the corner of his mouth. "Humph."

"You fire their asses?" he asked in a different tone.

"One of them." She explained her reasoning, and he nodded.

"Sounds like what I would have done, too."

She shouldn't be reassured by that, but was, just as she'd been by Colin's approval. The truth was, she'd risen from detective to lieutenant not much over eight months ago, with nothing in between. She'd worked with trainees before, but had no real supervisory experience, so this had been a gigantic jump for her. She'd been gaining in confidence, but still had her moments.

"Good you slapped the patrol officer, too," Clay added. "If she didn't know better than to accept the two macho idiots' invitation, she should have."

"No kidding."

A pair of boys bicycled past, one chasing the other, both of them pedaling for all they were worth.

"Why the uniform?" Jane asked.

"Seemed appropriate, the way I keep having to deal with other jurisdictions." He took a long drink. "Cool, too."

Jane had trouble tearing her gaze from his throat, working as he swallowed. Beads of sweat ran down it, one heading for the hollow at the base. She'd never seen him without his shirt. Back when they dated, their kisses had gotten pretty steamy, but she had always called a halt before they actually started shedding clothes. Now…well, she was a little bit sorry.

"If you keep looking at me like that, I'm going to have to kiss you."

To her shock, she realized he was watching her, heat in his eyes. Responding to what *he* saw in *her* eyes.

Great timing, she thought, turning her head to cut off the sight of him altogether.

Remember what a jerk he was yesterday? Does that ring any bells?

She thought she heard a faint sigh from beside her.

"I had a call first thing this morning from the FBI." His voice was neutral. "They had what sounded like a promising tip. We checked it out. Believe it or not, it was another domestic. Uglier than the last one, though, because this father wasn't supposed to have any visitation at all. He was sexually molesting the girl."

Sexually molesting was one of the things Jane had been trying very hard not to think about in relation to Bree, even though she knew it was a horrifyingly realistic possibility. Maybe the most realistic possibility, assuming she'd stopped a car to ask for help, and the driver had instead abducted her.

Suddenly stricken, Jane thought, *I should want Clay to be right. Because—if he is—it means whoever has Bree took her for some other reason.*

Any other reason would be better, wouldn't it?

"You okay?" He laid a big hand over hers lying on her thigh.

His touch felt so good. He made her feel safe, and that scared her as much as anything. She couldn't forget he'd humiliated her. She hadn't felt safe at all, standing there listening to those salacious hoots as every one of the men he was talking to thought about what *he'd* like to do to her.

Somehow, though, she knew he'd never do anything like that again. Not to her, and not to any other woman.

"I'm okay." She took a deep breath. "At least you rescued another girl."

"Yeah. It's good the publicity about Bree is making people pay attention to their instincts."

"The little girl… Is she all right?"

"Mostly." He sounded reserved enough she sneaked a glance to see a grim set to his mouth.

"Oh, no."

He didn't say anything.

"Do you think Bree's dead?" Jane asked.

"No." He scowled at her. "No, I don't, damn it!"

His anger shouldn't have reassured her, but did.

She gave a small nod, and looked down to see his hand still covered hers and had tightened. After a moment, she turned hers to return his clasp.

They sat sipping the iced coffee without talking for what had to be five minutes. Jane felt peculiar. People did pass on the path; a few even glanced at them. She wondered what they thought, a uniformed police officer holding hands with a woman in a public park. She found she didn't much care.

Clay finally made a grumbly sound in his throat and said, "I'd better be getting back."

"Me, too. Or getting there, at least. Drew and I were going to meet up at the hospital." She suspected she was late, but didn't much care about that, either.

He tossed his cup into a nearby trash container, and she followed suit. "Good shot," he murmured.

Clay finally let go of her, stretching his arms above his head, popping and crackling, before he groaned and rose to his feet. He took her hand and drew her to her feet, pulling her close to him as he'd done during that last, tumultuous scene at the café.

His eyes, so sharp and startlingly blue, searched hers. "You okay if I kiss you?"

Was she? she wondered in a miniburst of panic caused most of all by the fact that right this second, she didn't care about her many qualms, either. She *wanted* to kiss him.

Not letting herself hesitate, Jane rose on tiptoe and blindly sought his mouth with hers. He groaned again, but this time the sound rose from deep in his chest. Their lips pressed together like two twelve-year-olds in their first kiss. Embarrassed at her awkwardness, Jane might have pulled back, but he didn't let her. His big hand slid around the back of her neck, anchoring her and squeezing in a way that felt unbelievably good. He gently rubbed his lips against hers, then nuzzled her. The next thing she knew, she'd let him in and his tongue was stroking hers. Her whole body weakened, a sensation she'd never felt before with any other man, and one she wasn't sure she liked. It was classic—she was melting, softening, ready to be pliant to meet his needs. But, oh, they felt like her needs, too.

"God, Jane," he muttered against her mouth. "Do you know how much I've missed you?"

She was a little shocked to realize how much she had missed him, too. She hadn't let herself think of it like that.

"I don't understand," she whispered, opening her eyes.

"I don't, either." He rested his forehead against hers and for a moment that was all they did—they leaned against each other, until her legs began to feel strong enough to hold her again, and she could carefully separate herself from him.

The expression on his rough-hewn face was strange, as if he felt as shaken as she did.

It was just a kiss, she tried to tell herself. Tame. He hadn't even groped her, although her breasts ached as if he had. Oh, God. Imagining his hand enclosing her breast, Jane felt a painful stab of longing.

"Whatever you're thinking," he said hoarsely, "don't."

"What?"

"You heard me. It's all I can do not to lay you on the grass as it is."

A cramp low in her belly told her she might not have resisted. "Anyone could see us."

"That's what's stopping me." Muscles in his jaw flexed. "Let's go."

They walked toward the parking lot in silence, Jane conscious of how hot her cheeks were. Wonderful. Where was her common sense? She and it needed to have a little chat.

Like a gentleman, Clay accompanied her to her car, waited while she got in, then said, "I'll see you at the hospital," and closed her door.

DREW WILSON DIDN'T even seem to notice that Clay was there, as far as he could tell.

He jumped to his feet as Clay and Jane entered the glass-walled room. "She squeezed my hand! I swear she did, Jane."

She smiled at him. "That's great."

Clay's eyes narrowed as he saw that Drew seemed to be reaching for her, but Jane adroitly slipped past him as if she hadn't noticed and stood at her sister's bedside.

"Her face looks more..." She seemed to grope for the right word.

Clay, who'd walked around to the other side, could see what she was getting at. *Alive* was the word that came to mind, but he doubted Jane or Drew would appreciate it. "Like she's only sleeping," he said.

Her grateful gaze met his. "Yes."

"How are we going to tell her about Bree?" Drew asked.

Clay couldn't help thinking the guy had made a fairly giant leap. Apparently he had sudden, unshakable faith that his wife would be opening her eyes any minute. Didn't he know she might be permanently damaged? *But, hell,* he thought, *if she was my wife, I might not be letting myself think about that, either.*

If this was Jane.

Don't go there, he warned himself. But, damn, *she* had kissed *him.* He couldn't be wrong about that. He didn't know how they'd gotten there, after yesterday's debacle, but it felt good. Unbelievably good.

"What's the doctor say?" Jane was asking.

Drew answered, and they went on speculating. Clay didn't even try to listen. He kept watching Jane, seeing hope soften features that had been too tight these past days, but noticing, too, that her gaze kept shying from his, and either she'd gotten some sun while they were at the park or she was blushing.

And I, he reminded himself, *am standing at the bed-*

side of a woman who is in a coma and who doesn't yet know her daughter is missing.

He wished like hell she *would* open her eyes. Clay was beginning to fear that any hope of finding Brianna Wilson was locked in the unconscious woman's brain.

"I need to get back to work," he said abruptly. "Jane, you'll let me know how it goes?"

Her eyes flashed to his. "Yes. Of course I will. And…and you'll call me if you learn anything?"

"You know I will."

He hated to leave, but had no choice. The worst part was this worm of jealousy eating at his gut, even though Clay knew—or thought he knew—he was being completely irrational. Jane was fond of her brother-in-law, was filled with sympathy and fellow feeling, that was all. He was probably imagining the vibe he got from Drew suggesting there was something more.

Well, he was willing to bet Jane had never kissed Drew the way she'd kissed Clay today. The memory relaxed him and even had him smiling as he left the hospital.

JANE TURNED ON the desktop computer and waited for it to hum to life. She could hear Disney's *The Little Mermaid* singing from the family room. Alexis claimed it was her absolute favorite movie, although Jane worried because there were some pretty scary scenes in it that might have new impact now.

Leaving the hospital to pick up Alexis, she'd casually asked Drew if he'd mind if she used his computer.

"Huh? Oh, sure," he'd said, and she wasn't even sure

he had really heard her. But she'd covered her ass, which was what she had been going for.

Not that she'd totally made up her mind then that she was going to do what Clay had asked of her. She still hadn't.

Really? Then what am I doing on my sister and brother-in-law's computer?

She could check her email, maybe play a computer game.

An unpleasant knot in her belly told her what she already knew: she *had* made up her mind. And, while she didn't expect Drew for a while, he could walk in the door at any time.

She'd already checked desk drawers for a checkbook, but failed to find one. Come to think of it, what had happened to Lissa's purse? She'd surely had it with her, and if either of them routinely carried the checkbook, it would be her.

Jane had heard her sister say she paid most of her bills online, though, and given her expertise with QuickBooks, Jane was guessing she kept track of her own finances the same way.

Turned out she was wrong. She found a budget that Lissa must have cooked up a while back, since it incorporated Drew's salary. It included after-school care for Brec and day care for Alexis, a really staggering amount that had Jane gaping. Had it really made sense for Lissa to keep working back when it meant *both* kids had to be in day care? A few calculations gave her the answer: no. But Lissa had scoffed at the idea of being a housewife.

Wow, Jane realized, *I wouldn't be able to afford to*

keep working if I had two kids, either. Not the kind of thing she'd thought about when she was halfway dreaming of having her own family. And—had her dreams included dropping her children off at a preschool every morning and not picking them up until six?

Abandoning the budget and hoping neither Drew nor Lissa would ever notice the program had been opened on a day when neither of them could have been sitting down at the computer, Jane went online. She scrolled down their list of favorites and found their bank. When she went to the log-in page, she found the user name was saved, thank goodness.

Again she dug through desk drawers, hoping Lissa kept the same kind of notebook Jane did at home, listing user names and passwords. She was about to give up when she caught a glimpse of something behind the monitor. It was a fat little green address book. Jane flipped it open.

Apprehension became triumph and then guilt. Yes, there it was—the keys for her to intrude unforgivably on her sister's life.

Her sister, who was in a coma. Her sister who had somehow lost her daughter.

And…she might find they did have substantial savings, enough to draw on for a few months and give themselves the time for Drew to find a job he really wanted. She'd be able to blow Clay's nebulous theory out of the water, which would give her great pleasure.

Lissa and Drew would never know what she'd done.

Jane typed in the password.

A minute later, she sat with her heart pounding, thinking, *Where on earth did Lissa get all that money?*

CHAPTER NINE

JANE TENSED AT the sound of the key in the lock, then the front door opening and closing. She'd been waiting for Drew. Since he'd spent all afternoon and evening at the hospital, she had guessed he wouldn't try to stay all night, too.

It had taken her a long time to decide what to do. Her first instinct was to call Clay—but if she didn't talk to Drew first, give *him* a chance to be honest with the police, she would be forever alienating herself from Drew and Lissa, no matter what else happened.

So she'd been sitting at the kitchen table, nursing a cup of tea and pretending to read, for close to two hours now. The tea, she suspected, was stone-cold.

"You're still up." Drew appeared in the kitchen doorway. Maybe it was the artificial lighting, but his face seemed to have a gray cast. Light glinted off the lenses of his wire-rimmed glasses, obscuring his eyes and giving her a chill.

What if he knew all about the mysterious deposits? Clay would say she was being naive to assume this *nice* man was innocent of wrongdoing.

She managed a smile of sorts. "I was hoping to talk to you."

"Can it wait until morning?" He took his glasses off and rubbed his eyes. The sight of them, bloodshot and puffy, reassured her. "I'm beat."

"No," she said. "This is…important."

It had occurred to her that he might ask her to leave the house after he heard what she had to say. She wouldn't altogether blame him.

Renewed panic rose in her. What if he did? If she was never again allowed to see Alexis and Bree—? But the thought slammed to a halt. She'd done this *for* Bree.

"Would you like a cup of tea? Or coffee?"

Drew shook his head as he pulled out a chair across from Jane. "I must have had ten cups of coffee today." After hooking his glasses back in place, he gazed at her in puzzlement. "What's up? Did something go on with Alexis?" His expression changed. "God! Did that sergeant call you?"

"Nothing like that," she said hastily. Although that wasn't entirely honest, since she had invaded Drew and Lissa's privacy at Clay's suggestion. "And Alexis is fine. She watched *The Little Mermaid* and went to bed without complaint. I think she's worn out from her day."

He nodded.

"Clay—Sergeant Renner—has talked to me about the investigation. I knew him before, you know. Just recently we were involved in an operation together."

Drew's expression grew warier.

"He tells me you've been evasive about your finances."

His muscles bunched and the hand she could see balled into a fist. "It's none of his goddamn business!"

Jane's throat tightened, but there was no going back. "I think you're wrong. What's more, I think *you* know it."

He stared at her.

"I went online tonight. I found your passwords and looked at your bank records." She absolutely could not tell what he was thinking. "Drew, there's a reason you don't want to tell Sergeant Renner anything."

"Lissa does all our banking and bill paying." There was something like fear in his eyes. "You know that."

"And you haven't wondered at all how she's kept paying the bills with you out of work."

"I get unemployment." When she didn't say anything, he made a guttural sound and bent his head. "Yeah, I wondered. She kept saying we were fine. Once she said—" He breathed deeply for a minute. "She said, wasn't it lucky *one* of us could actually earn the money we needed."

"What did you think she meant by that?" Jane asked, almost gently.

He shook his head. "I thought it was a dig, that's all."

"Did you?"

Now his brown eyes held open anguish. "She was smug. Like—" His Adam's apple worked. "I don't know. She was up to something."

"Like what?" Did he share her fear that Lissa was embezzling from Stillwell Trucking? How else could she be coming up with that kind of money? The thought horrified Jane. *My sister, the crook.*

The worse part was—Jane could actually see it, if Lissa thought for some reason she was entitled.

Drew only shook his head. Hard.

After that, no matter what she said, he wouldn't answer. If it wasn't embezzling he feared, she began to wonder, what could it be? Did he imagine Lissa had become a high-class hooker? Was she out enough in the evening that it was possible?

"Drew," Jane said at last, "you have to tell Sergeant Renner. Whatever Lissa has been up to may have something to do with Bree's disappearance." She hesitated. "I know you love Lissa."

"I'm not so sure I do anymore," he said in a stifled voice.

Jane felt a lurch underneath her breastbone. Did that mean he *was* looking at her with different eyes? And… if the marriage failed, what would that do to the girls?

Or to Alexis, if they were too late to save Bree?

No! She couldn't let herself think anything like that.

Drew's eyes met hers. "If I don't tell him, you will. That's what you're saying, isn't it?"

She wanted to say "no, this is your decision," but it would have been a lie. "Yes."

He nodded. "Should I wait until morning?"

Her gaze found the clock on the microwave. "It's only nine-thirty." Seeing his instinctive resistance, she said, "Bree has been gone for over three days now, Drew. That's…a really long time."

A shudder grabbed him. She wasn't sure it wasn't a dry sob. "All right," he said dully. "Will you sit in?"

"If it's okay with Clay."

"Thank you." He fumbled at his waist and came up with his phone. When she told him the number, he dialed.

IT WAS JANE who let Clay in, her expression somber. The living room beyond her was dark, light coming from the kitchen and creating a nimbus around her hair, loose for once and tumbling over her shoulders. The brother-in-law was nowhere in sight.

"He didn't decide to talk to me on his own, did he?" Clay asked, keeping his voice low, paying attention to the shadows in her eyes. He sure as hell didn't want her to guess how indecently triumphant he felt because she had made the choice he'd known she would. The unsettling thing was, he wasn't thinking she'd chosen him over her sister and brother-in-law. He knew better, and didn't even mind. What she'd done was proof she was the clearheaded, dedicated cop he'd believed her to be.

Exactly what he *hadn't* wanted her to be, back last fall when they dated.

Clay didn't like being confused.

"He…didn't argue," Jane said quietly.

"Okay." Watching while she closed and locked the front door, he thought of the saying about the barn door. There wasn't much left to protect in this house.

No—not true. Drew Wilson had another daughter.

"Alexis asleep?" he asked.

"Yes. Pray she stays that way."

Jane had changed clothes since he'd seen her that morning, making him wonder if this was what she slept in. The pants were a loose, thin cotton knit, nothing meant to be sexy but nicely outlining the firm globes of her ass as she walked away from him. Clay stumbled over the thought. Would it offend her? Was *ass* derogatory? Hell. Did he want to get involved with a woman who had him tangled up over a choice of words? It wasn't as if he could help noticing her ass. Butt. Whatever. All he knew was that his hands tingled with the desire to get a good handful.

When she faced him, the baggy T-shirt she wore had clung to her more-than-generous breasts, as well. He wanted a handful of those, too. And a mouthful.

And this was *not* what he should be thinking about, considering he might finally be getting a break in this investigation. All he'd had to do was see Jane's face to know Drew wasn't about to show him monthly statements proving that his wife had scrimped so skillfully, she'd somehow managed to pay the bills with their vastly reduced income.

Drew sat at the table in the kitchen, shoulders slumped and head hanging. His hair poked out every which direction, as if he hadn't combed it in recent memory. His chin was at least two days from a shave, too. At the sound of their footsteps, he lifted his head slowly, the effort seeming huge.

"Thank you for calling me," Clay said.

Jane pulled up a chair and he did the same. A small pile of printed pages sat beside Drew's hand. Clay recognized the familiar format of a bank statement on the top page.

"I guess I didn't want to know," Drew said heavily. He pushed the papers across the table. "If I said anything, suggested I take a shit job as a fill-in, Lissa kept telling me not to worry, that she was handling it."

It. A hell of a vague word, Clay couldn't help thinking. "What was she handling?" he asked.

Bleary, bewildered brown eyes met his. "Bringing in plenty of money."

"How?"

He shook his head slowly and kept shaking it, as if he couldn't stop. "I don't know."

Jane moved. Only a little, but Clay looked at her.

Drew seemed sunk in apathy. After a quick glance at him, Jane said, "You know how these days, with on-line banking, you can open photocopies of the checks you deposited or wrote?" She waited for Clay's nod.

He did know, but from investigative work. Personally, he paid his bills the old-fashioned way and kept a checkbook the old-fashioned way, too. He wasn't sure he liked the idea of having his financial information out there for anyone to hack into. Jane, he thought, would probably consider him a dinosaur.

"The extra money all came from personal checks." She didn't like this any better than her brother-in-law did, but her eyes met Clay's. He hated seeing the hint of shame in them, as though she was responsible for her sister's failings because she'd raised her. "All written by James Stillwell."

Well, well. Somehow, he wasn't surprised. "I don't suppose they could have been forged," he said thoughtfully.

"I don't see how." Jane was trying to hide how she felt about this, but emotions leaked through nonetheless. He knew she hadn't wanted to betray her sister—but she was the one who felt betrayed now, by the little sister she'd mothered. "Over the past three months, there

have been five sizable checks. Not consecutive numbers. There's something wrong if he hasn't missed the
checks or the money. Finding out where the money went
wouldn't have been hard either, given that Stillwell uses
the same bank Drew and Lissa do."

Clay bent his head and studied the statements she'd
printed off, slowly flipping through, concentrating on
deposits. Damn, that was one hell of a supplemental
income. Melissa Wilson had had good reason to insist
she was "handling it."

"Funny Mr. Stillwell never mentioned how generous he was being to his bookkeeper." He regretted the
words the minute he said them, even before he saw the
way Drew squeezed his eyes shut. Clay had a bad feeling Drew thought his wife was earning the extra bucks
on her back. And he supposed it was possible. Lissa was
a looker, no question, and Stillwell a sleaze enough to
think it was fine and dandy to pay for sex, taking ad-
vantage of a young mother's desperation.

But Clay didn't believe it. The picture he was getting of Melissa Wilson didn't fit the description of a
desperate young mother, for starters. He was beginning to wonder if she wasn't essentially amoral. Jane
didn't want to think that, and he understood why. The
husband didn't want to believe it, either, but he knew
enough to be getting the idea that he wished he was
married to the other sister.

Clay's mouth tightened. *Sorry, buddy. Not happening.*

"Mr. Wilson," he said, rising to his feet, "I appreciate you coming forward with this information. I realize
this must feel like an invasion of your privacy. It has to

have been difficult for you, on top of everything else you're going through."

Drew stared at him so blindly, Clay wondered what—or who—he was really seeing. After a too-long moment, he nodded.

"I assume I can take these statements with me? I can assure you any information that doesn't pertain to the investigation will be kept confidential."

After another distinct pause, Drew nodded.

Clay bent his head politely. "Good night, then."

Jane got up, her worried gaze on her brother-in-law. "I'll see you out."

Neither of them said anything until she had released the dead bolt and opened the door.

As he stepped out, she said, "You'll talk to Stillwell tomorrow?"

"First thing." Seeing her expression, he said, "And yes, I'll let you know what I learn. Although I'm betting he lies through his teeth."

"I still don't understand."

"I don't, either." Unable to resist temptation, he slid his hand under the heavy fall of her hair to gently squeeze her nape. "I may be barking up the wrong tree."

She nodded, then shook her head in contradiction. "At least we know your instincts were right."

"I'd say I wished they hadn't been, except—"

Her distress took a chunk out of his heart muscle. "For Bree," she said, so softly he saw her lips shape the words more than heard them.

"Yeah. Damn. Come here."

She came.

Believing it to be what she needed, all he did was

hold her. He laid his cheek against the top of her head, savoring the springy feel of her curls, the pillow of her breasts against him, but most of all the trust it took for her to lean on him like this. Trust he knew he hadn't yet earned.

Finally she rubbed her cheek on his shirt, making him wonder if she was drying tears on him, then straightened, her eyes shadowed and her smile wry.

"I wonder if Drew will ever forgive me."

Clay stiffened. The whole time she'd been resting in his arms, had she been thinking about her brother-in-law? "If we find his daughter, does it matter?"

Jane hesitated long enough to bother him. "No," she said softly, at last. "Of course not."

Pity twisted inside him, replacing the sting he'd felt. "I'm sorry, Jane. This sucks."

"It does," she said on a sigh. She tried another smile, not much better. "Good night, Clay."

"Yeah." He bent his head and kissed her cheek, cushiony, soft and fragrant. "Get some sleep." He had to turn and go. This wasn't the moment for anything more.

She was still standing there in the open doorway when he got in his Jeep, and even when he backed out into the street, but the house was dark the last time he looked back.

"WHY WOULD YOU be interested in my financial relationship to one of my employees?" Stillwell asked in what appeared to be genuine surprise. That, or he was a hell of an actor, which was Clay's guess. "If any crime was committed, Mrs. Wilson was the victim."

He hadn't looked real happy to see Clay waiting outside his building when he arrived at eight-thirty. Clay had given some serious thought to going straight to his house last night, or knocking on the door at 7:00 a.m. or so, but had held on to his patience by a thread. He knew damn well that if he went to a judge right now asking for a warrant, he'd be met with bewilderment. Sure, something irregular was going on—but was it a crime? Did it have anything to do with the crime that *had* been committed? He couldn't prove a thing yet, and in all honesty didn't know.

"When I'm investigating, I look for any anomaly," he explained. "The financial situation of the Wilsons raised a red flag for me right away."

Stillwell leaned back in his desk chair, appearing comfortable and only mildly concerned. Avuncular, Clay thought. The guy had it down to an art form.

"Of course," Clay continued, testing the waters, "we're hoping that Mrs. Wilson will soon be able to tell us herself what happened. Had you heard she's showing distinct signs of improvement?"

The blue eyes remained guileless. "Yes, I stopped by again yesterday. Spoke to Drew, in fact. He sounded quite encouraged."

"So is Lieutenant Vahalik, Mrs. Wilson's sister."

"Melissa has mentioned that her sister is a police-woman." This time there was something different in his eyes—some secret amusement? "For sisters, they don't seem to have much in common."

"Oh, I don't know," Clay murmured, hiding his deep antipathy. "They both love those two girls. The lieutenant is dreading having to tell her sister that Brianna is missing."

There was a flicker of something, but it came and went too fast to be read with any accuracy. "Indeed," Stillwell said, shaking his head. "That will be distressing." He raised his eyebrows. "Unless you have reason to believe you might be able to find young Brianna before her mother regains consciousness?"

"That's my hope. Perhaps you can help me now by explaining these extra payments to Mrs. Wilson."

He looked surprised. "It's certainly no secret. She's a valued employee. When I learned her husband was having difficulty finding a new job and they might lose their home, I offered a personal loan. My hope is that, by carrying them for now, it will give Mr. Wilson time to wait for the right job locally."

"You care that much about a bookkeeper."

Stillwell shook his head. "Sergeant Renner, I can tell you're not a businessman. What's made Stillwell Trucking a success is the employees. I have very little turnover. When someone good comes to work for me, I try to keep him—or, in this case, her. In my experience, retaining the best employees is critical. I can readily afford the help I've given the Wilsons. He's an engineer. Once he's working again, he'll make good money. We can work out a payment schedule."

"And if he takes a job out of the area?"

"Then I'll still expect to be repaid," Stillwell said, some steel in his voice. "At some point, if his unemployment continues, I'll set a deadline. For now, I think of it as making an investment in the future."

Clay still didn't like the guy, but, damn it, his explanation sounded almost reasonable. Generous as all getout, of course, but there might actually be something to his theory that the company's success depended on retaining solid employees. And yeah, he probably could afford the amount he'd given Lissa without missing it.

Clay asked a few more questions, and found that Stillwell had asked Melissa to keep the loan private for obvious reasons; he wouldn't be willing to do the same for every employee, and didn't want to create hard feelings. He at least pretended to be dismayed to learn that she hadn't told her husband where the money was coming from.

He looked straight at Clay when he said, "Please tell Mr. Wilson the loan is personal, but my relationship with his wife is not."

"I'll do that," Clay agreed. "Thank you for your candor."

"You're very welcome." He stood and held out his hand, which Clay felt compelled to shake. "If there was anything at all I could do to bring Brianna Wilson home, you may be sure I'd do it."

Clay didn't have a lot of choice but to leave. Walking out to his Cherokee, he turned his head to watch a semi carefully maneuvering to back up to one of the loading docks. A man on the ground was using hand signals to guide the driver. A couple of others waited inside the bay to load or unload. Other trucks were already in place. Most, he supposed, picked up their loads elsewhere.

It was an interesting business, he reflected. Keeping track of what truck was where at every moment must present a challenge. Stillwell probably wished he had a radar screen like on a naval destroyer, so that he could watch the moving blips.

The attempt to distract himself only worked so long.

Sitting behind the wheel, Clay didn't start the engine immediately. Frustration weighed on him. He wasn't looking forward to telling Jane she'd violated her principles for information that had provided no help at all.

He wasn't 100 percent sure he believed James Stillwell was really that far thinking or altruistic. He'd told Jane he expected to be fed a lie, and he couldn't be sure that wasn't what had happened. But he was left with no reason to pursue this line of inquiry, no excuse for a warrant. Nothing but a niggle that insisted Melissa Wilson must have had a reason *not* to tell her husband about the loan so kindly extended by her employer. Think of how awkward it would be to spring it on him later—*Dear, did I mention how much money I borrowed while telling you I was "handling" everything?*

But if she'd embezzled from the company, why wouldn't Stillwell have called the cops, or, at the very least, fired her ass? No businessman liked looking stupid. Too often, they didn't prosecute. But if that was the case, why would he lie now? Why was he stopping so devotedly by the hospital to check on his bookkeeper's recovery? More employee relations? Hard to believe.

Away from James Stillwell's ultrasincere persona, Clay's dissatisfaction was growing. Too bad he was utterly devoid of ideas for what to do next.

Crap, he thought. What was he supposed to do? Hope some tip panned out? Hope Melissa Wilson opened her eyes and cried, "I saw John Doe grab my daughter!"

If there was one thing Clay hated, it was waiting. Taking a passive role.

His fingers tightened on the steering wheel and he swore aloud, viciously and at length.

FEELING DAZED, JANE set her phone down on the dresser. A loan? Lissa had done nothing worse than borrow money from her boss without telling Drew?

And, oh, God, think what I did to find that out.

She wanted to be mad at Clay. She *really* wanted to be mad at him, but couldn't. He'd been right—of course he had—to find out where the money had come from. The unexplained income was the one oddity in Lissa's recent life, a logical possible explanation for her equally odd behavior Saturday leading up to the accident.

Talking to Clay, Jane had wanted to know why Stillwell hadn't told Clay about the loan the first time they talked.

"He claims it didn't occur to him. At the time, he had no reason to think her accident was anything but an accident." The reluctance in his voice came through. "It makes sense."

"Why would he loan her so much money?" she asked.

Clay relayed an explanation about retaining quality employees, etc. etc. "And I kind of got the feeling the money is a drop in the bucket for him," he added.

"I told you I saw his house," Jane admitted. "He's got to be loaded."

"You going to the hospital today?"

"Yes."

She waited for him to tell her he'd stop by, or ask if they could have lunch together, but he only, rather curtly, said he'd be in touch and ended the call. When she thought about it, she realized how distant he'd sounded from the beginning.

He wouldn't have lied, would he? Found something out he didn't want to tell her? Did he assume she'd share anything he said with Drew?

Or... Suddenly she felt sick. Today, he didn't need anything from her. Had lunch and coffee and the phone calls and, dear God, the kiss been a little more manipulation on his part? If so—she'd totally fallen for the whole "you can trust me" shtick.

Shuddering, she told herself she was jumping to conclusions. Clay might just have had something on his mind. Known he wouldn't have time to see her today. She'd think a lot less of him if he *didn't* focus on finding Bree.

But the queasiness lingered, especially when it occurred to her she was going to have to tell Drew what Clay had learned. *Oh, Lissa, why didn't you tell him what you were doing?* But Jane could guess. Her sister really had enjoyed being the competent one, being in charge. She'd probably reveled in being able to make decisions without any input at all from Drew. Had she actually been *happy* that he had been humbled by being jobless?

Jane was a little staggered to discover how readily she could attribute awful motives to her sister. How much...she didn't like her?

But I do love her. Don't I?

Right this minute, she wasn't entirely sure.

A COUPLE OF hours later, despite everything, Jane felt a thrill when she squeezed Lissa's hand and Lissa squeezed back.

"Oh, my God," she whispered. "Lissa? Can you hear me? Squeeze my hand again if you can."

Nothing happened. Still, she had a huge lump in her throat. Part of her that she hadn't wanted to acknowledge had begun to believe Lissa was gone, that she wouldn't be back in any way her family would recognize. But this was so…tangible.

Tears burned in her eyes. She was crowded with memories—walking her little sister to class, holding her hand in the packed hallway. Lissa getting into bed with her the night after their parents' last, explosive fight, after Mom shouted, "I'm gone!" and went, not even stopping to say goodbye to either girl. Lissa's hand had slipped into Jane's that night, too, and she'd whispered, "I'm scared." Jane was scared, too, scared spitless. Literally. She remembered having to work up enough saliva to allow herself to whisper reassurance to the skinny little girl who didn't have anyone but her now.

Other times, too, when they'd thrown themselves into each other's arms after they had fought, or after Dad had hurt one of them. The times Jane had let him hurt her so that Lissa could slip away. Lissa hardly ever said, "I love you," but sometimes, when she watched Jane put ice on bruises or welts, she would.

Of course I love her, she thought, and bent to kiss her sister's forehead and feel the stir of an exhalation.

"Please wake up," she murmured. "Bree needs you, Lissa. I hope you can hear me. Please wake up."

She could have sworn her sister's eyelids fluttered, as if she was trying, but then…nothing.

CHAPTER TEN

CLAY WAS JUST coming out of the john at sheriff's head-quarters when his phone rang. His father, he saw with a jolt of alarm, who never called during the day.

Remembering what he'd told Jane about his mother, how the ever-present fear her cancer would recur had faded without him noticing, he thought, *Shit, not Mom.*

"Dad?"

"Rumor has it the missing Wilson kid is your case."

The way his heart had skipped a few beats, Clay battled momentary lightheadedness. He leaned a shoulder against the wall in the broad hallway. "That's why you called?"

"Why else would I?"

"Because you'd been injured. Because Mom—" He couldn't bring himself to say it.

"Didn't you just talk to your mother?"

"Yeah." He cleared his throat. "But that was a week ago."

"Why would you think anything like that?" Strangely, Chuck Renner sounded angry.

"The other day I was telling someone about Mom's cancer. Brought it to mind, that's all."

"Who would you talk to about your mother?"

A conclave of a couple of punks, one of Clay's detectives and a woman in a suit who was probably a defense attorney was taking place twenty feet or so away. Clay turned his back. "I'm…seeing someone," he said, keeping his voice down even as he wondered what in hell he was doing. "Women ask about things like that."

"Yeah, she a looker?" His father laughed. "Must be, you always liked big tits."

Tits? Oh, crap, it was Jane's voice he was hearing, burning with fury. *No, it's a rack, isn't it?*

"I like her." He cleared some roughness from his voice. "She's smart, she—"

"Got you by the short hairs, boy," his father sneered. "What's this big-titted gal do? Don't tell me you got lucky and she's a masseuse." He drew the word out, elongated it to make it obscene.

My father, the asshole. Clay shook his head in disbelief. Why had he thought for a minute he could talk to him?

"She's a cop, Dad. A good one. She was in on that operation I was involved in a few weeks ago."

"The raid?"

"She went in first. She's…" He bent his head and kneaded the back of his neck. "Brianna Wilson is her niece."

"What would you want with a woman like that?" His father sounded like he really wanted to know. "You gonna ask her to frisk you when you're in bed? Cuff you? You like a woman pretending to be a man?"

"Jane doesn't pretend anything," he heard himself

say. "She doesn't have to. She's a lieutenant for Angel Butte P.D. Outranks us both, Dad."

"That's what you want to go home and snuggle with at night?" His father snorted derisively. "You sure she doesn't have a dick to go with the tits?"

Clay stood frozen, thinking, *How many times have I talked like this?*

Suddenly impatient, he pushed away from the wall. "There a point to this call? If not, I've got a little girl to find."

"Maybe you should ask your lady cop to help," his father jeered, "since you don't seem to be getting anywhere on your own."

"Tell Mom I'll be calling," Clay said curtly, and ended the call.

Sometimes he couldn't believe he'd been fool enough to emulate this man.

Yeah, he thought, but this conversation had been his father at his worst. If that was him, through and through, Clay probably wouldn't be speaking to him at all. But it wasn't. He and Dad had had a lot of good times together, too. Despite the long hours every cop worked, Dad had spent hours patiently pitching or catching the ball as Clay and his brother had each played baseball, first Little League, then high school. Throwing a football. Clay remembered his father installing a couple of floodlights out in the backyard so they could keep playing ball after dark. His grin would flash as night fell and he declared, "Time to turn on the stadium lights."

He'd taught them to ride their bikes, to rebuild automotive engines, to cast a fishing line and handle a gun. Yeah, eventually he'd also taught them some majorly screwed-up attitudes about women—but mostly that had come later.

Clay fumbled toward remembering the first times his father had shocked him. He thought now that some of it was a kind of swaggering, like he'd been doing himself that day in the squad room when Jane overheard. As he'd grown into manhood—and probably his brother after him—Dad had done a lot more swaggering. It was as if he perceived a threat of some kind coming from a younger male in his own home. Maybe some of the shit he talked was his way of asserting he was a real man and his kids didn't yet measure up.

Looked at that way—his posturing was pathetic, Clay thought with faint shock. For the first time, he had to wonder how much of that crap his father actually believed. He suspected he'd never know for sure.

I will not be like that.

The vow was grimly taken.

And, damn, he wished the whole conversation hadn't started with a lie on his part, one implying he and Jane had something going.

His phone rang again and he gritted his teeth, but the number that appeared wasn't his father's. Instead it was FBI agent Ed Solomon's.

Clay's pulse quickened. "Ed?"

"We might have something."

Instead of continuing into the detectives' room, he turned to pace back down the hall. "Tell me."

IT WAS EVENING before he had a minute to do more than think about Jane. Discovering at close to eight that he was starved, he had the fleeting impulse to call her and— What? Invite her out to dinner? Someplace with white tablecloths and lit by candlelight, maybe? Sure. She's sick with fear because the little girl she loves is missing, and he's thinking about a romantic evening concluding with sex?

Except…he wasn't. The realization came as a shock. What he'd been thinking was that he wanted to talk to her. Hold her hand. Watch the play of emotions on her face. Let her draw whatever she needed from him, the way he had when he'd left the Wilson house last night.

He swore under his breath. He was such a goner, and over a woman who, at the very least, had terribly mixed feelings where he was concerned.

He couldn't help himself, though. He fumbled for his phone in the dark interior of his Jeep, scrolling for her number once the screen lit up.

"Clay?" she answered after the second ring.

He hated hearing her eagerness and hadn't let himself remember that every time he dialed her number, he raised her hopes and then crushed them.

"Nothing new," he hastened to say. Same way he had to begin every conversation with her these days. "Maybe I shouldn't have called."

Her breath hitched. At least, he thought that was what the sound was. "No." All the strain she felt was in her voice. "I mean, I'm glad you called." She gave an odd sounding laugh. "Did you know I was at the Raynors' for something like twenty-four hours before we figured out where Matt was being held?"

Wondering where she was going with this, he'd have given a lot to be able to see her face. "No."

"Alec and Julia both were…distraught. I felt really

sorry for her. He could *do* something, at least. You know? She was stuck waiting. I thought, I don't ever want that to be me. I even felt a little smug, because I'm a bad-ass cop. Of course that meant I'd never be the little woman, pacing the house praying for good news."

Her utter misery, wrapped in wry understanding of her own nature, did painful things to his heart.

"You know," he said, "you're still a cop. No, Bree wasn't snatched in your jurisdiction. But I'm open to ideas if you have any. I'm not trying to shut you out, Jane."

This silence, he wasn't sure how to interpret. Not until she said, "Thank you for saying that." The next rasping breath might have been a sob. "I would give anything to have a useful idea." Her voice shook. "Right now, I'm...paralyzed with fear. I don't know how Alec made decisions the way he did."

Clay hadn't been so sure Alec Raynor *should* have been making decisions involving the rescue of his own nephew, a boy he seemed to love more like a son. He'd seen that the man was on the ragged edge of control, barely keeping himself together. The impressive thing was, he'd done it. Clay had gained a great deal of admiration for Angel Butte police chief Alec Raynor, formerly of the LAPD.

"Being the one stuck waiting wouldn't sit well with me, either," he admitted. "You're doing better than I would."

"I'm about to fall apart," she said so quietly he barely heard her. "If it weren't for Alexis needing me..."

He pinched the bridge of his nose between thumb and forefinger, squeezing until it hurt. "God, Jane."

"I don't know why I'm telling you this."

"I called because I wanted to hear your voice. To listen to you."

"Did you—" She hesitated. "Was there anything you wanted to tell me?"

He hadn't even known, but yeah. He'd wanted to tell her about the conversation with his father. Which was a stupid idea. *My father wanted to know how big your tits are.* Right. That was what he needed to say to her. The whole topic was made worse by the fact she undeniably *had* big breasts.

Am I that predictable? he asked himself. His jaw muscles spasmed.

No, damn it! He'd been powerfully drawn to her long before she'd faced him and he'd seen her figure.

"Drew home?" he asked on impulse.

"No, he's at the hospital. Why?"

"I'm going to grab a bite to eat somewhere. I thought maybe if you wouldn't be leaving your niece alone, you'd come along and keep me company."

There was a small silence. "Alexis has gone to bed," Jane said. "I made spaghetti for dinner and have tons of leftovers. If you want to come by, I could heat some up for you."

"Are you sure?"

"I'm sure."

"That sounds way better than a burger and fries." He reached for the key in the ignition. "I'm on my way, just leaving headquarters."

She must have heard the roar of the engine, because she laughed. "See you."

Ten minutes later, he rapped lightly on the Wilsons'

front door, not wanting to ring the bell and wake the kid. Jane opened it almost immediately.

God, she looked good, he thought, with the hunger that seemed to be with him all the time lately. Tonight she wore a snug T-shirt and an airy, midcalf-length skirt. Her hair cascaded from an elastic capturing it on the crown of her head, and her feet were bare. He could hardly tear his gaze from those small, bare feet with unpainted toenails and high arches. They looked... innocent. He tried to imagine her painting her toenails and using one of those foam gizmos his last girlfriend had to separate the toes while she worked, and felt pretty confident Jane always had better things to do.

When he shook his head slightly and looked at her face again, her cheeks were a little pink. His gaping must have been really obvious.

"Come in," she said, stepping back.

One inhalation and he had to swallow saliva. "Man, it smells good."

She chuckled. "I don't do a lot of cooking, but spaghetti is one of my specialties. It was my mother's—" Her grimace echoed some of what he'd been feeling lately. "I really hate saying that."

He kissed her cheek, resisting the desire to nuzzle. Even so, her hair tickled his face. "If your mother's recipe tastes as good as it smells, you should take pride in the one legacy from her."

"Speaks your stomach," she said lightly, leading the way to the kitchen.

"Your brother-in-law won't mind me being here?" Clay said to her back.

She glanced over her shoulder. "Why would he?"

Because he wants you and guesses I'm a threat? "It's his house," he settled for saying.

"I told him we'd known each other before. Even worked together once."

In the kitchen, she shooed him to a chair at the table and smiled when he asked for milk instead of a beer or wine. He relaxed, watching her bustle. Doing what a woman should, his father would say.

His father could go to hell.

She'd not only heated up a generous serving of spaghetti, she'd cooked some green beans and warmed a couple of slabs of garlic bread, all of which she set in front of him.

"You're not hungry?"

"I ate."

"Enough?"

Their eyes met. She made a face. "I don't seem to have much appetite. I would have said I ate more when I was stressed, but this time—" One shoulder lifted. "It's not like I can't afford to lose weight."

"You don't need to," Clay blurted.

Her gaze turned shy. "Thank you. If, um, that was a compliment."

"It was." He sounded hoarse. He wanted to say more. Like, "your body is perfect." But this wasn't the time, any more than it had been the time to invite her out for that candlelit dinner.

This was better anyway, it occurred to him. She'd never offered to cook for him back when they were going out.

He picked up the fork and started eating, trying not to gobble or dribble sauce down his shirtfront or otherwise embarrass himself. It felt a little strange, eating while she watched.

"You sounded funny when you called," she said suddenly. "Like…I don't know. Something had gone sour?"

He used the napkin. "No. Nothing like that. The day was frustrating, that's all. Once I thought we might have caught a break—" Seeing her expression, he shook his head. "It was in one way. A witness came forward, a guy who passed your sister's SUV after it had gone off the road. He's been away on a business trip, just got back and saw the headlines. He says when he went by the accident, he was going to stop, then saw that someone else already had so he kept going."

Jane stared at him, her lips parted and her eyes big and hopeful despite what he'd already said about frustration.

"All he remembers is that it was a sedan, silver, he thinks. A guy—probably a man although he won't swear to it, was bending over the trunk of the car, like he'd put something in. The way he stood blocked the make of the car and the license plate. He mostly kept his back turned, but waved our witness on. The witness admits he was mostly gaping at the sight of someone slumped over the wheel of the Venza that had gone off the road. You know what people are like, passing car accidents."

She nodded.

"This guy figured an aide car must already be on the way."

"Can't he guess at what make of car it was?"

"The best he could do was good-size. Some kind of luxury model. Maybe a Lexus, he said first, then downgraded to a Camry or an Accord or… The man? Well, no, he didn't see a face or even hair color. More just the gesture waving him on. He didn't see a kid, but knows the man closed the trunk once he was by. Trouble is, he really wasn't paying attention. Even in the rearview mirror, it was the damaged vehicle and the unconscious person that held his attention."

"Oh, no." Jane looked sick. "He put Bree in the trunk."

Any other woman, he might have tried to reassure. Reminded her they couldn't be sure of anything. But he couldn't believe Jane would want him to soft-soap the harsh reality. She wasn't like other women he'd known.

"If this guy grabbed Brianna, it's unlikely he helped her into the backseat and fastened her belt for her."

Jane's eyes were fixed desperately on him. "She wouldn't have gone."

"Actually, it's possible she would have." Clay had given this a lot of thought. "She's only seven. If the guy seemed to be trying to help, it might have seemed safer to get in his car than stand beside the road or stay in a vehicle that was tilting toward the creek. Seeing her mother unconscious was probably scary. And what if she knew the man who'd stopped?"

"Knew him?" she breathed in what he could tell was horror.

"This is harking back to my theory that what happened wasn't really an accident. That there was a reason your sister was out on 253rd, maybe to see someone. Doing something she didn't want to tell her husband. Brianna might not have understood what was going on, if, say, her mom suddenly stepped on the gas because she had a bad feeling about whatever she'd intended to do."

"Lissa let herself get distracted calling Drew." He'd been right about Jane; despite her distress, she jumped off from his speculation into some of her own. "She might not have noticed whatever it was until too late." Then she focused sharply on him. "But you're satisfied that the money thing didn't lead anywhere."

Clay shook his head. "I wouldn't go that far. Stillwell's explanation sounded logical enough to have me thinking, okay, maybe. But, damn, it was a lot of money to risk loaning to an employee who would never be able to pay it back out of her own salary. I asked if he'd made her sign a promissory note, but he said it was more informal than that."

"It wouldn't break him if he didn't get the money back."

"No, but this is a guy who has built a fantastically successful company from the ground up. You can't tell me he did it by casually loaning money even to trusted employees with no proof they were supposed to pay it back."

She processed that, blinking a couple of times. "No. You're right."

"And then," he continued, feeling cruel, "there's the question of why she didn't tell Drew about the money. Unless…" He stopped, wishing he'd stopped while he was ahead. He had a bad feeling she wouldn't react well to what he was thinking, and right now he didn't want to tangle with her over the faith and affection she felt for the man whose house she was currently staying in.

But Jane said slowly, "Unless Drew did know. That's

what you're wondering, isn't it? If all that shock and dismay was an act."

"It crossed my mind." He took a quick bite, in case she tossed him out on his ear.

Of course she was shaking her head. "I don't believe it."

"Yeah, no kidding," Clay muttered.

Her eyes narrowed. "What's that supposed to mean?"

A smart man would say something tactful, like, "You know I have to consider all possibilities. This isn't personal." Turned out, where she was concerned he wasn't smart. What came out of his mouth was, "Drew's too nice to lie, right? And of course he's such a good guy, he'd never hurt a fly."

Her mouth formed an O of astonishment that transmuted into anger. She shoved her chair back from the table. "What is your problem?" she snapped. "You've had it in for Drew from the beginning. There's nothing you'd like better than to book him, is there?"

"That's not true."

"It is! You don't listen to me at all. I *know* this man."

"How well, Jane?" His fork clattered to his plate and he leaned forward, feeling his lips draw back in something like a snarl. "Because what I'm hearing is a whole lot more *knowing* than you should have for a guy married to your sister."

Dark color mounted her cheeks. "You actually think I'd—?" She was almost incoherent, but kept her voice to more like a hiss than a yell. Apparently she hadn't forgotten her sleeping niece. "You're disgusting." She looked at him like he was a cockroach she was about to stomp. "I can't believe I offered you dinner."

Belatedly, he tried for cop neutral. "Jane, I can't rule your brother-in-law out because you insist he's nice."

She looked at him with dislike. "But you could try trusting me as a character witness."

Well, shit. He clenched and unclenched his teeth a couple of times while he tried to decide whether honesty would pay—or not. "I admit your relationship with him rubs me the wrong way," he finally admitted.

"So you've decided he tried to knock off his wife."

"I never said that—"

"Really?" Jane said, scathing.

"I have to wonder." Frustration twisted in his belly. "It's my goddamn job to wonder!"

"Lower your voice!" she snapped. "And wondering is one thing, a vendetta is another."

"There's no vendetta." He had a moment of desperation. *Please let me be telling the truth.* "I'm trying my damnedest to be fair."

She had sunk back into her chair, but that was the only sign she was relenting. "I don't understand," she admitted. "Why do you have to 'try'? What do you have *against* Drew?"

Did she really not get it? he wondered incredulously. He hadn't been subtle. "You, what else?" he said.

She simply stared at him.

His throat felt tight, and he wasn't sure he could say anything else. Clay pushed back his chair and stood, going around the table. He held out his hand. "Jane."

She blinked at him.

"Come here," he said huskily.

After a suspended moment, she rose to her feet. Her

gaze was wary, but she let him envelop her hand in his
and tug her forward.

"I keep thinking about this." He bent and gently
bumped his forehead to hers. "I want to put my hands
on you. I want to kiss you."

He suited action to words, capturing her mouth
with his, kissing her more aggressively than he probably should have. Trying to convey without words what
he was afraid to say right out. Either in acquiescence
or surprise, her lips parted, letting his tongue plunge
deep. Instantly aroused, he pulled her tight against him,
gripping the fullness of her hip with one hand while the
other slid under the fall of her ponytail and angled her
head so he could devour her mouth. His blood roared
in his ears. He wanted to think she was kissing him
back but couldn't be sure. Damn, how he needed her.

But even though sheer need had almost drowned his
voice of reason, he started listening to it. What was he
going to do, lay her on the vinyl floor and start strip-
ping off her clothes? If that candlelit dinner was out,
sex would be yet a bigger mistake, even assuming she
went along with it.

Although it hurt to do, he began to ease back, gen-
tling the kiss and relaxing his hold on her until finally
he rubbed his cheek against hers, wincing at the rasp
that told him he'd probably scraped her softer skin.

Somehow, Clay discovered when he lifted his head
and looked down at her dazed face, the tightness in his
throat hadn't eased at all.

"I don't like knowing you're living here with him,"
he told her gruffly. "You'd never sleep with your sis-

ter's husband. I know that. But…there's something there with you two. You can't tell me there isn't."

She jerked away from him and turned her back. He could tell she was breathing hard. Standing so close, he was struck by her fragility: her shoulders so much narrower and finer boned than his and the slenderness of her neck, especially vulnerable from behind. Then there was the very feminine curve of waist and hips. The Jane he knew was tough and determined, but he had trouble reconciling those qualities with her sweet face and womanly body. Knowing that women did the job and did it well—that Jane was one of those women—bumped up against everything he'd grown up believing. That feminine and tough didn't go together. That women should be protected, not trusted in the line of fire.

In turmoil, he knew she'd never stand for this primitive need he had to claim her as *his*. But how was he supposed to get past it, even if she'd give him a second chance?

He was feeling helpless when she turned to face him again, her chin held unnaturally high.

"You haven't eaten much."

He glanced back at his plate. "You're not kicking me out?"

"Not yet."

Clay nodded and went back to his place.

"I have to go check on Alexis." She wasn't gone long. She sat back down, watching as he ate. Clay told himself he was lucky.

"We used to date."

His head came up. "What?"

"Drew and I." Her eyes were defiant. "He and I were seeing each other before— No." She gave a twisted smile. "When. *When* I introduced him to my sister."

"He ditched you?"

"That's one way to put it."

"And you continue to think he's a nice guy?" Clay said in disbelief.

Her chin still jutted at him. She was clinging to her pride. "He is a nice guy. One who couldn't help falling in love with Lissa. She's beautiful, you know. Vibrant. Plus, most men have trouble with what I do for a living." *And you're one of them,* her eyes reminded him.

Clay grappled with this history, trying to read the emotions she didn't want to share. "Weren't you hurt? Mad?"

"Yes to both, but—" she hesitated "—not as much as if I'd really been in love, or anything like that. The truth is, I liked Drew. I enjoyed spending an evening out with him. But we were more like friends than anything. We didn't have a lot of chemistry."

"He's looking at you lately as though he's changed his mind." Clay couldn't seem to help the way his voice hardened.

Jane shook her head. "I don't see that." But he'd seen the flicker of something in her eyes. She wasn't being completely truthful. "He's relying on me right now, that's all. He knows how much I love the girls."

He stayed silent and resumed eating.

"We're friends, that's all," she insisted.

"Okay." He knew damn well how irrational he was being. Of course she was allying herself with Drew. Right now, her brother-in-law needed her. Unless he was behind his wife's accident and his daughter's disappearance, he had to be scared to death. Grieving, and not in any shape to give a five-year-old girl what she needed. Admitting all that to himself made Clay feel ashamed. He'd been an idiot. He did know Jane would never start something with her sister's husband. His jealousy was another primitive response, illogical, not reasoned out. Jane Vahalik seemed to bring out those qualities in him, ones he hadn't even known he possessed. Old-fashioned views about men and women were one thing, but irrational emotions that seized control were something else again.

"I'm sorry." He got it out, although *he* wasn't being totally truthful now, either. He wasn't going to like it any better the next time he saw Jane with her arms around Drew Wilson and his around her.

She scrutinized him so carefully, he had a bad feeling she was seeing more than he wanted her to. "He's been acting a little weird," she said unexpectedly. "I've been uncomfortable a couple of times. It's not like he's come on to me or anything. Just…as if he's wondering. I think he's really scared for Lissa right now, but angry at her, too. He can't even ask her why she lied to him."

Clay nodded. He understood the anger just fine. Nothing he'd learned so far about Melissa Wilson suggested she was likable. He'd begun to speculate on how she and Jane could have grown up to be so different from each other. In particular, they had different ways of relating to men. Had to be something to do with their father. That relationship had left Jane having trouble trusting, if Clay was reading her right, but her sister seemed instead to feel some contempt for the male half of the species.

Or only for her husband?

What Clay couldn't decide was what any of this had to do with the current problem: her maybe/maybe not accident and the disappearance of seven-year-old Brianna. No—he knew. If the accident was just that, and Brianna had been abducted by a random predator, Melissa's character was irrelevant. It was a case of shit happening. He felt sure Jane's sister would be as fierce in defense of her child as Jane would have been, whatever other differences they had. Only if Melissa had gotten herself into a fix that had gone tragically wrong did her character become relevant to the investigation.

Separating what was relevant from what wasn't had become hard for him because he wanted to know everything about Jane, and that included her family dynamics.

Clay thought again about the phone call with his father that had triggered his call to her in turn. Could he tell her about it without getting her back up? He wished he had any idea what she was thinking right now.

"This is the best meal I've had in weeks," he said.

She smiled a little. "I'm glad."

"Especially these past days. I eat nothing but crap when I'm head down in an investigation."

"I know what you mean."

"When you're not married, there's nothing to pull you home, no one to remind you that you have a life outside the job."

"Was your father the same? Or did having a family make a difference with him?"

So she was curious about him, too. Some of Clay's edginess subsided.

"He's never been a detective. He stayed on the patrol side. He claims that's 'real' police work. Protecting people on a day-to-day basis. Being a first responder."

Jane nodded. "I can see that, but I like puzzles."

Clay did, too.

"I like the deeper involvement we have." Jane was still pursuing her train of thought. "Your father's like an E.R. doc, and we're more like, I don't know, oncologists."

Clay grinned. "Following a case to the death? Calling us surgeons might be a better analogy. We slice out the damaged tissue, allowing the body to heal."

She flashed a smile that made her beautiful for that moment. He hadn't seen her free of the effects of stress since last fall, before he'd blown it. "That's good," she exclaimed. "You're right."

His momentary jubilation faded. He pushed his empty plate away. "I wish I knew where to cut."

"I do, too," she said in a stifled voice, the delight gone as if it had never been. "I would give anything…"

"I know." He reached across the table to cover her small fist with his hand. He felt her quiver.

"If Bree's dead—"

She might well be, either because as a witness to an assault she was too great a threat, or because a sexual predator had grabbed her and was now, after too many goddamn days, done with her. Still, Clay's gut kept saying no. He thought the girl was being held for some other reason, most likely to put pressure on her father or mother. No, it almost had to be her mother, assuming she surfaced from the coma; Drew had agreed to a phone tap early on, in case there was a ransom call, but there'd been nothing. Unless someone had slipped him a note or bumped into him in the hospital corridor to mutter a message.... But had his behavior changed in any significant way? Clay couldn't see it.

His silence was answer enough. Jane's throat worked, but her eyes stayed dry. He wasn't used to feeling such pride in anyone. She was a gutsy woman.

"My father called," he said, surprising himself. *Not smart.* But it was too late. "He knew I was working Bree's disappearance."

"Did he give you a hard time for not finding her yet?" So she remembered what he'd said about his father's competitiveness.

"We didn't get there." Oh, damn, he was going to do it. "I told him about you."

Her eyes widened.

"He couldn't imagine why I'd be interested in a woman cop. Said some vulgar crap. I realized I've been hearing the same kind of things all my life."

"We want to admire our parents." Her voice was thick. "Accepting we can't is devastating."

Of all people, she knew. A mother who'd abandoned her, a father who had hurt her.

Different way, but I hurt her, too. The reminder told him he should leave, now.

He stood, too abruptly, and carried his plate and empty glass to the sink. He rinsed them, then added them to the dirty dishes in the dishwasher. Then he faced Jane. "I'd better go."

"All right," she said, sounding bewildered, and for good reason.

She trailed him to the front door, where he paused. Damn it, her bare toes were curling, as if the tile entryway floor was cold. "I shouldn't have told you what my father said."

"You didn't, not really."

His mouth quirked up in a smile that held no amusement at all. "I said enough—you can guess."

"Clay…" She touched his arm, only fleetingly, but he felt it like a burn. "You're not responsible for your father's beliefs or behavior."

"Only for when I echo them," he said flatly.

Her expression was odd now. "You're changing."

"I guess I am," he said after a minute. "Is it too late, Jane?" Hearing himself, he thought, *God, I'm begging.*

She didn't answer directly. "I don't understand why you want me." Her eyes were shadowed as she studied him, tiny furrows pleating her forehead. "Am I just a challenge?"

"No." He couldn't seem to stop his hands from cupping her face. He loved the cushiony feel of her cheeks, the warmth of her breath. "God, no. It's you, that's all."

She lifted her hands to cover his. "Three weeks ago I'd have said it was too late."

He grunted at the memory of their confrontations before and after the raid. "You did say."

"Now…you confuse me, Clay. But I want to believe you can accept me the way I am."

He wanted to believe he could, too.

He made a sound, one that seemed to provide a trigger for her, too. The next moment his arms had closed hard around her, and she'd surged onto tiptoes so her mouth could meet his.

CHAPTER ELEVEN

"ALEXIS ALREADY EATEN?" Jane accepted part of the morning newspaper from Drew and reached for her tea.

He made an assenting noise.

The front section—good. After a sip, she scanned the front page quickly, then again.

"We're not on the front page anymore."

The panic in her voice was enough to penetrate Drew's preoccupation. He slowly lifted his head. "What?"

She repeated herself.

He stared at her without comprehension. "What difference does it make?"

How could he not see? "People will start forgetting. Thinking about other headlines, other crimes. They'll quit paying as much attention if they happen to see a little girl who might be Bree. The tips will slow and eventually stop."

"None of them have helped anyway."

"But one might." Had Clay noticed? Of course he had, she realized, but there was only so much he could do to keep interest alive. Any development would renew attention from the media, but there hadn't been one. The closest they'd come was the witness who had been so busy gaping at an accident scene, he hadn't paid any attention to the man who was abducting a little girl. "We need people to see her face *every day*. It's... It might be Bree's only hope."

Drew's expression told her he now got it. "But what can we do?" he asked, sounding helpless.

"An appeal for help." She'd thought about it earlier, but hadn't seen then that it would make a difference. Now it might. "We could even offer a reward."

"Where am I supposed to get the money?" Bitterness tinged his voice.

"I have savings. It doesn't have to be huge to draw attention. If we're lucky, someone else—maybe Stillwell—will chip in. In fact, I could call and ask him."

"You think the guy would give more, when he's already been funding my family?" More of that bitterness.

"It would be good PR for him." She hesitated. "Let me talk to Clay first. Then I'll make some calls, try to set it up. If you're willing."

"Of course I am." Anguish made his words guttural. "You might have to tell me what to say."

"All right." She laid her hand over his, then was sorry when he grabbed on and held tight, as if she was his lifeline. Before Clay, it had never occurred to her Drew was feeling any sexual interest in her. She still wasn't sure she believed it, since he hadn't been all that excited about her even before she introduced him to her sister. In retrospect, she'd been glad. If she'd had sex with him, adjusting to him as a brother-in-law would have been a whole lot more awkward. She glanced at the clock. "I'll call Clay right now," she said, using it as an excuse to draw her hand away.

He nodded and watched as she reached for her phone. She'd have rather talked without Drew eavesdropping, but didn't see how she could gracefully excuse herself.

Clay answered right away, and listened as she explained what she wanted to do.

"I was going to suggest it in another day or two," he said. "We've got to keep interest stirred."

"What would you think of me going to Mr. Stillwell and asking if he'd match what I can afford to offer as a reward?"

He was quiet for a minute. "You know he won't be able to turn you down," he said at last, restraint in his voice.

"Is it a bad idea?"

"No." He was thinking it through, she could tell. "You said you'd met him."

"Yes, in passing."

"I don't see how it can hurt. You don't have to tell him you know about the loans to your sister. In fact, your asking might reassure him you *don't* know about those payments."

"Okay."

"Go for it," he decided. "Do you want me to set up a press conference?"

Her relief surprised her. She'd done it often enough before, just not with herself as the focus.

"If you don't mind," she said. "But why don't you wait until I try to talk to Stillwell?"

"Call me back," Clay said.

She was put right through to Lissa's boss. Her plea

wasn't as eloquent as she'd have liked to have made it, but she had no sooner finished than he said, "Of course I will. I'm ashamed I didn't think of offering a reward sooner. I suspect I can afford it better than you can. Keep your ten thousand, Lieutenant Vahalik. Let me offer the entire twenty. Or more, if you think a larger amount will make a difference."

"No." Her every instinct revolted. Maybe because she shared some of Clay's suspicion of this man? What if the reward was all for show, and really he knew exactly where Bree was? No, she told herself; what could possibly have motivated him? Still, she wanted to do this herself. For the sister she'd raised. "Let's keep it as a match. I…need to feel as if I'm doing something to help." She made no effort to prevent the hitch in her voice.

"I understand." He sounded sympathetic. "However you want to handle it. If there's anything else I can do…"

"I can't think of anything right now, but I'll let you know if that changes. Thank you, Mr. Stillwell. This is generous of you."

"It's nothing." He sounded almost brusque, as if he didn't want thanks. "I have a granddaughter, you know."

"Yes. I met her." She thanked him again, whether he wanted it or not, and then, still under Drew's gaze, called Clay back. He promised to let her know as soon as he'd set a time and place for the press conference.

"What kind of vibe did you get from Stillwell?" he asked.

"Nothing off. He seemed genuinely concerned and was kind."

She was beginning to be able to interpret Clay's grunts. This one said, *Maybe*.

Half an hour later, he got back to her. 1:00 p.m. in front of the sheriff's department headquarters. "I thought about staging it where your sister went off the road, but that might look like grandstanding, and given there's no shoulder, asking everyone to park along it isn't the best idea."

Of course, he hadn't hesitated when he called out search and rescue, but in this case, Jane agreed. "Besides, that's so close to the Hales'."

There was a pause. "Not likely to impact them, but you're right."

"*Are* you still getting tips?"

"They've slowed down drastically yesterday and today." His voice was gentle as he gave her the bad news.

"You said you checked out known pedophiles."

Horror filled Drew's eyes at the reminder of their worst fear. He drew his head back, as if he was a turtle wanting to retreat into his shell. Jane was sorry to have opened her big mouth in front of him, although the possibility had to be with him at all times anyway, as it was with her.

"Nothing jumped out at us," Clay said. "It would have been incredibly bad luck if one of them had been passing at the exact right moment."

But awful things involving bad luck did happen. They both knew that.

"Will you be there?" she asked. "I mean, this afternoon?"

"Of course I will." There was an indefinable note in

his voice. Tenderness, instead of the businesslike tone she'd expect? "I'll make a statement once you and Drew are done, reinforcing the message."

"Okay." She took a deep breath. "We'll see you then."

She and Drew agreed to split up for now. He was going to take Alexis to her day camp then go straight to the hospital, while Jane wanted to go by her apartment, at least briefly. At the very least, she needed to grab some clothes suitable for the press conference and maybe trade out some of the others, but promised to join Drew at the hospital later.

"Lissa was looking so much better," he said, almost but not quite sounding hopeful. "Maybe today."

Jane managed a smile and touched his arm, but fleetingly this time. "Soon."

THE SIGHT OF Lissa's face twitching, her lips momentarily parting, her eyelids flickering, no longer convinced Drew she was really on the verge of waking up. He wanted that, no matter how angry he was at her. For her sake, of course, because he knew love was still part of the confused mix he felt. The idea of all her fire and vitality stilled forever seemed impossible. Mostly, though, he ached for her to regain consciousness so they could ask her about Bree.

One of his greatest fears was she would know nothing. If Bree had been snatched after the SUV went off the road, which seemed likeliest, Lissa *wouldn't* have seen anything. She'd probably lost consciousness the moment her head hit the glass.

But she could damn well explain why she'd lied to him about where she was going, he thought with a deep-down coldness that wasn't like him. And why she was out on an obscure country road that went nowhere she should want to be.

Why she had endangered their child.

But he knew she'd claim *he* had done that, and he already felt guilty enough. If only he hadn't insisted she take Bree...

I didn't know. How could I know?

He had known something was wrong, though. A whole lot had been wrong for weeks, if not months. They hadn't made love in...three weeks or more, and that had been only the once and she'd acquiesced with initial reluctance. He had told himself she was tired because she'd been working extra hours, which was *his* fault. That, as their financial manager, she'd been feeling the stress of their reduced income. Because he'd felt inadequate, he hadn't questioned why so much else had changed.

He'd been a coward.

No more, he thought. He could tell that cop despised him, and Drew didn't blame him. It bothered him more that Jane must feel the same. How could she help it? He'd willfully buried his head in the sand.

Coward.

He and Jane had somehow built a friendship despite the way he'd treated her after he met Lissa. Until recently, he hadn't known how much he valued her friendship. He hadn't even noticed that a small voice in his head had been whispering, *You made a mistake.*

Jane, he was beginning to think, was worth ten of her more vivid, charismatic sister.

Then he looked at his wife's face and closed his eyes in pain. *No.* He loved her still. He did.

He thought he could love Jane, too, but…not the same way.

Increasingly, Drew suspected Lissa didn't love *him,* not anymore. He hadn't wanted to acknowledge even so much as that suspicion, so…he hadn't.

Coward.

He took out his wallet and removed the accordion insert that held photos. A wedding picture. He flipped past that, as well as another of Lissa, until he came to one of her holding a newborn Bree. So small and helpless, with more hair than any newborn ought to have. Jane's hair. He had another of Bree at about two, taken before Christmas that year to send to his parents, as well as to be framed on the mantel in the house he and Lissa had just bought. The most recent one he had was Bree's school picture from last year. She looked…cautious in it. Alexis was grinning or making a silly face in every picture they ever took, but not Bree. He gazed at his eldest daughter for a long time, until he couldn't see it anymore through the tears.

It was too damned hot to wait outside for Jane's arrival, but Clay paced near a window that looked out on the parking lot.

He saw her brother-in-law first, and was glad when she didn't get out of his car. She must be driving herself, then.

Drew hovered near the front steps, not looking as if he was sure where he should go or what he should do, then saw something that made him hustle inside.

Clay craned his neck. A television news van, with the satellite dish atop, was rolling in. He was glad to see it. Announcing a press conference was one thing, but there was no guarantee anyone would actually show up. Something more exciting might arise.

And in this case…Bree Wilson was undeniably becoming old news. Only her age and the horror every parent felt had kept her disappearance as prominent on the news as it had been for this long.

Clay went to meet Drew, who shook his hand but was reserved. He'd obviously shaved and used something to slick his hair into obedience, but Clay couldn't help noticing how he'd aged in less than a week. As distraught as he'd been that first day when he came in to report his wife and daughter missing, he had still looked like a young man. Lines hardly visible on his face then had now deepened to crevasses. His eyes had the thousand-yard stare of a man who had forgotten how to sleep. He kept blinking, either because his eyes burned or because he wasn't focusing well. Clay felt renewed pity.

"Jane on her way?" he asked.

"Yes. She ran into someone she knew on the way out of the hospital, but she can't be far behind me."

"Good," he said. "We'll set up on the steps so the sign is right behind us, to emphasize that the weight of the sheriff's department is behind you and to reinforce the message that viewers who know anything should call us." He kept talking, trying to prep Drew, but wasn't sure how much he said was getting through.

Out of the corner of his eye, he saw a black Yukon pull into the parking lot. A moment later, Jane walked in, her gaze locking onto Clay as though no one else was in the room. He tried to repress his reaction to her and greet her calmly.

He suspected she'd encouraged her brother-in-law to wear a dress shirt and slacks but to skip the tie. His choice of attire made him look serious, but not so together he'd be off-putting to other parents who couldn't imagine getting up in the morning and getting dressed at all if their child was missing. Jane had worn slacks and a short-sleeve rust-colored blouse that he thought was silk. She'd tried to tame her hair, this time with a pair of tortoiseshell combs that held it back from her face. He thought she'd applied some makeup, too. The fact he noticed told him how rarely she wore any. She carried a folder, and he wondered what was in it.

He repeated some of what he'd told Drew, and she only nodded at information she must already know. He'd been keeping an eye out over her shoulder and saw quite a cluster of reporters and camera operators outside. They waited in front of a podium the department used when making statements.

"Looks like we're ready," Clay said. "Who wants to go first?"

The two looked at each other. "I will," Jane said, and Drew nodded. Then she opened the manila folder and drew out a large color printout of a photo of Brianna, one he hadn't seen. She wore a bathing suit, her nose was a little sunburned and she was laughing. "Can we tape this to the front of the podium?" she asked. "Where they can't help seeing it?"

"Good idea." He grabbed a tape dispenser from the nearest desk, then held the door open for Jane and Drew.

The murmur of voices went silent while he carefully

centered and aligned the photo, then taped it in place. They were all looking at it, he was glad to see.

He then stepped up to the podium, introduced himself even though everyone there knew him and explained that Brianna Wilson's aunt and father each had brief statements to make, after which he and they would take a few questions.

Jane took his place. She gripped the podium on each side, her knuckles white. Not, he knew, because speaking in public made her nervous, but because this time it mattered so much.

"We're here today," she said, her voice pitched to reach even curiosity seekers who'd paused at the back of the pack, "to ask the public to remain alert to any glimpse of my niece, Brianna Wilson. As the days pass, it becomes too easy for people who don't know her to put her out of their minds. For those of us who love her—" Her voice cracked. Her fingers tightened. "We cannot forget for an instant. Brianna should be—we pray will be—starting second grade this coming week. She's smart, a little shy, intensely loyal to her friends. She must have been terrified to see her mother injured, and more terrified yet by whatever happened next." She vibrated with intensity as her gaze moved from face to face. "Please, *please,* don't forget Brianna. Watch for her. Pay attention if something seems wrong at a house in your neighborhood or at the end of your road. Brianna is somewhere, and her only hope is *you.*" She talked some more, ending with the offer of a twenty-thousand-dollar reward to be paid to anyone coming forward with information that led to finding her niece.

Then she stepped back and let Drew speak. His voice

was ragged as he echoed her plea, breaking down several times. By the end, tears ran down his ravaged face and fogged his glasses. The huge lenses of the cameras captured it all.

Moved even though he'd orchestrated this whole thing, Clay squeezed Drew's shoulder as he backed blindly away, then got his own message across. Who to call. Phone numbers for tips. A promise to honor anonymity when possible.

The first questions were about Melissa's condition. Clay answered those himself, sounding more confident than he felt when he said they anticipated she would regain consciousness within the next day or two. He sensed Jane's quick glance and hoped it didn't show too much surprise. He wasn't exactly setting her sister up as bait…but he wanted to alarm the assailant, if there had been one.

"Lieutenant Vahalik," a woman from a Bend television station called, "have you been working this investigation at all?"

Clay tensed. Of course she'd been recognized.

"The accident and presumed abduction happened outside my jurisdiction." She gestured toward the bronze placard beside the entry doors that said Butte County Sheriff's Department. "As I'm sure you're aware, the sheriff's department and the Angel Butte Police Department work closely together. Sergeant Renner and I were already acquainted. I feel very fortunate he is heading this investigation. I trust he will be as thorough as I would be."

"How does it feel to be a victim's family member instead of an investigator?" someone else asked.

Clay hated questions like that. What did they *think* it felt like? He especially didn't like this attempt to get Jane to bare herself for the entertainment of their viewing audiences. It was all he could do to stay impassive and not intervene, which he knew she wouldn't appreciate.

She met the reporter's gaze, her own naked. "I am terrified and heartbroken. That's how it feels. I do believe I have always treated the family of victims with empathy, so I'm not sure what will change in the future beyond, of course, having a deeper sense of what they're going through."

Clay didn't let anyone else jump in. He wound the thing down with a repeat of the phone numbers for reporting any sighting of Brianna Wilson or any knowledge whatsoever of her whereabouts.

Then he ushered Drew and Jane inside and led them to a small conference room, where he was able to shut the door. Drew sagged into a chair and buried his face in his hands. Jane laid a gentle hand on his back and rubbed. Clay resisted the need to do the same for her.

"You both did a good job," he said. "I think you had exactly the effect you wanted. I'm predicting Brianna's photo will be back above the fold on page one tomorrow, and on the local news on every station tonight." He didn't add, "for a day or two." Until fresh news crowded it out again.

Drew lifted his head long enough to cast a desperate glance at Clay. "No one has seen anything yet."

"They will," Clay said with more confidence than he felt.

"It's our best hope," Jane said, but her voice was so soft he knew she feared that hope was a faint one.

He left them long enough to get cold drinks from a machine. The sugar and caffeine seemed to revive Drew, who finally asked if the reporters would be gone. Clay went out to look and came back to say that the coast was clear. Drew left after telling Jane he was going back to the hospital, but would pick Alexis up himself.

"I'll see you later at home, then," she told him, watching as he left.

Then she turned to Clay, her expression bleak. "I want to think we did some good."

Aware of the expanse of glass that allowed people to see in, he couldn't take her in his arms the way he wanted. "You did everything you possibly could," he said, feeling how inadequate the words were.

"Will you just have to wait for tips?" she asked.

"I'm most hopeful your sister will be able to tell us something. But, no. I'm going back to Stillwell Trucking to talk to coworkers. I'm going to interview your sister's friends. Could she have been involved with a man? Up to something else? Someone must know."

"Wouldn't Drew have guessed— ?"

For once, she was neither tough nor cynical. The glimpse of her despair gutted him.

"I think he did," Clay said quietly.

He expected argument but didn't get one. After a moment, she nodded, her usual energy subdued. "I'll let you get back to work."

"Can you get away for a while tonight, Jane?" he asked, voice raw. "Maybe I could feed you dinner."

"You mean…go out?" She sounded uncertain.

"I was thinking I could cook. Since you fed me last night."

"You mean…at your place?" She shook her head and his heart sank until she said, "That's a dumb thing to ask. Where else are you going to cook? On a grill at the park?"

He let himself smile. "Well, we could."

"I think I've been stared at enough for one day." She wrinkled her nose. "If you mean it, I'd like that. Unless something happens."

He thought she was blushing. "That goes without saying," he said easily, and it did. They were both cops; something quite often happened to interrupt previously made plans. Clay had dated more than one woman who thought his profession was sexy until she got tired of him canceling on her. He guessed men would be even less understanding of a woman who constantly put her job ahead of a dinner date.

In this case, though, he knew they were both hoping something would come up—a promising tip, or her sister opening her eyes.

They agreed she'd drive herself to his house, and set a time. Then he walked her out, feeling a complicated stew of emotions that ranged from compassion at her pain to triumph because, for whatever reason, it seemed she might be giving him a second chance after all. He took the chance of kissing her cheek before she got into her macho black Yukon. At his last glimpse of her, she was definitely blushing.

JANE'S GAZE LINGERED on the Peruvian rug that hung above the river rock fireplace in Clay's log home. He'd surprised her in so many ways tonight, she was still reeling.

The log house in the woods wasn't a surprise; especially after becoming disenchanted with him, she'd relegated him to the stereotype of a redneck backcountry jerk, and a log cabin fit with that image. What didn't fit was the interior. For one thing, his space was spotlessly clean, and not as if he'd hastily stashed the empty beer cans, pizza boxes and dirty socks out of sight for her benefit. Instead she had the sense an orderly environment was important to him. That didn't mean he hadn't enriched it. She'd been taken aback by tall built-in shelves filled with books covering a huge gamut of subjects. His stereo system and speakers were impressive, but the television was small, and from its location, appeared to be an afterthought. A tall clay sculpture filling one corner was abstract and kept catching her eye. An antique copper boiling kettle held a pile of newspapers and kindling by the fireplace. The furnishings were simple, 19th-century antiques, well cared for. One huge, glorious framed photo was taken across Sparks Lake to what she recognized as South Sister. Otherwise, he'd hung a watercolor of black-eyed Susans in bloom.

He didn't offer her the classic bachelor fare of a grilled steak and baked potato for dinner, either. Instead he cooked chicken in a red wine sauce spiced heavily with marjoram over brown rice, with green beans that were currently in season.

Jane kept wondering over dinner whether he had any idea that he'd confounded her. She hadn't gotten to know him when they first dated nearly as well as she'd thought she had. Had she already been nursing preconceptions? Or had Clay been protecting himself, either consciously or unconsciously? He certainly hadn't invited her to his home.

He was the one to steer the conversation while he cooked and then while eating. They discussed national politics first, then the local electoral races.

"Does everyone in the department assume Sheriff Brock will be reelected?" she asked.

Eugene Brock was the incumbent Butte County sheriff, the one in danger of being ousted in November by her boss, Colin McAllister. Jane was aware that Colin and the Angel Butte police chief, Alec Raynor, both despised Brock.

Clay smiled at her question. "We're very careful not to talk about it. Personally? I think he'll lose. The dirty politics were a mistake."

Jane nodded. Someone on Brock's campaign staff had learned that Angel Butte mayor Noah Chandler had blacklisted Brock's main opponent, Colin, back when the city police chief job was open. Unfortunately for Brock, the mayor had come out strongly in support of Colin and explained in a way people understood why he'd made a decision then that no longer applied. Raynor was also enthusiastically supporting Colin, as were many of the county's most prominent citizens.

"My boss isn't popular among his officers," Clay said after a moment, his gaze resting on her. "He hasn't fought for funding the way Raynor is doing in Angel Butte. Training and manpower is inadequate. As a result, deputies screw up more often than they should. There's been a culture that encourages contempt for minorities and unnecessary violence. There may be deputies who are afraid of change. The rest of us are hoping for it."

He had to trust her to have told her so much. His views could damage his career if Brock did win re-election.

"You'll like working for Colin if he wins," she said. "I'll miss him."

"He's the one who promoted you."

The restraint in his voice told her he'd heard the rumors implying she must have slept her way into the job. How else could a mere woman get so far, so fast?

"I felt unqualified," she admitted, without telling him there were still times when she wasn't sure she was up to the job. "Some people thought he should have gone outside the department to hire. Things had gotten so bad at that point, we'd lost a lot of people who had the seniority and experience to step in. He claims to have been impressed with how I handled the investigation into the payoffs we discovered Chief Bystrom had been accepting."

"That had to have been tough." Clay cradled a coffee mug in one large hand. "With him your boss, and you only a detective."

She was grateful he didn't add that she was a woman. If he'd said, "only a woman," she'd have had to walk out.

"The thing is, I despised Bystrom," she said in a burst of honesty. "If I'd had any respect for him at all, it would have been way harder to grill him."

Clay laughed. "I only wish I had the chance to look into Brock's activities."

Once, she'd have been shocked. As it was, she simply raised her eyebrows. "You think he's corrupt?"

He waggled one hand. "I've wondered, that's all. What I know is that he's lazy and incompetent."

"Bystrom was both those things, too."

"I'll be voting for your boss."

"I'll tell him after the election, if he wins."

"Since I can't, without looking like I'm apple polishing?"

Jane chuckled. "Right."

His mouth had a curve, but his eyes were serious. "Do you expect to have a shot at his job?"

"Captain? Wow. No." Then she noticed how still he was holding himself, and felt a surge of disappointment. "You'd hate it if I got another promotion, wouldn't you?"

His expression didn't change. "I didn't say that."

"You didn't have to." She started to gather herself. "It's time I be getting home."

"No." Clay leaned forward, pushing his empty plate away, the intensity deepening the blue of his eyes. "I didn't say that, and I didn't mean it. I really was just curious."

"Not competitive." She didn't believe him.

"Would I feel a sting if my—" the hesitation was so slight she almost missed it "—girlfriend outranked me by that much? Sure." He shrugged. "I could live with it. What you've accomplished is amazing—a woman facing down men who share the attitude I grew up with. The longer I know you, the more I admire you."

Her chest was suddenly so tight it hurt. The burning in the back of her eyes told her she was perilously close to tears. Right. Tears would really impress him.

The thought that came to her then almost took her breath away. *Maybe I don't have to impress him.*

"I always make those assumptions with men," she said, shocked both by the realization and by her willingness to say it out loud, here and now, to *this* man. "I didn't know I was doing it. *I'm* the one who's competitive. Who thinks every guy I know resents my success."

"Because so many of them do? Or did your father belittle you as a girl?"

She shouldn't have been surprised by his perception, but she was. "Maybe both. Dad was a really unhappy, angry man. Nothing I did ever impressed him."

"Jane..." He hesitated, then asked quietly, "Did he sexually molest your sister?"

Stunned, she could only stare at him.

Suddenly he was on his feet, torment altering his face. "Or you?"

She closed her eyes. "Not me," she whispered. "But Lissa...I think he did. Oh, God." She bent over, holding her stomach. "I tried so hard to keep her away from him."

CHAPTER TWELVE

"How did you know?" Jane asked him.

The way she'd almost crumpled, the shock and misery on her face now, battered Clay with emotions. The need to protect her was paramount, more powerful than he'd ever felt. The contradictions in this woman—her vulnerability coupled with her strength and competence—had him on a knife-edge. The last thing she'd want was him to promise he'd never let anyone hurt her again, however much he wanted to. How was a man with his core beliefs supposed to deal with a woman like her?

He wished he had a clue.

But a thought jabbed at him. Maybe his core beliefs weren't the same as they'd always been. Maybe the seismic shift in him wasn't as shallow as he'd thought; maybe it had gone bedrock deep.

Yeah, he thought, disconcerted. It could be.

Lissa. That was who they were talking about. Not him.

"I didn't know." He had persuaded Jane to move from the table to the big leather sofa. He'd sat beside her, but gave himself enough space to see her as they talked. "It really was a guess."

"You don't even know Lissa." Her expression was almost hostile. Her instincts, he guessed, were to be defensive. This was a secret she'd kept for a very long time.

"In a way, I do," Clay pointed out. "From what you've said about her, what Drew has said. Other people, too. Her relationship with you is classic. She knows you tried to save her and is grateful, but she's also angry because sometimes you couldn't. I get the feeling she holds men in contempt, but also glories in her power over them. And maybe in the looks that bring her attention, even though those looks also were the cause of something so bad happening to her."

"Yes." Any defensiveness had collapsed. "She was conflicted with Dad. Sometimes creeping around him, scared of him, but sometimes wrapping him around her little finger and spiteful to me because *she* could and I couldn't. I think—" She took a deep breath that had him tightening his grip on her hand. "I think it started when she wasn't very old. *I* wasn't old enough to suspect. It wasn't until later—"

"But she never told you."

Jane shook her head. "I…hinted a few times and she would blow up. I'm still not positive."

"It's only a suspicion on my part. We may both be wrong."

"But it would explain things about her. Her need to hold the upper hand." She paused. "I asked once if she wanted a little boy, and Lissa said she was praying to have only girls. She didn't know if she could deal with a boy. She was really vehement."

That was his Jane—clear-sighted even at her most distraught. He was disconcerted again by the pride he felt in her.

"You never got any hint your father looked at you that way?"

"No." She shrugged. "He talked about how at least he had one beautiful daughter."

"Damn him," Clay said with such force her eyes dilated.

"Sometimes I hated him." She bit her lip. "I wanted to believe it didn't hurt when he said things like that." She made a funny sound he thought might be intended as a laugh. "I don't know why I'm telling you all this. I sound so pathetic."

"No." His throat wanted to close, but he kept talking anyway. "I've never known a woman as strong as you."

"Strong."

He couldn't tell if that was disbelieving or sad. Had she become strong precisely *because* she believed her father that she'd never be feminine or beautiful in anyone's eyes and this was her compensation?

"Your father was wrong." The words came out raw. "You are beautiful. That first time I saw you, I couldn't take my eyes off you."

Her eyes, glorious and unblinking, never left his.

"Thank God he was such an idiot. Thank God he never wanted you."

"Lissa—" Tears overflowed, but she didn't seem to notice. "I tried so hard to keep her safe." Her tongue swiped her lips. She must have tasted the salt of her tears, because she lifted a hand in disbelief to find her face wet. "I never—" Her mouth worked. Formed an O of anguish.

He caught her as she collapsed. Held her tight as she sobbed. Clay wondered if she'd ever let herself cry like this when she was a girl, trying so hard to be the adult, the protector, even though she must have known deep inside she was bound to fail.

He rocked her, his hands moving ceaselessly in an effort to comfort. Cheek pressed to her head, Clay had a bad feeling he was crying, too. He couldn't remember the last time he had. Not since he was a young boy. His father would have been scathing if he'd ever seen his son shed a tear.

Had Jane's wounds healed as scars that barely twinged, or had they only scabbed over? He imagined them breaking open every time she saw her sister. No wonder she had given so much to her nieces, even though they already had two parents. She saw it as a chance to keep them, at least, safe. Irrational though it would be, she must feel now as if she'd failed Bree. Mostly she'd held herself together, but guessing how she was torturing herself with guilt tore something open in Clay.

"Oh, Jane," he murmured. "Sweetheart. You've had to hold so much in. Let it out. It's okay."

She didn't cry as long as she should have. Of course she didn't. She must hate losing control as much as he did. More, maybe. Jane had been trying to save not only her sister, but herself. Her scumbag of a father, Clay couldn't let himself forget, might not have sexually molested her, but he had hit her.

His own need for self-control felt petty in comparison. An ego thing.

A memory swept over him, stunningly real. He knew exactly how he'd felt at that moment, trying not to quail from his father.

"You gonna let me goad you, boy?" Dad, right in his face, stabbing Clay's chest with a forefinger. "Are you?" He sneered. "Sure you are. You don't have the guts to stare me down, do you? Huh? Do you?"

He shut down the memory. There were a thousand like it lurking inside him somewhere. Not abusive— Dad would have said he was toughening his kid up— but suggesting he'd felt a need to dominate Clay from early on. Seen him as a threat, maybe, only because he was male?

Clay shook his head. He wasn't going to let his father impact his psyche anymore, not if he could help it.

Jane pulled away from him, swiping furiously at her cheeks. "I'm sorry. I don't know what got into me. I need—" Breaking off midsentence, she fled for his bathroom.

Clay carefully wiped beneath his eyes to be sure no moisture lingered, then stacked his feet on the coffee table and laid his arms along the back of the sofa, staying firmly planted on the middle cushion. Maybe he should clear the table or start cleaning the kitchen— but he intended to be right here when Jane reappeared.

When she did, her face was puffy and splotched with red. Any trace of makeup was long gone. She looked painfully self-conscious as she hovered in the middle of the main room.

"I really ought to be going. Drew might want to go back to the hospital."

"Don't go yet." Clay held out a hand, tenderness and desire tangling into a huge knot beneath his breastbone. "Come sit with me."

Longing and wariness did visible battle on her face. He waited to see which would win. After a moment, she took a small step toward him, then another, a doe approaching a waterhole despite the fear of predators. He didn't want to pressure her, so he didn't urge her, just smiled wryly. At last she came and perched at the end of the sofa, her back straight and her hands clasped on her lap like the prim, good girl he suspected she'd been growing up. When she wasn't warrior woman defending her sister, that was.

He gave passing thought to asking what had killed her father, who'd likely only been—what, in his forties when he died? But then Clay decided he didn't want to know. His life was spent upholding the law, but if one of the son of a bitch's daughters had figured out a way to off him without getting caught, he had a feeling he'd be applauding.

"You okay?" he said finally.

Even though she hadn't let her back touch the sofa, her mane of hair brushed his hand behind her. "I'm fine. Really. I guess everything is just getting to me."

He didn't have to move his hand very much to stroke her hair, at first lightly, then letting his fingers search for the curve of her head. He crushed a handful of curls and watched them rebound the moment he loosened his fist. Jane had stiffened slightly, but didn't move.

"You're entitled." He smiled, noticing how her few

pale freckles stood out along with the blotches. "You have a redhead's skin."

She wrinkled her nose at him. "I sunburn easily."

He tugged gently on her hair. "Come here."

She gave him a look that was somehow desperate before relaxing with a sigh against him. "I shouldn't."

"Yeah, you should." He nuzzled her cheek and nibbled on her earlobe.

"I swore I was never going to trust you again."

"You can."

She tilted her head so she could see his face. "You keep saying that."

"Because I mean it." Really a promise, the words had a weight. *To have and to hold.* Damn, he thought, without as much shock as there should have been.

"You've been...really nice."

A week ago—a few days ago—he'd have been stupid enough to say something caustic like "You mean I'm as nice as your brother-in-law?" At least he'd learned something.

"I don't like seeing you hurt," he said huskily.

She blinked hard a couple of times, as if she was about to cry again, but then she gave a wobbly smile. "Okay."

He framed her face with his hands. "What's that mean? Okay?"

She was trying hard to see down deep inside him, to those places he rarely even acknowledged to himself. His skin prickled, as if nerves were exposed, but he held still and let her look.

Finally she slipped her arms around his neck. "It means I want you to kiss me."

"Aah." God, he wanted her. "I can do that."

He kept it gentle at first, as searching as her gaze had been, but with more give and take. He tempted her with his tongue and waited for hers to chase his down. When she sucked on his lower lip, he groaned, his patience abandoning him.

Lifting and turning her, he set her on his lap so she straddled him. Her splotches were fading, he saw. Her lips were damp and a little swollen now. Wrapping the back of her neck with one hand, he pulled her close for a kiss that got a whole lot more serious. It was deep and hungry. His hips lifted, and she adjusted so she rubbed the hard length of his erection. Her knees tightened on him.

He pulled the combs from her hair so it cascaded free, then fumbled for the buttons on her blouse. She tugged his T-shirt up and he paused in his task enough to let her pull the shirt over his head. It was hard to concentrate when she immediately splayed her hands on his chest, tracing the contours of muscle and bone, testing the response of his nipples. He hadn't known they were so sensitive.

At last her blouse fell open, exposing a rather sturdy white bra. Her hands went still and she looked down. "If I'd known," she said, sounding embarrassed, "I would have worn something prettier for you."

He tried to laugh. "I think this is sexier. It's a Jane bra."

"I could take offense—" But she lost interest in doing so, because he'd unhooked the back and was drawing the bra down her arms.

Her breasts were the most erotic thing he'd ever

seen, a bounty, the swell of female flesh so generous he doubted his hands would encompass them. The skin was close enough to translucent, he could see a faint tracery of blue veins. Her nipples, more pink than brown, were drawn into tight peaks. He bent her back over his arm and licked first one, then the other.

Jane whimpered.

"Beautiful," he whispered, and drew one nipple into his mouth and suckled.

Her hips rocked. The fingers of one hand formed a fist in his hair. Her back arched to thrust her breasts at him. He was so damn hard it was painful. He wasn't sure he could make it upstairs. He transferred his attention to her other breast, and she made more sounds, ones that intensified his arousal.

With a raw sound of his own, he lifted her off him and groped for the button at her waistband. He was long past finesse, but he managed, and stripped her of slacks and panties until they caught on her shoes. By that time, she was trying to work down the zipper of his trousers at the same time. The light touch of her fingers was better than anything he'd ever felt.

Too good. Once he had her clothes dealt with, he took over yanking off his own, grabbing his wallet on the way, finding the thin packet.

Only then did he see the flash of what might be hurt. "Lucky you keep one handy, I guess." Her tone was flip.

"I put it in here when you let me kiss you. When you kissed me. Jane."

Her eyes lifted to his.

"I haven't been carrying condoms. There hasn't been anyone else since I met you," he said.

Shock widened her eyes, and then he saw such vulnerability it damn near stopped his heart. "You're serious," she whispered.

"I'm serious." He couldn't help sounding guttural, but wasn't sure he wanted her to know yet quite how serious he was. For her it would seem too fast. Him, he'd been waiting for her.

She quivered. "You keep making me cry. I never cry!"

"Don't. Not now." He sought her mouth desperately. "That's the last thing I want."

He should take his time, savor her richly feminine body, but he couldn't. He'd waited too long.

Clay bore her back onto the sofa, kneading a breast, then sliding his hand down over her belly to the tangle of curls the same shade of chestnut as those on her head. Finding her slick heat, stroking until she was moaning and trying to pull him over her.

He managed then to get the condom on, although he wasn't sure how. He tried to come down on her carefully. For all her lush curves, she was still a small woman, even dainty, and he was a big man. She pressed one knee against the back of the sofa, and he hooked an arm beneath her other leg, lifting it and spreading her. He pushed inside, gritting his teeth at the mind-blowing pleasure of the tight fit, trying to give her time to adjust even though all he wanted was to plunge hard and deep. He lifted his head to look at her, finding her head tipped back, her eyes closed, her lips parted.

"Jane."

Dazed and yet filled with tumult, her eyes opened.

"All right?" he managed to ask.

Her "yes" was barely a sigh, but it was enough. He seated himself deep, felt her fingernails bite into his back, and began to move. Usually he closed his eyes. He had better control that way, but this time he wanted to see her.

For a moment they watched each other as their bodies danced and did battle. Only when he saw astonishment on her face and heard her whisper, "Clay," as her spasms started did he bury his face into that mass of hair and let himself go. Every muscle in his body tightened and locked as he came in a powerful rush that went on and on.

In the aftermath, he tried to roll enough to take some of his weight on his shoulder, but movement above that seemed to be beyond him. It was a while before he even realized he had a mouthful of Jane's hair. Somehow that struck him as so funny he began to laugh as he tried to spit it out.

She jerked, then shoved at him. "What...?"

Clay managed to lift his head enough to grin down at her. It was probably a stupid, loopy, besotted smile, but he didn't care. "Your hair was trying to smother me."

She giggled and tried to corral it with one hand. "I'm sorry. It's impossible."

"It's glorious." He let his head flop back down.

"I'm glad you think so." She sounded shy.

"In case you haven't noticed, I'm sold on all of you." He squeezed her hip then slid his hand upward until he could capture a breast.

"Except..." It was hardly more than an exhalation, so soft he wasn't sure he'd heard.

He shoved himself up on his elbow so he could see her. "Except what?"

Suddenly she was flaring defiance at him. "Except for the fact I sometimes put on a tactical vest and distract the *real* cops by insisting on going where you don't think any woman should go."

"Damn it, Jane—!"

"It's true!"

"It was true." He didn't know any other way to say it. He'd wounded her then more than he'd realized.

She had been pushing at him, but now her hands went still. "It's only been a few weeks."

The muscles in his shoulders tightened. "I want you. The woman you are."

"That's…hard for me to believe." There was the sadness again.

Was this her way of retreating? Clay had to wonder. Did she need to pull back? Or when she'd said she would never trust him again, had she meant it?

"Give me a chance," he said.

Her eyes were anxious again. "What do you call this?" She waved at their bodies, still tangled together.

"If you don't trust me, it's sex," he said flatly.

She swallowed. "This isn't easy for me."

It wasn't easy for him, either. Clay knew he still had internal battles to wage. He wouldn't like seeing her put herself in danger in the future any better than he had three weeks ago. Maybe because she was a woman; maybe because of how he felt about her. Part of him wished she was a teacher, an attorney, an administrative assistant, a biologist. Damn near anything but a cop. He wasn't sure he could keep his mouth shut if the situation arose.

The pride he also felt was the new and unsettling part.

"Give me a chance," he repeated.

"I am," she said softly. After a discernible pause, "I think I am."

"All right." He tried to smooth the roughness from his voice, too. "We'll take it as we go, Jane."

He managed to heave himself off her, although then his butt stuck to the leather of the sofa and he watched her wince as she unglued herself enough to sit up, too.

"Next time, let's make it to bed," he suggested.

Her gaze flashed to him, but to his surprise she chuckled. "Or you can take the bottom."

He leaned over and kissed her, hard and fast. "I know you can't stay, but I wish you could."

"I wish, too," she said, so wistfully he knew she was remembering everything she'd been able, too fleetingly, to forget.

Clay went to the bathroom to discard the condom and returned to find her already half dressed and struggling into her bra. He watched with regret as her gorgeous breasts were covered, then resigned himself to getting dressed, too.

He refused her offer to help him clean the kitchen, wishing she wasn't the one who had a dark drive ahead of her. He didn't share that thought with her, though. He could imagine her incredulity. Chances were, like any cop, she'd spent years patrolling at night, getting out of her squad car to step into the middle of domestic violence scenes or gang turf wars. And no, he didn't like picturing any of that.

For the first time, he was glad she was a lieutenant, and largely confined behind a desk.

Something else he wasn't going to say.

She found the two hair combs, one on the coffee table, the other almost under the sofa, then retired to his bathroom to put herself back together.

When she was ready, Clay walked her out to her SUV, putting a hand out to stop her before he got in so he could kiss her again. She made a throaty sound and kissed him back, but both of them made a conscious effort to keep it light.

She got in and reached for the door handle, but didn't close it right away.

"Do you know where you're planning to start tomorrow?" she asked, with that renewed anxiety.

"Yeah." He'd thought about it earlier, before Jane arrived. "Stillwell Trucking. We'll see what kind of welcome I get."

"Instead of Lissa's friends?"

Inspiration hit him. "I was thinking I might leave that to you."

With only the porch light and a half-moon, he couldn't see her face well, but her surprise still showed. "You mean that?"

"I have a feeling you're as good a detective as I am." He wished he'd thought of this sooner. "What's more, I'm guessing your sister's women friends might talk to you more openly than they would to me."

She nodded, said, "I'll start first thing in the morning. Thank you, Clay," and finally drove away. He stood out in the dark watching until the last flicker of red taillight disappeared, reluctant to go back into his too-empty house.

BY NOON THE next day, Jane had talked to half a dozen of her sister's friends, although it developed that *friends* wasn't quite the right word for most, who were closer to acquaintances—current or former coworkers, or mothers of one of Bree's or Alexis's friends. Jane had left messages for others who were likely at work.

Drew called once to say, "She's making sounds, Jane. Not quite words, but…"

"She's going to wake up." Jane had begun to believe it. She only wished it wasn't taking so long. This was Friday. Six days since Bree had vanished so completely, no one at all had seen her since.

"Yeah, I think so, too," he said abruptly, and ended the call.

Her relief was huge when Clay called. She'd felt stupidly girlie that morning when she awakened, thinking about their lovemaking, wondering how much of what he'd said he had really meant, hoping he'd call. Her stomach had been in a knot ever since, even though she had discovered she didn't doubt him as much as she should, given his history.

She kept seeing the way he'd looked at her when he'd said, *I want you. The woman you are.* And then he'd asked her to join the investigation even though her doing so was against the rules.

He asked because I'm a woman, and he thought Lissa's friends would talk to me.

Maybe. But he must have women deputies he could have had make the same calls.

"Hi," she said shyly.

"I wish we'd woken up together."

She wished they had, too. Instead she'd tossed and turned, and had to get up twice with Alexis. Then she'd sat across the breakfast table from Drew instead of Clay.

"You know I couldn't stay."

He grunted acknowledgement. "Getting anywhere?"

"Without learning anything useful."

"Don't suppose you can meet for a quick lunch."

"Sure." She went for casually pleased. "When and where?"

Ten minutes later, she walked into Subway and found him waiting. The sight of him, as always, stirred something in her. He was so solid. Not exactly handsome, but a man every woman noticed. Maybe more so today because of the weapon and badge he wore at his belt.

Probably because he was official, he only kissed her cheek, though his smile was intimate. Then they ordered, and took their sandwiches to a table in the back where they weren't likely to be overheard.

Unwrapping his sandwich, he said, "How far did you get?"

She told him about the conversations. "I'll try to reach the others this evening. They're probably at work. But I actually talked to two of the women I thought of as Lissa's close friends. They do spa days, shop together, that kind of thing."

He nodded, his blue eyes intent on her face even as he took a bite.

"One of them admitted that Lissa grumbled about

Drew sometimes. Then she hurried to say, 'But you know how it is. Just because we're friends and she could. Not like anything was really wrong.'" Jane shook her head. "Money worries? 'Gee, Lissa didn't say anything.' Only ten days ago they went for a mani-pedi at the spa at Arrow Lake, which is not cheap."

"A what?" Clay stopped in the act of lifting the sandwich to his mouth again.

"A manicure and pedicure? You know. Fingernails and toenails? And usually you get a foot and hand massage, too?"

"Do *you* do that?"

"Um…" She looked down at her unpainted nails, cut short. "Do I *look* like I do?"

Clay's gaze followed hers. "No, thank God."

Jane rolled her eyes. "It probably feels great. A lot of women have jobs where they feel like they need to be decorative. And plenty of men *like* long red fingernails."

"Not this one." He resumed eating.

Jane felt a surge of pleasure. What was it he'd said? He was sold on *all* of her? Not exactly poetic, but… she didn't really want poetry. She wouldn't trust it, especially from a man like him. Apparently he was sold even on her fingernails, kept utilitarian short.

"Good to know."

A smile crinkled the skin beside his eyes.

"It's funny," she said, returning to her original thought. "Lissa was always the social one, part of the in crowd. The phone rang all the time for her. But now I'm thinking how shallow most of her relationships were." She frowned. "Are."

He didn't have to say that avoiding emotional intimacy was also classic behavior for a woman with her history.

"What about you?" she asked. "How did your morning go?"

In between bites, he told her. She finally had the chance to start eating.

"Stillwell wasn't pleased to see me. He professed not to understand why I'm treating a woman who lies unconscious in the hospital as a suspect." He grimaced. "Not that you haven't said the same."

"Not recently."

"No." He went on to say that Lissa's boss had understood why he needed to interview Lissa's coworkers. "Mostly it was a waste of time. I got the same thing you did. I was told how bubbly she is, how much fun. A couple of the women were obviously taken by Lissa's husband." He sounded wry. "And what *darling* daughters. I heard how devoted a mother she is."

"I actually think she is. It's...one of her redeeming qualities. Her not wanting to take Bree along on an errand is really unusual. I mean, she didn't want to be a stay-at-home mom. She insisted she'd go out of her mind, but she does spend a ton of time with them."

Clay seemed to accept what she said. "The one place the vibes weren't quite as warm and fuzzy was, interestingly enough, in the finance department. An overblown description for an office with a grand total of three employees. They have a temp filling in for your sister right now," he added.

On a spasm of grief, Jane wondered if Lissa would ever be going back to work at Stillwell Trucking. Or to work at all. She bowed her head momentarily, concentrating on poking a tomato slice back into the roll.

"This time Ms. Bitterman, the other bookkeeper, sounded a little catty. I didn't get the impression they liked each other much."

"I've had the impression Lissa didn't like her," Jane admitted. "She didn't think Betty Jean did a fair share of the work. Lissa thought Mr. Stillwell should let her go."

"Did she call the boss mister? Not by his first name?"

"No, it was always Mr. Stillwell."

He nodded. "Arnett, the accountant, was irritated I was wasting his time. He's not a real friendly guy. I may be mistaken, but I'd swear I caught a flash of intense dislike for your sister before he hid it with impatience."

"But…how does it matter? Do you picture either of them forcing Lissa off the road and then abducting Bree? Why would they?"

"Betty Jean, no. Arnett… I've got to tell you, my impression is he's cold enough to do anything he thinks he has to. Why, though, that's another story. What I didn't get from anyone at the company was the sense Lissa had anything going with Arnett, or any other man, for that matter." He wadded up the wrappings. "No hint of an affair from any of her friends?"

Jane shook her head. "Nope."

"All right. Keep at it." He rolled his shoulders as if the muscles were tight. "Goddamn, I wish she could talk to us."

"Drew thinks any minute. He said she's making noises that aren't quite words."

"That's good." His tone was encouraging, but his

eyes said as clearly as words that Lissa might never speak coherently again.

Suddenly losing her appetite, Jane set down the heel of her sandwich and bundled it into the wrappings, ready to throw away.

"Now what?" she asked, hopelessness stealing over her again.

Clay's gaze met hers. "Your sister has been in a position to see the money trail at Stillwell Trucking. Stillwell was a little too alarmed today. I think he's dirty. I don't know how, but I'm going to start poking around."

She stared at him. She'd spent a good part of the last year investigating the messy world of drug trafficking. Law enforcement attention had mostly been focused on private airfields and the small planes flying in and out, but trucking... That was another form of transportation, one that rarely caused a second glance.

"What if it's drugs?" she said.

Clay smiled. There was no light of humor in his eyes. She couldn't help thinking that his expression was wolfish. "Great minds think alike. Stillwell bragged to me about how his trucks run from the Mexican border north to the Canadian. He'd be perfectly situated."

"You're thinking Lissa saw something she shouldn't have."

"Maybe."

His response was unexpansive, but it was all he'd say. Jane needed to get to the hospital, Clay back to work, so they parted in the parking lot, Clay kissing her lightly on the lips this time, his last words, "I'll call."

She watched him stride away, wishing she was going with him instead of to the hospital.

CHAPTER THIRTEEN

"A LOT OF people are pulling for you, Lissa," Jane said softly.

Because she'd been busy all day, she had come to the hospital after dinner to sit with her sister. She thought Drew, so exhausted he almost looked worse than his wife, had been relieved at Jane's offer to take his place. With Lissa's coma so light, Drew wanted someone with her as much as possible. Jane agreed. It really seemed now as if Lissa was responding to their voices, if not to what they were saying. Her fingers tightened on theirs, she tossed her head on the pillow, she made sounds, from whispery quiet to guttural. Sometimes she looked as if she was fighting her way free.

Please.

"We need your help," she said, watching her sister's face. "No, not we. *Bree* needs you."

Lissa opened her eyes.

"Lissa?" Jane's voice cracked. "Oh, my God. You're awake."

Her sister's lips moved but nothing came out. Then she worked her mouth as if it was too dry to be functional.

"A sip of water? Is that what you'd like?"

Jane swore those lips formed a *yes*. She'd brought a water bottle with her she hadn't yet opened. Now she took the top off and slid her hand behind her sister's neck to help her lift her head slightly. She was careful to give only a few sips, although Lissa seemed to want more.

"You really are awake," she said then, and discovered her faith had been shakier than she'd known. "Let me tell the nurse."

A flurry of activity ensued, and she had to step back out of the way. A doctor came in to examine Lissa, and for a while there were several people around the bed blocking Jane's view. She saw enough to know that Lissa's eyes had remained open, though, and that she'd croaked a few words.

Drew. She had to call Drew.

And Clay.

Jane withdrew from ICU and paced in the empty corridor outside as she dialed.

"Drew? She's awake." She had to tell him she didn't yet know how clearheaded Lissa was, only that she'd looked as if she recognized Jane, had been able to drink water, and had said a few words. "It's early enough, maybe you could arrange for Alexis to spend the night with one of her friends. Tomorrow's Saturday, so most of the parents won't be working."

"I'll make calls," he said, sounding frenzied. "There must be someone."

Jane phoned Clay next, who sounded pleased to hear her voice until she told him why she was calling, at which point he became all cop.

"You haven't had a chance to ask any questions yet?"

"No, of course not! I don't even know yet whether she's suffered brain damage. I just thought you'd like to know."

"Do you want me to come?" he asked.

Yes. She was stunned at how much she did. Not because he could pry information from her sister, but because her own emotions were in turmoil and she wanted him there, holding her hand. Looking at her with those understanding blue eyes and saying whatever she needed to hear.

The strength of her longing was enough to add crispness to her voice. "No, there's no point yet. At the very least, she's bound to be confused. I'll let you know when it might be possible for her to be questioned."

"The sooner the better, you know."

"I do know." She resented the sharpness in his voice. Did he think she could forget Bree for one single minute?

Except…she had. Ashamed, she knew that when she was making love with Clay, she hadn't thought of anyone but him. Bree was either dead or being held somewhere, terrified, and Aunt Jane had been indulging herself in passion.

"I have to go," she said abruptly.

"Call me. No matter what. I want to hear how she is, and—" there was a hesitation "—how you are." His voice had softened.

He was never entirely cop with her. "Okay." She had to clear her throat. "I'll let you know in a couple of hours how it's going."

His "goodbye" was gentle, stirring up all the complicated feelings Jane had for and about him. Trying to block them out, she put her phone on her belt and hurried back into ICU.

The doctor had gone, and only one nurse remained at Lissa's bedside. The nurse, middle-aged and likable, beamed at Jane. "She asked for you."

"Really?" Jane took her sister's hand. Lissa's fingers curled around hers. Her eyes had been closed, but now they fluttered open again.

"Janie?"

When they were little girls, that was what Lissa had called her. It had been so many years since Jane had heard that. Her heart lurched. Was Lissa lost in the past?

"Yeah," she said huskily. "It's me. Oh, Liss. How are you?"

"Head…ache," her sister whispered.

"I bet." She surveyed Lissa's face. "You hit your head really hard. You've still got a whopper of a black eye, you know. Well, not black so much anymore. More purple. If you were looking in a mirror, you'd be reaching for the concealer."

Lissa's mouth curved into a smile. It felt like a miracle.

"I called Drew. He'll be here in a few minutes. He was with you all day." Her smile probably wobbled. "I'm the evening shift."

"Thank…you."

"I'll leave you alone," the nurse said kindly, and disappeared toward the nurses' station.

"Hos…pi…tal?" Lissa seemed to be having to frame words one syllable at a time.

"Yes. You had an accident." She tried to talk slowly,

waiting for comprehension. "You went off the road. Shrubbery stopped your Venza, but not suddenly enough to make the air bag deploy. Because of the angle you ended up tilted at, you hit your head on the side window. It knocked you out."

"Oh." Lissa seemed to be trying to remember and failing. Finally, her eyes drifted shut.

Jane hardly breathed, watching her sister. Apprehension filled her. Had Lissa slipped back into a coma? Was she asleep? A sense of urgency pounded at Jane, but it was obvious Lissa was in no condition to answer questions. She wanted to wake her, evoke a response, just to make sure she *hadn't* reverted to the coma, but also knew that Lissa would have to take her recovery slowly. Probably she'd been exhausted by as much effort as she'd already made.

And really, she'd done splendidly, Jane told herself. Lissa had been…present. Aware of her surroundings. She knew Jane. Her eyes had seemed to acknowledge her understanding of why Drew had sat at her side all day, and was now rushing to the hospital again. They could all lay to rest their worst fears. She truly seemed like herself.

Suddenly chilled, Jane thought, No, this wasn't their worst fear at all. That had to do with Bree, not Lissa.

She ended up sitting silently, unable to take her gaze from her sister's face, doing nothing but watching her breathe. Worrying. It must have been half an hour when she heard quick footsteps beyond the cubicle. She was already rising to her feet when Drew rushed in.

His eyes searched her face, then his wife's. "Lissa?" His voice was loud, and Lissa started. Her eyes opened again, and she stared wildly around before she fixed on Drew's face.

"God, Lissa." He stumbled to the chair Jane had been sitting in earlier, and almost fell onto it. He sounded... shattered, as if he was jubilant but terrified, too. Jane didn't blame him.

Part of her thought she ought to leave them alone, give them some privacy. But another part of her—Lieutenant Vahalik—didn't want to. Didn't entirely trust Drew to be honest about everything Lissa admitted to him. She felt a tiny twinge of guilt at her earlier hurt when Clay had transformed in an instant to detective instead of lover. She of all people should understand.

So instead of leaving, she backed away, hovering near the foot of the bed in the doorway in hopes of being unobtrusive. It must have worked, because Drew and Lissa focused utterly on each other.

"You're awake." He touched his wife's face, his fingers shaking. "I can't believe it."

"Head." She tried to lift her own hand.

Drew captured it in his.

"It's been a week. Almost a week. Do you know how scared I've been?"

Her head moved slightly on the pillow. *No.*

"Do you remember me talking to you?"

Ripples across her forehead indicated confusion. "Not...sure."

"No." He laughed, a sound as distraught as his expression when he'd first arrived. "Of course you don't. Sweetheart, do you remember...?"

Jane tensed.

"'Member?" her sister mumbled.

"The accident? Anything about it?"

"No-o." Lissa drew the word out, as if unsure even of that much.

"I shouldn't push you. It's just—" He jolted and his head turned until he was looking at Jane. So he hadn't entirely forgotten her presence.

She shook her head slightly in answer to the question he seemed to be asking.

Instinct said they had to give Lissa time. With her confusion so apparent, she was unlikely to be able to tell them anything useful. And upsetting her might slow her recovery. What if her distress was so great she had to be sedated?

"Not yet," Jane murmured, and he nodded even though his expression was still wild enough, she wasn't entirely sure she trusted him not to press for answers.

Lissa seemed content to hold his hand. She drifted off to sleep again, and finally he gently placed her hand on the bedcover and stood. Jane stepped outside and he followed.

"I'm going to stay," he said.

Her sense of urgency hadn't abated, but she didn't believe that half an hour or even two hours from now Lissa was going to wake up remembering all and demanding to know where Bree was.

"I think we should let her rest," Jane said. "Even a few words seem to tire her. I understand why you need to stay, but I'd suggest you don't do anything for now but comfort her if she seems to need it. We may see a big improvement by morning."

He looked back through the open doorway to the bed. "All right. I will sit for a little while."

"Alexis?"

"She's at her friend Zoe's house. She'll be fine. Zoe's mother said she could keep her all day tomorrow if I needed to be at the hospital."

"Good. Well, then, I think I'll leave the two of you alone."

Worry quickened on his face and he stepped too close to her. "You aren't going home, are you? I mean, I hope you'll stay at our place. We can talk later."

"For tonight, at least." Caution made her add, "I may not wait up for you, though. I know it's ridiculously early, but I haven't been sleeping well. I'm ready to crash."

He'd visibly relaxed. "I know what you mean. That's fine. I'll see you at breakfast, then?"

It was a question, one she had to answer, even though she wasn't sure she wanted to know what he had to say. Probably he just hoped to have someone to listen as he babbled out his relief, but...Clay had made her nervous and more aware that Drew *was* sending some mixed signals.

"Sure," she said easily. "Drive carefully when you head home. You've got to be at the end of your rope."

"I guess I am." He suddenly gave an exultant grin. "She's herself, Jane." He drew her into a quick, hard hug, then went back into the small glass-fronted room.

Jane walked out, hoping she was doing the right thing leaving him. Before she even stepped out into the parking lot, she was calling Clay.

BY THE TIME Jane called him again midmorning, Clay's tension had stretched to the point where he couldn't even sit at his desk. He prowled instead, making everyone else edgy.

Tips had picked up again after the press conference, keeping his small task force busy on the phones. He'd sent officers out to check further into a few, but none struck him as especially promising, certainly not enough to get him excited.

He'd occupied himself talking again to the witness who'd actually seen the car that had been stopped at the accident. Clay took with him pictures he'd printed out in color of luxury sedans. There were a lot of more ordinary four-door sedans, but in his experience, people's first impressions tended to be accurate. The car might not turn out to have been a Lexus, but he was betting it was something in that class.

The guy was clearly embarrassed to have been so unobservant. Mumbling something about not being a car guy, he flipped through the sheaf of pages, starting with Audi at the top and Volvo at the bottom, then the second tier of slightly more modest models, from Acura to the Toyota Avalon. A few of them he shook his head decisively over, but in the end he had to admit he didn't know.

Clay thanked him and went back to the station, where he sat at his computer and pulled up DMV records. He started with James Stillwell, who, he learned, drove a 2013 Land Rover. The second car, in his wife's name, was a BMW, but a model that was too small to fit the witness's description, and red besides.

Glenn Arnett clearly wasn't hurting for money, either. He'd gone for an even bigger SUV, the Cadillac Escalade, in a dark blue. The family's second car was a hybrid, a Prius, and they were also registered as owning a vintage Mustang. The sixteen-year-old son had a brand-new Mini Cooper, presumably a gift from Daddy.

That was when, frustrated, Clay started pacing. He wanted to go to the hospital, give Melissa Wilson a good, hard shake and say, "What the hell were you up to, and where's your daughter?"

And to think, he usually considered himself a patient man.

Thank God for Jane's call. "Neither of us have said anything yet," she told him, "but she's seeming more aware. She asked how damaged her Venza was."

"I'm on my way," he said.

As irritable and restless as he'd been, Clay imagined everyone in the department was happy to see him leave.

During the short drive, he chafed at every stoplight. Somewhere along the way, he realized his eagerness wasn't just for the chance to question Melissa. He wanted to see Jane, too. Even though he'd talked to her several times yesterday, that wasn't the same as being with her. Yeah, he'd finally gotten naked with her, but he was all too well aware she still had a lot of hesitations where he was concerned.

Seemed he wasn't patient where Jane was concerned, either. Or maybe that wasn't really the issue, it occurred to him. What he really hated was uncertainty. And, yeah, lack of control.

When Clay arrived at the hospital, he spotted Jane and Drew right away. They sat close to each other in the waiting area outside ICU. His head was bent close to hers, and their hands were clasped. Clay was better able to suppress the flare of jealousy than the last time he'd seen a similar scene, but it was there, clenching his stomach.

At the sound of his footfalls, Jane looked up. He thought he saw relief on her face, which untied some of his own tension. Of course she wasn't turning to her brother-in-law, not after having made love with Clay. And sure as hell not when her sister would need her husband so much.

Lissa, it turned out, was sleeping. They'd decided to wait out here for him. No, she hadn't yet asked about the girls, and neither of them had said anything. They'd probably been dreading that moment.

"Thank you for waiting," he said. He restrained the urge to kiss Jane, but he did lay a hand on her back as the three of them entered ICU together.

The nurse emerging from Lissa's small room looked as if she'd like to protest the *en masse* invasion, but her gaze flicked to the badge at his belt and, after only a brief hesitation and crimped lips, she stepped aside without saying anything. Like every other person in the tri-county area, she must know about the missing girl.

Lissa still didn't look like the beautiful woman she'd been in the family photos, not with the ugly bruising and the remains of swelling, but even before she opened her eyes, Clay could see significant change. It was obvious she *was* sleeping, and not unconscious.

Drew went right to her side and took her hand. "Liss," he said softly.

Her lashes fluttered several times and then her eyes opened, focusing on her husband's face. After a moment they roved, finding first Jane's and then Clay's. She kept staring at him, the stranger at the foot of her bed.

Her eyes were a color that, like Jane's, could be labeled hazel, but were closer to brown flecked with some gold and green. He hadn't been able to tell from the photo.

"Mrs. Wilson," he said, nodding to her. "I'm Sergeant Brenner with the Butte County Sheriff's Department."

Puzzlement crinkled her forehead, but she murmured, "Sergeant."

"I'm glad to see you recovering."

"Thank you."

Jane, he saw from the corner of his eye, had moved around the bed to stand at her sister's side, opposite Drew. Protectively?

"I'm hoping you'll be able to answer some questions." He paused. Lissa's expression didn't change at all, but he still felt sure she was bracing herself. "Do you remember the accident?"

"No," she said faintly. "Jane and Drew told me, but…" She trailed off.

"Did they say where it occurred?"

Something flared in her eyes, but she shook her head slightly.

"253rd." He described the location. "Are you familiar with the Bear Creek area?"

"No." She turned her head to look at her husband. "Why would I be there?"

"That's what we need to know, Mrs. Wilson." Clay hardened his voice. "Do you recall that your daughter Bree was with you in the vehicle when you went off the road?"

Her eyes, wildly dilating, met his again. "*What?*

Was… She wasn't hurt, was she?" That gave her an excuse to turn a pleading look on her husband.

His mouth opened, then closed. His Adam's apple bobbed.

Clay ruthlessly intervened. "We don't know. She has been missing since the accident. If you dropped her off somewhere beforehand, we need to know."

She broke into wild sobs. Jane took a step closer to the bed and bent over to smooth a hand over her sister's forehead. "Shh. We'll find her, Liss. We will." She glared at Clay, all her conflict written in her expression. Anguish and anger and doubt.

He might understand the anger, but it pissed him off anyway. Was he the only one here whose first priority was Brianna, seven years old and vulnerable in a way her mother wasn't? If so, it was a goddamn irony, considering he was the only one of them who had never met the kid.

"Where is she?" Lissa was sobbing. Her whole body thrashed. A nurse rushed into the room and condemned him with her stare, but when he jerked his head peremptorily toward the door, she reluctantly withdrew.

"Where?" Lissa cried. "Oh, God! Lexie! Is Lexie all right?"

"Lexie is fine," her husband soothed her. "But Bree—" His voice broke. "We need your help, Liss. You have to tell us if you know anything."

"How could I? If…if she wandered away or…or someone took her when I was unconscious?"

Her husband and sister swabbed at her tears and kept saying useless things like, "Of course we understand. We'll find her. But if there's anything at all you remember...?"

Disgusted, Clay interrupted. "Mrs. Wilson, I really need to know why you lied to your husband." She broke off midsob. There was pure fear on her face, he'd swear it. "You told him were running a brief errand, to Rite Aid. But you never went there at all. Instead you ended up ten miles away on an obscure country road, where you were apparently driving at high speed with your daughter in the vehicle with you. If we knew why you were there and whether you were being pursued, we might have a chance of finding out who took your daughter and why."

"I don't remember anything!" she cried. "Why would I lie? How can you say that?" Her face crumpled theatrically as she peered up at her husband. Tears rolled down her cheeks. She looked damn pathetic, between her expression, the bruises and the tears. "You don't believe him, do you, Drew?" She was heading toward hysteria. "You know I wouldn't—"

"You're still confused," Jane began, but the glance Clay flicked at her sliced off the rest of what she'd meant to say.

"You were acting strange," Drew said, in an oddly neutral voice. "You didn't want to take Bree with you. And you didn't go to Rite Aid—"

Her wild stare swung between them. "How do you know?"

"We've interviewed every clerk working last Saturday," Clay said. "No one saw you. You didn't make a purchase."

"But...maybe I didn't find what I wanted."

"It was a quiet day at the store. The clerks were quite certain they'd have seen you if you'd come in. Your picture and Brianna's have been plastered all over the newspapers and the television news. Two of the clerks remembered you from other times you shopped there. Not a single customer has called to say, 'But I saw them at Rite Aid.'"

"I might have gotten a call—"

"We've looked at your phone records. The only call made to or from your mobile phone that day is the one *you* made, telling your husband you'd forgotten to purchase an item he'd asked you to pick up at Rite Aid. That call was likely made moments before the accident."

Powerful emotions were working under this woman's too-slick surface. He couldn't tell which one would win.

"I don't remember anything!" she screamed. "Bree— oh, God, Bree." She threw herself onto her side and fell into a storm of weeping.

After a telling moment of hesitation, Drew reached for her and began to murmur to her in a soft voice.

Frustrated, Clay knew he wasn't going to get anything out of her. Without a word, he turned and walked out. He heard footsteps behind him and knew Jane had followed.

They were no sooner through the double, swinging doors when she snapped, "You knew how she'd react when she found out Bree was missing! You might have gotten somewhere with sympathy."

"Sympathy?" He spun to face her, glad they were alone out here for the moment. "You think that's what she needed?"

"Yes!"

He was in love with her, and she was confronting him as if he was the enemy. Good to know, he thought viciously.

He took a step closer until he loomed over her. "Tell me you didn't believe her."

Jane wasn't the woman to back down. Her chin rose a notch and, if anything, she thrust it toward him, her expression fulminating. "I told you how confused she is! Of course she went nuts when she found out her daughter is missing! What, you expected her to give it cool, collected thought? Really?"

His lip curled. "You're a detective, and you don't know an act when you see one?"

"Maybe you're the one who doesn't know genuine emotion when you see it."

Man, she was looking at him as if she despised him. In her eyes, he'd been brutal. Had she really bought that hysterical, woe-is-me shit, hook, line and sinker? He couldn't believe it.

It took him a minute to unclench his jaw. "You know what, Jane? Your sister started lying from the minute I asked the first question. She may not have known Brianna was missing. She might not even remember the accident itself." Keeping his voice level was a challenge. "But she knew damn well why she was out on 253rd. I think she has a real good idea who took Bree and why. And I'll be back to talk to her, whether you like it or not." His scathing look swept over Jane's flushed face. "But you go on back in there and pat her hand some more, if that makes you feel better."

Her mouth opened in clear indignation, but nothing came out.

Clay was too mad to do anything but leave. Hoping she'd call after him, but knowing she wouldn't.

CHAPTER FOURTEEN

A₦ ɪɴᴀʀᴛɪᴄᴜʟᴀᴛᴇ ꜱᴏᴜɴᴅ of fury escaped Jane's throat as she watched Clay stalk out. All she could think was, she'd *known* what a jackass he could be. So why was she surprised? And…disappointed?

So much churned inside her, she was afraid to move. She was afraid she'd do some damage if she did. Slamming her fist into a wall appealed to her as it never had before.

She must have stood there for five minutes before her stomach began to hurt so much, she stumbled over to the chairs and sank onto one, bending over into a near-fetal position.

Oh, Lissa. Then, with greater anguish, *Bree.* And finally, *Clay.*

She rocked, torn by so many emotions she could hardly grab onto any one as it spun by. She'd needed Clay to—

Understand. That was it. Be here for her.

Find Bree. Even in her misery, she knew that was what she needed most from him.

And that was what he'd been trying to do.

I sabotaged him, she realized. Even Drew had done

better than she had. Lissa had been able to see and hear his doubt. But her sister the cop? *I wanted to jump between her and her attacker. Hold her. Comfort her.*

Because that's what I always did.

The painful cramping in her stomach wasn't letting up. She kept flashing back to that last expression on Clay's face, so different from the way he'd looked at her lately. She didn't mind the anger as much as she did the disgust.

God help her, she *deserved* his disdain.

He was right. Lissa had lied. First to last, she'd lied. And Jane had known on one level, even as she locked into automatic defense mode.

How many times had she done that? How many times had she backed Lissa when she didn't deserve it? Jane thought wretchedly, *What I did was enabling.* Maybe *she* was responsible for the calculating, manipulative woman her sister had become.

She'd thought she was giving love and support, and now she knew how blind she'd been. Clinging to an illusion of closeness, of love given in return when maybe there never was any.

Her mind had begun to work with cold clarity. How often had Lissa played her? If she didn't truly love Jane, did she love anyone?

Even Bree?

Jane discovered she'd sat up straighter and was staring at an uninteresting landscape that hung on the wall.

No, that wasn't right. She'd seen the expression on her sister's face when she looked at her daughters. Heard her laughter, her terror when one of them did something reckless. Of course she loved Alexis and Bree.

Jane closed her eyes. *And me. Of course she loves me.* Maybe not the way Jane wanted to be loved. She was the one who needed a closeness that Lissa didn't. Partly because Lissa had a family and Jane didn't.

A conclusion reached, she walled it off. This wasn't about her. It was about Bree.

Jane believed Lissa *hadn't* known Bree had been snatched. Her shock and horror had been genuine. So... why hadn't she leaped to tell them anything she could that would bring Bree safely home?

Why had she lied, and without even pausing to think it through? If she'd been having an affair, say, would hiding it come ahead of getting Bree back? Jane frowned. No—unless Lissa knew full well that whoever had snatched Bree wouldn't hurt her.

What other reason could explain her decision to lie? Fear, of course.

Because she knew her silence was all that kept Bree safe. Alive. Somehow, the minute she'd been told that Bree had been snatched, she'd understood what had happened and why.

Only—why had she driven out past the Bear Creek county park in the first place? If it was to meet someone, she couldn't have been that afraid of him or her, or she surely wouldn't have gone once she'd been compelled to take Bree with her.

But something had happened. Had she actually stopped, then saw something that made her panic? Panicked even before she stopped, and decided to step on the gas and get out of there?

Which parts did she remember, and which were still hazy for her?

The pain in Jane's stomach intensified as she thought about how she'd blown it with Clay. He'd shown such trust in her. Treated her with the respect she'd wanted from him. And her? The first time he'd really needed her backing—the first time she'd had to make a choice between him and Lissa—she'd gone with knee-jerk outrage and defensiveness. Either he was steaming right now, or he'd written her off.

She'd rather think he was mad than so disgusted he no longer gave a damn.

Feeling very old suddenly, Jane tried to figure out what to do next. Go back in and see what was happening with Lissa? Call Clay and hope he'd listen to an apology?

Clay, of course, but, oh, she didn't want to do this.

GIVEN THAT THIS was Labor Day weekend, a drive that should have taken ten minutes took closer to twenty. Tourists had multiplied like mosquitoes in May. It seemed as if everyone on the road was driving like an idiot, too. If he hadn't been within the Angel Butte city limits for most of the way, and therefore out of his own jurisdiction, Clay would have been tempted to hit the siren and issue a few tickets.

When his phone rang and Clay saw Jane's number, he muted the ring with a single, hard stab. Let her leave a message. Right now, he didn't want to talk to her.

He knew he'd get over it. Knew he'd even forgive her, because he understood the pressure she was under and that her sister still claimed her first loyalty. But, goddamn it, he didn't like it.

He'd just parked and opened the door of his Cherokee when she called. Now, instead of getting out, he waited for the hum that would tell him he had a new voice mail message.

It came quickly. Teeth clenched, he typed in his password and listened.

"I'm hoping we can talk, Clay." She sounded dignified and repressed. "No matter what, I owe you an apology. I suppose…" The silence stretched, until he expected the beep that would tell him she had hung up without finishing. But finally she said softly, "I wanted to believe her." This time she was gone.

He groaned and bumped his head several times against the headrest. Call her? Or let himself cool down?

"Shit," he said aloud, and touched Reply. A moment later, her phone was ringing.

"Clay?" She sounded surprised. She hadn't expected him to call back.

"Yeah." He cleared his throat.

"You got my message?"

"Yeah," he said again. "I owe you an apology, too." This was hard to say. "I think I had to push your sister. But I was an asshole to you. I wanted—" Hell. He hadn't meant to say that.

Of course she picked up on it. "You wanted?"

"Your cooperation," he said, even though that wasn't what he'd really wanted. "I was frustrated, too. It's been a week, Jane. The chances of getting your niece back are diminishing by the minute."

"I know." Her voice was small.

"You have any suggestions?"

"I'm waiting to talk to Drew. Maybe I'm wrong, but

I think she's more likely to crack if he's the one applying the pressure."

She was admitting, more directly than she had with the apology, that she, too, knew her sister had lied. If this was anyone else, he'd have felt victorious. Instead he wished she didn't have to face such a cruel truth.

Setting his emotions aside, Clay thought about the scene in ICU. He pictured how Jane's sister had responded when her husband had expressed doubt. She'd been shocked. She had never imagined he wouldn't believe every word out of her mouth. Maybe from arrogance, maybe habit. It was pretty clear Drew had been blinding himself to his wife's behavior for a while. His jumping in and insisting she take their daughter with her on her supposed errand might have been his first rebellion against her recent dominance. From what he'd said, she had been furious—but she'd been the one to surrender.

"I think you're right," he said slowly. "If he won't do it, what about you?"

"I don't see that working." Jane sounded sad. "I told you we haven't been getting along very well. Even if we'd been doing better lately, she has this pattern of lashing out at me whenever I'm giving her advice she doesn't want, or she imagines I'm asserting some kind of big-sister authority. Me trying might be the worst thing we could do."

"All right." The uncomfortable density in his chest told him he'd already let go of his anger. He wished she was here, or he was there. He wanted to be able to put his arms around her. "Do you want me there?" he asked.

"Um…let me talk to Drew and see what he thinks."

If she'd heard Clay's double meaning, she wasn't letting on. "Lissa really *was* hysterical. She's still at the stage where she conks out after about ten minutes of conversation. We need to let her rest."

He grunted reluctant agreement.

"I'll call."

His hand tightened on the phone. "I'll be waiting."

She said goodbye and was gone.

Crap. He'd be pacing again.

DREW HADN'T KNOWN he was capable of such anger. He had always been laid-back. There was a time he'd considered being easygoing a virtue. The contrast between their personalities might explain why he'd fallen so hard for Lissa when he met her. He bored himself sometimes. He knew she'd never bore him.

Lately, though, he'd had to admit to himself that he and Lissa weren't equal partners, or anything close to it. He'd deferred, without even noticing he was doing it, because she was stronger. That might not ever have mattered—he might never even have become aware it was happening—if she had loved him as much as he loved her. If she'd wanted what was best for them, and for their family.

He wasn't sure there was an *us* anymore. Nor was he sure he wanted there to be. He had been praying for her to come out of the coma, partly for her sake, but most of all so she could help them find Bree.

And then she'd lied. The woman he had loved was protecting herself at their child's expense. The fact that she could do so was unthinkable to him. He would die for either of their daughters. He would have died for *her.* Today, even as he'd soothed her back to sleep, he kept thinking he didn't know her at all.

Right at this moment, he came close to hating her.

Once she was asleep, he told Jane he'd be back in a few hours and went for a drive. He followed Highway 31 southeast into drier country, glad of the lack of traffic. He could almost empty his mind when he concentrated on shifting, pretended to take in his surroundings. Part of him wanted to keep going. Eventually he'd cross the border into California. Lissa had checked out for days. Why couldn't he?

Because Alexis needed him. Bree might need him. Because he didn't think he could stand it if Jane thought he was weak.

He was almost back to Angel Butte when he took an impulsive turn, following signs to the Arrow Lake Resort, but continuing on past it and the airport. He and Lissa had taken the girls swimming here—not last summer, but the previous one, he thought.

Without having consciously made the decision, he found himself on 253rd, passing the Bear Creek picnic area, where some kind of large family gathering seemed to be going on. A huge banner he couldn't quite read hung between two pine trees. The crowd of people was a blur, colorful, cheerful even without him being able to hear the laughter. Drew stared for a minute, his foot lifting from the gas pedal, before he accelerated again and left it behind.

Torn vegetation made it obvious where Lissa had gone off the road. Just past it, he parked on the shoulder and walked back, looking in horror at the deep furrows and the gouges in the trunks of two small trees. If they hadn't stopped the Venza's descent—

How much worse could it have been? A quick death for Bree might have been better than whatever had happened to her. Pain slammed into him. He threw back his head until muscles and tendons strained and a shout ripped from his throat.

If the people at the campground heard, what would they think? He didn't care.

Once he started back toward town, Drew was vaguely surprised to discover he was hungry. He didn't want to go into a restaurant; people would recognize him and might ask questions. Even if all they did was express sympathy, he couldn't take it. Instead he went to Taco Time, using the outside window and keeping his face averted as he paid for and accepted his food. Parked at the far corner of the lot, he gobbled, shocking himself until he thought back to the past few days and remembered how little he'd actually eaten. Thank God Alexis was being taken care of. He knew he was running out of internal resources. He had been living in the belief that Lissa would open her eyes and tell them how they could find Bree.

Now…now he felt as if he was hardening inside. Changing. He suspected he would never be the same man he'd been.

JANE HAD GONE home and cleaned house. If Lissa woke up, no one from her family would be there. So what, Jane thought vengefully. She knew it wasn't in her to be supportive right now. Like Drew, she had needed to get away.

Eventually she took a short nap on her own bed, then a shower. She had reached for her hair dryer when her phone rang.

"I'm back at the hospital." It was Drew. His voice was unnaturally calm. "I'm ready to talk to her. Do you want to be here?"

"Yes. Give me ten minutes."

"All right." He paused. "Do we need to have Sergeant Renner here, too?"

She'd thought about it. "No. I think we have a better chance of getting answers from Lissa if he *isn't* there."

"I think so, too," he agreed.

She should at least tell Clay what they were going to do, she thought during the drive. He might agree to let them do this alone...but he might not, too. She wasn't prepared to take the risk.

A guilty conscience gripped her as she walked back into the hospital a short time later, her feet knowing the way to ICU without conscious direction from her. Past the escalator. Long hall that widened in front of some windows looking out on a small courtyard. Double doors.

No, she told herself, relaxing, of course Clay wouldn't mind. She thought he'd given her tacit permission to go ahead. He might have lost some trust in her today, but not all of it.

Drew stood when he saw her coming. Jane thought about hugging him, but something in his expression stopped her. She had never seen him so grim. So she only nodded, and they went in together.

"Oh," one of the nurses said with a smile. "She's been asking for you both."

Jane forced a smile of sorts. Drew didn't even manage that much.

Lissa was awake, plucking fretfully at her blanket. Her gaze flew to their faces, her eyes widening at whatever she saw there.

"Why are you looking at me like that? Both of you. Oh, God." She sounded as if she was about to hyperventilate. "Not Bree."

"Do you care?" Drew asked, his tone one of clinical interest. He advanced to his usual place at the side of the bed, but didn't bend down to kiss her or even take her hand.

Jane stopped at the foot.

"How can you say that?" Lissa cried.

"At first," Drew said, "we thought Bree must have stopped a car to ask for help. That she was unlucky enough to have fallen victim to a child molester. Every police department in central Oregon has been pursuing tips phoned in by the public. Do you know how many curly-haired girls Bree's age there are?"

His wife stared at him as if she was mesmerized. Jane wasn't even sure she was breathing.

"Do you know how I've felt, imagining my little girl in the hands of someone like that?"

Lissa said nothing.

He leaned toward her. "I was angry when Sergeant Renner began to speculate on other possibilities. Ones that meant you were involved in some wrongdoing. Not my wife, I insisted." His voice became deadlier with every word. "But there was the fact you were so determined to go to Rite Aid by yourself. And the fact you never got there at all, although when you phoned me, you implied you'd been, but had just forgotten the athlete's foot powder."

Lissa opened her mouth, then closed it.

"There was the puzzle of why the accident happened where it did. What were you doing out there?"

Still, she only stared, but her expression was stricken.

"Then he got to asking about our finances. How were we paying the bills, with me having been laid off for so many months? Didn't we have a heck of a steep mortgage? Car payments, too. My wife was handling all that, I said. But I've been asking, haven't I, Lissa? And you've been blowing me off. I still didn't have the guts to actually look, but Jane did. She pulled up our bank account. Saw what nice bonuses you've been getting lately."

Lissa gaped at Jane. "How could you?" she whispered.

He flattened his hands on the mattress and bent forward, his lips drawn back from his teeth. "What did you do to earn that money, Lissa? You *will* tell me."

"I…I… Nothing!" she almost screamed. "Not what you're thinking!"

"You don't know what I'm thinking."

"I didn't want us to lose the house!"

"But we were going to sell it anyway once I got a new job." He straightened and his voice went flat. "Or did you have no intention of moving, no matter what I did?"

"No!" Lissa was gasping and crying now. "Drew, what is *wrong* with you? Why are you treating me this way?"

"Because one of us has to care about Bree," he said

with such contempt even Jane stared at him with astonishment, "and it's obviously not going to be you."

"How can you say that? I love her! I *can't* tell you, or…or…" Her face contorted. "What if he kills her?" she wailed, before she flung herself onto her side, curling into a fetal position.

Jane had had broken ribs once. That was what this felt like, every breath agony.

"Who?" Drew asked hoarsely. "Who is 'he'?"

Lissa was either crying too hard to answer, or was refusing to.

"James Stillwell," Jane heard herself say. "That's who wrote those checks to you."

Her sister's head bobbed. "He said…he said he wanted to help, with Drew out of work…" she mumbled.

"But he wasn't being good-hearted, was he?" Jane said, her voice as cold and hard as Drew's had been. "Were you doing something illegal for him?"

"Or were you his mistress?" Drew didn't sound as if he minded either way. "You sure didn't care whether I was in your bed or not."

"No!" She unloosened the clench of her body enough to stare up at him in wild-eyed despair. "I wouldn't do that. No!"

Drew looked down at his wife as if he hated her. "Does he have Bree, Lissa?"

"Yes!" she yelled, then sobbed. "Yes," she said more quietly. "I think so. He must."

"Why? Why did he take her?" Drew's face worked, and he ran a hand over it. "Does he like little girls?"

"No! No. Nothing like that. It's me. Oh, God. It's me." Lissa was winding down, the terrified understanding in every word making Jane's skin prickle and burn as if she'd brushed against poison oak.

Lissa uncurled and leaned against the pillows. Now she was staring at some dreadful vision neither Drew nor Jane could see. She seemed unaware of the tears and snot streaking her cheeks and upper lip. "I think he was going to kill me," she said dully. "He'd been giving me checks at work. Then he said he was afraid someone would notice. He claimed he and his wife were going to be at her sister's house on Bear Creek and that I could come by Saturday. Only…only when I got to the address he gave me, I saw it was this rundown cabin that looked as if it was vacant. I've met his wife's sister. This wasn't anyplace she'd live." She shuddered. "It's so…deserted out there. There wasn't any traffic at all, and there were a few driveways, but I couldn't even really see the houses, and I got scared. So I kept going. I should have turned into the picnic area. At least there were people there. But I thought I could just keep going and make my way home. I was calling you—" her gaze flicked to Drew "—when this car came up really fast behind me. I can still see it in the rearview mirror. And…that's the last thing I remember. Except Bree." Her voice was so soft, both Drew and Jane leaned forward. "She was screaming. I can hear her."

Her husband swore. His eyes had sunk so deep in his head, they were hardly visible behind the glint of his glasses. "Why was he paying you, Lissa? You have to tell us."

She closed her eyes. "Glenn called in sick one day. I went in to look for something on his computer, and I saw he'd left his laptop, too. I was curious. I couldn't understand why he worked on it sometimes in the office instead of his PC. Of course it was password protected, but I tried a bunch of things, and… Well, he'd used his daughter's birthday." She looked at Drew. "We'd talked about our kids' birthdays. You know."

Dread held Jane utterly still.

"He had QuickBooks on there, but I could see right away that nothing was the same as what I worked on. Truck routing is computerized, too, you know." She waited, and Drew nodded. "That was on the laptop, too, only there were routes and dates I'd never seen before. I don't know whether they're just hiding some income, or whether they're transporting something illegal, but I thought—"

"You'd blackmail them," Drew said.

Finally she looked at him, her expression piteous. "Finding out, right when we needed extra money, it seemed like it was meant to be. Anyway, I've *earned* more than I was paid. Stillwell is a creep! He talks about how we're all one big family, but really most of us are nothing to him. Nothing," she spat. "Do you know how much Glenn makes? And we do practically the same thing! Well, if he can make that much, I thought I deserved it, too!"

Now Jane was the one to close her eyes. How had Lissa developed this sense of entitlement? She and Drew had had such a good life, and all the time she'd been seething because she was sure she deserved more.

"Did you really think he'd just pay you forever?" she asked with disbelief.

"He paid Glenn," Lissa said sullenly.

"Who is a CPA. Who would earn way more than you

no matter where he worked." Then she shook her head. Why was she wasting time? "Who was in the car behind you, Lissa? Was it Stillwell?"

Now Lissa looked scared. "Who else could it have been?"

"If Stillwell Trucking is running drugs, he has some ugly people on his payroll. He could have sent anyone. Somehow, he doesn't look like a guy who'd do his own dirty work."

"I was supposed to come alone," Lissa whispered. "I thought—I'd leave Bree in the car. Nobody would pay attention to a kid."

"Whoever it was, he saw you go by. Maybe hesitate and look down the driveway, then decide you weren't going to stop. So he came after you. You freaked and went sailing off the road. Maybe he was going to kill you, only those two hikers popped out and started running up the road to see if anyone was hurt. He might not have been able to get down to you, but Bree had scrambled out and he was able to grab her. He probably hoped you were dead, but decided he needed some insurance. With you in a coma, they couldn't let her go."

Lissa's eyes welled with fresh tears. "Is she dead?"

"I don't know. I don't see how they can ever let her go. She's old enough to be able to identify whoever it was who grabbed her."

Drew turned his head to look at her. His expression was terrible. "Why hasn't anybody found her body?"

Jane pressed her lips together and shook her head. "I have to call Clay."

Lissa gasped. "Wait! You can't tell him!"

Jane walked out.

CHAPTER FIFTEEN

CLAY LISTENED IN silence to Jane's terse recitation, hearing the deep distress she was trying to hide.

"I'm sorry," he said gently. He had to step quickly aside when two deputies wrestled a struggling, handcuffed man past him in the corridor outside the detective unit.

If Jane heard the screamed obscenities, she didn't remark on it. Instead, after a pool of silence, she said only, "Thank you."

He shoved a hand through his hair. "You know I have to talk to her."

"Be my guest." There was a hint of her more familiar tartness, if flavored with something darker than usual.

"Are you still at the hospital?" he asked.

"In the parking lot."

"Wait for me?"

"You want me there?"

"Yeah." Of course he did. Hadn't she noticed he always wanted her there?

"Okay," she said softly. "I'll see you in the waiting area."

He hit the traffic lights right this time and made it

back to the hospital in under ten minutes. Jane was standing looking out the window at the small courtyard surrounded by the hospital. When he walked up behind her, he could see through the glass and courtyard to the cafeteria on the other side.

"Hey," he said, voice gravelly, and she turned and went into his arms as if it was the most natural place in the world for her.

She let him hold her for only a minute, but he felt better for it and hoped she did, too. Looking down at her, though, he saw that all the distress he'd heard was in her eyes. Damn, she'd lost weight this past week. Beneath her eyes were purplish bruises. But her head was high, her shoulders squared. This was Jane. Of course she was keeping herself together.

"Drew still in there?" he asked.

Jane shook her head. "He walked out without even seeing me. He's…taking this hard."

Clay could understand. He wondered whether Jane's brother-in-law would stand by his wife. Or was he so terrified for his daughter, he wasn't thinking yet beyond that?

Once they stood at Melissa Wilson's bedside, Clay couldn't tell if she was sleeping or not. He felt no compunction at waking her.

"Mrs. Wilson."

Her lashes fluttered then lifted. Oh, yeah—she was deeply afraid, although he had no idea whether it was for herself or for her child.

In case she didn't hold up for long, he asked first about last Saturday.

She wasn't sure of the make of the car that had pursued her, only that it was a sedan, and silver. To her credit, she seemed to be struggling for any detail. "Something nice" was what she came up with.

"Picture the driver. I know you didn't get a good look, but you might have seen more than you know. Think about hair color."

Her eyes widened. "I don't know…" The uncertainty in her voice gave him a clue that she was taken aback by what she did remember. "I think," she said very slowly, "it might have been dark."

Which meant it likely hadn't been the president and owner of Stillwell Trucking behind her. Clay would have been surprised if it was. Guys like Stillwell didn't get their hands bloody.

He asked her more questions. What about height, for example. Her brow crinkled. Tall, she thought, and he could see her increasing shock. James Stillwell wasn't even average height.

Finally, he backed her up to the day she'd prowled through the information on Arnett's laptop. She gave him more details than Jane had.

"Mrs. Wilson," he said at last, "you cannot tell anyone you've revealed anything at all to us. If Brianna is still being held to ensure your silence, the slightest suspicion that you've talked could be a death sentence for her. Do you understand?"

She was shaking. Her teeth chattered, but she nodded. "Yes, I…I do. I understand."

Very conscious of Jane standing quietly beside him, but not allowing himself to look at her, he asked, "Have you spoken to Mr. Stillwell since you regained consciousness?"

Lissa shook her head. "He keeps coming by, but the nurses let only family in."

"All right. I'll reinforce that restriction. Are they putting phone calls through?"

"Not yet. But…one of the nurses said they may move me to a regular hospital room later today or tomorrow."

"I'm going to ask they hold off, or we'll stop visitors and calls to you in the new room, too."

"Oh, God." Her eyes pleaded with him. "How will you find her?"

"I have some ideas," he said, hoping he wasn't lying, "but we can't afford for her captors to panic."

Jane stirred. "What if Mr. Stillwell *is* allowed to see Lissa the next time he comes? If she tells him she won't say a word, might he let Bree go?"

With both women looking at him with such desperation, he didn't want to say this, but knew he had to. "I doubt it. My guess is that, right now, Stillwell and Arnett are thinking about doing some housecleaning. I want to make sure they don't have a chance to finish up."

"Bree…" Lissa whispered.

He inclined his head to her, seeing that her suffering was genuine. "She's my first priority. Count on it."

With a hand on Jane's back, Clay steered her out. He paused only to speak to the nurse, asking that the no-visitor rule be maintained and requesting to be informed before Melissa was moved, then kept Jane walking until they were in the parking lot by his Jeep, where he could be sure they wouldn't be overheard.

"Can I trust her to keep her mouth shut?" he asked bluntly.

Jane blinked. "Yes." Her voice firmed. "Yes, I'm sure you can."

"All right. Stillwell Trucking is inside the Angel Butte city limits. I need to talk to your boss."

"Colin?"

"Maybe Alec, too." He nodded at his Jeep. "Come with me?"

"Yes. Thank you."

When they walked into the city's public safety building a few minutes later, heads turned. Clay realized it was Jane drawing the attention. Maybe because she was dressed so casually, in cropped chinos, sandals and a lime-green, cap-sleeve T-shirt with a Celtic design on the front. He'd noticed the shirt the minute she faced him back at the hospital, because it fit so snugly over her breasts, the swirled design unintentionally echoing the rich swell beneath. She might not wear a uniform to work, but he'd seen what she did wear, and it didn't look anything like this.

But maybe it wasn't the clothes at all. It might be the exhaustion and stress so clearly marked on her usually gentle, serene face.

They took the elevator and went to Chief Raynor's office, where the P.A. looked surprised but ushered them in after only a few words said on the phone.

Raynor, a greyhound-lean, dark-haired man, rose from behind his desk and came around to shake hands and study Jane. "Lieutenant." Lines of perturbation showed on his face. "You don't look as if you've had good news."

She gave a small, twisted smile. "I think I'll let Sergeant Renner tell you about it."

Raynor raised those dark brows at Clay, who said, "I was hoping we could speak to Captain McAllister and you together."

Eyes of the darkest brown he'd ever seen assessed him before the chief nodded. "Sit," he told them, nodding toward a conversation area at one side of his large office even as he reached for his phone.

Jane sank immediately onto one chair and stared at her hands. Staying on his feet, Clay studied a large oil or acrylic painting hanging on the wall, a disturbing damn thing that fragmented when he tried to see it as a whole, but suggested violence.

"He's on his way," Raynor said behind him. "Coffee?"

Clay turned. "I could use a cup. Thank you."

Jane shook her head. He suspected she could use a boost of caffeine, too, but for all he knew, she'd been swilling the stuff nonstop this morning.

Colin McAllister and the coffee arrived simultaneously. Everyone settled in a semicircle around a low table.

Clay began to talk, bringing the two men up-to-date. "I don't want to move on the trucking company until we find Brianna," he said, "but I also don't want them to have a chance to bury all evidence of wrongdoing."

"If we raid the place, they'll kill the girl," Raynor said flatly.

Jane couldn't prevent a small, anguished sound. All three men gave her quick, apologetic looks.

"They may still have hopes they can shut Mrs. Wilson up," Clay said. "Her daughter is the lever as long as Mrs. Wilson is in the hospital and they can't get to her."

Nods all around. Jane stared at him.

"I think it's safe to say she'll have another accident once she's released."

More nods.

"I'm going to hunt for that little girl like I've never hunted for anyone in my life," Clay said grimly. "Some possible locations may be within the city limits...."

Raynor shook his head. "You have my blessing. Just let us know what you need from us."

"I'd like Lieutenant Vahalik to continue working with me."

The police chief's expression was kind when he turned his gaze to her. "Jane?"

"Yes. Of course," she said tightly.

"I'm also hoping Angel Butte P.D. will be prepared to move on the company the second we locate Brianna Wilson," Clay continued. "Don't give the bastards time to feed a single piece of paper in a shredder. We need that laptop."

He was gratified by the expressions he saw on both Raynor's and McAllister's faces.

"Colin will put together a team," Raynor said. "We'll be sure there are no leaks." He hesitated. "Have you considered bringing Stillwell and the accountant in now? Leaning on them?"

"There have to be other people in the company active in their side business. I doubt either of them are guarding Brianna, for example. If we alarm them at all, we'll be putting her at risk."

McAllister, who had been listening attentively but not saying much, finally spoke up. "I agree."

Raynor didn't argue. He simply nodded. "You going for a tap on phones?"

"That's at the top of my list. Mrs. Wilson's statement should give us grounds. I'd like to get the phones at the trucking company as well as the two men's personal phones."

McAllister suggested a judge who tended to be liberal with this kind of warrant, and Clay nodded. He'd heard good things about the judge, a woman appointed to the bench not that long ago. "I appreciate your cooperation." He swallowed the last of his coffee and stood. "I'll stay in close touch."

Everyone else rose, too. The police chief clapped him on the back. "You know I owe you one," he said with a small nod.

"Your nephew doing okay?"

"Yeah." Raynor actually smiled, if crookedly. "He had some nightmares, but nothing you wouldn't expect. He's thinking he might go into law enforcement."

Clay couldn't help a chuckle, despite his dark mood. "Somehow, that doesn't surprise me."

"Not sure his mother is thrilled," the chief said, sounding amused, "but she figures he's got plenty of years to change his mind."

The boy's mother, Clay knew, was now Alec Raynor's wife.

Colin walked Jane and Clay out, the three of them discussing the makeup of the team and how they'd proceed once they got the okay from Clay. Nobody said, *What if you don't find Brianna?*

Clay wasn't ready to seriously consider the possibility she was dead. He hadn't been kidding when he said finding the little girl was his first priority. He'd have given his all in any case—but this wasn't any case. He was looking for Jane's niece.

JANE WAS GRATEFUL for the chance to *do* something, even if it was research on a computer.

While Clay put together what he needed for the warrant and then left for the courthouse to get a signature, she had started with all property owned by Stillwell Trucking, then by Stillwell himself. Jane dived into the task, lacking faith that men as smart as James Stillwell and Glenn Arnett would be stupid enough to chat on the phone about their hostage and where they had her stashed. If they were really involved deeply in transporting illegal drugs, they would be aware of the risk of wiretaps. Jane knew Clay had to try, but she had a bad feeling they wouldn't find Bree that way.

Stillwell Trucking, she learned, leased some loading bays and storage berths in western Oregon and in other states, but nothing that sounded probable. The company's headquarters in Angel Butte was huge, of course, but neither of them could imagine he would take the risk of stowing a little girl there.

James Stillwell and his wife owned a home in one of the wealthiest enclaves in the county, one with a spectacular view northwest toward The Sisters and Mount Bachelor. He also owned a condo at a resort on Century Drive close to the ski area at Mount Bachelor. Turned out the place was time-share, and the Stillwells' condo was actually rented out to other people a good deal of the time. The rental agent told her eagerly that it happened to be available for the coming week, and Jane asked if she could see it.

She had to listen to a spiel about the extraordinary amenities the resort offered owners.

"Unlikely," she told Clay upon his return, when he set down his phone from a call of his own, "but one of us had better check it out."

She moved on to property in the wife's name, then the son's and daughter's. The daughter's and son-in-law's names registered nowhere local. They lived in Minneapolis. The son, though, worked for his father's company, supervising operations on the west side of the state. He owned a home in Portland and, interestingly enough, a cabin on Clear Lake not ten miles from Angel Butte.

She underscored the address twice with a heavy hand.

Clay was clearly frustrated. The Arnetts appeared not to own any resort or investment properties at all, only a home in the gracious Old Town of Angel Butte, but not one that was riverfront.

"They have a daughter at Pomona College in southern California," he reported. "Looks like Daddy is forking out forty thousand dollars plus a year for her education, and he's still got another kid to go."

"Good reason to bend his morals a little," Jane muttered.

Clay shook his head in disbelief. "That's one hell of a lot of money for a college education."

He'd gotten his hands on a list of employees, although there was always the possibility there were more being paid under the table.

Like Lissa, Jane thought, wincing.

She was trying *not* to think about her sister. For one thing, she couldn't afford to be paralyzed by guilt. She knew eventually she'd have to come to terms with her own responsibility for Lissa's elastic morals, but not now. *Once Bree was safe.*

Clay gave her other names to research. Stillwell Trucking had a sizable security department, which might be legitimate, of course, but might not, too.

Drew called midafternoon to tell her he was at home. "I can't talk to Lissa right now," he said, in a voice that seemed flattened by exhaustion and the fury of emotions burned down to ashes.

"I don't blame you," she said. "I feel the same."

Clay had turned from his computer and was watching her. "Drew," she mouthed to him, and he nodded.

She told Drew she was doing some research for Clay.

"You coming back to the house tonight?" Drew asked.

She hesitated. "Do you need me?"

"I don't know if I'm ready to talk yet, but your company would be welcome. I've picked Alexis up, too."

That speared her with another form of guilt. She hadn't thought of her youngest niece today at all.

Seeing something on her face, Clay scribbled on a piece of paper and pushed it across to her.

Have dinner with me tonight. Stay?

Oh, God. She wanted to.

"Jane?" Drew prompted.

"I won't make it for dinner," she said, having yet another attack of guilt. Drew was her friend. If he'd ever needed her, it was now.

He ditched me. He chose Lissa.

Yes, but…

"I can't promise," she said finally. "Don't worry if I don't make it."

There was a silence. Then, "It's Renner, isn't it?"

Okay, damn it, she would not feel guilty about this. "Yes," she said.

"I'll see you when I see you, then." And he was gone.

She set down her phone.

"Yes what?" Clay asked.

"He wanted to know if I was having dinner with you."

"What business is it of his?"

"I am living with him at the moment. More or less," she added hastily. "With him and Alexis." She was immediately annoyed with herself for feeling she had to justify anything she did to Clay *or* Drew.

She turned back to the computer.

"I thought we'd check out a few of these properties," Clay said. "We can grab dinner while we're out or go back to my place."

"All right. Do you have anything promising?"

"Hard to say when I don't know which employees might be involved."

"They could be renting someplace," she said in sudden frustration. "Using a barn, like Matt Raynor's kidnappers did. There must be vacant properties around."

The hard look Clay had had on his face while he listened to her phone conversation was gone, replaced with sympathy and shared frustration. "I thought we'd start with a drive out Bear Creek way. I can't imagine they'd hold Brianna in the cabin where your sister was supposed to meet up with Stillwell, but we have to look."

She'd been thinking about that. "They're unlikely to have planned in advance for anything like this. I mean, Lissa was supposed to be alone. Unless they intended to grab her—" She shook her head. "But why would they?"

"That's why I'm concentrating on owned properties," Clay agreed. "You don't drive up and down country roads looking for a vacant house when you've got a kid stowed in the trunk of your car and you've got to be having a major panic attack. If there was a plan B, I doubt this was it."

That made sense. At the same time, she couldn't imagine anyone who would be a logical suspect being willing to hold a kidnap victim at a property with his name on it.

But what were the alternatives?

Clay spent some time assigning officers to check out addresses on his list. Jane eavesdropped on his instructions—they were to drive personal vehicles only, and to go home if necessary to change out of uniforms. If they found anything of interest, they were to call him immediately rather than make a move.

Once his cluster of detectives and deputies broke apart to fan out across two counties, Clay and she were able to leave. He drove, stopping at her apartment so she could change to jeans and boots and get her Ruger from her small gun safe.

In between Clay taking calls, the two of them got a look at a dozen possible properties, some surrepti-

tiously, some—like the time-share condominium—
directly. One by one, they checked them off the list.

The vacant cabin on Bear Creek was even more
run-down than Lissa had described it. Uninhabitable,
in Jane's opinion. She and Clay had left his Jeep at
the county park and made their way along the creek,
then through the woods, until they reached the clear-
ing where it stood.

"Cover me," he said finally, despite the sagging roof
that made it unlikely anyone would try to hold a captive inside. Nodding, Jane gripped her weapon while he
moved swiftly across the open ground to flatten himself on the back wall of the ramshackle cabin. Watching
him, she was struck again by the grace and athletic ease
of his stride. If she'd gone instead, she'd probably have
stepped on half a dozen dry branches that would have
cracked loudly, but Clay managed to move silently. Like
the soldier he'd been, she remembered, accustomed to
ghosting through enemy territory.

When she realized suddenly that he'd edged up to
a window, glanced in and was shaking his head at her
as he walked openly back in her direction, Jane was
embarrassed to realize how wholly she'd let herself be
distracted.

She holstered her weapon and raised her eyebrows
when he got near, hoping her cheeks hadn't flushed.

"One room," he reported. "Floor's rotting."

"I wonder how they knew it was a good place to
meet," Jane said thoughtfully.

His brows drew together. "Good question. I didn't
recognize the property owner's name, but I'll dig
deeper."

The sun was setting when, hungry and discouraged, they bought a pizza and took it back to Clay's cabin in the woods. While he got out plates and drinks, she escaped to his bathroom to clean up. She'd acquired a long scratch across her upper arm from a careless encounter with a branch that wasn't as flexible as she'd thought it would be. She gently washed it and used antiseptic she found in his medicine cabinet to bathe it, wincing at the sting. Then she took her hair out of the ponytail, brushed it with her fingers and put it back. Not a whole lot of improvement, she was afraid, inspecting herself in the mirror, but there was only so much she could do.

Clay's gaze went straight to the scratch. "Got you good," he observed.

She made a face at him as she sat down at the table and reached for a soda. "It's not fair. You're way bigger than I am, and no vegetation got in *your* way."

He grinned. "I had some serious training, you know. I told you I was an army ranger, didn't I?"

She nodded. She'd found the idea he had been special forces disturbing on a lot of levels.

"I grew up hiking, fishing, hunting, too," he added. "Even did some mountain climbing."

"Do you still hunt?" she asked, not sure she approved. Hypocritical though that was, when she was reaching for a slice of pizza with Canadian bacon on it.

And, oh, wow, it tasted good.

"No, that was Dad's thing. I prefer to buy my meat at the supermarket." Clay's mouth quirked. "I must have gotten that from my mother. I could see the dread in her eyes when we showed up with a dead deer in the bed of the pickup truck. I don't know if she was thinking about Bambi, or merely trying to figure out what she'd do with all those strange cuts of meat, but she wasn't enthusiastic. I don't think Dad ever noticed," he added reflectively.

"My father was not an outdoorsman," Jane said, wiping her fingers on a napkin. "I got excited when I biked to the park in town."

Clay nudged the pizza toward her. "That's actually as nice a stand of old-growth trees as you'll find anywhere."

"I thought it was spooky when I was a kid."

He polished off a slice of pizza. "Isn't that where Captain McAllister's wife was abducted when she was a teenager?"

"Yes. Did you hear about the bones that turned up last fall when a crew took down some of the trees infested with beetles?"

"Yeah. Hey." He looked interested. "Was it your investigation that early on?"

As they ate, she told him about it—finding a backpack with a pitiful store of belongings that turned out to be all a boy had owned in the world. A picture of himself with his mother, the Purple Heart his father had earned in Vietnam before dying over there. The poor kid had been killed the same night Maddie Dubeau had been attacked and disappeared so completely, it was as if she'd vanished from the face of the earth.

Like Bree, Jane thought with a shiver.

With his sharp gaze, Clay noticed. "You okay?"

"I was thinking of the parallel with Bree."

"Not the same," he said, in the gentle voice that

broke down her defenses. "Maddie—she's Nell now, isn't she?—came upon a genuine psychopath."

"My boss," she reminded him. Lieutenant Brewer had headed Investigative Services for the ABPD until the investigation she and Colin McAllister conducted closed in on him. Colin had shot the man he'd considered friend and mentor while she had braced herself and gripped Colin by the belt to keep him from falling out of the open door of the helicopter as he lined up the shot.

Clay's face darkened. "It's the worst when our own goes bad."

She couldn't argue. Finding out this past year how many cops, both city and county, had been on the payroll of drug traffickers had sent a shock wave through the local law enforcement community.

Clay pushed his plate away with an abrupt, almost angry movement. "Damn. I wish we didn't have to let up tonight."

Jane's meal suddenly felt indigestible. "Where do we go next?" she said.

"We keep looking. Other employees. Relatives. Friends."

"Because friends or relatives are eager to lend their ski cabin to hold a kidnapped child."

He looked sardonic. "Some people's friends might not be."

He couldn't very well say *your* friends or relatives might not be. Because they now knew what her closest relative was capable of doing.

"But these mostly look like such ordinary people," she argued, determined to prove her original point. "I mean, take Glenn Arnett. His daughter is at one of the top liberal arts colleges in the nation. He's a CPA. When I went online, I found a newspaper article about his wife chairing a fund-raiser for the senior center. Do you really think she knows how her husband is paying that college tuition?"

"Probably not," Clay admitted. "You're right. You have to wonder if people like Stillwell and his pet accountant even think of themselves as criminals. Maybe to them it's just business."

"Shouldn't we have someone following Stillwell and Arnett?" she asked abruptly.

"We're monitoring the comings and goings at the trucking company right now, including theirs." He sounded cautious. "Outside that... My guess is they're both keeping a healthy distance from a kidnapped child."

"Maybe." She'd been thinking, though. "Drug running is one thing, murder and kidnapping another."

His eyebrows rose. "They do tend to go hand in hand."

"That's true, but we don't have any reason to think Stillwell has ever had to commit either crime before."

"Granted," Clay said after a moment.

"So he's not likely to keep a strongman on the payroll."

His mouth twitched, as though he was amused by her description. "If our suspicions are right, he's in an ugly business. My bet is that he's had to do some intimidating or worse by now. A trucker who wants a raise or else, say. There might well be someone on the payroll who has arranged accidents for him."

"But this is different," she argued. "Closer to home.

And a little girl." Was it really him she was trying to convince? Or herself.

"I'll give you that," he said. "I've met some major scumbags who wouldn't consider killing a cute seven-year-old kid."

"So what if it's only the two of them who knew about Lissa's blackmail? How many people would they *want* to know that they'd screwed up and let some book-keeper see information that jeopardized the whole enterprise? If they're transporting illegal drugs, they're working with some rough people who expect discretion and competence. Stillwell and Arnett could have been desperate enough to decide to kill Lissa themselves. Keep the whole thing quiet. Maybe they intended it to look like an accident. When that didn't work out... well, plan B went into effect, but they're still trying to handle it on their own."

She half expected Clay to instantly discount her theory, but instead she could see him clicking through the possibilities, weighing them against what he knew about the two men.

"Yeah," he said at last. "I can see it. All right. You know there's some risk they'll spot a tail." He paused, watching her.

He was right—they'd been going to great lengths to avoid doing anything that would panic either Stillwell or Arnett. Even so...they *couldn't* let Bree go. If they hadn't already realized that kidnapping a kid had been really dumb, they were going to have an epiphany any minute. Being caught with Bree in their hands was the worst thing that could happen to them right now.

She gave a mental gulp but nodded.

Clay gave a small nod, warmth and sympathy in his eyes. "I'll put someone on them tomorrow. You and I can take over when they cut out of work."

She smiled at him. "Good."

"In the meantime," he stood and came around the table to pull her to her feet, "I'd like to kiss you." His voice had become husky.

"I can't stay," she said hastily. "Drew really does need someone he can talk to." Seeing Clay's frown, she laid a finger over her lips. "But I think I can spare another hour."

He groaned and rested his forehead against hers. "I guess I can settle for that."

"I feel guilty."

He lifted his head. "Because your niece is still missing and you don't feel like you should grab even a few minutes of happiness?"

She nodded.

"You know there's nothing more we can do tonight."

"I do know."

"Damn, Jane," he muttered, bending to press soft kisses on her forehead. "Do you know how much I want to wake up in the morning with you?"

Her heart gave a quick, hard squeeze. "No. But…I'd like that, too."

"Soon," he said against her lips.

"Yes," she whispered, just before his mouth claimed hers.

CHAPTER SIXTEEN

THE DRIVE-THROUGH at McDonald's? Really?

Nothing Jane had heard about Glenn Arnett made her think he was a fast-food kind of guy, but who knew? According to the deputies who'd spent the day in visual distance of Stillwell Trucking, neither he nor Stillwell had left the building since their arrivals that day at 8:12 a.m. and 7:43 a.m., respectively. Maybe Glenn had forgotten his lunch and was starved. Maybe his wife was planning a dinner party and he detested the entrée she'd insisted on.

Seeing that a couple of bags were being passed to him, Jane amended her speculation. Maybe he was taking dinner home.

Jane bent her head and pretended to be digging in her purse when the Escalade started forward almost directly toward where she was parked at the curb, signaled and made a left then accelerated away from her.

Her phone rang. Clay.

"Stillwell went by the hospital," he said tersely. "He's in there right now."

"Even if he gets in to Lissa…"

"What about Drew?"

"I primed him to tell anyone who asks that she doesn't remember what happened," Jane said.

"What's really worrying me are the nurses. We could have been overheard talking to your sister."

Oh, God. Jane didn't remember paying attention at all to whether anyone else was near. "Surely they're expected to be discreet."

His grunt echoed what she knew to be true—people liked to talk, and they especially liked to talk when they knew something no one else did.

"You got anything?" he asked.

"Arnett went through the McDonald's drive-through."

A moment of blank silence was followed by, "You're kidding."

"Nope. But we're moving again."

"All right." He was gone.

At the moment, the dark blue Escalade appeared to be en route to the Arnetts' home. Which was probably exactly where he was going, Jane thought, fear swooping toward her, a hawk casting a dark shadow as it descended.

This was going to be a bust. Jane knew it. She would spend the entire evening sitting a block from Arnett's house waiting for something to happen that never would. Of course a CPA wasn't checking daily on a kidnapped kid! Assuming he even knew about the kidnapping. Once Lissa had started blackmailing Stillwell, he'd probably made a phone call and said, "Take care of her." He might be agitated now because whoever was supposed to do the job had failed so abysmally, but that didn't mean he knew anything about Bree's whereabouts or what Lissa had seen or not seen.

And Arnett? Drug traffickers hired muscle for the ugly stuff; they didn't send their accountant, for heaven's sake.

She and Clay were running out of ideas. *Oh, Bree.*

She tuned sharply back in when she realized the Escalade had not made the logical turn to take Glenn Arnett to his house a block from the Deschutes River in Old Town Angel Butte. Instead he was continuing sedately toward the outskirts of town.

Taking the burgers and fries to his son at work? She had no idea if the boy—Josh, if memory served her— even had an after-school job.

But they passed the city limits, generously drawn after last year's annexation, and Jane was forced to drop even farther back as cars she'd been hovering behind turned off. The road narrowed and acquired a yellow line down the middle. There'd been some development out here, but mostly of houses on at least one-acre lots. The land was becoming forested, which meant as the road wound, she lost sight of the Escalade. Plus side was, he would be less likely to notice her behind him.

She came around a bend and her pulse picked up when she saw only open road ahead. No—another road turned off to the right only. A flicker of red brake lights reassured her, and she turned, too. Now there was no other vehicle between them. She told herself he'd have no reason to guess she was working the case or that he was a suspect, and even if he did, he was unlikely to know what she drove. Besides, half the people in central Oregon drove sports utility vehicles of one kind or another.

It was another half a mile before he turned again, this

time into a driveway that cut through a stand of ponderosa pines beyond which was a vast swath of lawn. Jane
slowed to verify that the Escalade was indeed slowing
and stopping in front of a two-story house with a steep
pitched roof and a three-car garage. She automatically
took in the address on the side of the mailbox before
she continued past, debating her next step.

Turn into the next driveway, she decided. With luck,
nobody would be home.

At least nobody was outside. Trees screened the
house from the neighbor's, enough that she doubted
Glenn would notice a vehicle parked here. She had to
get out and walk partway through the narrow band of
woods to see him on the porch, the bags from McDonald's in his hand. She couldn't tell whether he was using
a key to let himself into the house, or whether someone
had opened the door. A moment later, he'd disappeared
inside and the door closed.

Her phone vibrated. Walking back to her Yukon, she
answered. "Clay?"

"Stillwell still hasn't come out," he said. "What about
Arnett?"

She told him where she was. He promised to call
back as soon as he had the owner's name. Jane took
the time to trot up to the front porch of the house she
sat in front of and ring the doorbell, manufacturing
a cover story as she waited. To her relief, no one appeared to be home.

Clay called before anything happened next door. A
Gerald and Helen Taylor owned the property in question. With Jane still on the line, Clay looked up DMV
records and was able to tell her that Gerald was sixty-

nine, his wife a year older. Clean driving records, no criminal history.

"Wait," she said, interrupting him midword. "The garage door is opening."

"Jane, can he see you?"

She ignored his alarmed question. "He's pushing a ride-on lawn mower out." Arnett disappeared into the recesses of the garage again and reemerged with a red gas can.

He'd changed clothes, she realized belatedly, and was now dressed for yard work.

"Okay, this is really strange."

"What's so strange? He gobbled a quick burger and fries and now he's going to mow the lawn."

"Gerald Taylor's lawn. Why would he do that?"

"Friends?"

"This is a really upscale house. People like this hire a lawn service when they're away, they don't ask their accountant buddy to stop by and mow."

"Crap," Clay said suddenly. "There's Stillwell. He's walking fast, and he doesn't look happy. He's getting into his Land Rover." Pause. "Already has his phone to his ear."

The mower next door started with a roar. Arnett's back was to her as he steered the mower in a straight line toward the far property line. As smooth as that lawn was, he couldn't be cutting more than a quarter inch or so. People who didn't water their lawns weren't having to bother mowing at all this late in the summer.

"Hold on," Jane said, set down the phone and grabbed her binoculars. There was definitely a vehicle in the garage. She wanted to see it. If she got a little closer…

"Jane?"

"I'll call you back," she said and cut the connection.

She made her way between trees, glad she didn't have to worry about whether she made noise or not. By the time she got into a better position to see into the garage, the mower was heading her way, and she tried to make herself skinny behind the bole of the largest tree. The roar grew louder as she stayed completely still, her body locked with tension. Then the sound changed subtly and she eased to the side to see that Glenn had started back the way he'd come.

Carefully, she lifted the binoculars, first surveying the house. Drapes and blinds at several of the windows were closed. Nobody was visible through the few uncovered windows.

Then she focused on the opening into the three-car garage.

What she saw sent her racing back to her SUV. She couldn't take a chance of the mower cutting out and Glenn overhearing her voice. She took a minute to do some online research before she called Clay back.

"Goddamn it!" he roared. "Where the hell did you go?"

"Clay, listen to me."

"No, you listen to me. I think Stillwell is on his way to the Taylors'. We're not five minutes away."

"Clay," she said, "I got a look into the garage. The first bay is empty. That's where Arnett took the mower out through. The one car I can see in there is a Lexus. And it's silver."

He swore again, then said, "Who are these people?"

"I think they're Glenn's parents-in-law. Remember I

mentioned that article in the paper about his wife chairing the event? I had this niggle of a memory and I just went back and looked it up again. Her name is Lois Taylor Arnett."

"What if Mom and Dad are away?" Clay had calmed down, but she didn't fool herself that he was relaxed. "Great place to stash the kid, and Glenn even has an excuse to go out there regularly."

"That's what I'm thinking."

"Where are you?"

She told him. Not a minute later, a vehicle turned into the Taylors' driveway. Through the trees, she saw it was a shiny SUV, a sort of pearlescent tan. Stillwell drove a Land Rover, she remembered.

Itching to sneak through the woods and get a better look, she waited for Clay's Jeep.

"Jane?"

She jumped six inches. He was standing right beside her open driver's side door. "You sneaked up on me!"

"I parked across the road. Let's get where we can see what's happening."

Once again she was reduced to trailing him through the narrow band of woods, wishing she had the ability to move as silently and surreptitiously as he did. His khaki-colored chinos and brown polo shirt were good camouflage, too. Her jeans and green T-shirt were subtly wrong, the green just a little too bright.

The ride-on mower abruptly fell silent and she winced as a branch cracked under her foot right then.

But when she followed Clay's example and knelt beside him as they reached the last hint of anything that could be called a blind, a clump of what she thought were salmonberries, she realized it didn't matter what she was wearing or what small sounds she'd made in getting close. The mower abandoned twenty feet away, the two men stood face-to-face in the driveway, engaged in an intense conversation. Neither was looking around.

Stillwell gestured sharply toward the house. Arnett scowled and appeared to argue. Stillwell's next gesture, a slice of his hand, was even more emphatic. Expression unhappy, Arnett nodded.

"Jesus," Clay murmured. "There's someone else in the house."

"What?"

"Eleven o'clock."

It had to be a bedroom window. She couldn't make out more than fingers parting the blinds enough for someone to watch the scene in the driveway.

Not a child, she realized right away, or probably even a woman. Whoever it was had to be tall.

"That son of a bitch is going to leave."

Jane switched her attention back to the driveway, where Stillwell was indeed backing away.

Glenn Arnett looked angry. He must have raised his voice, because, straining, Jane caught a few words. "Why am I…?"

"Because you're the idiot who left your laptop where anyone could browse through it," Clay said under his breath.

James Stillwell snapped a reply she couldn't make out, got into his Land Rover, backed in a semicircle and drove away. Arnett watched him go, his face suffused with fiery red and his hands knotted into fists.

Clay lowered his binoculars, his expression grim. "I should have called for backup. Hell. A warrant."

"You think he was just ordered to get rid of her."

His gaze met hers squarely. "You have a different interpretation?"

After a moment, she shook her head. Her heart drummed. Not only did they lack backup, they also had no idea how many people were in that house, how well armed they were, even in what part of the house Bree was being held. They each had one handgun, one magazine each, no flash bangs to confuse their opponents or any other embroidery on the basics.

With sudden terror, she knew Clay would insist they wait. He hadn't wanted her being part of the raid to rescue Matt Raynor. He'd never accept her, a woman, as his partner in a high-risk operation like this one, where they'd be going in blind.

A low, viciously uttered expletive came to her ears. She switched her panicked gaze to Glenn Arnett in time to see him swing around and stalk toward the open garage.

"Clay," she whispered. Begged, when her whole body strained to tear across the swath of lawn and follow Arnett into the dim interior of the garage.

CLAY COULD NOT freaking believe this was happening. Gazing down at Jane's face, radiating intensity and desperation, he allowed himself one stricken moment of fear.

He could lose her. Have to watch her go down.

There was no chance to try for more complete intelligence, summon backup, arm themselves better. He'd give anything for a tactical vest—for Jane. He had one in the back of his Jeep…but Arnett was disappearing from sight, and they couldn't spare even the couple of minutes it would take him to make his way to the road and back.

Either Arnett would prove to have enough conscience that he wouldn't be able to bring himself to kill a little girl, or he'd do it fast, to get it over with. Or, hell, he'd order whatever scumbag was upstairs to kill the kid, so he could convince himself his own hands were still clean.

No time to do anything but go. Clay shoved the fear for Jane down deep. He couldn't afford it right now. The truth was, he knew he was damn lucky he wasn't here alone. Or—worse—that Jane was here alone. At least they'd had practice at this kind of rescue operation, Clay reasoned. And whether he liked the idea of her in danger or not, he'd seen her in action and knew she was good.

He had the fleeting memory of thinking he wanted her at his side pretty much always. *Watch what you wish for.*

Yeah…but he couldn't offhand think of another cop he'd rather have at his back.

The soft sound of the door at the back of the garage opening and closing came to him.

"Shit," he said again, and grabbed his cell phone. "Raynor?" he said a moment later. "I think you need to move on Stillwell Trucking. Now."

Relief transformed Jane's face.

"You found the girl?" Raynor asked.

"We think so. One way or another, they're going to

know in the next two minutes that we're onto them. I suspect Stillwell is on his way back to the office to begin that shredding we talked about."

"Then we'll beat him there." Chief Raynor sounded satisfied. "Good luck."

"Thanks." Clay raised his eyebrows at Jane as he stowed the phone. "You ready?"

"Yes!"

Clay grabbed her, kissed her hard, then said, "Let's do it."

No one was visible now through the window upstairs. He saw no movement behind any others. He turned and ran, hearing Jane close behind. He stopped to one side of the open garage door and waited until she flattened herself on the other. Then, weapons drawn, they went in together.

The garage was utterly silent, a couple of overhead bulbs on, a small square of sunlight at the far end where there was a window. A white SUV was parked on the other side of the Lexus. At the back of the empty bay was a closed interior door.

Clay jerked his head toward it. Jane nodded. They moved swiftly and silently across the concrete floor. There were two steps up to the door. Clay went first, turning the knob slowly, easing the door open a crack. All he could see was a white interior wall.

"Arnett?" a man called, voice sounding hollow in the way they did in a building with high ceilings. "That you?"

"Yeah, I'm on my way up." The second voice wasn't coming from far away.

Clay opened the door and stepped into a hallway,

turning with his weapon held ready in both hands. Jane followed. Out of the corner of his eye he saw her flatten a hand on the door to make sure it closed slowly and silently.

Clay didn't even have to signal. They both moved down the hall to where they could see open space. A living room with vaulted ceiling, a vast kitchen and a slate-tiled entry all converged with a staircase.

In theory, he and Jane should clear this floor, make sure they weren't leaving anyone behind them, but a driving sense of urgency told him they didn't have time. He kept remembering looking at Glenn Arnett and *knowing* on a subliminal level that the guy was utterly cold-blooded. He might not want to murder a child; he'd raised two of his own after all. But he'd see the act as what he had to do to protect his children, his wife, the privileged life he had built.

The staircase was clear. Clay could hear voices upstairs now. Two? More?

He raised two fingers. Jane frowned and held up three. After a moment, Clay grimaced. They'd find what they found.

Too bad this wasn't a mansion with a back staircase for the servants. They had no choice but to openly climb the stairs and hope no one hovered above in the hall.

Yeah, and hope Arnett didn't head straight for wherever he had Bree stashed and shoot her before Clay and Jane could get that far.

The two of them climbed side by side. A faint creak came from under his feet, or maybe hers. They both froze momentarily. Heard nothing from above but low male voices.

Would Arnett go for something as messy as a gun-shot? This was his parents-in-law's house. He was sophisticated enough to know it was difficult to im-possible to ensure no trace of blood had seeped into a crack behind molding or soaked the carpet pad and subflooring beneath it.

Maybe he'd carry her out with the plan of doing it elsewhere.

There was a creak and a scraping sound. Somebody swore.

Jesus, Clay thought. Chilled, it occurred to him that one twist of Arnett's hands would break a seven-year-old child's neck. From the alarm Clay saw on Jane's face, she was thinking something similar.

Taller than her, he was the first to see the hallway. Empty.

"Clear," he mouthed to her, and they took the last few steps faster, then started down the hall.

"Man, I don't want anything to do with this," a man's voice said, close enough to raise the hair on Clay's nape. "I thought we were going to let the kid go."

"Yeah? You sure she hasn't seen your face?"

The barrel of Jane's Ruger swiveled toward the last doorway on their right. Master bedroom, Clay thought. It would have its own bathroom. Logical place to stash a hostage. Usually en suite bathroom doors didn't have even a push-button lock. The door would open inward, though. The men had blocked it somehow from the out-side. Removing that impediment was taking them the minute or two that kept them too distracted to watch out for anyone else entering the house.

Clay reached the door. Flattened himself against the

wall beside it, Jane hovering. After a moment, he took a quick look. Only two men were visible. One—Arnett— had his back to Clay. The other had stepped aside, but had his head turned to watch Arnett, who was shifting a piece of plywood away from the doorway.

"This is a damned nuisance," Arnett was grumbling.

"*You* think it's a nuisance?" the second man said. "You're not the one who had to drag that chest of drawers back and forth."

Clay held up two fingers to Jane, but bent his head and murmured in her ear, "Can't see the whole room."

She nodded.

"I'll go for them. You sweep the room."

Another nod.

Clay went fast through the doorway to clear the way for Jane. "Police!" he said loudly. "Put your hands in the air!"

A gun went off. The bullet slapped into the wallboard so close, Clay felt the sting of wood and gypsum shrapnel. He didn't let himself take his eyes from the two men who were his targets. At his back, Jane fired and Clay heard a grunt of pain. She was yelling something, but he ignored that, too.

The man with Arnett was snatching a handgun off the bed.

"Put the weapon down," Clay ordered as he crossed the width of the bedroom. It lifted toward him and he squeezed the trigger. Once. Twice. The son of a bitch went down, the gun falling from his hand. Glenn Arnett had flattened himself with his back to the bathroom door and his arms over his head

"Don't shoot! Don't shoot!"

"Down," Clay snapped. He used his foot to shove the big black handgun under the bed, where no one could dive for it. "On the floor. That's it. Spread-eagle."

Once Arnett was facedown, his fingers gripped the pile of the oat-colored carpet tight enough to rip fibers free.

"You have cuffs?" Jane asked.

"Back pocket." The scum sprawled a few feet away from Arnett was bleeding, but he wasn't dead. Clay kept his weapon trained on both men.

He felt Jane's hand slide into his pocket and pull the plastic handcuff ties out. Too bad he only had one set.

A moment later, he heard her voice. "Backup requested." She was on the phone. He listened as she gave the address, told the dispatcher that two men had suffered gunshot wounds, aide cars requested.

The next moment she raced past Clay and around Glenn Arnett and reached for the bathroom doorknob.

Clay moved so he could cover all three men.

"Bree?" Jane called, her voice shaking. "Are you in there? It's Aunt Jane. I don't want to scare you coming in."

The silence chilled Clay. He didn't even want to know what it did to Jane.

What if she wasn't here? What if—?

"Is it really you?" came a small voice.

A sob of relief escaped Jane and she shoved the bathroom door open. "Bree. Oh, Bree. Oh, my God. Look at you. Oh, Bree." Tears thickened her voice. Clay saw her fall to her knees and then all but crawl to where a small figure was squeezed behind the toilet.

Clay felt a sting in his own eyes. Only the rage that filled him kept him from breaking down.

"You're slime," he said gutturally, when Arnett turned his head so he didn't have to watch the reunion taking place within. "Your life as you know it is over."

"I came to see what was going on in the house," he cried. "This wasn't me. It was Stillwell. He knew the house was empty and he's been using it. I saw somebody upstairs—"

"Save the bullshit for your attorney."

The first, distant sound of a siren came to Clay's ears as he began, "You have the right to remain silent."

JANE SAT ON the bathroom floor, her back to a wall, and held her niece who clung to her as if she was a lifebuoy in a raging ocean.

Bree cried in horrible, gulping sobs of terror she had been suppressing. "I thought you'd *never* come!" she wailed at one point.

Jane knew her own cheeks were wet, too. "It took us a long time to find you," she explained, then went back to murmuring things like, "Oh, Bree. I've been so scared."

In her first, sweeping assessment, she hadn't been able to tell whether the little girl had been hurt. Bree had looked so small, so skinny, her hair tangled and wild, her expression torn between disbelief and hope. And then she'd wriggled out from behind the toilet and thrown herself at Jane, the small body smacking against Jane's and knocking her back on her butt.

Since then, all Jane could do was hold her and wait for the storm to abate. Thank God, Clay had remained in her line of sight, most of his attention on the three men he held at gunpoint, but every so often his gaze shifted to hers and she saw everything she felt in his eyes.

"Oh, sweetheart. Your mom and dad have been so scared, too. I can hardly wait to tell them you're safe and coming home."

Bree went very still before she rubbed her face on Jane's T-shirt and cautiously peered up from between swollen lids. "Mommy isn't dead?" she whispered. "I thought she was dead."

"No." Jane bent her head and kissed her forehead. "She was knocked out, and it was days before she woke up and could tell us what she remembered. But she's going to be fine, Bree. I promise."

"Oh." The wiry body in her arms sagged and Bree laid her cheek back against Jane's breast.

Voices brought her head up. The bedroom suddenly swarmed with EMTs and uniformed deputies. Glenn Arnett was pulled roughly to his feet, handcuffed and led away. The medics applied bandages to the two injured men, shifted them onto gurneys, lifted them and then they disappeared, too.

Jane realized with a funny feeling of panic that she had lost sight of Clay. But no sooner did she think that than he filled the bathroom doorway, something in his hand.

"Nice to meet you, Brianna Wilson," he said, in an astonishingly gentle voice. He held out his phone. "I kind of thought the two of you might want to make a call."

A spurt of tears blinded Jane. Coming into the bathroom and crouching right beside them, Clay gave a low chuckle. "How about if I get Bree's daddy on the line for you?"

Jane's head bobbed. Bree was staring at Clay with that same look of dazed hope.

A moment later, Jane heard a ring, then a second. On the fourth, Drew answered.

"Sergeant Renner?" His voice sounded far away.

Clay carefully wrapped Bree's fingers around the phone. She raised it to her ear.

"Daddy?" she whispered. "Daddy, it's me."

CHAPTER SEVENTEEN

"Jane found Bree." Drew stood beside his wife's bed. His voice was rough with emotion. "She's okay, Lissa. She's safe."

She stared at him incredulously. Tears welled in her eyes and began to overflow, dripping toward her ears and the pillow. "Then it's all over?" she whispered.

"Over?" He really never had known this woman. It was odd to feel such a strange detachment where she was concerned. "It's not over for Bree. Who knows what they did to her? What aftereffects she'll suffer?" He made a gruff sound. "For me? No, I think it's safe to say nothing will ever be the same for me. It's not even over for your sister, or for Sergeant Renner. They both shot and wounded men to rescue Bree. They took some chances today and their careers may be impacted." His jaw muscles flexed. "And it's especially not over for you, Liss. You admitted to extortion. Chances are good you'll be arrested, tried and convicted. No juror or judge is going to be sympathetic, not after hearing that you knew your employer was running illegal drugs and, instead of going to authorities, you decided you deserved a cut of the money he was earning."

Her mouth worked. Shock and the sheen of tears made her eyes even more beautiful. Drew was not moved.

"But...I thought..."

"What? That Sergeant Renner would feel sorry for you because you got banged on the head and had to worry about your daughter for a few days?"

He didn't remember ever stunning her speechless before.

"I've got to go," he said. "Bree's being brought into the emergency room. Jane wants her checked over. I need to be there when she arrives."

Jane herself wasn't coming with Bree. Because they'd discharged their weapons, she had explained, both she and Clay had to stay on scene. A young female deputy was bringing Bree. Jane had promised to follow as soon as she could.

"Will you bring her...?" Lissa pleaded.

"Yeah. Bree will want to see you. She told me she thought you were dead."

His back was to her when she said, "I thought I was doing the right thing for us."

Drew closed his eyes for a moment, swallowed and turned. He felt so much he couldn't identify it all, and yet at the same time was curiously empty of the emotions he might expect to feel.

"Nothing you did was for us." Her face was stricken, stunned again; he wondered if it was all an act. "There hasn't been any 'us' for a long time, has there, Lissa?"

"But...does this mean you're...you're *leaving* me?" The way she had to fumble for words, he could tell this much shock was genuine.

Until now, he hadn't even known he'd decided. Not that long ago, he'd thought if she regained consciousness and Bree was home safe, he could forgive Lissa anything. He'd been wrong.

"Yes, I am. Not right away. As long as you're out on bail, you can stay at the house. In the guest room. We'll try to figure out how to pay for an attorney for you. But the house is going up for sale as soon as I can get it listed. The next decent job offer I get, I'm taking. And when I move, the girls are going with me. You're not a fit mother," he finished, flatly.

"You can't—" Washed with tears, her face contorted.

"I can," he said, and walked out on her. It was like ripping away a body part. Excruciatingly painful, and yet…freeing.

They had been married for nine years, and she was a stranger.

He left ICU, his steps hastening until he was almost running. Bree was safe. He would soon be able to hold her.

Miracles happened.

SEVERAL EXHAUSTING HOURS later, night had fallen when Clay walked Jane to her SUV, which had been moved by a deputy from the neighbor's property to the long driveway of the Taylor house.

Things would have gone much worse, she was convinced, if Alec Raynor hadn't arrived to support Jane by his mere presence and to assure Clay's lieutenant that, yes, he had loaned Lieutenant Vahalik to a joint operation. He kept repeating that he knew it was unusual to allow her to participate in an investigation on a matter pertaining to her own family, but he had felt confident she would maintain her professionalism. He'd explained that, in conjunction with Sergeant Renner and Lieutenant Vahalik's recent actions, Captain McAllister and a team had moved on Stillwell Trucking and Glenn Arnett's home, using already secured search warrants. He had added that he understood Mr. Arnett's laptop computer was providing a wealth of information that suggested illegal activities, or, at the very least, evidence that considerable income had been hidden from Internal Revenue Service scrutiny. Word had gone out to the state patrol in five states suggesting that any trucks belonging to the company be stopped and thoroughly searched, preferably using drug-sniffing dogs.

She and Clay had been asked to explain every move they had made over the past several days, every decision made, every thought, then had to repeat themselves. And do it again. She had a suspicion they would both have been in deep shit were it not for the obviously successful result of their impromptu rescue operation. Bree was safe with her father. After the length of time she'd been missing, nobody had really believed she would be recovered alive.

It helped, too, that all three men she and Clay had brought down were vociferously blaming each other and James Stillwell. Or that Jane and Clay both had heard one of the men insist he wanted no part in hurting Bree, while Arnett had retorted, "You sure she hasn't seen your face?"

Stillwell had been picked up and, of course, was proclaiming ignorance of all activities concerning Melissa Wilson, her missing child and the evidence that his company's trucks had been moving unnamed cargo on a regular basis. He insisted Mrs. Wilson was lying, that the checks he had written to her were loans, as he had described to Sergeant Renner. Nobody was very interested in his denials. How much of the extra income had made its way into his own bank accounts would be uncovered by forensic accountants.

Arnett's wife was reportedly in shock.

Thank God, Jane and Clay had finally been allowed to leave. She didn't remember ever having been so exhausted. Her knees were actually wobbly. Alec Raynor had walked partway out with them, bent his head in what looked like respect and said, "Good work tonight, Jane, Clay," after which he'd gotten into his SUV and departed.

Clay had asked her for a lift to his Jeep, which was still tucked away somewhere down the road. Thus Jane turned right out of the driveway rather than toward town. A moment later, her headlights picked out the glint of metal, where his vehicle was pulled into a mostly overgrown track that went nowhere.

She pulled in behind it.

Clay looked at her, the dashboard lights doing little to illuminate the craggy planes of his face. "Will you come home with me, Jane?"

"I promised Bree—"

"You can't tell me she isn't tucked into bed by now."

"And there's Lissa," she said weakly.

Clay didn't say anything.

Somehow she hadn't expected the moment of truth to arrive so soon. She'd dimly thought Clay would call tomorrow and ask her out. But *her* truth was that she wanted nothing else in the world right now so much as to go home with him. To climb into bed with him, make love with him, wake in the morning with him.

"Let me call Drew," she said, then waited a suspicious moment to find out whether Clay would get bullish and possessive.

He only nodded.

Drew answered right away. "Bree's asleep," he reported. "She asked Alexis to sleep with her. They're all cuddled up together."

"She's really all right."

"Yeah." He sounded as bemused and jubilant both as she felt. "According to the doctor, there's no sign she was molested or that anyone hit her. She lost some weight. Sounds like they only fed her once a day. Given that she was in a bathroom, she did a pretty good job keeping herself clean. She even found a toothbrush. No hairbrush or comb, though. It took me a while to work the knots out of her hair."

"Did Lissa get to see her?"

"It was quite a reunion." He was quiet for a moment. "Our marriage is over, Jane."

Understanding tangled with grief. "I thought it might be."

"I told her she can expect to be arrested. I'll do my best to help with legal expenses, but otherwise I'm done."

Despite everything, tears stung Jane's eyes. "I don't blame you."

"I expected to hear from you sooner. You're not in trouble, are you?"

"I'm not sure yet," she admitted. "But I don't think

so. Clay might be in more trouble for letting me get involved the way he did."

"Tell him thank you," her brother-in-law said, voice husky. "If not for him—"

"I'll tell him." Her decision wasn't all that hard to make. "I'm spending the night at his place."

"I thought you might be." She heard resignation in Drew's voice. "Bree'll want to see you in the morning."

"I want to see her, too. Um…you know she'll probably have nightmares."

"They're both tucked into my bed. I wanted them close tonight."

"I'll see you in the morning, then."

"I owe you thanks, too, Jane."

"No. I love Bree, you know that."

"I do know." His voice had softened. "See you."

She ended the call and looked at Clay. "Okay."

"Good." He smiled. "Follow me?"

She nodded dumbly, even as she wondered what had happened to all her doubts about him. Did she really believe he'd changed so much from the man who'd stood in the bull pen summing up the size of her breasts with his hands while verbally reducing her to nothing but a sex object?

He leaned over, kissed her cheek and got out, striding into the deeper shadows where he had parked.

Yes. Yes, she trusted him.

Jane didn't even want to think about how much he could hurt her if it turned out she was wrong.

"Is IT CRASS of me to tell you I'm starved?" Clay asked, as soon as he let them in his front door. He wanted her desperately, but something told him they both needed to decompress.

"I gave thought to detouring through a fast-food place. Lunch is a distant memory."

"Let me see what I've got." He led the way to the kitchen, conscious of a deep sense of satisfaction that she was here and apparently prepared to stay the night.

Was it too soon to ask if she'd stay *every* night from here on out?

Was he sure that was what he wanted?

Stupid question; he was pretty sure he'd been a goner from his first sight of her face. Look how long he'd been celibate, waiting for her.

They decided on a lasagna from the grocery store freezer case, agreeing that the speed it could be heated in the microwave trumped all other considerations. Jane made a salad while he sliced a loaf of sourdough bread, buttered it and rubbed it with a clove of garlic he'd crushed.

Watching him, she smiled impishly, that small dimple appearing. "And here I thought you were the kind of man who'd use garlic salt."

"Gourmet all the way, that's me."

She made a face at him. "Is this the moment to confess that, ninety percent of the time, I eat microwaveable meals?"

"Too late. I know you can cook."

"You know…? Oh, the spaghetti."

"Gave yourself away." The microwave dinged and he slid the lasagna in its disposable plastic container onto a cork-backed tile and carried it to the table.

A minute later, they were both dishing up and diving in. Clay kept an eye on her, glad to see the stress falling away as she ate and also sipped cautiously at the merlot he'd opened.

She'd eaten only half the food on her plate when she suddenly set down her fork. "I can't believe we found her. I wouldn't let myself consciously think it, but—"

Even now, she couldn't say it.

"You thought she was dead. That we were too late."

"Didn't you?"

Clay shook his head. "No. You put your finger on it when you pointed out that Stillwell and Arnett were amateurs, in a way. They were committing a crime, but bloodlessly, from a distance. Add some extra truck runs, turn a blind eye, put the money through some gymnastics so its origins weren't obvious. Your sister didn't use her head when she thought she could manipulate them, though. They only had three choices at that point—pay her, potentially forever, shut down the illegal part of the business and lose that really nice extra money, or shut her up. Even then, I'm betting they were too squeamish to talk about killing her. 'Take care of her' was probably as blunt as their vocabulary got."

"It was Arnett who was supposed to do it, wasn't it?"

"That's my guess," he agreed. "Don't know if anybody has found a gun yet, or whether he had something else in mind. Maybe figured he could make her death look like an accident. When she didn't keep the rendezvous and instead kept right on going, he probably panicked. Seeing her go off the road, that must have looked like providence. Given just a minute, he could have smashed her head a little harder against the glass, broken her neck, who knows."

Jane shuddered. "But instead, he discovered she hadn't come alone."

"Worse yet, Bree must have jumped out when she saw her mom unconscious and bleeding and scrambled up to the road. He might have killed her, too, tossed her down the bank, then finished off your sister. Only instead, he's suddenly got these hikers popping out down the road and running along the shoulder toward him. Another car's coming. All he can think to do is grab Bree, stuff her in the trunk and take off. He's sweating and praying Lissa is dead."

"But then they find out she's not."

"Right. They deluded themselves that Bree was insurance, until reality sank in and they realized there was no way they could ever let this kid go. Bree probably did see Arnett before he grabbed her, and she might even have recognized him from one of those company picnics."

"I'm assuming somebody has asked her questions by now."

"It doesn't really matter whether she recognized him or not. How could he be sure? What if he'd screwed up and there was something in the bathroom, like an old prescription bottle with his mother-in-law's name on it? As frantic as he was by then, I doubt he did much but toss her in there, figure out how to keep her from getting out and then call his boss to confess to a disaster in the making."

One thing they had learned this evening: Lois Arnett said her parents had been gone for much of the summer on their dream trip, driving their RV to Alaska and back. Glenn had told her he'd gone by the Taylors' house to check on it and that the yard looked like hell. He'd fired the landscapers and promised her he'd get the lawn and flower beds back in shape before her parents returned toward the end of September.

Reportedly, she had sounded shell-shocked when she said, "He wouldn't let me help. He said Mom and Dad had been good to him, and this was something he could do as payback."

The detective who had interviewed her believed she'd been genuinely ignorant of her husband's activities. Clay felt a little sorry for her and for their kids. He wondered if the daughter was going to be able to stay at her expensive private college.

Clay pushed his chair back from the table now and held out a hand to Jane. "Hey. Come here."

She'd regained enough spirit to eye him suspiciously. "Is that an order?"

He chuckled. "I figure I'm too big to sit on your lap."

Her chin came back down. "You'd squish me." She went to him, wriggling a couple of times to settle herself comfortably on his thighs, then leaning against him with a long sigh.

He rubbed his cheek against her hair and wrapped both arms around her. He was aroused, and she must know he was, but for the moment he didn't feel any sense of urgency. Just having her here was enough. Holding her. He felt a sense of rightness, of peace, and guessed from the almost boneless way she curled into him she felt something similar.

They sat there for a couple of minutes before he tipped his head so he could see her face. "Better?"

"Yes. Although it's all… I don't even know. Overwhelming. I mean, I'm relieved, but—" her shoulders moved "—Lissa has totally screwed up her life. And… and I want to fix it for her, but I can't."

"Do you really want to?"

Jane was quiet for a bit. "No," she admitted finally, her voice soft and sad. "I always made excuses for her. You know? But this time…I can't."

"No," he murmured, hurting for her.

"I wonder—"

A spark of temper had him lifting his head. "Don't say you wonder whether this is *your* fault in some way."

Jane pushed away from him, one hand planted on his chest. "I wasn't going to! Although, shouldn't I? I mean, I mostly raised her."

"And did your damnedest to fix everything that was wrong." He knew he sounded hard, but how else to stamp down on her guilt?

Instead of getting mad, she sagged. "I did. I tried so hard."

"Damn it." He gathered her close again, nuzzling aside hair so he could kiss her temple. "I don't think I can stand to see you beat yourself up."

"Well, I wasn't going to," she said with dignity. "What I was really going to say was that I wonder how much I blinded myself to. I wanted to believe there was just tension between the two of us. But I was mostly satisfied. I mean, look at her, she has a great marriage, fantastic kids, likes her job. So what if she resents me?"

"Most of those years, what you saw probably *was* the truth. Your sister did have fantastic kids, and probably a pretty good marriage, and, yeah, a job that satisfied her."

"What I never knew is that she wanted more, and had no moral governor to stop her."

Jane nestled her head into the crook of his neck.

Sensing her need for silence, Clay gave it to her.

"Maybe I should cut her off," she said finally, "but I don't think I can."

"Tell me you don't plan to bankrupt yourself to pay for her legal defense."

"No." This sigh stirred every corpuscle in his body. "She doesn't deserve that."

Hell, no, she didn't. Once Clay wouldn't have seen parallels with himself. Now he had no trouble understanding how you could love someone who was undeserving. No, he wouldn't be cutting his father off, either.

But he also understood that he needed to love a woman who he liked and admired, whose opinion he valued. That wasn't something he'd ever seen in his parents' marriage. He wasn't sure he'd even believed anything better was possible.

Until Jane.

He kissed her cheek and laid it on the line. "I love you, Jane."

She went so still, he'd swear she had quit breathing. Finally she shifted on his thighs until she could see his face. "You mean that."

"Yeah." Hell, he had a lump the size of a chestnut in his throat. "You know I do."

She searched his face, her expression...enigmatic. He absolutely could not tell what she was thinking. Waiting to find out was killing him.

"You...disappointed me," she said, so softly he wouldn't have heard her if she'd still been sitting on the other side of the table. He started to open his mouth, but she stopped him with her forefinger laid on his lips. "You hurt me," she finished, even more quietly.

"I know I did." His voice sounded as if it was being dragged over gravel and he was bleeding. "I'll never forget the expression on your face."

"When we first met, I thought—" Jane shrugged awkwardly. "I thought maybe I'd finally gotten lucky. You made me feel things."

He squeezed his eyes shut for a painful moment. "I know."

"So…who are you, Clay?"

He suddenly realized he was fighting for his life here. He had to get this right.

"I think you know that, too," he said finally. "You've helped me uncover the man I can be. I've had to slough off a lot of the crap I was taught growing up. Earlier…" He hesitated. "I was thinking how good it is to love someone who *does* deserve everything I can give her. I love my parents, but I always hold something back. The women I used to get involved with—the relationships replicated my parents'. I never felt a lot of respect for any of them. They might not have known that consciously, but somewhere inside they probably did. You challenge me. I like that," he said simply, then shook his head. "No. I *love* that. I love you." He swallowed, feeling defenseless and hating it, but knowing there was no choice but to bare himself. Not if he was to earn her trust. "I want you to love me more than I can ever remember wanting anything."

Her eyes filled with tears. "I do, Clay. Of course I

do. You couldn't have hurt me so much if I hadn't been falling in love with you even back then."

"God," he said, and kissed her. The way their lips met was hungry and desperate, but also gentle. He ached with an emotion he hardly recognized, but could only label as tenderness. Lust was there, but then it always was when Jane was near. His tongue touched the soft places in her mouth, and hers did the same in his. Eventually he rained kisses along her jaw, over her plush cheek, onto the bridge of her nose, the closed lids of her eyes. "I love you," he whispered. "I love you."

Tasting the salt of her tears scared him, but she was smiling radiantly when he pulled back to see what had gone wrong. Jane sniffed and swiped at her cheeks. "I swear I'm not a crybaby. I should be mad that you make me cry."

Clay laughed, bending to touch his forehead to hers. "It's only fair. I was thinking a minute ago that around you I feel like I've lost a few layers of skin and every nerve is exposed."

She blinked. "That sounds painful."

"No." His mouth tilted up, if wryly. "Frightening."

"Oh," she breathed, her eyes such pools of emotion, he had the stupidly sappy idea he could keep looking into them forever.

Sappy, maybe. Not stupid.

"I swore years ago—" She put on the brakes.

He nuzzled her cheek and ear. "Tell me."

"That I wouldn't let anyone make me cry."

And now he could. Not only could—*did*. Clay couldn't decide how that made him feel.

"I've bitched about my childhood," he said, "but it

was idyllic compared to yours. How your sister came out the way she did, I get. How you came out the way you did…" He shook his head. "You're amazing, Jane."

She scrubbed her face on his shirt. "Damn it, you're doing it again!"

"I don't want to date, do an occasional overnight."

That made her go still in his arms again, although she didn't raise her head to look at him.

"I want you to move in. I want you to start thinking about marrying me."

After a suspended moment, she did meet his eyes. "Wow."

"Is that a good wow, or an I'm-freaked one?"

"I don't know." She frowned. "Why should I move in with you? Did you ever think about moving in with me?"

Suddenly he was smiling. "You live in an apartment. I have a log house in the woods. My place is better than your place."

The frown deepened into a scowl temporarily, then dissolved, although she was trying not to smile. "Okay. I'll give you that."

"How about the marriage part of my proposition?"

"Were you asking?"

"I will be the second I think you're receptive."

"Scared to take a chance?"

He chuckled. "Jane Vahalik, I love you. Will you marry me?"

Her expression was unexpectedly grave. "Do you want to have children?"

Didn't she? "Yeah," he said cautiously. "I guess I do."

"I suppose you assume I'll be content to stay home with them."

"Ah."

Her eyes narrowed. "What's that supposed to mean?"

"You're challenging me. Again. Yes, Jane, I expect you to take care of yourself and our children when you're pregnant, by not taking part in operations that hold any risk whatsoever. As for raising the kids, we'll do it together. We can take turns. We can both go to half time and juggle our schedules. No, I do not assume you'll become a happy homemaker." He gently kissed her. "That's not you. You'd go nuts. Hell, *I'd* go nuts. We'll work it out, okay?"

"You're not conning me."

Somehow he kept smiling. "You're the best cop I've ever worked with. If we can rescue kidnapped children together, we ought to be able to raise our own together, too, shouldn't we?"

Her arms tightened around his neck and she pressed a kiss to his jaw. "You keep saying what I want to hear."

His temper rose, but only as a cover for the vulnerability and fear beneath. Maybe once you blew it bad enough, there wasn't any regaining lost ground.

"And you don't believe me."

"No, I do," She looked at him, her own expression unguarded. "That scares me. I've had people on the job I could trust, but otherwise—" she gave another of those funny shrugs that didn't convey what she probably thought they did "—not so much."

Her mother. Her father. Lissa. Damn, even Drew.

"I know," Clay said huskily. "Jane, I'll probably screw up. I've got conditioned responses." He grimaced.

"You've probably already figured out I'm possessive. Protective. Sometimes I'll open my mouth without thinking. But in the big ways, I swear I won't let you down. And I'll never dismiss you or your opinion."

She let out one small sniff. "Was that a real proposal?"

Relief felt like a shot of whiskey in his gut. "Yeah."

"Then yes. I love you, too, Clay Renner. And I can't think of anyone I'd rather have at my back, either."

Exultant, he surged to his feet and swung her high. She was laughing as he lowered her slowly. His own smile had died by the time he let her feet touch the floor.

"Can we make love now?" he asked, low and somehow not patient at all anymore.

She lifted her face to his. "Please."

Could life get any better than this? Clay really doubted it.

EPILOGUE

VALENTINE'S DAY WAS almost on them when Jane was summoned to Alec Raynor's office.

"The chief would like to speak to you," his administrative assistant told her on the phone.

Walking upstairs and down the hall, Jane did an automatic search for dire possibilities.

Someone had complained about her. Someone *important* had complained about her. But she couldn't think of anyone she'd recently offended. And even Mayor Noah Chandler and his wife had come to Jane and Clay's wedding.

She would be served advance notice that her job wouldn't be held for her if she were to go on maternity leave.

Okay, that was silly—the city's human resources department would chew up and spit out anyone, including the police chief, who dared do or say anything that politically incorrect.

Or—God—could this have something to do with Lissa's upcoming trial? But surely any news like that would have come from Drew or Lissa's attorney.

Jane brooded as the elevator rose. Drew had recently accepted a job in the Portland area, but he and the kids hadn't yet moved. A subdued Lissa had told Jane she had hopes of a reconciliation, but Jane couldn't see it happening. For all that he was supporting his wife through her legal challenges, Drew had withdrawn emotionally from her. He wasn't the man he'd been. Jane wasn't even sure a reconciliation would be the best thing for the girls. And for Bree, at least, the move might give her a chance to let go of some of her fears. Jane mostly regretted the fact that she wouldn't be able to see Bree and Alexis as often.

Shaking off her thoughts about her sister's fractured family, she stepped out of the elevator.

But then, right outside Raynor's office, she froze midstep. Could this summons be about Colin's so-far unfilled job? He had, to no one's surprise, won the election and taken office as Butte County Sheriff. Three months had passed. Jane had been involved in the interviews of half a dozen applicants for captain of investigative and support services, but if Chief Raynor had offered the job to any of them, he hadn't told her.

Maybe that was his news. Or…no. She couldn't imagine he'd been considering her, too, without discussing it with her, but…he might be getting desperate. Especially if he *had* offered the job to a couple of those candidates and they'd chosen not to take it.

She gulped. An offer to her would definitely qualify as a dire possibility. It was something she'd love…ten or fifteen years from now. If Raynor were to make it now,

Clay's masculine pride would be threatened, although at least now she had the confidence in him to know he'd get over it and even be proud of her. But saying no… That would hurt a little. Even though the timing was wrong in lots of ways, including the fact she had begun to suspect the past few days that she was pregnant. In fact, she'd resolved to stop at Rite Aid on the way home and pick up a home pregnancy kit to find out. She'd been nursing a bubble of excitement all day, thinking about it. This fall, she'd turned thirty-five. Clay would be thirty-seven in March. They'd decided they wanted at least two children, and shouldn't delay starting their family. She knew how excited he'd be.

Jane realized she'd been standing here staring at the closed door with *Police Chief* printed in gold on the frosted inset window. Dumb. Probably Raynor only wanted to make her aware of some new procedure.

She strode in, and the assistant glanced up. "Lieutenant. Go on in, he's expecting you."

"Thanks."

She opened the inner door to find that Chief Raynor wasn't alone. Colin McAllister was with him. Raynor half sat on his desk, one foot braced on the floor. Colin sprawled in one of the chairs facing him.

"Colin," she said in surprise. "Or should I say, Sheriff?"

He laughed. "Don't you dare. Nell does when she's annoyed at me."

Jane smiled. "What's up?"

"I don't know." He nodded at her boss. "He insisted on waiting with his news until you got here."

Raynor's dark good looks had always intimidated her a little, although not as much since she'd seen him scared out of his skull when his nephew was kidnapped. He didn't smile often, though, and hardly ever openly grinned.

"We have one more guest coming." He tilted his head. "I think that's him now."

Their esteemed mayor walked in the door, his eyebrows raised. "I'm a busy man. What's this about?"

"Not too busy for this." Raynor's smile grew. "I just got off the phone with my contact at the DEA. They are finally moving ahead to try my not-so-esteemed predecessor."

"About goddamned time," Chandler grumbled, while Colin whooped and Jane smiled.

"And get this," the chief continued. "They have a money trail straight to Roberto Perez's organization."

Perez was the head of the Mexican and southern California drug cartel responsible for the kidnapping of Matt Raynor. They had been applying pressure on Alec Raynor to keep him from testifying at a trial in Los Angeles, a leftover from his former job with the LAPD.

"He has a witness willing to tie those payments to warnings about police raids, and the dates correlate with times when carefully planned operations went inexplicably wrong." All the major law enforcement agencies in central Oregon were part of a coalition to battle illicit drug trafficking. Former police chief Gary Bystrom would have had the knowledge needed to betray his allies and his own department.

"So they're not getting him just for tax evasion," Chandler said with deep satisfaction.

"Nope." Raynor gave a laundry list of charges. Even if Bystrom was only convicted on a few of them, he'd be spending a whole lot of time in prison.

"Bet his tan will fade." Colin sounded downright vengeful. He'd spent years trying to keep the department effective despite Bystrom's laziness and tendency to ass-kiss city council members rather than support his own officers…and, as they all eventually learned, his corruption. "His wife might as well sell his fishing waders and skis at a garage sale, for all the use he'll get out of them."

Raynor crossed his arms and smiled at them. "I'd like to invite you all, along with your respective spouses, to join Julia and me at Chandler's Brew Pub tonight for dinner. Seems like the news deserves a celebration."

All agreed. In an undertone, Chief Raynor asked Jane to stay for a minute. Colin and Noah Chandler departed together, apparently friendly at least, if not friends, after their former rivalry.

Her stomach tightened. Please, not some crap that would ruin an amazingly good day she hoped would get better once she peed on a stick.

His expression was once again serious, although his stance remained relaxed. "Jane, I thought you should be the first to know that I've hired a replacement for Colin. He'll be starting on March 15."

Whew was all she could think. No need for regrets—
and her workload would ease a whole lot once she
wasn't trying to do her job and half of another one,
too. Running for office had pulled Colin away a whole
lot, even before he won the election and officially resigned. Since then, even inadequately filling the vac-
uum had been a huge challenge.

"Have I met him?" she asked politely.

"Yes. And recommended him. Reid Sawyer."

The man's face materialized immediately in her
memory. Jane nodded.

"Good. I'll look forward to his start date."

"You and me both," Raynor said fervently, and they
shared crooked smiles of understanding. "Then I'll see
you at six at Chandler's," he added.

Accepting her dismissal, she left, thinking about
Reid Sawyer. He was a big man with a remote air that
reminded her of Clay back when he'd been suppressing
his emotions. Maybe because of that resemblance, she
hadn't been intimidated by Sawyer. Jane did remember
wondering why he wanted the job when he was rising in
the ranks in one of the largest sheriff's departments in
the nation, and in an urban setting. Plus—the climate in
southern California was way better. Why choose what
had to seem like a backwater town to him? There had
to be something he wasn't telling them.

With so much else crowding for her attention, she
shrugged off the thought. Everyone had personal reasons for making a move. Sawyer's weren't her business.
Shrugging off speculation wasn't hard.

She'd been working such long hours lately, surely no one would object if she left early. There was a home pregnancy kit on the pharmacy shelf with her name on it.

* * * * *

Look for the next
THE MYSTERIES OF ANGEL BUTTE
book by Janice Kay Johnson!

Coming in September 2014 from
Harlequin Superromance.

MAKING IT TO 25

CHAPTER ONE

ANN GORDON PICKED up one of the photos spread across her coffee table and smiled at the sight of her eldest daughter, Dani, dressed as the Mad Hatter for *Alice in Wonderland*. Just yesterday, it seemed, but actually seven years ago. Dani was a senior in college this year, no longer a fifteen-year-old who dreamed of becoming a Broadway star.

Oh, and there was Jessie, caked with mud but grinning triumphantly as she ran from a soccer field. Ann set that one down and reached for another, and another. All gripped her heart. Letting go was so hard.

Letting go of her children, and of her husband.

She was engaged in one of the world's saddest tasks: the official separation of lives. Family photos divided in half, so she and Jack could each treasure the memory of their daughters' childhoods. She was plucking out the best photos to make copies so that she could put together an album for him. She hadn't gotten very far, because each picture brought back a flood of memories...memories she found herself drowning in.

The hardest was looking at ones that included him, blue eyes narrowed in amusement, dark hair rumpled, a toddler on his back or a teenager encircled by his arm.

He had been so handsome. Was so handsome, she admitted to herself, even with a touch of silver in his hair.

The phone rang, and Ann was grateful for the interruption. Somehow she wasn't at all surprised to find the caller was Jessie. Her youngest had always had a gift for reading her mind.

"Sweetie! What's up?"

"Nothing," her daughter said. "Mara went home for the weekend, and I guess I had a pang of homesickness. What are you doing?"

"Going through boxes of pictures. I promised your father I'd make him an album of photos of you guys."

"Really?" Jessie sounded alarmed. "That sounds so..."

"So?" Ann nudged, when her nineteen-year-old daughter hesitated.

"Permanent."

She bit her lip. "Honey...I'm afraid it *is*. I haven't even talked to your dad in months. We email once in a while...."

"He came up last week. He had business, I guess, and he took me to dinner."

How did he look? caught on her tongue. How pathetic that would sound. "That's nice," she said instead.

"I always thought you two were happy!" Jessie wailed.

Ann had thought they were, too. Maybe they had been, while they had the girls to glue the family together. She and Jack had chattered during the four-hour drive home from Portland after they'd left Jessie in the dorm room with the strange girl who would become her new best friend. What would Jessie end up majoring in?

they had speculated. Would she leave big assignments until the last minute, like she'd always tended to do?

They had chuckled at the image of the dorm room, knee-deep in clutter on Jessie's half, neat as a pin on her roommate's. Perhaps it was natural that they'd talked only about the girls on such a momentous day, when they'd opened their hands to let their youngest go free.

It wasn't until the next day, and the day after, that the silences began to develop. Silences both a little sad and yet restful at first. "The house is so quiet," one of them would say. *They* were quiet, too, because they didn't have a thing to say to each other. How long had it been since the two of them had spent any real time together? Ann felt as if, working the long hours he did, Jack had made a choice many years ago: be a real father or a husband. He'd chosen to be a father. Their children knew him. She didn't.

She *wanted* him to be a great father to their children; she just didn't understand why he couldn't have saved a sliver of himself for her. But he hadn't.

All they'd talked about in private times was family, she realized in those months after they left Jessie at college. In the early years, he'd told her about his cases, but he hadn't in so long, she couldn't remember the last time. He'd never seemed interested in what she did at the art gallery once she went back to work; never had time to attend openings or meet her new colleagues and friends. They weren't *friends* anymore. Not the way a husband and wife should be.

Four months after they'd left their daughter waving outside the dorm, Jack had looked across the breakfast table and said, "I feel like I'm living with a stranger."

"It's only taken you fifteen years to notice," Ann had said.

They had both been weirdly distant, agreeing that they'd drifted apart. He packed and left that day, coming back only once after he'd rented an apartment for the official dividing of possessions, during which they continued to be terribly polite. That was when she'd promised to divide the photos, too. It had taken her almost a year to keep the promise.

"I think we *were* happy," she told her daughter now. "We didn't notice how much we'd grown apart until you and Dani were both gone. It happens, honey."

"I don't want it to happen to my mom and dad!"

"I'm sorry" was all she could say.

"What made you start going through pictures?" Jessie demanded.

Because this week would have been their anniversary. Because she was dreading the day, and needed to feel as if she was taking charge of her life before it came.

"I'm just…starting to clean things out."

Hearing what she didn't say, her daughter gasped. "You wouldn't move!"

"I haven't made any decisions. Right now, I'm just trying to get rid of things, cut down on clutter."

"It's home!" Jessie declared, tears in her voice. "You can't sell the house."

Ann soothed and reassured without making any promises, eventually ending the call with a promise to come for a visit herself in a few weeks.

After hanging up, she decided to leave the latest box of photos for another day and go to bed. Turning out lights, heading upstairs, she felt the quiet, empty rooms around her.

Selling would be hard. She and Jack had bought the generous two-story, white clapboard house with hardwood floors and a big yard on Mercer Island when she was pregnant with Jessie. Even Dani didn't remember living anywhere else.

The house was so full of memories: the dent beside the garage door where she had backed into the house on her very first solo drive; the faint lines on the wall in the upstairs hall where Ann had marked their growth spurts; Dani's room, still so girlie, the shelves filled with stuffed animals and favorite childhood books; Jessie's room almost boyish with sports trophies and posters of rock stars.

How can I leave the home where I raised my children?

The trouble was, Jack was ever present in this house, too. His place at the table, his chair in the living room, the closed door to his home office. His side of the bed, his closet in the master bedroom—empty. The ghost of his laugh. The house was filled with him, and Ann could hardly bear it.

She knew, practically, the house was too big for her. Neither girl was likely to come home for more than another summer or two. It was absurd for her to rattle around in a 3,500-square-foot house.

Ann was still conflicted, but in her heart she knew the time was coming. That was why she'd started cleaning out closets, finishing tasks long left undone, planning for the day when she or Jack filed for divorce.

Over the next few days, still resolved, she left a pile of negatives at the grocery store to have prints made and went to the craft store to choose a couple of albums. Each day, she would go home to the big empty house, eat dinner alone in the silence, and finish sorting boxes—working her way back through basketball camps and ballet rehearsals, birthday parties and Christmas morning gift opening.

The following Thursday, she was in her office at the art gallery she co-owned and managed when her assistant buzzed. "Someone from Clackamas College on line one."

On a squeeze of alarm, Ann reached for the phone. "Ann Gordon speaking."

"Mrs. Gordon, this is Nelson Shields. I'm the president of Clackamas College."

Her pulse bounced, then raced. The president of the college? Why would the president be calling her?

"Is something wrong?" Her throat clogged. "Jessie... Is Jessie all right?"

His hesitation terrified her.

"We believe she's okay right now, but...Mrs. Gordon, I'm afraid I have frightening news." He took a breath. "Jessie has been taken hostage, along with several other students, by a disgruntled former employee of the college. He has a bomb, and is threatening to kill the students."

"Hostage?" she whispered. "Kill...Jessie?"

CHAPTER TWO

THE MOMENT JACK'S car pulled into the driveway, Ann flew out the front door. He met her halfway to the porch, his arms open. She flung herself into them, grateful to be held. She hadn't cried yet, but was suddenly torn by a sob.

"I'm so scared."

"Me, too," he murmured, his cheek against her hair. "Our Jessie."

He let her cry, and when they finally separated, she saw that his eyes were red, too. Either her not-yet ex-husband had aged in the nine months since she'd seen him, or her call with the terrifying news had carved those lines in his face.

Jessie taken hostage with other students at the college by an angry ex-employee with a bomb. How much scarier could it get than that?

Jack studied her, too, and she knew he would see similar changes in her. The strain alone made her feel as if she'd shatter if someone tapped her shoulder. The tears would have made her blotchy and puffy. She didn't care.

"Did you pack a bag?" he asked.

She nodded. "I'll go get it and lock up."

They'd decided to fly to Portland to shave a couple of hours off the trip. A small voice in Ann's head whispered, *What difference does it make if you're there, outside the building where Jessie is held? You can't do anything.* But she refused to listen. She had to believe that once they were there, they'd think of something. Jessie needed them and they were coming.

During the drive to the SeaTac airport, she repeated everything the college president had told her, as closely as she could remember. Jack interjected with a few terse questions. She saw that his knuckles were white, his fingers wrapped tightly around the steering wheel.

He drove with near-reckless speed, and she leaned forward against her seat belt, wanting him to go faster. He parked at the airport and they raced in, barely making it through security in time to join the tail end of the line to board their flight. The time before the plane began to inch away from the gate was agonizing for Ann. She heard a small, muffled sound, and realized a whimper had escaped her.

Jack's big hand closed over hers, and she returned his clasp as the plane slowly taxied to the runway.

Faster. Please, faster.

"How long since we've held hands?" he asked unexpectedly.

Torn from her silent effort to will the pilot to take off, Ann looked down at their entwined hands. "I…" She shook her head. "I don't know. A long time."

She felt self-conscious suddenly, but didn't withdraw her hand. Nor did Jack let go of hers.

"Maybe if we'd held hands more often…"

"How could we? You were never around." The moment the acid words were out, she regretted them. This was no time for recriminations. They couldn't change the past. For Jessie, they needed to be able to depend on each other. "I'm sorry," she said.

Jack shook his head. "No, you're right."

"We've said everything. There's no point in repeating ourselves."

He looked at her, eyes grave. "Did we say everything? It seems to me the problem was that we quit talking."

"I guess we just didn't care enough to bother." Pain squeezed her heart. "Jack, can we not do this? Not now?"

His eyes closed for a moment, and then he nodded. "You're right. My turn to be sorry, Ann."

"It's okay," she whispered.

He searched her face for another minute, and she wondered what he was thinking. But he said only, "Thank God, we're taking off."

The plane began its rush forward, followed by the improbable moment of becoming airborne. During the steep climb, Ann let go of Jack's hand to grip her armrests. *Hold on, Jessie. We're coming.*

They had leveled off and the flight attendant had begun to serve drinks before Jack said, "I saw her last week."

"I know. She called a couple of nights ago. I was thinking about her, and the phone rang." Ann smiled with difficulty. "She's always had a gift that way."

"I remember. No letter from her at summer camp, and you were ready to go charging up there."

"And the phone rang." Ann laughed, but tears also stung her eyes. "She said, 'Mom, I can *feel* you worrying. Quit, already!'"

"She knows you too well."

Ann shook her head. "Dani does, too, but she doesn't sense things…at least not like Jessie does."

He was silent for a moment, his forehead furrowed. "Do you think she knows we're on our way?"

"Oh, yes." She had no doubt. "Mommy and Daddy to the rescue."

Both shook their head when the flight attendant paused to ask what they'd like to drink. "Nothing, thank you," Jack said.

She turned to the passengers seated across the aisle.

"She called me Daddy the other day." Jack's voice was gravelly. "It…got to me. I realized neither of the girls have called me that in a long time."

"No." Ann was the one, this time, to reach for his hand. "I haven't heard *Mommy* in years."

His grip hurt, it was so tight, but she didn't mind. When was the last time he'd needed anything from her, even so minor as a reassuring hand to hold?

"I didn't even think about it, but…did you call Dani?"

Their oldest went to school in southern California.

"No. I thought, what's the point? If we have to…" She stopped, unable to go on.

Jack swore. "We won't have to. Not the way you're thinking. I won't let that bastard hurt my little girl."

The girls had always believed their daddy walked on water. Right this minute, Jessie might be thinking, *Once Daddy is here…*

But what could Jack do? Desperation ran cold through her. What could *she* do? She and Jack hadn't even been able to save their marriage! Twenty-four years, and they'd given up. They hadn't even been able to make it to their silver wedding anniversary. Didn't that prove they weren't supermom and dad?

"Will you call?" she said suddenly. "Find out if..." Her throat closed. *If anything had changed. If Jessie was still "okay."*

Jack nodded and reached for the air phone provided by the airline. She took the number from her purse that the college president had given her, then sat rigid while he dialed and had a brief conversation. At the end, he shook his head at her. "Still a standoff."

Tears wet her face. "Oh, Jack. I want..." She didn't have to finish.

"I want, too," he said roughly.

For Jessie to be safe. No, more than that: to go back to a time when their family was together and safe, before the house had gotten so quiet.

CHAPTER THREE

JACK HAD DECLINED the college president's offer to have them met at the airport. He rented a car and they drove straight to the administrative building.

The last time I was here, Ann thought in a daze, *I was dropping Jessie off for fall semester.* Not with her husband, the way she had the year before, but alone, a single mother.

Now...now her daughter was being held hostage by a crazy former college employee who wanted to make some kind of point she didn't understand. And after they'd agreed to separate after twenty-four years of marriage, Ann was seeing Jack for the first time in nine months because their youngest daughter needed them.

They went straight to the students' union, where the standoff was taking place. Jack parked a couple of blocks away, well back from the police cordon, and they walked. The sight of a dozen police cars, SWAT team members dressed in black and heavily armed, and even—*oh, God!*—what she knew must be a sniper atop the science building shook Ann to her core.

Jack's arm closed around her and he said a profanity she'd never heard him use. She understood. She'd been frightened, but in her heart had thought they could do something. But this scene was out of a television drama. How could it be real? Nineteen-year-old Jessie inside, held by a man with a bomb?

They spotted Nelson Shields, the lanky college president with blond hair turning to silver, talking to a group of people. When they saw him begin to walk away, they hurried to catch up.

Ann remembered thinking he was almost too smooth. Now the ragged edges showed.

After they introduced themselves, he began, "A negotiator has opened talks with Lansky."

"Who *is* this man?" Jack asked.

"A janitor. He was caught going through a student's drawers in her dorm room, and, of course, we fired him." He shook his head. "You never expect anything like this."

"What is it he wants?" Ann was trembling.

"He has yet to make any demands."

Jack was staring past him at the low, stuccoed building. "How is he guarding the whole students' union building?"

The president turned, too. "He isn't. He's got the post office." He pointed, and Ann remembered that the students' union was actually four wings surrounding a courtyard. "There's no access from inside the other wings," the college president continued. "Only from the street side and the courtyard. The windows are few and tiny. Unfortunately—" he sounded thoughtful "—the building is ideal for holding the SWAT team off."

That first fall, Ann had gone with her when Jessie collected the combination for her mailbox. Now she pictured the long skinny front room, little more than a corridor lined by old-fashioned mailboxes, interrupted by one door where students asked for packages too big to fit in their boxes.

It was apparently in that back area where the enraged ex-janitor held the students. "We think he has them locked in the small room at the end where supplies are stored and packages kept secure. No windows. He claims he has a bomb rigged to go off. He says he has a gun, too."

For the first time, Ann saw the cluster of other couples, the women crying, the men embracing their wives. Other parents.

"How many students are in there?" she whispered.

"We believe he has eleven. It was just bad luck, bad timing for the students who were picking up mail."

"Oh, no." Ann pressed her hand to her mouth. "I sent her a care package."

Jack's arm tightened around her. "It's not your fault."

"No, but if I hadn't…"

He swung her to face him. "Ann, you sent her a package out of love. Don't think for a second you're to blame. Maybe the damn thing hasn't even come! Maybe Jessie just walked a friend over to check *her* box."

Ann drew a ragged breath. "Yes. You're right. Maybe it *hasn't* come. I didn't mail it until Monday."

He pressed a kiss to her forehead, then drew back.

"We can't do anything, can we?" he asked the president.

"It's in the hands of the negotiator. If you want to join the other parents over there —" he nodded toward the tableau on the lawn, well back from the cordon "—the lieutenant is giving regular updates."

Jack nodded abruptly and, hand on Ann's back, guided her toward the group of other parents. The college had set up chairs in small groups, and a long table—the kind they used for parent weekend lunches—held a coffee urn, tubs full of sodas and water bottles, and even food that looked untouched.

A few other parents greeted them. No one, it seemed, knew any more than Jack and Ann did.

She counted, and realized that not every hostage's parents had yet arrived. Langdon College was a nationally ranked liberal-arts school, with students from virtually every state. Imagine if she'd lived in Boston when she'd gotten that morning's call.

"How can we do nothing but wait?" Jack asked as soon as they were alone.

Staring at the students' union, Ann said, "It's almost worse here, isn't it?"

He nodded. "Somehow I spent the morning focused on getting here. I had a goal."

"That's exactly it," she agreed, grateful to have her despair put into words. "As long as there was something to *do*..."

"We could hold on." He moved his shoulders in a way she recognized as his attempt to ease unbearable tension. "Do you want a cup of coffee?"

"Coffee?" How mundane that sounded! Ann shook her head no. "Maybe later. It's nice of them to provide it."

"Nice?" Jack's voice was savage. "We pay them forty thousand dollars a year to keep our daughter safe, remember?"

"That's not fair," she said. "That's not what we pay them for."

He rubbed the back of his neck. "You're right. Funny, I didn't like it when Jessie looked at Columbia. New

York City. She'd get mugged, she'd get…" He broke off. "I was so relieved when she chose Clackamas."

Ann touched his hand. "We can't keep them safe forever, Jack. No matter how hard we try."

His face was ravaged. "But that's my job!"

"No. Your job was to love the girls, and you did." She could say that without reservation; he'd been a wonderful father.

Just not a wonderful husband.

"Something's happening," he said suddenly.

He was right. There was a stir in the police lines, raised voices. Another hostage's mother gasped. Ann reached for Jack even as he reached for her.

From the crowd on the other side of the cordon, a SWAT team member glanced toward the parents, then began to come forward, face grim.

CHAPTER FOUR

"SOMEHOW HE CAUGHT sight of the sniper on the roof," the police lieutenant told the gathered parents. "He's threatening to kill a student if we don't pull him off."

"You're doing as he asks, aren't you?" someone begged.

"We've had some dispute, but...yes. We don't believe he really wants to kill anyone. We're just going to wait him out."

Ann listened with disbelief. Somehow she'd wandered into a television drama, only this was real.

Despite the nine months since they'd separated, it felt natural to be standing close to Jack, to feel his hand resting on her lower back. A high-powered attorney, somehow he'd never found time for her once they had children, but she'd always known that in other ways she could depend on him.

The lieutenant went back to the police line and the parents of the student hostages huddled to discuss, with an edge of hysteria, whether the police were competent and how irresponsible the college had been not to recognize such a borderline personality in one of their own employees.

They were scared, just as Ann and Jack were. Eventually the group drifted apart, and the two of them found lawn chairs set up by the school under the shade of an enormous old maple tree. It was just one of the trees that made the campus so beautiful, along with the hundred-year-old clock tower and the ivy-covered brick buildings.

"Aren't they replacing the students' union building?" Jack asked.

Ann nodded. "This one is way too small. It doesn't fit architecturally, either. They've actually broken ground over beyond the tennis courts."

If the new SUB had been open this fall, she couldn't help thinking, this janitor—Lansky, was that his name?—might not have been able to hold so many students so readily. He couldn't have barricaded himself in the way he had here.

Jack appeared lost in his thoughts. Perhaps fifteen minutes went by before he said, "Their births, Jessie's and Dani's, were two of the most amazing days of my life."

Her eyes stung. "Mine, too."

"I remember thinking, *we* did this. You and I."

She'd thought the same, not knowing that the extraordinary feat of having two beautiful, smart, funny, affectionate daughters would also spell the end of the closeness that she and Jack had shared.

But she couldn't say, *What went wrong? We were so in love.* They'd already given up, she and Jack. They couldn't stay in love, but they could continue to be the parents they'd always been.

"I thought I was scared when Jessie took the header off her bike that time. Remember?"

How could she forget? "That neighbor boy came

screaming up the driveway. She was unconscious on the sidewalk."

"I blamed myself for taking the training wheels off too soon," Jack said.

Ann stared at him. "I didn't know that. I was wailing, and you just took charge. Like always."

His mouth twisted. "I can't stand not to be in control. You know that. But that doesn't mean I'm not afraid... freaking out underneath."

"You've always been so strong."

He grunted, his gaze on the police line and the low, white building beyond. "All pretense. God, Ann— how could you of all people not know how scared I was underneath?"

Shaken, she asked, "How could I know, if you never told me? I always thought..." She shook her head. "I think I fell in love with you in the first place because you were so sure of your values and what you wanted out of life. You never got rattled!" A small laugh choked her. "Except when I told you on the way to the hospital that I thought Jessie was coming right that minute."

His head turned, and his blue eyes met hers. "I've never driven so fast in my life."

Ann frowned, hearing what she'd just said. "Is that why you never admitted to being as vulnerable as the rest of us? Because you thought that's why I loved you?"

"You just said as much. It *is* why you loved me."

"It's one of a million reasons why I loved you! And honestly..." She paused. What an odd time to be telling each other such truths. "I admired your self-control, but sometimes I wanted so much to see it shatter. I hated being so emotional in comparison. And then sometimes I wondered..." She stopped.

His narrowed gaze fixed intently on her face. "You wondered?" he prodded.

"Whether you loved me as much as I did you."

Oh, Lord, she thought in shock. That was why she hadn't been more surprised by his gradual withdrawal from their former closeness after the girls were born. Maybe, deep inside, she'd always believed she wouldn't be able to hold on to him forever.

"Oh, I loved you as much." His voice was husky. "So much, I was a coward. You could admit to being vulnerable. I never could."

"Why are you telling me this now?" she asked, straight out.

He grimaced, tiredness around his eyes. "This," he said simply, gesturing toward the police cordon. "For once, I'm too damned scared to pretend."

"Oh, Jack," Ann whispered. "What if…?"

"No what-ifs!" he said, gritting his teeth. "These negotiators are good at what they do. They'll talk this guy out."

"If he gives her half a chance, *Jessie* will talk him into surrendering."

Some of the strain on Jack's lean face lightened. "You know she's talking."

Saying Jessie never quit talking was an old family joke. She'd been an incredible chatterbox as a preschooler, and into her teenage years had even talked in her sleep.

"And she has such a kind heart." Ann looked toward the building where her daughter was in danger. "She undoubtedly feels sorry for him, despite everything."

"She probably does, doesn't she?" Jack's hand came

out to grip hers with bruising strength. "God, Ann. How will we survive if things go wrong?"

We? They hadn't survived, not as a unit. How would she survive? How would he? She didn't know.

She didn't let either her voice or gaze falter. "You're the one who said no what-ifs, remember? We have to have faith."

His eyes were red-rimmed. "I lost my faith when I lost you fifteen years ago."

Stunned, she said, "What are you talking about?"

"Isn't that when you quit giving a damn?"

They stared at each other. "I thought," she said carefully, "that's when *you* quit giving a damn."

CHAPTER FIVE

JACK AND ANN sat on white plastic chairs in the dappled shade under a maple tree, waiting while a police negotiator tried to persuade the crazed ex-employee of the college to release their daughter.

Only fear could have gotten them talking like this. Could have made Jack Gordon talk about feelings he'd buried for fifteen years or more.

"You changed, Ann. You shut me out," he insisted.

Her mouth actually fell open. "*I* shut *you* out! How could I shut out someone who was never home?"

"Do you know how tough it was to walk out of the office because Jessie had a T-ball game? To pick up Dani from jazz dance? I was afraid I was sacrificing the chance to make partner, but you—all of you—were more important."

Wondering what alternate universe she'd wandered into, Ann retorted, "I've never said you weren't a great dad. You were. Are. But all of your free time was for the girls. Sure, you could take a couple of hours off to referee a basketball game. You just couldn't manage it so we could have an evening out by ourselves. Most of the time, you got home after I'd gone to bed and left before I was up. The only way I could see you was to schedule another activity for Dani or Jessie!"

His voice rose. "I couldn't do both! You made it pretty damn clear that their events weren't optional."

"*I* made it clear?" She sounded like an idiot, echoing him again, but she was too stupefied to do anything else. Now everything was *her* fault?

"They were always counting on their daddy being there. You'd be sure I knew that." He was agitated enough to stand, walk a couple of steps away, turn back to face her. He'd left his suit jacket in the car and had now tugged his tie loose and unbuttoned the throat of his white dress shirt. Her dark-haired, blue-eyed husband had never looked handsomer than he did now, jaw muscles knotted, mouth compressed.

"Jeez, Ann! If I couldn't make it, I'd know I wasn't measuring up in your eyes."

"What are you talking about? I knew you couldn't get away sometimes. I never expected you to say, 'Your Honor, can we recess at two o'clock this afternoon? My five-year-old has a school play.' That's why I stayed home for so many years!"

Jack's expression softened. "You were a great mother. I just got the distinct impression that my only worth in your eyes was as the breadwinner and father. I wanted to matter with you, Ann, even if that was the only way I could do it."

They both knew they were revisiting arguments they'd already had. It all seemed so petty, when their nineteen-year-old daughter's life was threatened by a nut with a bomb, but Ann could no more have stopped herself from arguing than she could have stayed home in Mercer Island instead of flying down here to be as close to Jessie as she could be.

Ann said hotly, "I'm not the one who could never seem to make an anniversary dinner. The one who shut himself in his den every night the minute the girls went to bed."

Jack shoved his hands in his pants pockets, perhaps to hide the fact they were fisted. "Those first years in the firm were killers. We both knew they would be. But we wanted financial success. And we didn't want to have to wait to have a family. How the hell did you think I could do everything?"

"I didn't ask for everything! Just a little piece of you. I wanted you to talk about your day. Tell me you thought I was beautiful, like you used to."

His eyes burned into Ann's. "I never quit wanting you. You know that."

Okay, she did; their sex life had stayed active until those last months, when the silence between them had made reaching for each other awkward.

After a moment, Jack rubbed a hand over his face, then swung away. "Damn it. I'm going to go find out what's happening."

He strode away before she could respond, and she was glad to see him go. She needed a minute to…well, process what he'd said. And what he'd implied.

Besides, she, too, was painfully aware that over an hour had passed since the SWAT team lieutenant had last come to update the parents who waited a safe distance back from the police cordon. "We'll wait him out," he'd said the last time, but for how long?

Ann didn't know which was worse: to continue to wait, the suspense excruciating, or to see the SWAT team prepare for an assault that might scare the guy into triggering the bomb.

Another father stood and followed Jack. Ann realized the other parents hadn't huddled the way she might have expected; instead, like Jack and Ann, they had separated into couples that clung together. The effort of talking to strangers was too much. Ann wondered if any of the others were divorced, or even separated, like she and Jack were.

And yet, of course, there was no one else she'd want beside her right now, while they waited to learn Jessie's fate.

When he came back with the other man, Jack spoke with the habit of authority, his raised voice carrying to every anxious mother and father. "They're talking with the guy. He's fluctuating between threats and remorse or just fear of what he's gotten himself into, the negotiator isn't sure. He's encouraging the remorse, soothing him when he threatens."

"What if he doesn't have a bomb at all?" someone asked.

Jack's voice roughened. "They secured a search warrant for his house. They found components and feel sure he did construct one."

Another father, balding, bearded and skinny, stood. "Do these guys even know for sure that our kids are alive?"

"Half an hour ago, they got him to hold the phone up and they heard muffled yells, so they think they're okay."

"You mean, *some* of them are okay," the balding man said.

He'd said only what they were all thinking. In the

silence that followed, everyone seemed to shrink back into themselves, the momentary cohesion dissolving.

Jack rejoined Ann.

"I need to say one final thing. About us. Our marriage," she said.

He waited, standing in front of her, his expression closed.

She lifted her chin. "I never cared that much about financial success. I would have rather had more of you and less money."

"You never knew what it was like to have less money." Jack's voice was harsh. "I did."

"So at least be honest. It was *you* who wanted that more than you wanted to spend time with me or Jessie and Dani."

He made a strangled sound of frustration. "Don't you get it, Ann? I didn't give a damn about myself! I just didn't want you ending up like my mother."

"You gave up our life together so I wouldn't end up a poor widow?" In disbelief, Ann shook her head.

"My father died of a heart attack when he was forty-eight. You know that. Did it ever occur to you my health—hereditarily speaking—may not be so hot?"

"I... You eat right." Her voice was thin, thready. "Your cholesterol has always been fine. And your blood pressure."

"He had no warning, either. My mother had to work two jobs to finish raising us kids. She'd hide it from us, but once in a while her exhaustion and despair showed. Being sure you were okay, the girls were okay, even if I dropped dead... Of course that mattered."

She stood slowly. "Jack, why didn't you ever *say?*"

"Oh, I said. You just didn't listen."

"Jack," she whispered.

"Water under the bridge." His voice had become distant again. "You were right. This isn't the time or place."

"But…"

"We've got to eat. I'll get us sandwiches." He walked away, leaving her shocked and, once again, silenced.

But, oh, in such a different way.

Maybe this *wasn't* the ideal time or place. But somehow they'd never found either, not even when they were still living together. The grounds of the college could be their only place; Jessie's hours of peril their only time.

CHAPTER SIX

Hour dragged into hour. Ann went no farther than the nearby science building to use the bathroom. She had to be there, outside the college students' union building, to be as close to Jessie as possible.

Most of the activity took place in the van where the negotiator huddled with a telephone and spoke to the enraged ex-employee. How do you negotiate with someone like that? she wondered. Did you lie, tell him he could walk out and go back to his life? Or would even that not be incentive, when that life had been wretched enough to drive him to this terrible act?

As many as fifty to one hundred college students stood outside the perimeter and stared, too—including Jessie's roommate, who approached Ann and Jack.

Dark-haired Mara, from Hawaii, rushed to give Ann a hug. Her brown eyes filled with tears. "I'm so scared!"

"We are, too," Ann whispered. "I didn't know...I was afraid you were in there, too."

The nineteen-year-old shook her head. "I was in class. I didn't even hear about this for a couple of hours!"

She sat and talked with them for a while about Jessie—what she'd been doing, thinking, reading, studying. "I don't know how she's ever going to decide what to major in. She loves her calculus class *and* her American lit class. Nobody, like nobody, loves both!"

Ann laughed, in a watery way. "I sure didn't love calculus."

"She never gets tired. Did you know she's playing rugby this fall?"

In surprise, Jack said, "What about soccer?"

"Rugby is only intramural so far," Ann said. "She just wanted to try it. Somehow she's managed to do both."

Managed. That sounded so terribly past tense. But she didn't want to correct herself, to remind Jack and Mara that Jessie might never get to manage anything again.

"The rugby teams really get into it." Mara sounded awed. "But she's, like, *fearless.*"

Involuntarily, all three looked toward the long, low building where Jessie was now held hostage, threatened by a man with his finger on the trigger of a bomb. Their golden girl, who'd always skated through life, cheerful, gifted and popular, had to be afraid to have discovered she wasn't immune from disaster.

Ann wished she'd never had to discover any such thing.

After Mara left, Ann said, "She's a nice girl. Jessie was lucky to get her as a roommate."

Please, please, let Jessie be lucky again.

Jack read her mind. "Jessie has always floated above every potential swamp. It sure made Dani mad."

Ann gave another of those laughs that felt as if it could become a sob so easily. "Dani always claimed Jessie was going to grow up and become a con artist, because she never got caught in her lies."

A grin pulled at Jack's mouth. "She did have a gift." His smile died. "*Does*. Does have a gift."

Now he was doing it, too.

"Jessie's okay." Ann didn't know if she believed herself, but she wanted to. "She's strong."

"Yeah. She's an amazing kid." He met Ann's eyes. "She's a lot like her mother."

Warmth in her chest, she said, "And her father. Maybe more like you, so sure of herself. I always thought she'd end up an attorney like you."

"We've already established that I'm not that sure of myself," he reminded her.

"I guess I'm having a little trouble believing that." She gave him a tremulous smile. "I was so astonished that you ever even looked at me. I suppose I never quite understood why you fell in love with me."

"In the first place, I thought you were the most beautiful woman I'd ever seen." His own smile was wry. "A cliché, but true. And then I found out you were also smart and empathetic. And your art! You shouldn't have quit painting, Ann."

She shook her head. "I wasn't good enough to make it."

"There you go again, undervaluing yourself. You could sketch a face and tell me more about that person than I ever would have seen with my own eyes. You're extraordinarily perceptive, Ann, in a world of people more interested in themselves than in anyone else."

His compliment brought equal measures of pleasure and grief. "Perceptive?" she said. "When apparently I never understood you at all?"

He turned his head away and stared toward the SUB. "Maybe I was a little afraid you'd see too much," he said quietly. "Maybe I was hiding."

She shifted in her chair to look directly at him. "What were you hiding?"

His voice wasn't his own; low and halting, he sounded younger, uncertain. "The fact that I was afraid I'd fail. That I'd be like my father and let you down, like he let my mother and us kids down."

"But…you've told me wonderful stories about your dad," Ann said in perplexity. "About building go-karts and rock hounding and coaching girls' softball for your sister's teams."

Jack shrugged. "Through a kid's eyes, he was a perfect father. But, you know, he wasn't ambitious enough to ever rise in the hierarchy anywhere he worked. And then he got laid off a few months before his heart attack."

Ann stared at him. "Jack, we all have strengths and weaknesses. Do you really believe that everything wonderful about him was negated because he wasn't hugely successful in the working world? Because he wasn't *ambitious?*"

He turned to look at her, his expression troubled. "I think Mom grew to hate him. He died and left us poor. That's all she remembered."

Ann liked his mother, but she was hearing about a far more bitter woman than the one she knew—the one who had benefited from Jack's financial success. "Had he kept her from developing a career of her own?"

"Well, women weren't as likely to have a career in those days. It was assumed she'd raise the kids, he'd bring home the paycheck."

"My aunt Regina retired as an executive from GE." Aunt Reggie and Uncle Charlie had raised three kids, as well.

"What are you saying?" Jack demanded. "That it was Mom's fault she didn't make enough money?"

"I'm saying maybe it wasn't fair for her to put that burden of blame on your dad—to the point where you grew up believing your only significant role in life was to make enough money so your widow and children would be well off after you were gone."

He shoved his fingers into his dark hair, wildly disheveling it. "God. When you put it that way…"

"Maybe we're all programmed by our parents, by family stories, in ways we don't understand."

"What about you?" Jack asked. "Why did you have trouble believing I could love you?"

Astonished, she realized she didn't know. Why had she always felt so sure Jack would discover someday that she wasn't worthy of him?

She'd just opened her mouth to speak when a bustle of activity on the police line brought both their heads around. "Oh, God," she whispered. "What's happening?"

Warm and strong, Jack's hand closed on hers. "Maybe something good."

The lieutenant, looking far more careworn than he had this morning, walked over to the parents, who all slowly stood, stiff and frightened.

"We've had a break," he announced. "Our guy has agreed to release one student who can verify that they're all fine."

Jack's hand almost crushed hers. Ann quit breathing. One student? Only one?

She looked around and saw on the other faces the same wild hope she felt.

Please. Let that one student be my child.

CHAPTER SEVEN

THE MAN WITH the bomb was going to release only one of the eleven kids he held hostage in the students' union building of the college. One. To speak for all the others—perhaps to be the only survivor of this horrific ordeal.

Ann so desperately wanted Jessie to be that one, and yet she felt guilty for the depths of her prayers. If Jessie walked out, every other parent here would have equally powerful hopes crushed.

As if caught in a dream, or a nightmare, they all followed the lieutenant to stand behind a police car with several SWAT team members dressed in black, wearing bulletproof vests.

Voices murmured and police radios crackled. "Out the back door."

Another mother said, "The student's coming out on the other side of the building! I'm going there." She turned blindly. They all started behind her.

Then, from one of the radios a man said, "No, wait! He thinks we've set a trap. They're coming out the front."

As stupidly as sheep being herded by the snapping teeth of a dog, the parents all swung around again.

Jack wrapped Ann in his arms, and she closed hers around his waist. They stood close, both their bodies twisted so they could see the door to the post office wing of the students' union building.

Nothing happened. The voices gradually died away until all that was left was the most awful hush. Everyone waited, stared, hoped and dreaded.

Ann began to think she couldn't bear another minute. Another second. She heard a stifled sob, then felt as much as heard Jack's sharp intake of breath when the door opened a crack. There was another pause. No one so much as moved.

Abruptly, the door swung open and a girl stumbled out and fell to her hands and knees. The door slammed shut and police swarmed forward, enveloping her and carrying her back to safety.

Two of the parents gasped and rushed forward. Ann stood frozen, trying to reconcile the picture in her head of her Jessie—tall, athletic, blonde and ponytailed, perhaps stumbling as she came out, but then running to her mother and father—with the snapshot her eyes had taken in of a petite girl with dark hair, short and spiky, and face blank with terror.

"Not Jessie," Jack murmured, and Ann realized that once again they'd been thinking in sync. He, too, was having trouble accepting that another child was safe, not theirs.

They waited until the lieutenant waved them over, at which point all the parents gathered around the sobbing girl, held in her father's arms. One of the police officers handed her a cloth and she mopped her face, then tried to compose herself.

"Everyone is okay. He said to say that, and it's true. He hasn't hurt anyone. We were just so scared!"

Names were called out. Bridget. Kirk. Aaron. Camille. She kept nodding her head yes. Everyone was fine. She didn't know all their names, but Kirk, he'd given her a drink from his water bottle, and Maureen had shared this bag of potato chips she'd just bought in the SUB cafe before checking her mail.

"Jessie," Ann finally said softly.

Jack's arm tightened.

The girl's face relaxed. "Jessie is awesome! She's been, like, talking to this guy?" Her voice rose as if it were a question. "Telling him the administration was mean to him, and we students would back him. You could tell he listened to her."

A police officer said, "I thought you students were locked in the back room. How were you talking to him?"

"He opened the door sometimes. At first he'd just rant. I think he wanted someone to talk to. You know? And then sometimes he'd stand right outside the door and talk to us through it."

Finally, she was led away, tucked between her mom and dad. Like all the other parents, Jack and Ann were left standing there, side by side.

"Jessie's okay," he said. "You heard her."

"Why couldn't she be quiet?" Ann asked him. Begged. "Stay out of sight?"

Sounding resigned, he said, "Because that wouldn't be Jessie. She's never let events control her."

No, of course she couldn't do that, not their take-charge daughter.

"This would be worse, in a way, if it was Dani," Jack added.

Yes, it would, Ann realized. Not that she loved Jessie less or Dani more, but their older daughter had always been more timid. Jessie, if she walked out safe and sound—*when* she walked out—would be less scarred, more able to regain her confidence. Dani's was more fragile to start with.

Ann nodded and let him lead her back toward the two white plastic chairs that sat under the maple tree.

"It's getting dark," he observed.

Startled, she looked around. He was right. Dusk was settling, purple-gray. Within half an hour, darkness would cloak the campus.

Ann and Jack sat and waited in silence. Evening brought a chill that raised goose bumps on her bare arms. Jack went to the car and returned with his suit jacket and a sweater she'd brought.

The police set up floodlights, creating a shockingly white light that made the darkness beyond its edge seem denser.

Ann could scarcely see Jack when she said, "My sister was Dad's favorite."

"What?" His head turned toward her, although she couldn't make out his expression.

"I think that's why I didn't believe someone as wonderful as you could possibly love me above everyone else. Because I always knew I was second best."

"You've said that, and he did seem closer to Marjorie." Jack sounded thoughtful. "But you and he seem to have an okay relationship."

"Oh, we do. Better, I think, once I was an adult, when I didn't need his approval so much. And it wasn't that he was mean or anything. It was more subtle than that. But I always knew. And Mom didn't have favorites, so I had nothing to balance it."

"Thus you've always had good friendships with other women, but men were another story."

The answer was so simple. How absurd that she'd

never seen it before. On some Freudian level, Jack had stood in for her father. At last, miraculously, she'd been the favorite. She just hadn't believed it would last.

"So you saw my long hours as waning interest," he continued, his familiar, well-loved voice close beside her in the darkness.

"Yes."

"Meantime, I was working so damned hard not to be my father, I didn't notice."

They really hadn't known each other at all, Ann saw. Twenty-four years and two children together, and they'd misunderstood so much.

His hand found hers. "We've been a pair of idiots, haven't we?"

Despite the ache of fear under her breastbone, Ann felt a stirring of hope. Could she trust it? Trust Jack and herself? Especially if...

No! She wouldn't think it. If she believed with all her heart that tonight, or tomorrow, or the next day, she would be able to hold her youngest daughter in her arms again, then it must come true. She wouldn't think about how hard it would be for her and Jack to overcome that kind of tragedy.

"I guess we have," she admitted. "And it took this to make us realize it."

They both looked at the closed door, stark under the bright white lights.

"Come out, come out," Jack murmured, with the singsong intonation of the childhood game.

Ann shivered.

CHAPTER EIGHT

THE POLICE CONVINCED all of the parents to go to hotel rooms the college had reserved for them to get some rest. The hostage taker in the students' union building apparently wanted to sleep.

"He said he won't talk to us until morning, and he's going to sleep with his hand on the trigger." The SWAT team lieutenant looked weary.

They all nodded, zombielike, and allowed themselves to be steered to their cars. Jack drove in silence. When the room key was handed to him, he stared stupidly at it for a minute. "They only gave us one room. Do you want me to ask for a second room?"

She shook her head. "I'd rather have you close if…" Her throat closed.

He nodded. She didn't have to finish.

If they call. If something happens. "Something," of course, was to remain undefined.

The room had only one queen-size bed. Ann didn't care. She brushed her teeth and loosely braided her hair but decided to sleep in her clothes. "In case," she said.

Jack nodded again and removed only his shoes before he lay down on the bed beside her. "This has been one hell of a day, hasn't it?"

She had to laugh, in a shaky way. "That's an understatement! I don't know if I can take another one like it."

He rolled onto his side so he could see her. "You'll take as many as you have to. I bet you'd storm the building if you could. You've always been amazingly fierce when it came to protecting the kids."

"But in the end, I can't do anything to save Jessie." Her eyes filled with tears for the first time in many hours. She hadn't even cried when the other student was released instead of their Jessie.

He reached for her, and as naturally as if they hadn't been separated for nine months, Ann went into his arms, her head finding its place on his broad shoulder. Mouth against her hair, he murmured, "Let yourself cry, love."

"I want Jessie here!" she wailed, clutching his shirtfront. "Not…not…" Tears poured out, hot and salty.

He kept smoothing her hair back from her face, wiping her wet cheeks, saying soft words that were exactly what she needed to hear.

In the end, worn down, she lay limp against him. "Crying without you was hard," she whispered. "I mean, when you left."

"I don't know what I was thinking." His arms tightened. "Ann…can we try again?"

She drew back, knowing her eyes were puffy and her face a mess but not caring. "Can you forgive me for pushing you away?"

"Is that what you did?"

"I think…" Ann bit her lip. "I think I used the kids to hold on to you. I thought you wouldn't leave me if you were involved enough in their lives."

A spasm of pain crossed his face. "Didn't we ever talk, even in the beginning?"

"Maybe." She tried to smile. "Maybe we *did* talk, and just didn't listen."

He made a rough sound in his throat and kissed her. Not with passion, although she knew he felt it for her, but with thanksgiving.

"I love you, Ann. I never stopped."

"Me, either." Her eyes welled with tears she had thought were spent. "We can go back to the beginning, and start again."

They kissed some more and whispered to each other until Ann abruptly fell asleep, midword.

When she awakened as suddenly and heard the deep, even breathing of someone else, she tensed, then remembered everything. Jack, her love. Jessie. Oh, God, Jessie.

Her eyes focused on the clock. It was 6:30 a.m. Gray light filtered around the window drapes. She moved, and Jack woke instantly.

"Did someone call?"

"No."

"Let's clean up and go see what's happening."

They parked again, seeing a scene virtually unchanged from the day before: a picturesque college campus marred by the police cordon surrounding the SUB. College officials had brought coffee and a continental breakfast. After hearing that the negotiator hadn't yet spoken to the man inside, Ann let Jack persuade her into nibbling on a muffin. She seemed unable to taste, but knew she had to eat to stay strong.

The other parents filtered back, gathering around the coffee urn.

Ann listened to snatches of conversation.

"Have you heard anything?"

"I dreamed the students overwhelmed him. I saw it clear as day, this swarm of them enveloping him."

They all heard a phone ring and turned in unison. It was in the SWAT team van. Through the open door, they could see the negotiator, a tall man with graying hair, talk on the phone. The conversation was brief. He hung up, spoke to the officers with him, and a buzz seemed to pass along the line of police officers.

A coffee cup dropped from one mother's hand onto the lawn. No one reacted.

The lieutenant came toward them, his face telling them he had good news. "He says none of this is the students' fault, and he's coming out."

They all broke into speech at once.

He held up his hand. "That's all we know."

The babble of voices broke off when the door behind which their sons and daughters had been held hostage for nearly twenty-four hours opened. Guns were leveled, but the first person out was a young woman. Behind her crowded other students. Ann searched for Jessie's bright blond head and saw her, right in the middle— next to the dumpy man with stubble on his jaw who had to be their captor.

The police rushed forward, and for a moment the students stood their ground, protecting the former janitor who had taken them captive. Then they parted, and the police handcuffed the small, frightened man who looked incapable of inciting so much fear and hustled him away. The students' heads turned.

"Mom?" one of them said. "Mom, Dad!" another cried. They raced to their parents.

"Jessie!" Ann met her halfway, more tears flowing. Jack's arms came around both of them, and they stood locked together, mother and daughter crying. No, Ann saw with a peek, *all* crying. Even Jack.

"You're here!" their nineteen-year-old daughter sniffed at last. "Both of you. I knew you would be."

"We've been so scared," Ann said.

Jessie pulled back, face tear-streaked but shining. "Well, me, too, but…it was amazing, Mom! I think *I* talked him into giving up! I couldn't believe it worked."

She was happy? Not traumatized? Ann stared at her in shock. She and Jack had been joking when they said Jessie was probably in there negotiating!

"I know what I'm going to major in now," she declared. "Psychology. Because, see, it was *interesting,* hearing how sad and angry he was and realizing that somebody could have helped him before. So he didn't do something like this."

Jack was the first to laugh. Ann joined him, hysteria only a millimeter away.

Now Jessie gaped at them. "Why's that funny?"

Jack controlled himself enough to say, "We've been terrified, and you—you've been finding your vocation."

On her dignity, their daughter lifted her chin. "I still don't think it's funny."

"No." Ann sobered. "No, it really isn't."

"I'm just trying to say that I'm okay. Everything's good."

"Yeah," Jack said. "I think it is."

Her eyes narrowed. "You've still got your arm around Mom."

He grinned at her. "Yes, I do."

Jessie squealed. "You're back together?"

He smiled down at Ann, and her heart swelled at

the look in his eyes. "We're going to try again," he murmured.

It came to her then; this was the day she'd dreaded. "Guess what?" Ann said. How fitting it seemed. "Today is our anniversary. Our twenty-fifth."

"So it is." He kissed her lightly, his lips promising more later, when they were alone. For her ears only, voice husky, he said, "Happy twenty-fifth." Then he wrapped his other arm around his daughter. "If the police need to talk to you, they can do it later. What do you say we go get some breakfast? And call Dani?"

Their daughter bounced, as if she was five years old. "I have *so* much to tell you!"

They smiled at each other, their eyes meeting in a moment of complete understanding. Possibly the first in their lives, Ann thought. But not the last.

After all, with a little luck they'd have another twenty-five years to finally get to know each other.

* * * * *

We hope you enjoyed reading

COP BY HER SIDE

and

MAKING IT TO 25

by JANICE KAY JOHNSON.

If you enjoyed these stories, then you'll love
Harlequin Superromance stories!

You want romance plus a bigger story!
Harlequin Superromance stories are filled with
powerful relationships that deliver a strong emotional
punch and a guaranteed happily ever after.

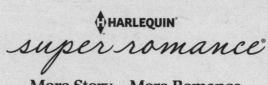

More Story...More Romance

Enjoy six *new* stories from
Harlequin Superromance every month!

Available wherever books and ebooks are sold.

A mistake that's meant to be...

The Sweetest September
by Liz Talley

All John Beauchamp wants is a simple life.
Then Shelby Mackey breezes in, announcing that
she's pregnant. Their one crazy night of passion has
changed everything.

Even though Shelby insists John doesn't have to be
involved, John can't let her go that easily. So when Shelby
agrees to stay in town temporarily, John's determined to
make that stay permanent—and as sweet as can be.

Get the first book in the
Home in Magnolia Bend miniseries!

**AVAILABLE AUGUST 2014,
WHEREVER BOOKS AND EBOOKS ARE SOLD.**

HARLEQUIN®

super romance®

More Story...More Romance

www.Harlequin.com

HSR60862

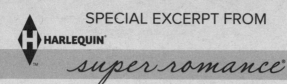
The Sweetest September

By Liz Talley

Shelby Mackey would have been happy
to *never* revisit the night she met
John Beauchamp. Well, that's not entirely true.
It was a good night…until the end. But now
avoiding him is no longer an option!

Read on for an exciting excerpt of the upcoming
book **THE SWEETEST SEPTEMBER**
by Liz Talley…

Shelby took a moment to take stock of the man she hadn't
seen since he'd slipped out that fateful night. John's boots
were streaked with mud and his dusty jeans had a hole in the
thigh. A kerchief hung from his back pocket. He looked like
a farmer.

She'd never thought a farmer could look, well, sexy. But
John Beauchamp had that going for him…not that she was
interested.

Been there. Done him. Got pregnant.

He looked down at her with cautious green eyes…like she
was a ticking bomb he had to disarm. "What are you doing
here?"

Shelby tried to calm the bats flapping in her stomach, but there was nothing to quiet them with. "Uh, it's complicated. We should talk privately."

He slid into the cart beside her, his thigh brushing hers. She scooted away. He noticed, but didn't say anything.

She glanced at him and then back at the workers still casting inquisitive looks their way.

John got the message and stepped on the accelerator.

Shelby yelped and grabbed the edge of the seat, nearly sliding across the cracked pleather seat and pitching onto the ground. John reached over and clasped her arm, saving her from that fate.

"You good?" he asked.

"Yeah," she said, finding her balance, her stomach pitching more at the thought of revealing why she sat beside him than at the actual bumpy ride.

So how did one do this?

Probably should just say it. Rip the bandage off. Pull the knife out. He probably already suspected why she'd come.

As they turned onto the adjacent path, Shelby took a deep breath and said, "I'm pregnant."

How will John react to the news?
Find out what's in store for these two—and the
baby— in THE SWEETEST SEPTEMBER
by Liz Talley, available August 2014 from
Harlequin® Superromance®.

Love is one unpredictable ride

Rodeo Dreams
by **Sarah M. Anderson**

Ride straight to the top of the rodeo circuit—that's June Spotted Elk's dream. Having danced with adversity in the male-dominated world of bull riding, she won't let anyone—not even a sexy, scarred stranger—get in her way.

Seasoned bull rider Travis Younkin knows what it's like to make it to the top and then hit the bottom. Back in the arena to resurrect his career, he can't afford a distraction like June. No matter how deeply the stubborn and beautiful rider gets to him.

Because he'll do anything for victory. But so will June.

**AVAILABLE AUGUST 2014,
WHEREVER BOOKS AND EBOOKS ARE SOLD.**

⬦HARLEQUIN®

super romance

More Story...More Romance
www.Harlequin.com

HSR60865